• • •

LUCY MAUD MONTGOMERY

ANNE OF THE ISLAND

AND

ANNE'S HOUSE OF DREAMS

COURAGE
BOOKS

an imprint of
RUNNING PRESS
Philadelphia • London

CK   RG

The text of *Anne of the Island* is reprinted from a first edition, published in 1915 by the L. C. Page Company in Boston, and made available through the courtesy of the Free Library of Philadelphia. The text of *Anne's House of Dreams* is reprinted from a first edition, published in 1917 by Frederick A. Stokes Company in New York. All spellings and punctuation are preserved as they appeared in the original editions, except for obvious typographical errors.

A longer version of the essay "'Kindred Spirits' All: Green Gables Revisited" by Carol Gay was published posthumously in the *Children's Literature Association Quarterly*, II (1986) and was reprinted in *Such a Simple Little Tale*, edited by Mavis Reimer and published by the Children's Literature Association and the Scarecrow Press, Metuchen, New Jersey and London, © 1992. It is excerpted here with the permission of her husband, Professor Thomas Gay.

"Anne of Green Gables" and "Diana Barry" are trademarks of the Anne of Green Gables Licensing Authority, Charlottetown, Prince Edward Island.

9   8   7   6   5   4   3   2   1

Digit on the right indicates the number of this printing

Library of Congress Cataloging-in-Publication Number 96-86275

ISBN 0-7624-0113-3

Cover design by Diane Miljat
Cover illustration by Larry Winborg
Edited by Elaine M. Bucher
Set in ITC Berkeley Oldstyle

Published by Courage Books, an imprint of
Running Press Book Publishers
125 South Twenty-second Street
Philadelphia, Pennsylvania 19103-4399

. . .

Contents

· · ·

LUCY MAUD MONTGOMERY

ANNE OF THE ISLAND

1
THE SHADOW OF CHANGE

"Harvest is ended and summer is gone," quoted Anne Shirley, gazing across the shorn fields dreamily. She and Diana Barry had been picking apples in the Green Gables orchard, but were now resting from their labors in a sunny corner, where airy fleets of thistledown drifted by on the wings of a wind that was still summer-sweet with the incense of ferns in the Haunted Wood.

But everything in the landscape around them spoke of autumn. The sea was roaring hollowly in the distance, the fields were bare and sere, scarfed with golden rod, the brook valley below Green Gables overflowed with asters of ethereal purple, and the Lake of Shining Waters was blue—blue—blue; not the changeful blue of spring, nor the pale azure of summer, but a clear, steadfast, serene blue, as if the water were past all moods and tenses of emotion and had settled down to a tranquillity unbroken by fickle dreams.

"It has been a nice summer," said Diana, twisting the new ring on her left hand with a smile. "And Miss Lavendar's wedding seemed to come as a sort of crown to it. I suppose Mr. and Mrs. Irving are on the Pacific coast now."

"It seems to me they have been gone long enough to go around the world," sighed Anne. "I can't believe it is only a week since they were married. Everything has changed. Miss Lavendar and Mr. and Mrs. Allan gone—how lonely the manse looks with the shutters all closed! I went past it last night, and it made me feel as if everybody in it had died."

"We'll never get another minister as nice as Mr. Allan," said

Diana, with gloomy conviction. "I suppose we'll have all kinds of supplies this winter, and half the Sundays no preaching at all. And you and Gilbert gone—it will be awfully dull."

"Fred will be here," insinuated Anne slyly.

"When is Mrs. Lynde going to move up?" asked Diana, as if she had not heard Anne's remark.

"Tomorrow. I'm glad she's coming—but it will be another change. Marilla and I cleared everything out of the spare room yesterday. Do you know, I hated to do it? Of course, it was silly—but it did seem as if we were committing sacrilege. That old spare room has always seemed like a shrine to me. When I was a child I thought it the most wonderful apartment in the world. You remember what a consuming desire I had to sleep in a spare room bed—but not the Green Gables spare room. Oh, no, never there! It would have been too terrible—I couldn't have slept a wink from awe. I never *walked* through that room when Marilla sent me in on an errand—no, indeed, I tiptoed through it and held my breath, as if I were in church, and felt relieved when I got out of it. The pictures of George Whitefield and the Duke of Wellington hung there, one on each side of the mirror, and frowned so sternly at me all the time I was in, especially if I dared peep in the mirror, which was the only one in the house that didn't twist my face a little. I always wondered how Marilla dared houseclean that room. And now it's not only cleaned but stripped bare. George Whitefield and the Duke have been relegated to the upstairs hall. 'So passes the glory of this world,'" concluded Anne, with a laugh in which there was a little note of regret. It is never pleasant to have our old shrines desecrated, even when we have outgrown them.

"I'll be so lonesome when you go," moaned Diana for the hundredth time. "And to think you go next week!"

"But we're together still," said Anne cheerily. "We mustn't let next week rob us of this week's joy. I hate the thought of going myself—home and I are such good friends. Talk of being lonesome! It's I who should groan. *You'll* be here with any number of your old friends—*and* Fred! While I shall be alone among strangers, not knowing a soul!"

"*Except* Gilbert—*and* Charlie Sloane," said Diana, imitating Anne's italics and slyness.

"Charlie Sloane will be a great comfort, of course," agreed Anne sarcastically; whereupon both those irresponsible damsels laughed. Diana knew exactly what Anne thought of Charlie Sloane; but, despite sundry confidential talks, she did *not* know just what Anne thought of Gilbert Blythe. To be sure, Anne herself did not know that.

"The boys may be boarding at the other end of Kingsport, for all I know," Anne went on. "I am glad I'm going to Redmond, and I am sure I shall like it after a while. But for the first few weeks I know I won't. I shan't even have the comfort of looking forward to the weekend visit home, as I had when I went to Queen's. Christmas will seem like a thousand years away."

"Everything is changing—or going to change," said Diana sadly. "I have a feeling that things will never be the same again, Anne."

"We have come to a parting of the ways, I suppose," said Anne thoughtfully. "We had to come to it. Do you think, Diana, that being grown-up is really as nice as we used to imagine it would be when we were children?"

"I don't know—there are *some* nice things about it," answered Diana, again caressing her ring with that little smile which always had the effect of making Anne feel suddenly left out and inexperienced. "But there are so many puzzling things, too. Sometimes I feel as if being grown-up just frightened me—and then I would give anything to be a little girl again."

"I suppose we'll get used to being grown-up in time," said Anne cheerfully. "There won't be so many unexpected things about it by and by—though, after all, I fancy it's the unexpected things that give spice to life. We're eighteen, Diana. In two more years we'll be twenty. When I was ten I thought twenty was a green old age. In no time you'll be a staid, middle-aged matron, and I shall be nice, old maid Aunt Anne, coming to visit you in vacations. You'll always keep a corner for me, won't you, Di darling? Not the spare room, of course,—old maids can't aspire to spare rooms, and I shall be as 'umble as *Uriah Heep*, and quite content with a little over-the-porch or off-the-parlor cubby hole."

"What nonsense you do talk, Anne," laughed Diana. "You'll marry somebody splendid and handsome and rich—and no spare room in Avonlea will be half gorgeous enough for you—and you'll turn up your nose at all the friends of your youth."

"That would be a pity; my nose is quite nice, but I fear turning it up would spoil it," said Anne, patting that shapely organ. "I haven't so many good features that I could afford to spoil those I have; so, even if I should marry the King of the Cannibal Islands, I promise you I won't turn up my nose at *you*, Diana."

With another gay laugh the girls separated, Diana to return to Orchard Slope, Anne to walk to the Post Office. She found a letter awaiting her there, and when Gilbert Blythe overtook her on the bridge over the Lake of Shining Waters she was sparkling with the excitement of it.

"Priscilla Grant is going to Redmond, too," she exclaimed. "Isn't that splendid? I hoped she would, but she didn't think her father would consent. He has, however, and we're to board together. I feel that I can face an army with banners—or all the professors of Redmond in one fell phalanx—with a chum like Priscilla by my side."

"I think we'll like Kingsport," said Gilbert. "It's a nice old burg, they tell me, and has the finest natural park in the world. I've heard that the scenery in it is magnificent."

"I wonder if it will be—can be—any more beautiful than this," murmured Anne, looking around her with the loving, enraptured eyes of those to whom "home" must always be the loveliest spot in the world, no matter what fairer lands may lie under alien stars.

They were leaning on the bridge of the old pond, drinking deep of the enchantment of the dusk, just at the spot where Anne had climbed from her sinking dory on the day Elaine floated down to Camelot. The fine, empurpling dye of sunset still stained the western skies, but the moon was rising and the water lay like a great, silver dream in her light. Remembrance wove a sweet and subtle spell over the two young creatures.

"You are very quiet, Anne," said Gilbert at last.

"I'm afraid to speak or move for fear all this wonderful beauty will vanish just like a broken silence," breathed Anne.

Gilbert suddenly laid his hand over the slender white one lying on the rail of the bridge. His hazel eyes deepened into darkness, his still boyish lips opened to say something of the dream and hope that thrilled his soul. But Anne snatched her hand away and turned quickly. The spell of the dusk was broken for her.

"I must go home," she exclaimed, with a rather overdone carelessness. "Marilla had a headache this afternoon, and I'm sure the twins will be in some dreadful mischief by this time. I really shouldn't have stayed away so long."

She chattered ceaselessly and inconsequentially until they reached the Green Gables lane. Poor Gilbert hardly had a chance to get a word in edgewise. Anne felt rather relieved when they parted. There had been a new, secret self-consciousness in her heart with regard to Gilbert, ever since that fleeting moment of revelation in the garden of Echo Lodge. Something alien had intruded into the old, perfect, school-day comradeship—something that threatened to mar it.

"I never felt glad to see Gilbert go before," she thought, half-resentfully, half-sorrowfully, as she walked alone up the lane. "Our friendship will be spoiled if he goes on with this nonsense. It mustn't be spoiled—I won't let it. Oh, *why* can't boys be just sensible!"

Anne had an uneasy doubt that it was not strictly "sensible" that she should still feel on her hand the warm pressure of Gilbert's, as distinctly as she had felt it for the swift second his had rested there; and still less sensible that the sensation was far from being an unpleasant one—very different from that which had attended a similar demonstration on Charlie Sloane's part, when she had been sitting out a dance with him at a White Sands party three nights before. Anne shivered over the disagreeable recollection. But all problems connected with infatuated swains vanished from her mind when she entered the homely, unsentimental atmosphere of the Green Gables kitchen where an eight-year-old boy was crying grievously on the sofa.

"What is the matter, Davy?" asked Anne, taking him up in her arms. "Where are Marilla and Dora?"

"Marilla's putting Dora to bed," sobbed Davy, "and I'm crying 'cause Dora fell down the outside cellar steps, heels over head, and scraped all the skin off her nose, and—"

"Oh, well, don't cry about it, dear. Of course, you are sorry for her, but crying won't help her any. She'll be all right tomorrow. Crying never helps any one, Davy-boy, and—"

"I ain't crying 'cause Dora fell down cellar," said Davy, cutting short Anne's well-meant preachment with increasing bitterness. "I'm crying 'cause I wasn't there to see her fall. I'm always missing some fun or other, seems to me."

"Oh, Davy!" Anne choked back an unholy shriek of laughter. "Would you call it fun to see poor little Dora fall down the steps and get hurt?"

"She wasn't *much* hurt," said Davy defiantly. "'Course, if she'd been killed I'd have been real sorry, Anne. But the Keiths ain't so easy killed. They're like the Blewetts, I guess. Herb Blewett fell off the hayloft last Wednesday, and rolled right down through the turnip chute into the box stall, where they had a fearful wild, cross horse, and rolled right under his heels. And still he got out alive, with only three bones broke. Mrs. Lynde says there are some folks you can't kill with a meat-axe. Is Mrs. Lynde coming here tomorrow, Anne?"

"Yes, Davy, and I hope you'll be always very nice and good to her."

"I'll be nice and good. But will she ever put me to bed at nights, Anne?"

"Perhaps. Why?"

"'Cause," said Davy very decidedly, "if she does I won't say my prayers before her like I do before you, Anne."

"Why not?"

"'Cause I don't think it would be nice to talk to God before strangers, Anne. Dora can say hers to Mrs. Lynde if she likes, but *I* won't. I'll wait till she's gone and then say 'em. Won't that be all right, Anne?"

"Yes, if you are sure you won't forget to say them, Davy-boy."

"Oh, I won't forget, you bet. I think saying my prayers is great fun. But it won't be as good fun saying them alone as saying them to you. I wish you'd stay home, Anne. I don't see what you want to go away and leave us for."

"I don't exactly *want* to, Davy, but I feel I ought to go."

"If you don't want to go you needn't. You're grown up. When *I'*m grown up I'm not going to do one single thing I don't want to do, Anne."

"All your life, Davy, you'll find yourself doing things you don't want to do."

"I won't," said Davy flatly. "Catch me! I have to do things I don't want to now, 'cause you and Marilla'll send me to bed if I don't. But when I grow up you can't do that, and there'll be nobody to tell me not to do things. Won't I have the time! Say, Anne, Milty Boulter says his mother says you're going to college to see if you can catch a man. Are you, Anne? I want to know."

For a second Anne burned with resentment. Then she laughed, reminding herself that Mrs. Boulter's crude vulgarity of thought and speech could not harm her.

"No, Davy, I'm not. I'm going to study and grow and learn about many things."

"What things?"

> "'Shoes and ships and sealing wax
> And cabbages and kings,'"

quoted Anne.

"But if you *did* want to catch a man how would you go about it? I want to know," persisted Davy, for whom the subject evidently possessed a certain fascination.

"You'd better ask Mrs. Boulter," said Anne thoughtlessly. "I think it's likely she knows more about the process than I do."

"I will, the next time I see her," said Davy gravely.

"Davy! If you do!" cried Anne, realizing her mistake.

"But you just told me to," protested Davy aggrieved.

"It's time you went to bed," decreed Anne, by way of getting out of the scrape.

After Davy had gone to bed Anne wandered down to Victoria Island and sat there alone, curtained with fire-spun, moonlit gloom, while the water laughed around her in a duet of brook and wind. Anne had always loved that brook. Many a dream had she spun over its sparkling water in days gone by. She forgot love-lorn youths, and the cayenne speeches of malicious neighbors, and all the problems of her girlish existence. In imagination she sailed over storied seas that wash the distant shining shores of "faëry lands forlorn," where lost Atlantis and Elysium lie, with the evening star for pilot, to the land of Heart's Desire. And she was richer in those dreams than in realities; for things seen pass away, but the things that are unseen are eternal.

2

GARLANDS OF AUTUMN

The following week sped swiftly, crowded with innumerable "last things," as Anne called them. Good-bye calls had to be made and received, being pleasant or otherwise, according to whether callers and called-upon were heartily in sympathy with Anne's hopes, or thought she was too much puffed-up over going to college and that it was their duty to "take her down a peg or two."

The A.V.I.S. gave a farewell party in honor of Anne and Gilbert one evening at the home of Josie Pye, choosing that place, partly because Mr. Pye's house was large and convenient, partly because it was strongly suspected that the Pye girls would have nothing to do with the affair if their offer of the house for the party was not accepted. It was a very pleasant little time, for the Pye girls were gracious, and said and did nothing to mar the harmony of the occasion—which was not according to their wont. Josie was unusually amiable—so much so that she even remarked condescendingly to Anne,

"Your new dress is rather becoming to you, Anne. Really, you look *almost pretty* in it."

"How kind of you to say so," responded Anne, with dancing eyes. Her sense of humor was developing, and the speeches that would have hurt her at fourteen were becoming merely food for amusement now. Josie suspected that Anne was laughing at her behind those wicked eyes; but she contented herself with whispering to Gertie, as they went downstairs, that Anne Shirley would put on more airs than ever now that she was going to college—you'd see!

All the "old crowd" was there, full of mirth and zest and youthful light-heartedness. Diana Barry, rosy and dimpled, shadowed by the faithful Fred; Jane Andrews, neat and sensible and plain; Ruby Gillis, looking her handsomest and brightest in a cream silk blouse, with red geraniums in her golden hair; Gilbert Blythe and Charlie Sloane, both trying to keep as near the elusive Anne as possible; Carrie Sloane, looking pale and melancholy because, so it was reported, her father would not allow Oliver Kimball to come near the place; Moody Spurgeon MacPherson, whose round face and objectionable ears were as round and objectionable as ever; and Billy Andrews, who sat in a corner all the evening, chuckled when any one spoke to him, and watched Anne Shirley with a grin of pleasure on his broad, freckled countenance.

Anne had known beforehand of the party, but she had not known that she and Gilbert were, as the founders of the Society, to be presented with a very complimentary "address" and "tokens of respect"—in her case a volume of Shakespeare's plays, in Gilbert's a fountain pen. She was so taken by surprise and pleased by the nice things said in the address, read in Moody Spurgeon's most solemn and ministerial tones, that the tears quite drowned the sparkle of her big gray eyes. She had worked hard and faithfully for the A.V.I.S., and it warmed the cockles of her heart that the members appreciated her efforts so sincerely. And they were all so nice and friendly and jolly—even the Pye girls had their merits; at that moment Anne loved all the world.

She enjoyed the evening tremendously, but the end of it rather spoiled all. Gilbert again made the mistake of saying something sentimental to her as they ate their supper on the moonlit verandah; and Anne, to punish him, was gracious to Charlie Sloane and allowed the latter to walk home with her. She found, however, that revenge hurts nobody quite so much as the one who tries to inflict it. Gilbert walked airily off with Ruby Gillis, and Anne could hear them laughing and talking gaily as they loitered along in the still, crisp autumn air. They were evidently having the best of good times, while she was horribly bored by Charlie Sloane, who talked unbrokenly on, and never, even by accident, said one thing that was worth listening to. Anne gave an occasional absent "yes" or "no," and thought how beautiful Ruby had looked that night, how very goggly Charlie's eyes were in the moonlight—worse even than by daylight—and that the world, somehow, wasn't quite such a nice place as she had believed it to be earlier in the evening.

"I'm just tired out—that is what is the matter with me," she said, when she thankfully found herself alone in her own room. And she honestly believed it was. But a certain little gush of joy, as from some secret, unknown spring, bubbled up in her heart the next evening, when she saw Gilbert striding down through the Haunted Wood and crossing the old log bridge with that firm, quick step of his. So Gilbert was not going to spend this last evening with Ruby Gillis after all!

"You look tired, Anne," he said.

"I am tired, and, worse than that, I'm disgruntled. I'm tired because I've been packing my trunk and sewing all day. But I'm disgruntled because six women have been here to say good-bye to me, and every one of the six managed to say something that seemed to take the color right out of life and leave it as gray and dismal and cheerless as a November morning."

"Spiteful old cats!" was Gilbert's elegant comment.

"Oh, no, they weren't," said Anne seriously. "That is just the trouble. If they had been spiteful cats I wouldn't have minded them. But they are all nice, kind, motherly souls, who like me and whom I like, and that is why what they said, or hinted, had such undue weight with me. They let me see they thought I was crazy going to Redmond and trying to take a B.A., and ever since I've been wondering if I am. Mrs. Peter Sloane sighed and said she hoped my strength would hold out till I got through; and at once I saw myself a hopeless victim of nervous prostration at the end of my third year; Mrs. Eben Wright said it must cost an awful lot to put in four years at Redmond; and I felt all over me that it was unpardonable in me to squander Marilla's money and my own on such a folly; Mrs. Jasper Bell said she hoped I wouldn't let college spoil me, as it did some people; and I felt in my bones that the end of my four Redmond years would see me a most insufferable creature, thinking I knew it all, and looking down on everything and everybody in Avonlea; Mrs. Elisha Wright said she understood that Redmond girls, especially those who be-longed to Kingsport, were 'dreadful dressy and stuck-up,' and she guessed I wouldn't feel much at home among them; and I saw myself, a snubbed, dowdy, humiliated country girl, shuffling through Redmond's classic halls in copper-toed boots."

Anne ended with a laugh and a sigh commingled. With her sensitive nature all disapproval had weight, even the dis-approval of those for whose opinions she had scant respect. For the time being life was savorless, and ambition had gone out like a snuffed candle.

"You surely don't care for what they said," protested Gilbert.

"You know exactly how narrow their outlook on life is, excellent creatures though they are. To do anything *they* have never done is anathema maranatha. You are the first Avonlea girl who has ever gone to college; and you know that all pioneers are considered to be afflicted with moonstruck madness."

"Oh, I know. But *feeling* is so different from *knowing*. My common sense tells me all you can say, but there are times when common sense has no power over me. Common nonsense takes possession of my soul. Really, after Mrs. Elisha went away I hardly had the heart to finish packing."

"You're just tired, Anne. Come, forget it all and take a walk with me—a ramble back through the woods beyond the marsh. There should be something there I want to show you."

"Should be! Don't you know if it is there?"

"No. I only know it should be, from something I saw there in spring. Come on. We'll pretend we are two children again and we'll go the way of the wind."

They started gaily off. Anne, remembering the unpleasantness of the preceding evening, was very nice to Gilbert; and Gilbert, who was learning wisdom, took care to be nothing save the schoolboy comrade again. Mrs. Lynde and Marilla watched them from the kitchen window.

"That'll be a match some day," Mrs. Lynde said approvingly.

Marilla winced slightly. In her heart she hoped it would, but it went against her grain to hear the matter spoken of in Mrs. Lynde's gossipy matter-of-fact way.

"They're only children yet," she said shortly.

Mrs. Lynde laughed good-naturedly.

"Anne is eighteen; I was married when I was that age. We old folks, Marilla, are too much given to thinking children never grow up, that's what. Anne is a young woman and Gilbert's a man, and he worships the ground she walks on, as any one can see. He's a fine fellow, and Anne can't do better. I hope she won't get any romantic nonsense into her head at Redmond. I don't approve of them co-educational places and never did, that's what.

I don't believe," concluded Mrs. Lynde solemnly, "that the students at such colleges ever do much else than flirt."

"They must study a little," said Marilla, with a smile.

"Precious little," sniffed Mrs. Rachel. "However, I think Anne will. She never was flirtatious. But she doesn't appreciate Gilbert at his full value, that's what. Oh, I know girls! Charlie Sloane is wild about her, too, but I'd never advise her to marry a Sloane. The Sloanes are good, honest, respectable people, of course. But when all's said and done they're *Sloanes*."

Marilla nodded. To an outsider, the statement that Sloanes were Sloanes might not be very illuminating, but she understood. Every village has such a family; good, honest, respectable people they may be, but *Sloanes* they are and must ever remain, though they speak with the tongues of men and angels.

Gilbert and Anne, happily unconscious that their future was thus being settled by Mrs. Rachel, were sauntering through the shadows of the Haunted Wood. Beyond, the harvest hills were basking in an amber sunset radiance, under a pale, aerial sky of rose and blue. The distant spruce groves were burnished bronze, and their long shadows barred the upland meadows. But around them a little wind sang among the fir tassels, and in it there was the note of autumn.

"This wood really is haunted now—by old memories," said Anne, stooping to gather a spray of ferns, bleached to waxen whiteness by frost. "It seems to me that the little girls Diana and I used to be play here still, and sit by the Dryad's Bubble in the twilights, trysting with the ghosts. Do you know, I can never go up this path in the dusk without feeling a bit of the old fright and shiver? There was one especially horrifying phantom which we created—the ghost of the murdered child that crept up behind you and laid cold fingers on yours. I confess that, to this day, I cannot help fancying its little, furtive footsteps behind me when I come here after nightfall. I'm not afraid of the White Lady or the headless man or the skeletons, but I wish I had never imagined that baby's ghost into existence. How angry Marilla and

Mrs. Barry were over that affair," concluded Anne, with reminis-
cent laughter.

The woods around the head of the marsh were full of purple
vistas, threaded with gossamers. Past a dour plantation of gnarled
spruces and a maple-fringed, sun-warm valley they found the
"something" Gilbert was looking for.

"Ah, here it is," he said with satisfaction.

"An apple tree—and away back here!" exclaimed Anne
delightedly.

"Yes, a veritable apple-bearing apple tree, too, here in the very
midst of pines and beeches, a mile away from any orchard. I was
here one day last spring and found it, all white with blossom. So I
resolved I'd come again in the fall and see if it had been apples.
See, it's loaded. They look good, too—tawny as russets but with a
dusky red cheek. Most wild seedlings are green and uninviting."

"I suppose it sprang years ago from some chance-sown seed,"
said Anne dreamily. "And how it has grown and flourished
and held its own here all alone among aliens, the brave determined thing!"

"Here's a fallen tree with a cushion of moss. Sit down, Anne—
it will serve for a woodland throne. I'll climb for some apples.
They all grow high—the tree had to reach up to the sunlight."

The apples proved to be delicious. Under the tawny skin was a
white, white flesh, faintly veined with red; and, besides their own
proper apple taste, they had a certain wild, delightful tang no
orchard-grown apple ever possessed.

"The fatal apple of Eden couldn't have had a rarer flavor,"
commented Anne. "But it's time we were going home. See, it was
twilight three minutes ago and now it's moonlight. What a pity
we couldn't have caught the moment of transformation. But such
moments never are caught, I suppose."

"Let's go back around the marsh and home by way of Lovers'
Lane. Do you feel as disgruntled now as when you started
out, Anne?"

"Not I. Those apples have been as manna to a hungry soul.

I feel that I shall love Redmond and have a splendid four years there."

"And after those four years—what?"

"Oh, there's another bend in the road at their end," answered Anne lightly. "I've no idea what may be around it—I don't want to have. It's nicer not to know."

Lovers' Lane was a dear place that night, still and mysteriously dim in the pale radiance of the moonlight. They loitered through it in a pleasant chummy silence, neither caring to talk.

"If Gilbert were always as he has been this evening how nice and simple everything would be," reflected Anne.

Gilbert was looking at Anne, as she walked along. In her light dress, with her slender delicacy, she made him think of a white iris.

"I wonder if I can ever make her care for me," he thought, with a pang of self-distrust.

3
GREETING AND FAREWELL

Charlie Sloane, Gilbert Blythe and Anne Shirley left Avonlea the following Monday morning. Anne had hoped for a fine day. Diana was to drive her to the station and they wanted this, their last drive together for some time, to be a pleasant one. But when Anne went to bed Sunday night the east wind was moaning around Green Gables with an ominous prophecy which was fulfilled in the morning. Anne awoke to find raindrops pattering against her window and shadowing the pond's gray surface with widening rings; hills and sea were hidden in mist, and the whole world seemed dim and dreary. Anne dressed in the cheerless gray dawn, for an early start was necessary to catch the boat train; she struggled against the tears that *would* well up in her eyes in spite of herself. She was leaving the home that was so dear to her, and something told her that she was leaving it forever, save as a holiday refuge. Things would never be the same again; coming back for vacations would not be living there. And oh, how dear and beloved everything was—that little white porch room, sacred to the dreams of girlhood, the old Snow Queen at the window, the brook in the hollow, the Dryad's Bubble, the Haunted Wood, and Lovers' Lane—all the thousand and one dear spots where memories of the old years bided. Could she ever be really happy anywhere else?

Breakfast at Green Gables that morning was a rather doleful meal. Davy, for the first time in his life probably, could not eat, but blubbered shamelessly over his porridge. Nobody else seemed to have much appetite, save Dora, who tucked away her rations comfortably. Dora, like the immortal and most prudent Charlotte, who "went on cutting bread and butter" when her frenzied lover's body had been carried past on a shutter, was one of those fortunate creatures who are seldom disturbed by anything. Even at eight it took a great deal to ruffle Dora's placidity. She was sorry Anne was going away, of course, but was that any reason why she should fail to appreciate a poached egg on toast? Not at all. And, seeing that Davy could not eat his, Dora ate it for him.

Promptly on time Diana appeared with horse and buggy, her rosy face glowing above her raincoat. The good-byes had to be said then somehow. Mrs. Lynde came in from her quarters to give Anne a hearty embrace and warn her to be careful of her health, whatever she did. Marilla, brusque and tearless, pecked Anne's cheek and said she supposed they'd hear from her when she got settled. A casual observer might have concluded that Anne's going mattered very little to her—unless said observer had happened to get a good look in her eyes. Dora kissed Anne primly and squeezed out two decorous little tears; but Davy, who had been crying on the back porch step ever since they rose from the table, refused to say good-bye at all. When he saw Anne coming towards him he sprang to his feet, bolted up the back stairs and hid in a clothes closet, out of which he would not come. His muffled howls were the last sounds Anne heard as she left Green Gables.

It rained heavily all the way to Bright River, to which station they had to go, since the branch line train from Carmody did not connect with the boat train. Charlie and Gilbert were on the station platform when they reached it, and the train was whistling. Anne had just time to get her ticket and trunk check, say a hurried farewell to Diana, and hasten on board. She wished she were going back with Diana to Avonlea; she knew she was going to die of homesickness. And oh, if only that dismal rain would stop pouring down as if the whole world were weeping over summer vanished and joys departed! Even Gilbert's presence brought her no comfort, for Charlie Sloane was there, too, and Sloanishness could be tolerated only in fine weather. It was absolutely insufferable in rain.

But when the boat steamed out of Charlottetown harbor things took a turn for the better. The rain ceased and the sun began to burst out goldenly now and again between the rents in the clouds, burnishing the gray seas with copper-hued radiance, and lighting up the mists that curtained the Island's red shores with gleams of gold foretokening a fine day after all. Besides, Charlie Sloane promptly became so seasick that he had to go below, and Anne and Gilbert were left alone on deck.

"I am very glad that all the Sloanes get seasick as soon as they go on water," thought Anne mercilessly. "I am sure I couldn't take my farewell look at the 'ould sod' with Charlie standing there pretending to look sentimentally at it, too."

"Well, we're off," remarked Gilbert unsentimentally.

"Yes, I feel like Byron's 'Childe Harold'—only it isn't really my 'native shore' that I'm watching," said Anne, winking her gray eyes vigorously. "Nova Scotia is that, I suppose. But one's native shore is the land one loves the best, and that's good old P.E.I. for me. I can't believe I didn't always live here. Those eleven years before I came seem like a bad dream. It's seven years since I crossed on this boat—the evening Mrs. Spencer brought me over from Hopetown. I can see myself, in that dreadful old wincey dress and faded sailor hat, exploring decks and cabins with enraptured curiosity. It was a fine evening; and how those red Island shores did gleam in the sunshine. Now I'm crossing the strait again. Oh, Gilbert, I do hope I'll like Redmond and Kingsport, but I'm sure I won't!"

"Where's all your philosophy gone, Anne?"

"It's all submerged under a great, swamping wave of loneliness and homesickness. I've longed for three years to go to Redmond—and now I'm going—and I wish I weren't! Never mind! I shall be cheerful and philosophical again after I have just one good cry. I *must* have that, 'as a went'—and I'll have to wait until I get into my boarding-house bed tonight, wherever it may be, before I can have it. Then Anne will be herself again. I wonder if Davy has come out of the closet yet."

It was nine that night when their train reached Kingsport, and they found themselves in the blue-white glare of the crowded station. Anne felt horribly bewildered, but a moment later she was seized by Priscilla Grant, who had come to Kingsport on Saturday.

"Here you are, beloved! And I suppose you're as tired as I was when I got here Saturday night."

"Tired! Priscilla, don't talk of it. I'm tired, and green, and provincial, and only about ten years old. For pity's sake take your poor, broken-down chum to some place where she can hear herself think."

"I'll take you right up to our boarding-house. I've a cab ready outside."

"It's such a blessing you're here, Prissy. If you weren't I think I should just sit down on my suitcase, here and now, and weep bitter tears. What a comfort one familiar face is in a howling wilderness of strangers!"

"Is that Gilbert Blythe over there, Anne? How he has grown up this past year! He was only a schoolboy when I taught in Carmody. And of course that's Charlie Sloane. *He* hasn't changed—couldn't! He looked just like that when he was born, and he'll look like that when he's eighty. This way, dear. We'll be home in twenty minutes."

"Home!" groaned Anne. "You mean we'll be in some horrible boarding-house, in a still more horrible hall bedroom, looking out on a dingy back yard."

"It isn't a horrible boarding-house, Anne-girl. Here's our cab. Hop in—the driver will get your trunk. Oh, yes, the boarding-house—it's really a very nice place of its kind, as you'll admit tomorrow morning when a good night's sleep has turned your blues rosy pink. It's a big, old fashioned, gray stone house on St. John Street, just a nice little constitutional from Redmond. It used to be the 'residence' of great folk, but fashion has deserted St. John Street and its houses only dream now of better days. They're so big that the people living in them have to take boarders just to fill up. At least, that is the reason our landladies are very anxious to impress on us. They're delicious, Anne—our landladies, I mean."

"How many are there?"

"Two. Miss Hannah Harvey and Miss Ada Harvey. They were born twins about fifty years ago."

"I can't get away from twins, it seems," smiled Anne. "Wherever I go they confront me."

"Oh, they're not twins now, dear. After they reached the age of thirty they never were twins again. Miss Hannah has grown old, not too gracefully, and Miss Ada has stayed thirty, less gracefully still. I don't know whether Miss Hannah can smile or not; I've never caught her at it so far, but Miss Ada smiles all the time and that's worse. However, they're nice, kind souls, and they take two boarders every year because Miss Hannah's economical soul cannot bear to 'waste room space'—not because they need to or have to, as Miss Ada has told me seven times since Saturday night. As for our rooms, I admit they are hall bedrooms, and mine does look out on the back yard. Your room is a front one and looks out on Old St. John's graveyard, which is just across the street."

"That sounds gruesome," shivered Anne. "I think I'd rather have the back yard view."

"Oh, no, you wouldn't. Wait and see. Old St. John's is a darling place. It's been a graveyard so long that it's ceased to be one and has become one of the sights of Kingsport. I was all through it yesterday for a pleasure exertion. There's a big stone wall and a row of enormous trees all round it, and rows of trees all through it, and the queerest old tombstones, with the queerest and quaintest inscriptions. You'll go there to study, Anne, see if you don't. Of course, nobody is ever buried there now. But a few years ago they put up a beautiful monument to the memory of Nova Scotian soldiers who fell in the Crimean War. It is just opposite the entrance gates and there's 'scope for imagination' in it, as you used to say. Here's your trunk at last—and the boys coming to say good-night. Must I really shake hands with Charlie Sloane, Anne? His hands are always so cold and fishy-feeling. We must ask them to call occasionally. Miss Hannah gravely told me we could have 'young gentlemen callers' two evenings in the week, if they went away at a reasonable hour; and Miss Ada asked me, smiling, please to be sure they didn't sit on her beautiful cushions. I promised to see to it; but goodness knows where else they *can* sit, unless they sit on the floor, for there are cushions on *everything*. Miss Ada even has an elaborate Battenburg one on top of the piano."

Anne was laughing by this time. Priscilla's gay chatter had the intended effect of cheering her up; homesickness vanished for the time being, and did not even return in full force when she finally found herself alone in her little bedroom. She went to her window and looked out. The street below was dim and quiet. Across it the moon was shining above the trees in Old St. John's, just behind the great dark head of the lion on the monument. Anne wondered if it could have been only that morning that she had left Green Gables. She had the sense of a long passage of time which one day of change and travel gives.

"I suppose that very moon is looking down on Green Gables now," she mused. "But I won't think about it—that way home-sickness lies. I'm not even going to have my good cry. I'll put that off to a more convenient season, and just now I'll go calmly and sensibly to bed and to sleep."

4
APRIL'S LADY

Kingsport is a quaint old town, hearking back to early Colonial days, and wrapped in its ancient atmosphere, as some fine old dame in garments fashioned like those of her youth. Here and there it sprouts out into modernity, but at heart it is still unspoiled; it is full of curious relics, and haloed by the romance of many legends of the past. Once it was a mere frontier station on the fringe of the wilderness, and those were the days when Indians kept life from being monotonous to the settlers. Then it grew to be a bone of contention between the British and the French, being occupied now by the one and now by the other, emerging from each occupation with some scar of battling nations branded on it.

It has in its park a martello tower, autographed all over by tourists, a dismantled old French fort on the hills beyond the town, and several antiquated cannon in its public squares. It has other historic spots also, which may be hunted out by the curious, and none is more quaint and delightful than Old St. John's Cemetery at the very core of the town, with streets of quiet, old-time houses on two sides, and busy, bustling, modern thoroughfares on the others. Every citizen of Kingsport feels a thrill of possessive pride in Old St. John's, for, if he be of any pretensions at all, he has an ancestor buried there, with a queer, crooked slab at his head, or else sprawling protectively over the grave, on which all the main facts of his history are recorded. For the most part no great art or skill was lavished on those old tombstones. The larger number are of roughly chiselled brown or gray native stone, and only in a few cases is there any attempt at ornamentation. Some are adorned with skull and cross-bones, and this grizzly decoration is frequently coupled with a cherub's head. Many are prostrate and in ruins. Into almost all Time's tooth has been gnawing, until some inscriptions have been completely effaced, and others can only be deciphered with difficulty.

The graveyard is very full and very bowery, for it is surrounded and intersected by rows of elms and willows, beneath whose shade the sleepers must lie very dreamlessly, forever crooned to by the winds and leaves over them, and quite undisturbed by the clamor of traffic just beyond.

Anne took the first of many rambles in Old St. John's the next afternoon. She and Priscilla had gone to Redmond in the forenoon and registered as students, after which there was nothing more to do that day. The girls gladly made their escape, for it was not exhilarating to be surrounded by crowds of strangers, most of whom had a rather alien appearance, as if not quite sure where they belonged.

The "freshettes" stood about in detached groups of two or three, looking askance at each other; the "freshies," wiser in their day and generation, had banded themselves together on the big staircase of the entrance hall, where they were shouting out glees with all the vigor of youthful lungs, as a species of defiance to their traditional enemies, the Sophomores, a few of whom were prowling loftily about, looking properly disdainful of the "unlicked cubs" on the stairs. Gilbert and Charlie were nowhere to be seen.

"Little did I think the day would ever come when I'd be glad of the sight of a Sloane," said Priscilla, as they crossed the campus, "but I'd welcome Charlie's goggle eyes almost ecstatically. At least, they'd be familiar eyes."

"Oh," sighed Anne. "I can't describe how I felt when I was standing there, waiting my turn to be registered—as insignificant as the teeniest drop in a most enormous bucket. It's bad enough to feel insignificant, but it's unbearable to have it grained into your soul that you will never, *can* never, be anything but insignificant, and that is how I did feel—as if I were invisible to the naked eye and some of those Sophs might step on me. I knew I would go down to my grave unwept, unhonored and unsung."

"Wait till next year," comforted Priscilla. "Then we'll be able to look as bored and sophisticated as any Sophomore of them all.

No doubt it is rather dreadful to feel insignificant; but I think it's better than to feel as big and awkward as I did—as if I were sprawled all over Redmond. That's how I felt—I suppose because I was a good two inches taller than any one else in the crowd. I wasn't afraid a Soph might walk over me; I was afraid they'd take me for an elephant, or an overgrown sample of a potato-fed Islander."

"I suppose the trouble is we can't forgive big Redmond for not being little Queen's," said Anne, gathering about her the shreds of her old cheerful philosophy to cover her nakedness of spirit. "When we left Queen's we knew everybody and had a place of our own. I suppose we have been unconsciously expecting to take life up at Redmond just where we left off at Queen's, and now we feel as if the ground had slipped from under our feet. I'm thankful that neither Mrs. Lynde nor Mrs. Elisha Wright know, or ever will know, my state of mind at present. They would exult in saying 'I told you so,' and be convinced it was the beginning of the end. Whereas it is just the end of the beginning."

"Exactly. That sounds more Anneish. In a little while we'll be acclimated and acquainted, and all will be well. Anne, did you notice the girl who stood alone just outside the door of the co-eds' dressing room all the morning—the pretty one with the brown eyes and crooked mouth?"

"Yes, I did. I noticed her particularly because she seemed the only creature there who *looked* as lonely and friendless as I *felt*. I had *you*, but she had no one."

"I think she felt pretty all-by-herselfish, too. Several times I saw her make a motion as if to cross over to us, but she never did it—too shy, I suppose. I wished she would come. If I hadn't felt so much like the aforesaid elephant I'd have gone to her. But I couldn't lumber across that big hall with all those boys howling on the stairs. She was the prettiest freshette I saw today, but probably favor is deceitful and even beauty is vain on your first day at Redmond," concluded Priscilla with a laugh.

"I'm going across to Old St. John's after lunch," said Anne. "I don't know that a graveyard is a very good place to go to get cheered up, but it seems the only get-at-able place where there are trees, and trees I must have. I'll sit on one of those old slabs and shut my eyes and imagine I'm in the Avonlea woods."

Anne did not do that, however, for she found enough of interest in Old St. John's to keep her eyes wide open. They went in by the entrance gates, past the simple, massive, stone arch surmounted by the great lion of England.

"'And on Inkerman yet the wild bramble is gory,
   And those bleak heights henceforth shall be famous in story,'"

quoted Anne, looking at it with a thrill. They found themselves in a dim, cool, green place where winds were fond of purring. Up and down the long grassy aisles they wandered, reading the quaint, voluminous epitaphs, carved in an age that had more leisure than our own.

"'Here lieth the body of Albert Crawford, Esq.,'" read Anne from a worn, gray slab, "'for many years Keeper of His Majesty's Ordnance at Kingsport. He served in the army till the peace of 1763, when he retired from bad health. He was a brave officer, the best of husbands, the best of fathers, the best of friends. He died October 29th, 1792, aged 84 years.' There's an epitaph for you, Prissy. There is certainly some 'scope for imagination' in it. How full such a life must have been of adventure! And as for his personal qualities, I'm sure human eulogy couldn't go further. I wonder if they told him he was all those best things while he was alive."

"Here's another," said Priscilla. "Listen—'To the memory of Alexander Ross, who died on the 22nd of September, 1840, aged 43 years. This is raised as a tribute of affection by one whom he served so faithfully for 27 years that he was regarded as a friend, deserving the fullest confidence and attachment.'"

"A very good epitaph," commented Anne thoughtfully. "I wouldn't wish a better. We are all servants of some sort, and if the fact that we are faithful can be truthfully inscribed on our tombstones nothing more need be added. Here's a sorrowful little gray stone, Prissy—'to the memory of a favorite child.' And here is another 'erected to the memory of one who is buried else-where.' I wonder where that unknown grave is. Really, Pris, the graveyards of today will never be as interesting as this. You were right—I shall come here often. I love it already. I see we're not alone here—there's a girl down at the end of this avenue."

"Yes, and I believe it's the very girl we saw at Redmond this morning. I've been watching her for five minutes. She has started to come up the avenue exactly half a dozen times, and half a dozen times has she turned and gone back. Either she's dread-fully shy or she has got something on her conscience. Let's go and meet her. It's easier to get acquainted in a graveyard than at Redmond, I believe."

They walked down the long grassy arcade towards the stranger, who was sitting on a gray slab under an enormous willow. She was certainly very pretty, with a vivid, irregular, be-witching type of prettiness. There was a gloss as of brown nuts on her satin-smooth hair and a soft, ripe glow on her round cheeks. Her eyes were big and brown and velvety, under oddly-pointed black brows, and her crooked mouth was rose-red. She wore a smart brown suit, with two very modish little shoes peep-ing from beneath it; and her hat of dull pink straw, wreathed with golden-brown poppies, had the indefinable, unmistakable air which pertains to the "creation" of an artist in millinery. Priscilla had a sudden stinging consciousness that her own hat had been trimmed by her village store milliner, and Anne wondered uncomfortably if the blouse she had made herself, and which Mrs. Lynde had fitted, looked *very* countrified and homemade besides the stranger's smart attire. For a moment both girls felt like turning back.

But they had already stopped and turned towards the gray slab. It was too late to retreat, for the brown-eyed girl had evidently concluded that they were coming to speak to her. In-stantly she sprang up and came forward with outstretched hand

and a gay, friendly smile in which there seemed not a shadow of
either shyness or burdened conscience.

"Oh, I want to know who you two girls are," she exclaimed
eagerly. "I've been *dying* to know. I saw you at Redmond this
morning. Say, wasn't it *awful* there? For the time I wished I had
stayed home and got married."

Anne and Priscilla both broke into unconstrained laughter at
this unexpected conclusion. The brown-eyed girl laughed, too.

"I really did. I *could* have, you know. Come, let's all sit down
on this gravestone and get acquainted. It won't be hard. I know
we're going to adore each other—I knew it as soon as I saw you
at Redmond this morning. I wanted so much to go right over and
hug you both."

"Why didn't you?" asked Priscilla.

"Because I simply couldn't make up my mind to do it. I never
can make up my mind about anything myself—I'm always afflicted with indecision. Just as soon as I decide to do something I feel
in my bones that another course would be the correct one. It's a
dreadful misfortune, but I was born that way, and there is no use
in blaming me for it, as some people do. So I couldn't make up
my mind to go and speak to you, much as I wanted to."

"We thought you were too shy," said Anne.

"No, no, dear. Shyness isn't among the many failings—or
virtues—of Philippa Gordon—Phil for short. Do call me Phil
right off. Now, what are your handles?"

"She's Priscilla Grant," said Anne, pointing.

"And *she's* Anne Shirley," said Priscilla, pointing in turn.

"And we're from the Island," said both together.

"I hail from Bolingbroke, Nova Scotia," said Philippa.

"Bolingbroke!" exclaimed Anne. "Why, that is where I was
born."

"Do you really mean it? Why, that makes you a Bluenose after all."

"No, it doesn't," retorted Anne. "Wasn't it Dan O'Connell who
said that if a man was born in a stable it didn't make him a horse?
I'm Island to the core."

"Well, I'm glad you were born in Bolingbroke anyway. It makes us kind of neighbors, doesn't it? And I like that, because when I tell you secrets it won't be as if I were telling them to a stranger. I *have* to tell them. I can't keep secrets—it's no use to try. That's my worst failing—that, and indecision, as aforesaid. Would you believe it?—it took me half an hour to decide what hat to wear when I was coming here—*here*, to a graveyard! At first I inclined to my brown one with the feather; but as soon as I put it on I thought this pink one with the floppy brim would be more becoming. When I got *it* pinned in place I liked the brown one better. At last I put them close together on the bed, shut my eyes, and jabbed with a hat pin. The pin speared the pink one, so I put it on. It is becoming, isn't it? Tell me, what do you think of my looks?"

At this naïve demand, made in a perfectly serious tone, Priscilla laughed again. But Anne said, impulsively squeezing Philippa's hand,

"We thought this morning that you were the prettiest girl we saw at Redmond."

Philippa's crooked mouth flashed into a bewitching crooked smile over very white teeth.

"I thought that myself," was her next astounding statement, "but I wanted some one else's opinion to bolster mine up. I can't decide even on my own appearance. Just as soon as I've decided that I'm pretty I begin to feel miserably that I'm not. Besides, I have a horrible old great-aunt who is always saying to me, with a mournful sigh, 'You were such a pretty baby. It's strange how children change when they grow up.' I adore aunts, but I detest great-aunts. Please tell me quite often that I am pretty, if you don't mind. I feel so much more comfortable when I can believe I'm pretty. And I'll be just as obliging to you if you want me to—I *can* be, with a clear conscience."

"Thanks," laughed Anne, "but Priscilla and I are so firmly convinced of our own good looks that we don't need any assurance about them, so you needn't trouble."

"Oh, you're laughing at me. I know you think I'm abominably vain, but I'm not. There really isn't one spark of vanity in me. And I'm never a bit grudging about paying compliments to other girls when they deserve them. I'm so glad I know you folks. I came up on Saturday and I've nearly died of homesickness ever since. It's a horrible feeling, isn't it? In Bolingbroke I'm an important personage, and in Kingsport I'm just nobody! There were times when I could feel my soul turning a delicate blue. Where do you hang out?"

"Thirty-eight St. John's Street."

"Better and better. Why, I'm just around the corner on Wallace Street. I don't like my boarding-house, though. It's bleak and lonesome, and my room looks out on such an unholy back yard. It's the ugliest place in the world. As for cats—well, surely *all* the Kingsport cats can't congregate there at night, but half of them must. I adore cats on hearth rugs, snoozing before nice, friendly fires, but cats in back yards at midnight are totally different animals. The first night I was here I cried all night, and so did the cats. You should have seen my nose in the morning. How I wished I had never left home!"

"I don't know how you managed to make up your mind to come to Redmond at all, if you are really such an undecided person," said amused Priscilla.

"Bless your heart, honey, I didn't. It was father who wanted me to come here. His heart was set on it—why, I don't know. It seems perfectly ridiculous to think of *me* studying for a B.A. degree, doesn't it? Not but what I can do it, all right. I have heaps of brains."

"Oh!" said Priscilla vaguely.

"Yes. But it's such hard work to use them. And B.A.'s are such learned, dignified, wise, solemn creatures—they must be. No, *I* didn't want to come to Redmond. I did it just to oblige father. He *is* such a duck. Besides, I knew if I stayed home I'd have to get married. Mother wanted that—wanted it decidedly. Mother has plenty of decision. But I really hated the thought of being married for a few years yet. I want to have heaps of fun before I settle down. And, ridiculous as the idea of my being a B.A. is, the idea of my being an old married woman is still more absurd, isn't it? I'm only eighteen. No, I concluded I would rather come to Redmond than be married. Besides, how could I ever have made up my mind which man to marry?"

"Were there so many?" laughed Anne.

"Heaps. The boys like me awfully—they really do. But there were only two that mattered. The rest were all too young and too poor. I must marry a rich man, you know."

"Why must you?"

"Honey, you couldn't imagine *me* being a poor man's wife, could you? I can't do a single useful thing, and I am *very* extravagant. Oh, no, my husband must have heaps of money. So that narrowed them down to two. But I couldn't decide between two any easier than between two hundred. I knew perfectly well that whichever one I chose I'd regret all my life that I hadn't married the other."

"Didn't you—love—either of them?" asked Anne, a little hesitatingly. It was not easy for her to speak to a stranger of the great mystery and transformation of life.

"Goodness, no. *I* couldn't love anybody. It isn't in me. Besides I wouldn't want to. Being in love makes you a perfect slave, *I* think. And it would give a man such power to hurt you. I'd be afraid. No, no, Alec and Alonzo are two dear boys, and I like them both so much that I really don't know which I like the better. That is the trouble. Alec is the best looking, of course, and I simply couldn't marry a man who wasn't handsome. He is good-tempered, too, and has lovely, curly, black hair. He's rather too perfect—I don't believe I'd like a perfect husband—somebody I could never find fault with."

"Then why not marry Alonzo?" asked Priscilla gravely.

"Think of marrying a name like Alonzo!" said Phil dolefully. "I don't believe I could endure it. But he has a classic nose, and it *would* be a comfort to have a nose in the family that could be depended on. I can't depend on mine. So far, it takes after the Gordon pattern, but I'm so afraid it will develop Byrne tendencies as I grow older. I examine it every day anxiously to make sure it's still Gordon. Mother was a Byrne and has the Byrne nose in the Byrnest degree. Wait till you see it. I adore nice noses. Your nose is awfully nice, Anne Shirley. Alonzo's nose nearly turned the balance in his favor. But *Alonzo*! No, I couldn't decide. If I could have done as I did with the hats—stood them both up together, shut my eyes, and jabbed with a hatpin—it would have been quite easy."

"What did Alec and Alonzo feel like when you came away?" queried Priscilla.

"Oh, they still have hope. I told them they'd have to wait till I could make up my mind. They're quite willing to wait. They both worship me, you know. Meanwhile, I intend to have a good time. I expect I shall have heaps of beaux at Redmond. I can't be happy unless I have, you know. But don't you think the freshmen are fearfully homely? I saw only one really handsome fellow among them. He went away before you came. I heard his chum call him Gilbert. His chum had eyes that stuck out *that far*. But you're not going yet, girls? Don't go yet."

"I think we must," said Anne, rather coldly. "It's getting late, and I've some work to do."

"But you'll both come to see me, won't you?" asked Philippa, getting up and putting an arm around each. "And let me come to see you. I want to be chummy with you. I've taken such a fancy to you both. And I haven't quite disgusted you with my frivolity, have I?"

"Not quite," laughed Anne, responding to Phil's squeeze, with a return of cordiality.

"Because I'm not half so silly as I seem on the surface, you know. You just accept Philippa Gordon, as the Lord made her, with all her faults, and I believe you'll come to like her. Isn't this graveyard a sweet place? I'd love to be buried here. Here's a grave I didn't see before—this one in the iron railing—oh, girls, look, see—the stone says it's the grave of a middy who was killed in the fight between the *Shannon* and the *Chesapeake*. Just fancy!"

Anne paused by the railing and looked at the worn stone, her pulses thrilling with sudden excitement. The old graveyard, with its over-arching trees and long aisles of shadows, faded from her sight. Instead, she saw the Kingsport Harbor of nearly a century agone. Out of the mist came slowly a great frigate, brilliant with "the meteor flag of England." Behind her was another, with a still, heroic form, wrapped in his own starry flag, lying on the quarter deck—the gallant Lawrence. Time's finger had turned back his pages, and that was the *Shannon* sailing triumphant up the bay with the *Chesapeake* as her prize.

"Come back, Anne Shirley—come back," laughed Philippa, pulling her arm. "You're a hundred years away from us. Come back."

Anne came back with a sigh; her eyes were shining softly.

"I've always loved that old story," she said, "and although the English won that victory, I think it was because of the brave, defeated commander I love it. This grave seems to bring it so near and make it so real. This poor little middy was only eighteen. He 'died of desperate wounds received in gallant action'—so reads his epitaph. It is such as a soldier might wish for."

Before she turned away, Anne unpinned the little cluster of purple pansies she wore and dropped it softly on the grave of the boy who had perished in the great sea-duel.

"Well, what do you think of our new friend?" asked Priscilla, when Phil had left them.

"I like her. There is something very lovable about her, in spite of all her nonsense. I believe, as she says herself, that she isn't half as silly as she sounds. She's a dear, kissable baby—and I don't know that she'll ever really grow up."

"I like her, too," said Priscilla decidedly. "She talks as much about boys as Ruby Gillis does. But it always enrages or sickens me to hear Ruby, whereas I just wanted to laugh good-naturedly at Phil. Now, what is the why of that?"

"There is a difference," said Anne meditatively. "I think it's because Ruby is really so *conscious* of boys. She plays at love and love-making. Besides, you feel, when she is boasting of her beaux that she is doing it to rub it well into you that you haven't half so many. Now, when Phil talks of her beaux it sounds as if she was just speaking of chums. She really looks upon boys as good comrades, and she is pleased when she has dozens of them tagging round, simply because she likes to be popular and to be thought popular. Even Alec and Alonzo—I'll never be able to think of those two names separately after this—are to her just two playfellows who want her to play with them all their lives. I'm glad we met her, and I'm glad we went to Old St. John's. I believe I've put forth a tiny soul-root into Kingsport soil this afternoon. I hope so. I hate to feel transplanted."

5
LETTERS FROM HOME

For the next three weeks Anne and Priscilla continued to feel as strangers in a strange land. Then, suddenly, everything seemed to fall into focus—Redmond, professors, classes, students, studies, social doings. Life became homogeneous again, instead of being made up of detached fragments. The Freshmen, instead of being a collection of unrelated individuals, found themselves a class, with a class spirit, a class yell, class interests, class antipathies and class ambitions. They won the day in the annual "Arts Rush" against the Sophomores, and thereby gained the respect of all the classes, and an enormous, confidence-giving opinion of themselves. For three years the Sophomores had won in the "rush"; that the victory of this year perched upon the Freshman's banner was attributed to the strategic generalship of Gilbert Blythe, who marshalled the campaign and originated certain new tactics, which demoralized the Sophs and swept the Freshmen to triumph. As a reward of merit he was elected president of the Freshman Class, a position of honor and responsibility—from a Fresh point of view, at least—coveted by many. He was also invited to join the "Lambs"—Redmondese for Lamba Theta—a compliment rarely paid to a Freshman. As a preparatory initiation ordeal he had to parade the principal business streets of Kingsport for a whole day wearing a sunbonnet and a voluminous kitchen apron of gaudily flowered calico. This he did cheerfully, doffing his sunbonnet with courtly grace when he met ladies of his acquaintance. Charlie Sloane, who had not been asked to join the Lambs, told Anne he did not see how Blythe could do it, and *he*, for his part, could never humiliate himself so.

"Fancy Charlie Sloane in a 'caliker' apron and a 'sun bunnit,'" giggled Priscilla. "He'd look exactly like his old Grandmother Sloane. Gilbert, now, looked as much like a man in them as in his own proper habiliments."

Anne and Priscilla found themselves in the thick of the social life of Redmond. That this came about so speedily was due in great measure to Philippa Gordon. Philippa was the daughter of a rich and well-known man, and belonged to an old and exclusive "Bluenose" family. This, combined with her beauty and charm—a charm acknowledged by all who met her—promptly opened the gates of all cliques, clubs and classes in Redmond to her; and where she went Anne and Priscilla went, too. Phil "adored" Anne and Priscilla, especially Anne. She was a loyal little soul, crystal-free from any form of snobbishness. "Love me, love my friends" seemed to be her unconscious motto. Without effort, she took them with her into her ever widening circle of acquaintanceship, and the two Avonlea girls found their social pathway at Redmond made very easy and pleasant for them, to the envy and wonderment of the other freshettes, who, lacking Philippa's sponsorship, were doomed to remain rather on the fringe of things during their first college year.

To Anne and Priscilla, with their more serious views of life, Phil remained the amusing, lovable baby she had seemed on their first meeting. Yet, as she said herself, she had "heaps" of brains. When or where she found time to study was a mystery, for she seemed always in demand for some kind of "fun," and her home evenings were crowded with callers. She had all the "beaux" that heart could desire, for nine-tenths of the Freshmen and a big fraction of all the other classes were rivals for her smiles. She was naïvely delighted over this, and gleefully recounted each new conquest to Anne and Priscilla, with comments that might have made the unlucky lover's ears burn fiercely.

"Alec and Alonzo don't seem to have any serious rival yet," remarked Anne, teasingly.

"Not one," agreed Philippa. "I write them both every week and tell them all about my young men here. I'm sure it must amuse them. But, of course, the one I like best I can't get. Gilbert Blythe won't take any notice of me, except to look at me as if I were a nice little kitten he'd like to pat. Too well I know the reason. I owe you a grudge, Queen Anne. I really ought to hate you and instead I love you madly, and I'm miserable if I don't see you every day. You're different from any girl I ever knew before. When you look at me in a certain way I feel what an insignificant, frivolous little beast I am, and I long to be better and wiser and stronger. And then I make good resolutions; but the first nice-looking mannie who comes my way knocks them all out of my head. Isn't college life magnificent? It's so funny to think I hated it that first day. But if I hadn't I might never got really acquainted with you. Anne, please tell me over again that you like me a little bit. I yearn to hear it."

"I like you a big bit—and I think you're a dear, sweet, adorable, velvety, clawless, little—kitten," laughed Anne, "but I don't see when you ever get time to learn your lessons."

Phil must have found time for she held her own in every class of her year. Even the grumpy old professor of Mathematics, who detested co-eds, and had bitterly opposed their admission to Redmond, couldn't floor her. She led the freshettes everywhere, except in English, where Anne Shirley left her far behind. Anne herself found the studies of her Freshman year very easy, thanks in great part to the steady work she and Gilbert had put in during those two past years in Avonlea. This left her more time for a social life which she thoroughly enjoyed. But never for a moment did she forget Avonlea and the friends there. To her, the happiest moments in each week were those in which letters came from home. It was not until she had got her first letters that she began to think she could ever like Kingsport or feel at home there. Before they came, Avonlea had seemed thousands of miles away; those letters brought it near and linked the old life to the new so closely that they began to seem one and the same, instead of two hopelessly segregated existences. The first batch contained six letters, from Jane Andrews, Ruby Gillis, Diana Barry, Marilla, Mrs. Lynde and Davy. Jane's was a copper-plate production, with every "t" nicely crossed and every "i" precisely dotted, and not an interesting sentence in it. She never mentioned the school, concerning which Anne was avid to hear; she never answered one of the questions Anne had asked in her letter. But she told Anne how many yards of lace she had recently crocheted, and the kind of weather they were having in Avonlea, and how she intended to have her new dress made, and the way she felt when her head ached. Ruby Gillis wrote a gushing epistle deploring Anne's absence, assuring her she was horribly missed in everything, asking what the Redmond "fellows" were like, and filling the rest with accounts of her own harrowing experiences with her numerous admirers. It was a silly, harmless letter, and Anne would have laughed over it had it not been for the postscript. "Gilbert seems to be enjoying Redmond, judging from his letters," wrote Ruby. "I don't think Charlie is so struck on it."

So Gilbert was writing to Ruby! Very well. He had a perfect right to, of course. Only—!! Anne did not know that Ruby had written the first letter and that Gilbert had answered it from mere courtesy. She tossed Ruby's letter aside contemptuously. But it took all Diana's breezy, newsy, delightful epistle to banish the sting of Ruby's postscript. Diana's letter contained a little too

much Fred, but was otherwise crowded and crossed with items
of interest, and Anne almost felt herself back in Avonlea while
reading it. Marilla's was a rather prim and colorless epistle,
severely innocent of gossip or emotion. Yet somehow it conveyed
to Anne a whiff of the wholesome, simple life at Green Gables,
with its savor of ancient peace, and the steadfast abiding love that
was there for her. Mrs. Lynde's letter was full of church news.
Having broken up housekeeping, Mrs. Lynde had more time than
ever to devote to church affairs and had flung herself into them
heart and soul. She was at present much worked up over the
poor "supplies" they were having in the vacant Avonlea pulpit.

"I don't believe any but fools enter the ministry nowadays,"
she wrote bitterly. "Such candidates as they have sent us, and
such stuff as they preach! Half of it ain't true, and, what's worse, it
ain't sound doctrine. The one we have now is the worst of the lot.
He mostly takes a text and preaches about something else. And
he says he doesn't believe all the heathen will be eternally lost.
The idea! If they won't all the money we've been giving to Foreign Missions will be clean wasted, that's what! Last Sunday night
he announced that next Sunday he'd preach on the axe-head that
swam. I think he'd better confine himself to the Bible and leave
sensational subjects alone. Things have come to a pretty pass if a
minister can't find enough in Holy Writ to preach about, that's
what. What church do you attend, Anne? I hope you go regularly.
People are apt to get so careless about church-going away from
home, and I understand college students are great sinners in this
respect. I'm told many of them actually study their lessons on
Sunday. I hope you'll never sink that low, Anne. Remember how
you were brought up. And be very careful what friends you
make. You never know what sort of creatures are in them colleges. Outwardly they may be as whited sepulchers and inwardly
as ravening wolves, that's what. You'd better not have anything to
say to any young man who isn't from the Island.

"I forgot to tell you what happened the day the minister called
here. It was the funniest thing I ever saw. I said to Marilla, 'If

Anne had been here wouldn't she have had a laugh?' Even Marilla laughed. You know he's a very short, fat little man with bow legs. Well, that old pig of Mr. Harrison's—the big, tall one—had wandered over here that day again and broke into the yard, and it got into the back porch, unbeknowns to us, and it was there when the minister appeared in the doorway. It made one wild bolt to get out, but there was nowhere to bolt to except between them bow legs. So there it went, and, being as it was so big and the minister so little, it took him clean off his feet and carried him away. His hat went one way and his cane another, just as Marilla and I got to the door. I'll never forget the look of him. And that poor pig was near scared to death. I'll never be able to read that account in the Bible of the swine that rushed madly down the steep place into the sea without seeing Mr. Harrison's pig careering down the hill with that minister. I guess the pig thought he had the Old Boy on his back instead of inside of him. I was thankful the twins weren't about. It wouldn't have been the right thing for them to have seen a minister in such an undignified predicament. Just before they got to the brook the minister jumped off or fell off. The pig rushed through the brook like mad and up through the woods. Marilla and I run down and helped the minister get up and brush his coat. He wasn't hurt, but he was mad. He seemed to hold Marilla and me responsible for it all, though we told him the pig didn't belong to us, and had been pestering us all summer. Besides, what did he come to the back door for? You'd never have caught Mr. Allan doing that. It'll be a long time before we get a man like Mr. Allan. But it's an ill wind that blows no good. We've never seen hoof or hair of that pig since, and it's my belief we never will.

"Things is pretty quiet in Avonlea. I don't find Green Gables as lonesome as I expected. I think I'll start another cotton warp quilt this winter. Mrs. Silas Sloane has a handsome new apple-leaf pattern.

"When I feel that I must have some excitement I read the murder trials in that Boston paper my niece sends me. I never used to do it, but they're real interesting. The States must be an awful place. I hope you'll never go there, Anne. But the way girls roam over the earth now is something terrible. It always makes me think of Satan in the Book of Job, going to and fro and walking up and down. I don't believe the Lord ever intended it, that's what.

"Davy has been pretty good since you went away. One day he was bad and Marilla punished him by making him wear Dora's apron all day, and then he went and cut all Dora's aprons up. I spanked him for that and then he went and chased my rooster to death.

"The MacPhersons have moved down to my place. She's a great housekeeper and very particular. She's rooted all my June lilies up because she says they make a garden look so untidy. Thomas set them lilies out when we were married. Her husband seems a nice sort of a man, but she can't get over being an old maid, that's what.

"Don't study too hard, and be sure and put your winter underclothes on as soon as the weather gets cool. Marilla worries a lot about you, but I tell her you've got a lot more sense than I ever thought you would have at one time, and that you'll be all right."

Davy's letter plunged into a grievance at the start.

"Dear anne, please write and tell marilla not to tie me to the rale of the bridge when I go fishing the boys make fun of me when she does. Its awful lonesome here without you but grate fun in school. Jane andrews is crosser than you. I scared mrs. lynde with a jacky lantern last nite. She was offel mad and she was mad cause I chased her old rooster round the yard till he fell down ded. I didn't mean to make him fall down ded. What made him die, anne, I want to know. Mrs lynde threw him into the pig pen she mite of sold him to mr. blair. mr. blair is giving 50 sense apeace for good ded roosters now. I herd mrs. lynde asking the minister to pray for her. What did she do that was so bad, anne, I want to know. I've got a kite with a magnificent tail, anne. Milty bolter told me a grate story in school yesterday. it is troo. old Joe

Mosey and Leon were playing cards one nite last week in the woods. The cards were on a stump and a big black man bigger than the trees come along and grabbed the cards and the stump and disapered with a noys like thunder. Ill bet they were skared. Milty says the black man was the old harry. was he, anne, I want to know. Mr. kimball over at spenservale is very sick and will have to go to the hospitable. please excuse me while I ask marilla if thats spelled rite. Marilla says its the silem he has to go to not the other place. He thinks he has a snake inside of him. whats it like to have a snake inside of you, anne. I want to know. mrs. lawrence bell is sick to. mrs. lynde says that all that is the matter with her is that she thinks too much about her insides."

"I wonder," said Anne, as she folded up her letters, "what Mrs. Lynde would think of Philippa."

6

IN THE PARK

"What are you going to do with yourselves today, girls?" asked Philippa, popping into Anne's room one Saturday afternoon.

"We are going for a walk in the park," answered Anne. "I ought to stay in and finish my blouse. But I couldn't sew on a day like this. There's something in the air that gets into my blood and makes a sort of glory in my soul. My fingers would twitch and I'd sew a crooked seam. So it's ho for the park and the pines."

"Does 'we' include any one but yourself and Priscilla?"

"Yes, it includes Gilbert and Charlie, and we'll be very glad if it will include you, also."

"But," said Philippa dolefully, "if I go I'll have to be gooseberry, and that will be a new experience for Philippa Gordon."

"Well, new experiences are broadening. Come along, and you'll be able to sympathize with all poor souls who have to play gooseberry often. But where are all the victims?"

"Oh, I was tired of them all and simply couldn't be bothered with any of them today. Besides, I've been feeling a little blue— just a pale, elusive azure. It isn't serious enough for anything darker. I wrote Alec and Alonzo last week. I put the letters into envelopes and addressed them, but I didn't seal them up. That evening something funny happened. That is, Alec would think it funny, but Alonzo wouldn't be likely to. I was in a hurry, so I snatched Alec's letter—as I thought—out of the envelope and scribbled down a postscript. Then I mailed both letters. I got Alonzo's reply this morning. Girls, I had put that postscript to *his* letter and he was furious. Of course he'll get over it—and I don't care if he doesn't—but it spoiled my day. So I thought I'd come to you darlings to get cheered up. After the football season opens I won't have any spare Saturday afternoons. I adore football. I've got the most gorgeous cap and sweater striped in Redmond colors to wear to the games. To be sure, a little way off I'll look like a walking barber's pole. Do you know that that Gilbert of yours has been elected Captain of the Freshman football team?"

"Yes, he told us so last evening," said Priscilla, seeing that outraged Anne would not answer. "He and Charlie were down. We knew they were coming, so we painstakingly put out of sight or out of reach all of Miss Ada's cushions. That very elaborate one with the raised embroidery I dropped on the floor in the corner behind the chair it was on. I thought it would be safe there. But would you believe it? Charlie Sloane made for that chair, noticed the cushion behind it, solemnly fished it up, and sat on it the whole evening. Such a wreck of a cushion as it was! Poor Miss Ada asked me today, still smiling, but oh, so reproachfully, why I had allowed it to be sat upon. I told her I hadn't—that it was a matter of predestination coupled with inveterate Sloanishness and I wasn't a match for both combined."

"Miss Ada's cushions are really getting on my nerves," said Anne. "She finished two new ones last week, stuffed and embroidered within an inch of their lives. There being absolutely no other cushionless place to put them she stood them up against the wall on the stair landing. They topple over half the time and if we come up or down the stairs in the dark we fall over them. Last Sunday, when Dr. Davis prayed for all those exposed to the perils of the sea, I added in thought 'and for all those who live in houses where cushions are loved not wisely but too well!' There! we're ready, and I see the boys coming through Old St. John's. Do you cast in your lot with us, Phil?"

"I'll go, if I can walk with Priscilla and Charlie. That will be a bearable degree of gooseberry. That Gilbert of yours is a darling, Anne, but why *does* he go around so much with Goggle-eyes?"

Anne stiffened. She had no great liking for Charlie Sloane; but he was of Avonlea, so no outsider had any business to laugh at him.

"Charlie and Gilbert have always been friends," she said coldly. "Charlie is a nice boy. He's not to blame for his eyes."

"Don't tell me that! He is! He must have done something dreadful in a previous existence to be punished with such eyes. Pris and I are going to have such sport with him this afternoon. We'll make fun of him to his face and he'll never know it."

Doubtless, "the abandoned P's," as Anne called them, did carry out their amiable intentions. But Sloane was blissfully ignorant; he thought he was quite a fine fellow to be walking with two such co-eds, especially Philippa Gordon, the class beauty and belle. It must surely impress Anne. She would see that some people appreciated him at his real value.

Gilbert and Anne loitered a little behind the others, enjoying the calm, still beauty of the autumn afternoon under the pines of the park, on the road that climbed and twisted around the harbor shore.

"The silence here is like a prayer, isn't it?" said Anne, her face upturned to the shining sky. "How I love the pines! They seem to strike their roots deep into the romance of all the ages. It is so comforting to creep away now and then for a good talk with them. I always feel so happy out here."

>"'And so in mountain solitudes o'ertaken
>   As by some spell divine,
>   Their cares drop from them like the needles shaken
>   From out the gusty pine,'"

quoted Gilbert.

"They make our little ambitions seem rather petty, don't they, Anne?"

"I think, if ever any great sorrow came to me, I would come to the pines for comfort," said Anne dreamily.

"I hope no great sorrow ever will come to you, Anne," said Gilbert, who could not connect the idea of sorrow with the vivid, joyous creature beside him, unwitting that those who can soar to the highest heights can also plunge to the deepest depths, and that the natures which enjoy most keenly are those which also suffer most sharply.

"But there must—sometime," mused Anne. "Life seems like a cup of glory held to my lips just now. But there must be some bitterness in it—there is in every cup. I shall taste mine some day. Well, I hope I shall be strong and brave to meet it. And I hope it won't be through my own fault that it will come. Do you remember what Dr. Davis said last Sunday evening—that the sorrows God sent us brought comfort and strength with them, while the sorrows we brought on ourselves, through folly or wickedness, were by far the hardest to bear? But we mustn't talk of sorrow on an afternoon like this. It's meant for the sheer joy of living, isn't it?"

"If I had my way I'd shut everything out of your life but happiness and pleasure, Anne," said Gilbert in the tone that meant "danger ahead."

"Then you would be very unwise," rejoined Anne hastily. "I'm sure no life can be properly developed and rounded out without some trial and sorrow—though I suppose it is only when we are pretty comfortable that we admit it. Come—the others have got to the pavilion and are beckoning to us."

They all sat down in the little pavilion to watch an autumn sunset of deep red fire and pallid gold. To their left lay Kingsport, its roofs and spires dim in their shroud of violet smoke. To their right lay the harbor, taking on tints of rose and copper as it stretched out into the sunset. Before them the water shimmered, satin smooth and silver gray, and beyond, clean shaven William's Island loomed out of the mist, guarding the town like a sturdy bulldog. Its lighthouse beacon flared through the mist like a baleful star, and was answered by another in the far horizon.

"Did you ever see such a strong-looking place?" asked Philippa. "I don't want William's Island especially, but I'm sure I couldn't get it if I did. Look at that sentry on the summit of the fort, right beside the flag. Doesn't he look as if he had stepped out of a romance?"

"Speaking of romance," said Priscilla, "we've been looking for heather—but, of course, we couldn't find any. It's too late in the season, I suppose."

"Heather!" exclaimed Anne. "Heather doesn't grow in America, does it?"

"There are just two patches of it in the whole continent," said Phil, "one right here in the park, and one somewhere else in Nova Scotia, I forget where. The famous Highland Regiment, the Black Watch, camped here one year, and, when the men shook out the straw of their beds in the spring, some seeds of heather took root."

"Oh, how delightful!" said enchanted Anne.

"Let's go home around by Spofford Avenue," suggested Gilbert. "We can see all 'the handsome houses where the wealthy nobles dwell.' Spofford Avenue is the finest residential street in Kingsport. Nobody can build on it unless he's a millionaire."

"Oh, do," said Phil. "There's a perfectly killing little place I want to show you, Anne. It wasn't built by a millionaire. It's the first place after you leave the park, and must have grown while Spofford Avenue was still a country road. It did grow—it wasn't built! I don't care for the houses on the Avenue. They're too brand new and plate-glassy. But this little spot is a dream—and its name—but wait till you see it."

They saw it as they walked up the pine-fringed hill from the park. Just on the crest, where Spofford Avenue petered out into a plain road, was a little white frame house with groups of pines on either side of it, stretching their arms protectingly over its low roof. It was covered with red and gold vines, through which its green-shuttered windows peeped. Before it was a tiny garden, surrounded by a low stone wall. October though it was, the garden was still very sweet with dear, old-fashioned, unworldly flowers and shrubs—sweet may, southern-wood, lemon verbena, alyssum, petunias, marigolds and chrysanthemums. A tiny brick wall, in herring-bone pattern, led from the gate to the front porch. The whole place might have been transplanted from some remote country village; yet there was something about it that made its nearest neighbor, the big lawn-encircled palace of a tobacco king, look exceedingly crude and showy and ill-bred by contrast. As Phil said, it was the difference between being born and being made.

"It's the dearest place I ever saw," said Anne delightedly. "It gives me one of my old, delightful, funny aches. It's dearer and quainter than even Miss Lavendar's stone house."

"It's the name I want you to notice especially," said Phil. "Look—in white letters, around the archway over the gate. 'Patty's Place,' isn't that killing? Especially on this Avenue of Pine-hursts and Elmwolds and Cedarcrofts? 'Patty's Place,' if you please! I adore it."

"Have you any idea who Patty is?" asked Priscilla.

"Patty Spofford is the name of the old lady who owns it, I've discovered. She lives there with her niece, and they've lived there for hundreds of years, more or less—maybe a little less, Anne. Exaggeration is merely a flight of poetic fancy. I understand that wealthy folk have tried to buy the lot time and again—it's really worth a small fortune now, you know—but 'Patty' won't sell upon any consideration. And there's an apple orchard behind the house in place of a back yard—you'll see it when we get a little past—a real apple orchard on Spofford Avenue!"

"I'm going to dream about 'Patty's Place' tonight," said Anne. "Why, I feel as if I belonged to it. I wonder if, by any chance, we'll ever see the inside of it."

"It isn't likely," said Priscilla.

Anne smiled mysteriously.

"No, it isn't likely. But I believe it will happen. I have a queer, creepy, crawly feeling—you can call it a presentiment, if you like—that 'Patty's Place' and I are going to be better acquainted yet."

7

HOME AGAIN

Those first three weeks at Redmond had seemed long; but the rest of the term flew by on wings of wind. Before they realized it the Redmond students found themselves in the grind of Christmas examinations, emerging therefrom more or less triumphantly. The honor of leading the Freshman classes fluctuated between Anne, Gilbert and Philippa; Priscilla did very well; Charlie Sloane scraped through respectably, and comported himself as complacently as if he had led in everything.

"I can't really believe that this time tomorrow I'll be in Green Gables," said Anne on the night before departure. "But I shall be. And you, Phil, will be in Bolingbroke with Alec and Alonzo."

"I'm longing to see them," admitted Phil, between the chocolatee she was nibbling. "They really are such dear boys, you know. Oh, I'm going to have a splendid time in the holidays. There's to be no end of dances and drives and general jamborees. I shall never forgive you, Queen Anne, for not coming home with me for the holidays."

"'Never' means three days with you, Phil. It was dear of you to ask me.—and I'd love to go to Bolingbroke some day. But I can't go this year—I *must* go home. You don't know how my heart longs for it."

"You won't have much of a time," said Phil scornfully. "There'll be one or two quilting parties, I suppose; and all the old gossips will talk you over to your face and behind your back. You'll die of lonesomeness, child."

"In Avonlea?" said Anne, highly amused.

"Now, if you'd come with me you'd have a perfectly gorgeous time. Bolingbroke would go wild over you, Queen Anne—your hair and your style and, oh, everything! You're so *different*. You'd be such a success—and I would bask in reflected glory—'not the rose but near the rose.' *Do* come, after all, Anne."

"Your picture of social triumphs is quite fascinating, Phil, but I'll paint one to off-set it. I'm going home to an old country farmhouse, once green, rather faded now, set among leafless apple orchards. There is a brook below and a December fir wood beyond, where I've heard harps swept by the fingers of rain and wind. There is a pond near by that will be gray and brooding now. There will be two oldish ladies in the house, one tall and thin, one short and fat; and there will be two twins, one a perfect model, the other what Mrs. Lynde calls a 'holy terror.' There will be a little room upstairs over the porch, where the old dreams hang thick, and a big, fat, glorious feather bed which will almost seem the height of luxury after a boarding house mattress. How do you like my picture, Phil?"

"It seems a very dull one," said Phil, with a grimace.

"Oh, but I've left out the transforming thing," said Anne softly. "There'll be love there, Phil—faithful, tender love, such as I'll never find anywhere else in the world—love that's waiting for *me*. That makes my picture a masterpiece, doesn't it, even if the colors are not very brilliant?"

Phil silently got up, tossed her box of chocolates away, went up to Anne, and put her arms about her.

"Anne, I wish I was like you," she said soberly.

Diana met Anne at the Carmody station the next night, and they drove home together under silent, star-sown depths of sky. Green Gables had a very festal appearance as they drove up the lane. There was a light in every window, the glow breaking out through the darkness like flame-red blossoms swung against the dark background of the Haunted Wood. And in the yard was a brave bonfire with two gay little figures dancing around it, one of which gave an unearthly yell as the buggy turned in under the poplars.

"Davy means that for an Indian war-whoop," said Diana. "Mr. Harrison's hired boy taught it to him, and he's been practicing it up to welcome you with. Mrs. Lynde says it has worn her nerves to a frazzle. He creeps up behind her, you know, and then lets go. He was determined to have a bonfire for you, too. He's been piling up dry branches for a fortnight and pestering Marilla to be let pour some kerosene oil over it before setting it on fire. I guess she did, by the smell, though Mrs. Lynde said up to the last that Davy would blow himself and everybody else up if he was let."

Anne was out of the buggy by this time, and Davy was rapturously hugging her knees, while even Dora was clinging to her hand.

"Isn't that a bully bonfire, Anne? Just let me show you how to poke it—see the sparks? I did it for you, Anne, 'cause I was so glad you were coming home."

The kitchen door opened and Marilla's spare form darkened against the inner light. She preferred to meet Anne in the shadows, for she was horribly afraid that she was going to cry with joy,—she, stern, repressed Marilla, who thought all display of deep emotion unseemly. Mrs. Lynde was behind her, sonsy, kindly, matronly, as of yore. The love that Anne had told Phil was waiting for her surrounded her and enfolded her with its blessing and its sweetness. Nothing, after all, could compare with old ties, old friends, and old Green Gables! How starry Anne's eyes were as they sat down to the loaded supper table, how pink her cheeks, how silver-clear her laughter! And Diana was going to stay all night, too. How like the dear old times it was! And the rosebud tea set graced the table! With Marilla the force of nature could no further go.

"I suppose you and Diana will now proceed to talk all night," said Marilla sarcastically, as the girls went upstairs. Marilla was always sarcastic after any self-betrayal.

"Yes," agreed Anne gaily, "but I'm going to put Davy to bed first. He insists on that."

"You bet," said Davy, as they went along the hall. "I want somebody to say my prayers to again. It's no fun saying them alone."

"You don't say them alone, Davy. God is always with you to hear you."

"Well, I can't see Him," objected Davy. "I want to pray to somebody I can see, but I *won't* say them to Mrs. Lynde or Marilla, there now!"

Nevertheless, when Davy was garbed in his gray flannel nighty, he did not seem in a hurry to begin. He stood before Anne, shuffling one bare foot over the other, and looked undecided.

"Come, dear, kneel down," said Anne.

Davy came and buried his head in Anne's lap, but he did not kneel down.

"Anne," he said in a muffled voice, "I don't feel like praying after all. I haven't felt like it for a week now. I—I *didn't* pray last night nor the night before."

"Why not, Davy?" asked Anne gently.

"You—you won't be mad if I tell you?" implored Davy.

Anne lifted the little gray-flannelled body on her knee and cuddled his head on her arm.

"Do I ever get 'mad' when you tell me things, Davy?"

"No-o-o, you never do. But you get sorry, and that's worse. You'll be awful sorry when I tell you this, Anne—and you'll be 'shamed of me, I s'pose."

"Have you done something naughty, Davy, and is that why you can't say your prayers?"

"No, I haven't done anything naughty—yet. But I want to do it."

"What is it, Davy?"

"I—I want to say a bad word, Anne," blurted out Davy, with a desperate effort. "I heard Mr. Harrison's hired boy say it one day last week, and ever since I've been wanting to say it *all* the time—even when I'm saying my prayers."

"Say it then, Davy."

Davy lifted his flushed face in amazement.

"But, Anne, it's an *awful* bad word."

"*Say it!*"

Davy gave her another incredulous look, then in a low voice he said the dreadful word. The next minute his face was burrowing against her.

"Oh, Anne, I'll never say it again—never. I'll never *want* to say it again. I knew it was bad, but I didn't s'pose it was so—so—I didn't s'pose it was like *that*."

"No, I don't think you'll ever want to say it again, Davy—or think it, either. And I wouldn't go about much with Mr. Harrison's hired boy if I were you."

"He can make bully war-whoops," said Davy a little regretfully.

"But you don't want your mind filled with bad words, do you, Davy—words that will poison it and drive out all that is good and manly?"

"No," said Davy, owl-eyed with introspection.

"Then don't go with those people who use them. And now do you feel as if you could say your prayers, Davy?"

"Oh, yes," said Davy, eagerly wriggling down on his knees, "I can say them now all right. I ain't scared now to say 'if I should die before I wake,' like I was when I was wanting to say that word."

Probably Anne and Diana did empty out their souls to each other that night, but no record of their confidences has been preserved. They both looked as fresh and bright-eyed at breakfast as only youth can look after unlawful hours of revelry and confession. There had been no snow up to this time, but as Diana crossed the old log bridge on her homeward way the white flakes were beginning to flutter down over the fields and woods, russet and gray in their dreamless sleep. Soon the far-away slopes and hills were dim and wraith-like through their gauzy scarfing, as if pale autumn had flung a misty bridal veil over her hair and was waiting for her wintry bridegroom. So they had a white Christmas after all, and a very pleasant day it was. In the forenoon letters and gifts came from Miss Lavendar and Paul; Anne opened them in the cheerful Green Gables kitchen, which was filled with what Davy, sniffing in ecstasy, called "pretty smells."

"Miss Lavendar and Mr. Irving are settled in their new home now," reported Anne. "I am sure Miss Lavendar is perfectly happy—I know it by the general tone of her letter—but there's a note from Charlotta the Fourth. She doesn't like Boston at all, and she is fearfully homesick. Miss Lavendar wants me to go through to Echo Lodge some day while I'm home and light a fire to air it, and see that the cushions aren't getting moldy. I think I'll get Diana to go over with me next week, and we can spend the evening with Theodora Dix. I want to see Theodora. By the way, is Ludovic Speed still going to see her?"

"They say so," said Marilla, "and he's likely to continue it. Folks have given up expecting that that courtship will ever arrive anywhere."

"I'd hurry him up a bit, if I was Theodora, that's what," said Mrs. Lynde. And there is not the slightest doubt but that she would.

There was also a characteristic scrawl from Philippa, full of Alec and Alonzo, what they said and what they did, and how they looked when they saw her.

"But I can't make up my mind yet which to marry," wrote Phil. "I do wish you had come with me to decide for me. Some one will have to. When I saw Alec my heart gave a great thump and I thought, 'He must be the right one.' And then, when Alonzo came, thump went my heart again. So that's no guide, though it should be, according to all the novels I've ever read. Now, Anne, *your* heart wouldn't thump for anybody but the genuine Prince Charming, would it? There must be something radically wrong with mine. But I'm having a perfectly gorgeous time. How I wish you were here! It's snowing today, and I'm rapturous. I was so afraid we'd have a green Christmas and I loathe them. You know, when Christmas is a dirty grayey-browney affair, looking as if it had been left over a hundred years ago and had been in soak ever since, it is called a *green* Christmas! Don't ask me why. As Lord Dundreary says 'there are thome thingth no fellow can underthtand.'

"Anne, did you ever get on a street car and then discover that you hadn't any money with you to pay your fare? I did, the other day. It's quite awful. I had a nickel with me when I got on the car. I thought it was in the left pocket of my coat. When I got settled down comfortably I felt for it. It wasn't there. I had a cold chill. I felt in the other pocket. Not there. I had another chill. Then I felt in a little inside pocket. All in vain. I had two chills at once.

"I took off my gloves, laid them on the seat, and went over all my pockets again. It was not there. I stood up and shook myself, and then looked on the floor. The car was full of people, who were going home from the opera, and they all stared at me, but I was past caring for a little thing like that.

"But I could not find my fare. I concluded I must have put it in my mouth and swallowed it inadvertently.

"I didn't know what to do. Would the conductor, I wondered, stop the car and put me off in ignominy and shame? Was it possible that I could convince him that I was merely the victim of my own absent-mindedness, and not an unprincipled creature trying to obtain a ride upon false pretenses? How I wished that Alec or Alonzo were there. But they weren't because I wanted them. If I *hadn't* wanted them they would have been there by the dozen. And I couldn't decide what to say to the conductor when he came around. As soon as I got one sentence of explanation mapped out in my mind I felt nobody could believe it and I must compose another. It seemed there was nothing to do but trust in Providence, and for all the comfort that gave me I might as well have been the old lady who, when told by the captain during a storm that she must put her trust in the Almighty exclaimed, 'Oh, Captain, is it as bad as that?'

"Just at the conventional moment, when all hope had fled,

and the conductor was holding out his box to the passenger next to me, I suddenly remembered where I had put that wretched coin of the realm. I hadn't swallowed it after all. I meekly fished it out of the index finger of my glove and poked it in the box. I smiled at everybody and felt that it was a beautiful world."

The visit to Echo Lodge was not the least pleasant of many pleasant holiday outings. Anne and Diana went back to it by the old way of the beech woods, carrying a lunch basket with them. Echo Lodge, which had been closed ever since Miss Lavendar's wedding, was briefly thrown open to wind and sunshine once more, and firelight glimmered again in the little rooms. The perfume of Miss Lavendar's rose bowl still filled the air. It was hardly possible to believe that Miss Lavendar would not come tripping in presently, with her brown eyes a-star with welcome, and that Charlotta the Fourth, blue of bow and wide of smile, would not pop through the door. Paul, too, seemed hovering around, with his fairy fancies.

"It really makes me feel a little bit like a ghost revisiting the old time glimpses of the moon," laughed Anne. "Let's go out and see if the echoes are at home. Bring the old horn. It is still behind the kitchen door."

The echoes were at home, over the white river, as silver-clear and multitudinous as ever; and when they had ceased to answer the girls locked up Echo Lodge again and went away in the perfect half hour that follows the rose and saffron of a winter sunset.

8
ANNE'S FIRST PROPOSAL

The old year did not slip away in a green twilight, with a pinky-yellow sunset. Instead, it went out with a wild, white bluster and blow. It was one of the nights when the storm-wind hurtles over the frozen meadows and black hollows, and moans around the eaves like a lost creature, and drives the snow sharply against the shaking panes.

"Just the sort of night people like to cuddle down between their blankets and count their mercies," said Anne to Jane Andrews, who had come up to spend the afternoon and stay all night. But when they were cuddled between their blankets, in Anne's little porch room, it was not her mercies of which Jane was thinking.

"Anne," she said very solemnly, "I want to tell you something. May I?"

Anne was feeling rather sleepy after the party Ruby Gillis had given the night before. She would much rather have gone to sleep than listen to Jane's confidences, which she was sure would bore her. She had no prophetic inkling of what was coming. Probably Jane was engaged, too; rumor averred that Ruby Gillis was engaged to the Spencervale schoolteacher, about whom all the girls were said to be quite wild.

"I'll soon be the only fancy-free maiden of our old quartette," thought Anne, drowsily. Aloud she said, "Of course."

"Anne," said Jane, still more solemnly, "what do you think of my brother Billy?"

Anne gasped over this unexpected question, and floundered helplessly in her thoughts. Goodness, what *did* she think of Billy Andrews? She had never thought *anything* about him—round-faced, stupid, perpetually smiling, good-natured Billy Andrews. Did *anybody* ever think about Billy Andrews?

"I—I don't understand, Jane," she stammered. "What do you mean—exactly?"

"Do you like Billy?" asked Jane bluntly.

"Why—why—yes, I like him, of course," gasped Anne, wondering if she were telling the literal truth. Certainly she did not *dislike* Billy. But could the indifferent tolerance with which she regarded him, when he happened to be in her range of vision, be considered positive enough for liking? *What* was Jane trying to elucidate?

"Would you like him for a husband?" asked Jane calmly.

"A husband!" Anne had been sitting up in bed, the better to wrestle with the problem of her exact opinion of Billy Andrews. Now she fell flatly back on her pillows, the very breath gone out of her. "*Whose* husband?"

"Yours, of course," answered Jane. "Billy wants to marry you. He's always been crazy about you—and now father has given him the upper farm in his own name and there's nothing to prevent him from getting married. But he's so shy he couldn't ask you himself if you'd have him, so he got me to do it. I'd rather not have, but he gave me no peace till I said I would, if I got a good chance. What do you think about it, Anne?"

Was it a dream? Was it one of those nightmare things in which you find yourself engaged or married to some one you hate or don't know, without the slightest idea how it ever came about? No, she, Anne Shirley, was lying there, wide awake, in her own bed, and Jane Andrews was beside her, calmly proposing for her brother Billy. Anne did not know whether she wanted to writhe or laugh; but she could do neither, for Jane's feelings must not be hurt.

"I—I couldn't marry Billy, you know, Jane," she managed to gasp. "Why, such an idea never occurred to me—never!"

"I don't suppose it did," agreed Jane. "Billy has always been far too shy to think of courting. But you might think it over, Anne. Billy is a good fellow. I must say that, if he *is* my brother. He has no bad habits and he's a great worker, and you can depend on him. 'A bird in the hand is worth two in the bush.' He told me to tell you he'd be quite willing to wait till you got through college, if you insisted, though he'd *rather* get married this spring before the planting begins. He'd always be very good to you, I'm sure, and you know, Anne, I'd love to have you for a sister."

"I can't marry Billy," said Anne decidedly. She had recovered her wits, and was even feeling a little angry. It was all so ridiculous. "There is no use thinking of it, Jane. I don't care anything for him in that way, and you must tell him so."

"Well, I didn't suppose you would," said Jane with a resigned sigh, feeling that she had done her best. "I told Billy I didn't believe it was a bit of use to ask you, but he insisted. Well, you've made your decision, Anne, and I hope you won't regret it."

Jane spoke rather coldly. She had been perfectly sure that the enamored Billy had no chance at all of inducing Anne to marry him. Nevertheless, she felt a little resentment that Anne Shirley, who was, after all, merely an adopted orphan, without kith or kin, should refuse *her* brother,—one of the Avonlea Andrews. Well, pride sometimes goes before a fall, Jane reflected ominously.

Anne permitted herself to smile in the darkness over the idea that she might ever regret not marrying Billy Andrews.

"I hope Billy won't feel very badly over it," she said nicely.

Jane made a movement as if she were tossing her head on the pillow.

"Oh, he won't break his heart. Billy has too much good sense for that. He likes Nettie Blewett pretty well, too, and mother would rather he married her than any one. She's such a good manager and saver. I think, when Billy is once sure you won't have him, he'll take Nettie. Please don't mention this to any one, will you, Anne?"

"Certainly not," said Anne, who had no desire whatever to publish abroad the fact that Billy Andrews wanted to marry her preferring her, when all was said and done, to Nettie Blewett. Nettie Blewett!

"And now I suppose we'd better go to sleep," suggested Jane.

To sleep went Jane easily and speedily; but, though very unlike MacBeth in most respects, she had certainly contrived to murder sleep for Anne. That proposed-to damsel lay on a wakeful pillow until the wee sma's, but her meditations were far from being romantic. It was not, however, until the next morning that she had an opportunity to indulge in a good laugh over the whole affair. When Jane had gone home—still with a hint of frost in voice and manner because Anne had declined so ungratefully and decidedly the honor of an alliance with the House of Andrews—Anne retreated to the porch room, shut the door, and had her laugh out at last.

"If I could only share the joke with some one!" she thought. "But I can't. Diana is the only one I'd want to tell, and, even if I hadn't sworn secrecy to Jane I can't tell Diana things now. She tells everything to Fred—I know she does. Well, I've had my first proposal. I supposed it would come some day—but I certainly never thought it would be by proxy. It's awfully funny—and yet there's a sting in it, too, somehow."

Anne knew quite well wherein the sting consisted, though she did not put it into words. She had had her secret dreams of the first time some one should ask her the great question. And it had, in those dreams, always been very romantic and beautiful: and the "some one" was to be very handsome and dark-eyed and distinguished-looking and eloquent, whether he were Prince Charming to be enraptured with "yes," or one to whom a regretful, beautifully worded, but hopeless refusal must be given. If the latter, the refusal was to be expressed so delicately that it would be next best thing to acceptance, and he would go away, after kissing her hand, assuring her of his unalterable, life-long devotion. And it would always be a beautiful memory, to be proud of and a little sad about, also.

And now, this thrilling experience had turned out to be merely grotesque. Billy Andrews had got his sister to propose for him because his father had given him the upper farm; and if Anne wouldn't "have him" Nettie Blewett would. There was romance for you with a vengeance! Anne laughed—and then sighed. The bloom had been brushed from one little maiden dream. Would the painful process go on until everything became prosaic and hum-drum?

9
AN UNWELCOME LOVER AND A WELCOME FRIEND

The second term at Redmond sped as quickly as had the first—"actually whizzed away," Philippa said. Anne enjoyed it thoroughly in all its phases—the stimulating class rivalry, the making and deepening of new and helpful friendships, the gay little social stunts, the doings of the various societies of which she was a member, the widening of horizons and interests. She studied hard, for she had made up her mind to win the Thorburn Scholarship in English. This being won, meant that she could come back to Redmond the next year without trenching on Marilla's small savings—something Anne was determined she would not do.

Gilbert, too, was in full chase after a scholarship, but found plenty of time for frequent calls at Thirty-eight, St. John's. He was Anne's escort at nearly all the college affairs, and she knew that their names were coupled in Redmond gossip. Anne raged over this but was helpless; she could not cast an old friend like Gilbert aside, especially when he had grown suddenly wise and wary, as behooved him in the dangerous proximity of more than one Redmond youth who would gladly have taken his place by the side of the slender, red-haired co-ed, whose gray eyes were as alluring as stars of evening. Anne was never attended by the crowd of willing victims who hovered around Philippa's conquering march through her Freshman year; but there was a lanky, brainy Freshie, a jolly, little, round Sophomore, and a tall, learned Junior who all liked to call at Thirty-eight, St. John's, and talk over 'ologies and 'isms, as well as lighter subjects, with Anne, in the be-cushioned parlor of that domicile. Gilbert did not love any of them, and he was exceedingly careful to give none of them the advantage over him by any untimely display of his real feelings Anne-ward. To her he had become again the boy-comrade of Avonlea days, and as such could hold his own against any smitten swain who had so far entered the lists against him. As a companion, Anne honestly acknowledged nobody could be so satisfactory as Gilbert; she was very glad, so she told herself, that he had evidently dropped all nonsensical ideas—though she spent considerable time secretly wondering why.

Only one disagreeable incident marred that winter. Charlie Sloane, sitting bolt upright on Miss Ada's most dearly beloved cushion, asked Anne one night if she would promise "to become Mrs. Charlie Sloane some day." Coming after Billy Andrews' proxy effort, this was not quite the shock to Anne's romantic sensibilities that it would otherwise have been; but it was certainly another heart-rending disillusion. She was angry, too, for she felt that she had never given Charlie the slightest encouragement to suppose such a thing possible. But what could you expect of a Sloane, as Mrs. Rachel Lynde would ask scornfully? Charlie's whole attitude, tone, air, words, fairly reeked with Sloanishness. He was conferring a great honor—no doubt whatever about that. And when Anne, utterly insensible to the honor, refused him, as delicately and considerately as she could—for even a Sloan had feelings which ought not to be unduly lacerated—Sloanishness still further betrayed itself. Charlie certainly did not take his dismissal as Anne's imaginary rejected suitors did. Instead, he became angry, and showed it; he said two or three quite nasty things; Anne's temper flashed up mutinously and she retorted with a cutting little speech whose keenness pierced even Charlie's protective Sloanishness and reached the quick; he caught up his hat and flung himself out of the house with a very red face; Anne rushed upstairs, falling twice over Miss Ada's cushions on the way, and threw herself on the bed, in tears of humiliation and rage. Had she actually stooped to quarrel with a Sloane? Was it possible anything Charlie Sloane could say had power to make her angry? Oh, this was degradation, indeed—worse even than being the rival of Nettie Blewett!

"I wish I need never see the horrible creature again," she sobbed vindictively into her pillows.

She could not avoid seeing him again, but the outraged

Charlie took care that it should not be at very close quarters. Miss Ada's cushions were henceforth safe from his depredations, and when he met Anne on the street, or in Redmond's halls, his bow was icy in the extreme. Relations between these two old schoolmates continued to be thus strained for nearly a year! Then Charlie transferred his blighted affections to a round, rosy, snub-nosed, blue-eyed, little Sophomore who appreciated them as they deserved, whereupon he forgave Anne and condescended to be civil to her again; in a patronizing manner intended to show her just what she had lost.

One day Anne scurried excitedly into Priscilla's room.

"Read that," she cried, tossing Priscilla a letter. "It's from Stella—and she's coming to Redmond next year—and what do you think of her idea? I think it's a perfectly splendid one, if we can only carry it out. Do you suppose we can, Pris?"

"I'll be better able to tell you when I find out what it is," said Priscilla, casting aside a Greek lexicon and taking up Stella's letter. Stella Maynard had been one of their chums at Queen's Academy and had been teaching school ever since.

"But I'm going to give it up, Anne dear," she wrote, "and go to college next year. As I took the third year at Queen's I can enter the Sophomore year. I'm tired of teaching in a back country school. Some day I'm going to write a treatise on 'The Trials of a Country Schoolmarm.' It will be a harrowing bit of realism. It seems to be the prevailing impression that we live in clover, and have nothing to do but draw our quarter's salary. My treatise shall tell the truth about us. Why, if a week should pass without some one telling me that I am doing easy work for big pay I would conclude that I might as well order my ascension robe 'immediately and to onct.' 'Well, you get your money easy,' some rate-payer will tell me, condescendingly. 'All you have to do is to sit there and hear lessons.' I used to argue the matter at first, but I'm wiser now. Facts are stubborn things, but, as some one has wisely said, not half so stubborn as fallacies. So I only smile loftily now in eloquent silence. Why, I have nine grades in my school and I have to teach a little of everything, from investigating the interiors of earthworms to the study of the solar system. My youngest pupil is four—his mother sends him to school to 'get him out of the way'—and my oldest is twenty—it 'suddenly struck him' that it would be easier to go to school and get an education than follow the plough any longer. In the wild effort to cram all sorts of research into six hours a day I don't wonder if the children feel like the little boy who was taken to see the biograph. 'I have to look for what's coming next before I know what went last,' he complained. I feel like that myself.

"And the letters I get, Anne! Tommy's mother writes me that Tommy is not coming on in arithmetic as fast as she would like. He is only in simple reduction yet, and Johnny Johnson is in fractions, and Johnny isn't half as smart as her Tommy, and she can't understand it. And Susy's father wants to know why Susy can't write a letter without misspelling half the words, and Dick's aunt wants me to change his seat, because that bad Brown boy he is sitting with is teaching him to say naughty words.

"As to the financial part—but I'll not begin on *that*. Those whom the gods wish to destroy they first make country schoolmarms!

"There, I feel better, after that growl. After all, I've enjoyed these past two years. But I'm coming to Redmond.

"And now, Anne, I've a little plan. You know how I loathe boarding. I've boarded for four years and I'm so tired of it. I don't feel like enduring three years more of it. Now, why can't you and Priscilla and I club together, rent a little house somewhere in Kingsport, and board ourselves? It would be cheaper than any other way. Of course, we would have to have a housekeeper and I have one ready on the spot. You've heard me speak of Aunt Jamesina? She's the sweetest aunt that ever lived, in spite of her name. She can't help that! She was called Jamesina because her father, whose name was James, was drowned at sea a month before she was born. I always call her Aunt Jimsie. Well, her only daughter has recently married and gone to the foreign mission field. Aunt Jamesina is left alone in a great big house, and she is horribly lonesome. She will come to Kingsport and keep house for us if we want her, and I know you'll both love her. The more I think of the plan the more I like it. We could have such good, independent times.

"Now, if you and Priscilla agree to it, wouldn't it be a good idea for you, who are on the spot, to look around and see if you can find a suitable house this spring? That would be better than leaving it till the fall. If you could get a furnished one so much the better, but if not, we can scare up a few sticks of furniture between us and old family friends with attics. Anyhow, decide as soon as you can and write me, so that Aunt Jamesina will know what plans to make for next year."

"I think it's a good idea," said Priscilla.

"So do I," agreed Anne delightedly. "Of course, we have a nice boarding-house here, but, when all's said and done, a boarding house isn't home. So let's go house-hunting at once, before exams come on."

"I'm afraid it will be hard enough to get a really suitable house," warned Priscilla. "Don't expect too much, Anne. Nice houses in nice localities will probably be away beyond our means. We'll likely have to content ourselves with a shabby little place on some street whereon live people whom to know is to be unknown, and make life inside compensate for the outside."

Accordingly they went house-hunting, but to find just what they wanted proved even harder than Priscilla had feared. Houses there were galore, furnished and unfurnished; but one was too big, another too small; this one too expensive, that one too far from Redmond. Exams were on and over; the last week of the term came and still their "house o' dreams" as Anne called it, remained a castle in the air.

"We shall have to give up and wait till the fall, I suppose," said Priscilla wearily, as they rambled through the park on one of April's darling days of breeze and blue, when the harbor was creaming and shimmering beneath the pearl-hued mists floating over it. "We may find some shack to shelter us then; and if not, boarding-houses we shall have always with us."

"I'm not going to worry about it just now, anyway, and spoil this lovely afternoon," said Anne, gazing around her with delight. The fresh chill air was faintly charged with the aroma of pine balsam, the sky above was crystal clear and blue—a great inverted cup of blessing. "Spring is singing in my blood today, and the lure of April is abroad on the air. I'm seeing visions and dreaming dreams, Pris. That's because the wind is from the west. I do love the west wind. It sings of hope and gladness, doesn't it? When the east wind blows I always think of sorrowful rain on the eaves and sad waves on a gray shore. When I get old I shall have rheumatism when the wind is east."

"And isn't it jolly when you discard furs and winter garments for the first time and sally forth, like this, in spring attire?" laughed Priscilla. "Don't you feel as if you had been made over new?"

"Everything is new in the spring," said Anne. "Springs themselves are always so new, too. No spring is ever just like any other spring. It always has something of its own to be its own peculiar sweetness. See how green the grass is around that little pond, and how the willow buds are bursting."

"And exams are over and gone—the time of Convocation will soon come—next Wednesday. This day next week we'll be home."

"I'm glad," said Anne dreamily. "There are so many things I want to do. I want to sit on the back porch steps and feel the breeze blowing down over Mr. Harrison's fields. I want to hunt ferns in the Haunted Wood and gather violets in Violet Vale. Do you remember the day of our golden picnic, Priscilla? I want to hear the frogs singing and the poplars whispering. But I've learned to love Kingsport, too, and I'm glad I'm coming back next fall. If I hadn't won the Thorburn I don't believe I could have. I *couldn't* take any of Marilla's little hoard."

"If we could only find a house!" sighed Priscilla. "Look over there at Kingsport, Anne—houses, houses everywhere, and not one for us."

"Stop it, Pris. 'The best is yet to be.' Like the old Roman, we'll find a house or build one. On a day like this there's no such word as fail in my bright lexicon."

They lingered in the park until sunset, living in the amazing miracle and glory and wonder of the springtide; and they went home as usual, by way of Spofford Avenue, that they might have the delight of looking at Patty's Place.

"I feel as if something mysterious were going to happen right away—'by the pricking of my thumbs,'" said Anne, as they went up the slope. "It's a nice story-bookish feeling. Why—why—why! Priscilla Grant, look over there and tell me if it's true, or am I seein' things?"

Priscilla looked. Anne's thumbs and eyes had not deceived her. Over the arched gateway of Patty's Place dangled a little, modest sign. It said "To Let, Furnished. Inquire Within."

"Priscilla," said Anne, in a whisper, "do you suppose it's possible that we could rent Patty's Place?"

"No, I don't," averred Priscilla. "It would be too good to be true. Fairy tales don't happen nowadays. I won't hope, Anne. The disappointment would be too awful to bear. They're sure to want more for it than we can afford. Remember, it's on Spofford Avenue."

"We must find out anyhow," said Anne resolutely. "It's too late to call this evening, but we'll come tomorrow. Oh, Pris, if we can get this darling spot! I've always felt that my fortunes were linked with Patty's Place, ever since I saw it first."

10
PATTY'S PLACE

The next evening found them treading resolutely the herring-bone walk through the tiny garden. The April wind was filling the pine trees with its roundelay, and the grove was alive with robins—great, plump, saucy fellows, strutting along the paths. The girls rang rather timidly, and were admitted by a grim and ancient handmaiden. The door opened directly into a large living room, where by a cheery little fire sat two other ladies, both of whom were also grim and ancient. Except that one looked to be about seventy and the other fifty, there seemed little difference between them. Each had amazingly big, light-blue eyes behind steel-rimmed spectacles; each wore a cap and a gray shawl; each was knitting without haste and without rest; each rocked placidly and looked at the girls without speaking; and just behind each sat a large white china dog, with round green spots all over it, a green nose and green ears. Those dogs captured Anne's fancy on the spot; they seemed like the twin guardian deities of Patty's Place.

For a few minutes nobody spoke. The girls were too nervous to find words, and neither the ancient ladies nor the china dogs seemed conversationally inclined. Anne glanced about the room. What a dear place it was! Another door opened out of it directly into the pine grove and the robins came boldly up on the very step. The floor was spotted with round, braided mats, such as Marilla made at Green Gables, but which were considered out of date everywhere else, even in Avonlea. And yet here they were on Spofford Avenue! A big, polished grandfather's clock ticked loudly and solemnly in a corner. There were delightful little cupboards over the mantel-piece, behind whose glass doors gleamed quaint bits of china. The walls were hung with old prints and silhouettes. In one corner the stairs went up, and at the first low turn was a long window with an inviting seat. It was all just as Anne had known it must be.

By this time the silence had grown too dreadful, and Priscilla nudged Anne to intimate that she *must* speak.

"We—we—saw by your sign that this house is to be let," said Anne faintly, addressing the older lady, who was evidently Miss Patty Spofford.

"Oh, yes," said Miss Patty. "I intended to take that sign down today."

"Then—then we are too late," said Anne sorrowfully. "You've let it to some one else?"

"No, but we have decided not to let it at all."

"Oh, I'm so sorry," exclaimed Anne impulsively. "I love this place so. I did hope we could have got it."

Then did Miss Patty lay down her knitting, take off her specs, rub them, put them on again, and for the first time look at Anne as at a human being. The other lady followed her example so perfectly that she might as well have been a reflection in a mirror.

"You *love* it," said Miss Patty with emphasis. "Does that mean that you really *love* it? Or that you merely like the looks of it? The girls nowadays indulge in such exaggerated statements that one never can tell what they *do* mean. It wasn't so in my young days. *Then* a girl did not say she *loved* turnips, in just the same tone as she might have said she loved her mother or her Savior."

Anne's conscience bore her up.

"I really do love it," she said gently. "I've loved it ever since I saw it last fall. My two college chums and I want to keep house next year instead of boarding so we are looking for a little place to rent; and when I saw that this house was to let I was so happy."

"If you love it, you can have it," said Miss Patty. "Maria and I decided today that we would not let it after all, because we did not like any of the people who have wanted it. We don't *have* to let it. We can afford to go to Europe even if we don't let it. It would help us out, but not for gold will I let my home pass into the possession of such people as have come here and looked at it.

You are different. I believe you do love it and will be good to it.
You can have it."

"If—if we can afford to pay what you ask for it," hesitated Anne.

Miss Patty named the amount required. Anne and Priscilla
looked at each other. Priscilla shook her head.

"I'm afraid we can't afford quite so much," said Anne, choking
back her disappointment. "You see, we are only college girls and
we are poor."

"What were you thinking you could afford?" demanded Miss
Patty, ceasing not to knit.

Anne named her amount. Miss Patty nodded gravely.

"That will do. As I told you, it is not strictly necessary that we
should let it at all. We are not rich, but we have enough to go to
Europe on. I have never been in Europe in my life, and never
expected or wanted to go. But my niece there, Maria Spofford,
has taken a fancy to go. Now, you know a young person like
Maria can't go globe-trotting alone."

"No—I—I suppose not," murmured Anne, seeing that Miss
Patty was quite solemnly in earnest.

"Of course not. So I have to go along to look after her. I expect
to enjoy it, too; I'm seventy years old, but I'm not tired of living
yet. I daresay I'd have gone to Europe before if the idea had
occurred to me. We shall be away for two years, perhaps three.
We sail in June and we shall send you the key, and leave all in
order for you to take possession when you choose. We shall pack
away a few things we prize especially, but all the rest will be left."

"Will you leave the china dogs?" asked Anne timidly.

"Would you like me to?"

"Oh, indeed, yes. They are delightful."

A pleased expression came into Miss Patty's face.

"I think a great deal of those dogs," she said proudly. "They
are over a hundred years old, and they have sat on either side of
this fireplace ever since my brother Aaron brought them from
London fifty years ago. Spofford Avenue was called after my
brother Aaron."

"A fine man he was," said Miss Maria, speaking for the first time. "Ah, you don't see the like of him nowadays."

"He was a good uncle to you, Maria," said Miss Patty, with evident emotion. "You do well to remember him."

"I shall always remember him," said Miss Maria solemnly. "I can see him, this minute, standing there before that fire, with his hands under his coat-tails, beaming on us."

Miss Maria took out her handkerchief and wiped her eyes; but Miss Patty came resolutely back from the regions of sentiment to those of business.

"I shall leave the dogs where they are, if you will promise to be very careful of them," she said. "Their names are Gog and Magog. Gog looks to the right and Magog to the left. And there's just one thing more. You don't object, I hope, to this house being called Patty's Place?"

"No, indeed. We think that is one of the nicest things about it."

"You have sense, I see," said Miss Patty in a tone of great satisfaction. "Would you believe it? All the people who came here to rent the house wanted to know if they couldn't take the name off the gate during their occupation of it. I told them roundly that the name went with the house. This has been Patty's Place ever since my brother Aaron left it to me in his will, and Patty's Place it shall remain until I die and Maria dies. After that happens the next possessor can call it any fool name he likes," concluded Miss Patty, much as she might have said, "After that—the deluge." "And now, wouldn't you like to go over the house and see it all before we consider the bargain made?"

Further exploration still further delighted the girls. Besides the big living room, there was a kitchen and a small bedroom downstairs. Upstairs were three rooms, one large and two small. Anne took an especial fancy to one of the small ones, looking out into the big pines, and hoped it would be hers. It was papered in pale blue and had a little, old-timey toilet table with sconces for candles. There was a diamond-paned window with a seat under the blue muslin frills that would be a satisfying spot for studying or dreaming.

"It's all so delicious that I know we are going to wake up and find it a fleeting vision of the night," said Priscilla as they went away.

"Miss Patty and Miss Maria are hardly such stuff as dreams are made of," laughed Anne. "Can you fancy them 'globe-trotting'—especially in those shawls and caps?"

"I suppose they'll take them off when they really begin to trot," said Priscilla, "but I know they'll take their knitting with them everywhere. They simply couldn't be parted from it. They will walk about Westminster Abbey and knit, I feel sure. Meanwhile, Anne, we shall be living in Patty's Place—*and* on Spofford Avenue. I feel like a millionairess even now."

"I feel like one of the morning stars that sang for joy, said Anne.

Phil Gordon crept into Thirty-eight, St. John's, that night and flung herself on Anne's bed.

"Girls, dear, I'm tired to death. I feel like the man without a country—or was it without a shadow? I forget which. Anyway, I've been packing up."

"And I suppose you are worn out because you couldn't decide which things to pack first, or where to put them," laughed Priscilla.

"E-zackly. And when I had got everything jammed in somehow, and my landlady and her maid had both sat on it while I locked it, I discovered I had packed a whole lot of things I wanted for Convocation at the very bottom. I had to unlock the old thing and poke and dive into it for an hour before I fished out what I wanted. I would get hold of something that felt like what I was looking for, and I'd yank it up, and it would be something else. No, Anne, I did NOT swear."

"I didn't say you did."

"Well, you looked it. But I admit my thoughts verged on the profane. And I have such a cold in the head—I can do nothing but sniffle, sigh and sneeze. Isn't that alliterative agony for you? Queen Anne, do say something to cheer me up."

"Remember that next Thursday night you'll be back in the land of Alec and Alonzo," suggested Anne.

Phil shook her head dolefully.

"More alliteration. No, I don't want Alec and Alonzo when I have a cold in the head. But what has happened you two? Now that I look at you closely you seem all lighted up with an internal iridescence. Why, you're actually *shining*! What's up?"

"We are going to live in Patty's Place next winter," said Anne triumphantly. "*Live*, mark you, not board! We've rented it, and Stella Maynard is coming, and her aunt is going to keep house for us."

Phil bounced up, wiped her nose, and fell on her knees before Anne.

"Girls—girls—let me come, too. Oh, I'll be so good. If there's no room for me I'll sleep in the little dog-house in the orchard— I've seen it. Only let me come."

"Get up, you goose."

"I won't stir off my marrow bones till you tell me I can live with you next winter."

Anne and Priscilla looked at each other. Then Anne said slowly.

"Phil dear, we'd love to have you. But we may as well speak plainly. I'm poor—Pris is poor—Stella Maynard is poor—our housekeeping will have to be very simple and our table plain. You'd have to live as we would. Now, you are rich and your boarding-house fare attests the fact."

"Oh, what do I care for that?" demanded Phil tragically. "Better a dinner of herbs where your chums are than a stalled ox in a lonely boarding-house. Don't think I'm *all* stomach, girls. I'll be willing to live on bread and water—with just a *leetle* jam—if you'll let me come."

"And then," continued Anne, "there will be a good deal of work to be done. Stella's aunt can't do it all. We all expect to have our chores to do. Now, you—"

"Toil not, neither do I spin," finished Philippa. "But I'll learn to do things. You'll only have to show me once. I *can* make my own bed to begin with. And remember that, though I can't cook,

I *can* keep my temper. That's something. And I *never* growl about the weather. That's more. Oh, please, please! I never wanted anything so much in my life—and this floor is awfully hard."

"There's just one more thing," said Priscilla resolutely. "You, Phil, as all Redmond knows, entertain callers almost every evening. Now, at Patty's Place we can't do that. We have decided that we shall be at home to our friends on Friday evenings only. If you come with us you'll have to abide by that rule."

"Well, you don't think I'll mind that, do you? Why, I'm glad of it. I knew I should have had some such rule myself, but I hadn't enough decision to make it or stick to it. When I can shuffle off the responsibility on you it will be a real relief. If you won't let me cast in my lot with you I'll die of the disappointment and then I'll come back and haunt you. I'll camp on the very doorstep of Patty's Place and you won't be able to go out or come in without falling over my spook."

Again Anne and Priscilla exchanged eloquent looks.

"Well," said Anne, "of course we can't promise to take you until we've consulted with Stella; but I don't think she'll object, and, as far as we are concerned, you may come and glad welcome."

"If you get tired of our simple life you can leave us, and no questions asked," added Priscilla.

Phil sprang up, hugged them both jubilantly, and went on her way rejoicing.

"I hope things will go right," said Priscilla soberly.

"We must *make* them go right," avowed Anne. "I think Phil will fit into our 'appy little 'ome very well."

"Oh, Phil's a dear to rattle round with and be chums. And, of course, the more there are of us the easier it will be on our slim purses. But how will she be to live with? You have to summer and winter with any one before you know if she's *livable* or not."

"Oh, well, we'll all be put to the test, as far as that goes. And we must quit us like sensible folk, living and let live. Phil isn't selfish, though she's a little thoughtless, and I believe we will all get on beautifully in Patty's Place."

11
THE ROUND OF LIFE

Anne was back in Avonlea with the luster of the Thorburn Scholarship on her brow. People told her she hadn't changed much, in a tone which hinted they were surprised and a little disappointed she hadn't. Avonlea had not changed, either. At least, so it seemed at first. But as Anne sat in the Green Gables pew, on the first Sunday after her return, and looked over the congregation, she saw several little changes which, all coming home to her at once, made her realize that time did not quite stand still, even in Avonlea. A new minister was in the pulpit. In the pews more that one familiar face was missing forever. Old "Uncle Abe," his prophesying over and done with, Mrs. Peter Sloane, who had sighed, it was to be hoped, for the last time, Timothy Cotton, who, as Mrs. Rachel Lynde said "had actually managed to die at last after practising at it for twenty years," and old Josiah Sloane, whom nobody knew in his coffin because he had his whiskers neatly trimmed, were all sleeping in the little graveyard behind the church. And Billy Andrews was married to Nettie Blewett! They "appeared out" that Sunday. When Billy, beaming with pride and happiness, showed his be-plumed and be-silked bride into the Harmon Andrews' pew, Anne dropped her lids to hide her dancing eyes. She recalled the stormy winter night of the Christmas holidays when Jane had proposed for Billy. He certainly had not broken his heart over his rejection. Anne wondered if Jane had also proposed to Nettie for him, or if he had mustered enough spunk to ask the fateful question himself. All the Andrews family seemed to share in his pride and pleasure, from Mrs. Harmon in the pew to Jane in the choir. Jane had resigned from the Avonlea school and intended to go West in the fall.

"Can't get a beau in Avonlea, that's what," said Mrs. Rachel Lynde scornfully. "*Says* she thinks she'll have better health out West. I never heard her health was poor before."

"Jane is a nice girl," Anne had said loyally. "She never tried to attract attention, as some did."

"Oh, she never chased the boys, if that's what you mean," said Mrs. Rachel. "But she'd like to be married, just as much as anybody, that's what. What else would take her out West to some forsaken place whose only recommendation is that men are plenty and women scarce? Don't you tell me!"

But it was not at Jane Anne gazed that day in dismay and surprise. It was at Ruby Gillis, who sat beside her in the choir. What had happened to Ruby? She was even handsomer than ever; but her blue eyes were too bright and lustrous, and the color of her cheeks was hectically brilliant; besides, she was very thin; the hands that held her hymn-book were almost transparent in their delicacy.

"Is Ruby Gillis ill?" Anne asked of Mrs. Lynde, as they went home from church.

"Ruby Gillis is dying of galloping consumption," said Mrs. Lynde bluntly. "Everybody knows it except herself and her family. *They* won't give in. If you ask *them*, she's perfectly well. She hasn't been able to teach since she had that attack of congestion in the winter, but she says she's going to teach again in the fall, and she's after the White Sands school. She'll be in her grave, poor girl, when White Sands school opens, that's what."

Anne listened in shocked silence. Ruby Gillis, her old schoolchum, dying? Could it be possible? Of late years they had grown apart; but the old tie of schoolgirl intimacy was there, and made itself felt sharply in the tug the news gave at Anne's heartstrings. Ruby, the brilliant, the merry, the coquettish! It was impossible to associate the thought of her with anything like death. She had greeted Anne with gay cordiality after church, and urged her to come up the next evening.

"I'll be away Tuesday and Wednesday evenings," she had whispered triumphantly. "There's a concert at Carmody and a party at White Sands. Herb Spencer's going to take me. He's my *latest*. Be sure to come up tomorrow. I'm dying for a good talk with you. I want to hear all about your doings at Redmond."

Anne knew that Ruby meant that she wanted to tell Anne all about her own recent flirtations, but she promised to go, and Diana offered to go with her.

"I've been wanting to go to see Ruby for a long while," she told Anne, when they left Green Gables the next evening, "but I really couldn't go alone. It's so awful to hear Ruby rattling on as she does, and pretending there is nothing the matter with her, even when she can hardly speak for coughing. She's fighting so hard for her life, and yet she hasn't any chance at all, they say."

The girls walked silently down the red, twilit road. The robins were singing vespers in the high tree-tops, filling the golden air with their jubilant voices. The silver fluting of the frogs came from marshes and ponds, over fields where seeds were beginning to stir with life and thrill to the sunshine and rain that had drifted over them. The air was fragrant with the wild, sweet, wholesome smell of young raspberry copses. White mists were hovering in the silent hollows and violet stars were shining bluely on the brooklands.

"What a beautiful sunset," said Diana. "Look, Anne, it's just like a land in itself, isn't it? That long, low bank of purple cloud is the shore, and the clear sky further on is like a golden sea."

"If we could sail to it in the moonshine boat Paul wrote of in his old composition—you remember?—how nice it would be," said Anne, rousing from her reverie. "Do you think we could find all our yesterdays there, Diana—all our old springs and blossoms? The beds of flowers that Paul saw there are the roses that have bloomed for us in the past?"

"Don't!" said Diana. "You make me feel as if we were old women with everything in life behind us."

"I think I've almost felt as if we were since I heard about poor Ruby," said Anne. "If it is true that she is dying any other sad thing might be true, too."

"You don't mind calling in at Elisha Wright's for a moment, do you?" asked Diana. "Mother asked me to leave this little dish of jelly for Aunt Atossa."

"Who is Aunt Atossa?"

"Oh, haven't you heard? She's Mrs. Samson Coates of Spencer-vale—Mrs. Elisha Wright's aunt. She's father's aunt, too. Her husband died last winter and she was left very poor and lonely, so the Wrights took her to live with them. Mother thought we ought to take her, but father put his foot down. Live with Aunt Atossa he would not."

"Is she so terrible?" asked Anne absently.

"You'll probably see what she's like before we can get away," said Diana significantly. "Father says she has a face like a hatchet—it cuts the air. But her tongue is sharper still."

Late as it was Aunt Atossa was cutting potato sets in the Wright kitchen. She wore a faded old wrapper, and her gray hair was decidedly untidy. Aunt Atossa did not like being "caught in a kilter," so she went out of her way to be disagreeable.

"Oh, so you're Anne Shirley?" she said, when Diana intro-duced Anne. "I've heard of you." Her tone implied that she had heard nothing good. "Mrs. Andrews was telling me you were home. She said you had improved a good deal."

There was no doubt Aunt Atossa thought there was plenty of room for further improvement. She ceased not from cutting sets with much energy.

"Is it any use to ask you to sit down?" she inquired sarcastical-ly. "Of course, there's nothing very entertaining here for you. The rest are all away."

"Mother sent you this little pot of rhubarb jelly," said Diana pleasantly. "She made it today and thought you might like some."

"Oh, thanks," said Aunt Atossa sourly. "I never fancy your mother's jelly—she always makes it too sweet. However, I'll try to worry some down. My appetite's been dreadful poor this spring. I'm far from well," continued Aunt Atossa solemnly, "but still I keep a-doing. People who can't work aren't wanted *here*. If it isn't too much trouble will you be condescending enough to set the jelly in the pantry? I'm in a hurry to get these spuds done to-night. I suppose you two *ladies* never do anything like this. You'd be afraid of spoiling your hands."

"I used to cut potato sets before we rented the farm," smiled Anne.

"I do it yet," laughed Diana. "I cut sets three days last week. Of course," she added teasingly, "I did my hands up in lemon juice and kid gloves every night after it."

Aunt Atossa sniffed.

"I suppose you got that notion out of some of those silly magazines you read so many of. I wonder your mother allows you. But she always spoiled you. We all thought when George married her she wouldn't be a suitable wife for him."

Aunt Atossa sighed heavily, as if all forebodings upon the occasion of George Barry's marriage had been amply and darkly fulfilled.

"Going, are you?" she inquired, as the girls rose. "Well, I suppose you can't find much amusement talking to an old woman like me. It's such a pity the boys ain't home."

"We want to run in and see Ruby Gillis a little while," explained Diana.

"Oh, anything does for an excuse, of course," said Aunt Atossa, amiably. "Just whip in and whip out before you have time to say how-do decently. It's college airs, I s'pose. You'd be wiser to keep away from Ruby Gillis. The doctors say consumption's catching. I always knew Ruby'd get something, gadding off to Boston last fall for a visit. People who ain't content to stay home always catch something."

"People who don't go visiting catch things, too. Sometimes they even die," said Diana solemnly.

"Then they don't have themselves to blame for it," retorted Aunt Atossa triumphantly. "I hear you are to be married in June, Diana."

"There is no truth in that report," said Diana, blushing.

"Well, don't put it off too long," said Aunt Atossa significantly. "You'll fade soon—you're all complexion and hair. And the

Wrights are terrible fickle. You ought to wear a hat, *Miss Shirley*. Your nose is freckling scandalous. My, but you *are* redheaded! Well, I s'pose we're all as the Lord made us! Give Marilla Cuthbert my respects. She's never been to see me since I come to Avonlea, but I s'pose I oughtn't to complain. The Cuthberts always did think themselves a cut higher than any one else round here."

"Oh, isn't she dreadful?" gasped Diana, as they escaped down the lane.

"She's worse than Miss Eliza Andrews," said Anne. "But then think of living all your life with a name like Atossa! Wouldn't it sour almost any one? She should have tried to imagine her name was Cordelia. It might have helped her a great deal. It certainly helped me in the days when I didn't like *Anne*."

"Josie Pye will be just like her when she grows up," said Diana. "Josie's mother and Aunt Atossa are cousins, you know. Oh, dear, I'm glad that's over. She's so malicious—she seems to put a bad flavor in everything. Father tells such a funny story about her. One time they had a minister in Spencervale who was a very good, spiritual man but very deaf. He couldn't hear any ordinary conversation at all. Well, they used to have a prayer meeting on Sunday evenings, and all the church members present would get up and pray in turn, or say a few words on some Bible verse. But one evening Aunt Atossa bounced up. She didn't either pray or preach. Instead, she lit into everybody else in the church and gave them a fearful raking down, calling them right out by name and telling them how they all had behaved, and casting up all the quarrels and scandals of the past ten years. Finally she wound up by saying that she was disgusted with Spencervale church and she never meant to darken its door again, and she hoped a fearful judgment would come upon it. Then she sat down out of breath, and the minister, who hadn't heard a word she said, immediately remarked, in a very devout voice, 'Amen! The Lord grant our dear sister's prayer!' You ought to hear father tell the story."

"Speaking of stories, Diana," remarked Anne, in a significant, confidential tone, "do you know that lately I have been wondering if I could write a short story—a story that would be good enough to be published?"

"Why, of course you could," said Diana, after she had grasped the amazing suggestion. "You used to write perfectly thrilling stories years ago in our old Story Club."

"Well, I hardly meant one of that kind of stories," smiled Anne. "I've been thinking about it a little of late, but I'm almost afraid to try, for, if I should fail, it would be too humiliating."

"I heard Priscilla say once that all Mrs. Morgan's first stories were rejected. But I'm sure yours wouldn't be, Anne, for it's likely editors have more sense nowadays."

"Margaret Burton, one of the Junior girls at Redmond, wrote a story last winter and it was published in the *Canadian Woman*. I really do think I could write one at least as good."

"And will you have it published in the *Canadian Woman*?"

"I might try one of the bigger magazines first. It all depends on what kind of a story I write."

"What is it to be about?"

"I don't know yet. I want to get hold of a good plot. I believe that is very necessary from an editor's point of view. The only thing I've settled on is the heroine's name. It is to be *Averil Lester*. Rather pretty, don't you think? Don't mention this to any one, Diana. I haven't told anybody but you and Mr. Harrison. *He* wasn't very encouraging—he said there was far too much trash written nowadays as it was, and he'd expected something better of me, after a year at college."

"What does Mr. Harrison know about it?" demanded Diana scornfully.

They found the Gillis home gay with lights and callers. Leonard Kimball, of Spencervale, and Morgan Bell, of Carmody, were glaring at each other across the parlor. Several merry girls had dropped in. Ruby was dressed in white and her eyes and cheeks were very brilliant. She laughed and chattered incessantly, and after the other girls had gone she took Anne upstairs to display her new summer dresses.

"I've a blue silk to make up yet, but it's a little heavy for summer wear. I think I'll leave it until the fall. I'm going to teach in White Sands, you know. How do you like my hat? That one you had on in church yesterday was real dinky. But I like something brighter for myself. Did you notice those two ridiculous boys downstairs? They've both come determined to sit each other out. I don't care a single bit about either of them, you know. Herb Spencer is the one I like. Sometimes I really do think's he's *Mr. Right*. At Christmas I thought the Spencervale schoolmaster was that. But I found out something about him that turned me against him. He nearly went insane when I turned him down. I wish those two boys hadn't come tonight. I wanted to have a nice good talk with you, Anne, and tell you such heaps of things. You and I were always good chums, weren't we?"

Ruby slipped her arm about Anne's waist with a shallow little laugh. But just for a moment their eyes met, and behind all the luster of Ruby's, Anne saw something that made her heart ache.

"Come up often, won't you, Anne?" whispered Ruby. "Come alone—I want you."

"Are you feeling quite well, Ruby?"

"Me! Why, I'm perfectly well. I never felt better in my life. Of course, that congestion last winter pulled me down a little. But just see my color. I don't look much like an invalid, I'm sure."

Ruby's voice was almost sharp. She pulled her arm away from Anne, as if in resentment, and ran downstairs, where she was gayer than ever, apparently so much absorbed in bantering her two swains that Diana and Anne felt rather out of it and soon went away.

12
"AVERIL'S ATONEMENT"

"What are you dreaming of, Anne?"

The two girls were loitering one evening in a fairy hollow of the brook. Ferns nodded in it, and little grasses were green, and wild pears hung finely-scented, white curtains around it.

Anne roused herself from her reverie with a happy sigh.

"I was thinking out my story, Diana."

"Oh, have you really begun it?" cried Diana, all alight with eager interest in a moment.

"Yes, I have only a few pages written, but I have it all pretty well thought out. I've had such a time to get a suitable plot. None of the plots that suggested themselves suited a girl named *Averil*."

"Couldn't you have changed her name?"

"No, the thing was impossible. I tried to, but I couldn't do it, any more than I could change yours. *Averil* was so real to me that no matter what other name I tried to give her I just thought of her as *Averil* behind it all. But finally I got a plot that matched her. Then came the excitement of choosing names for all my characters. You have no idea how fascinating that is. I've lain awake for hours thinking over those names. The hero's name is *Perceval Dalrymple*."

"Have you named *all* the characters?" asked Diana wistfully. "If you hadn't I was going to ask you to let me name *one*—just some unimportant person. I'd feel as if I had a share in the story then."

"You may name the little hired boy who lived with the *Lesters*," conceded Anne. "He is not very important, but he is the only one left unnamed."

"Call him *Raymond Fitzosborne*," suggested Diana, who had a store of such names laid away in her memory, relics of the old "Story Club," which she and Anne and Jane Andrews and Ruby Gillis had had in their schooldays.

Anne shook her head doubtfully.

"I'm afraid that is too aristocratic a name for a chore boy, Diana. I couldn't imagine a Fitzosborne feeding pigs and picking up chips, could you?"

Diana didn't see why, if you had an imagination at all, you couldn't stretch it to that extent; but probably Anne knew best, and the chore boy was finally christened *Robert Ray*, to be called *Bobby* should occasion require.

"How much do you suppose you'll get for it?" asked Diana.

But Anne had not thought about this at all. She was in pursuit of fame, not filthy lucre, and her literary dreams were as yet untainted by mercenary considerations.

"You'll let me read it, won't you?" pleaded Diana.

"When it is finished I'll read it to you and Mr. Harrison, and I shall want you to criticize it *severely*. No one else shall see it until it is published."

"How are you going to end it—happily or unhappily?"

"I'm not sure. I'd like it to end unhappily, because that would be so much more romantic. But I understand editors have a prejudice against sad endings. I heard Professor Hamilton say once that nobody but a genius should try to write an unhappy ending. And," concluded Anne modestly, "I'm anything but a genius."

"Oh, I like happy endings best. You'd better let him marry her," said Diana, who, especially since her engagement to Fred, thought this was how every story should end.

"But you like to cry over stories?"

"Oh, yes, in the middle of them. But I like everything to come right at last."

"I must have *one* pathetic scene in it," said Anne thoughtfully. "I might let *Robert Ray* be injured in an accident and have a death scene."

"No, you mustn't kill *Bobby* off," declared Diana, laughing. "He belongs to me and I want him to live and flourish. Kill somebody else if you have to."

For the next fortnight Anne writhed or revelled, according to mood, in her literary pursuits. Now she would be jubilant over a brilliant idea, now despairing because some contrary character would *not* behave properly. Diana could not understand this.

"*Make* them do as you want them to," she said.

"I can't," mourned Anne. "Averil is such an unmanagable heroine. She *will* do and say things I never meant her to. Then that spoils everything that went before and I have to write it all over again."

Finally, however, the story was finished, and Anne read it to Diana in the seclusion of the porch gable. She had achieved her "pathetic scene" without sacrificing *Robert Ray*, and she kept a watchful eye on Diana as she read it. Diana rose to the occasion and cried properly; but, when the end came, she looked a little disappointed.

"Why did you kill *Maurice Lennox*?" she asked reproachfully.

"He was the villain," protested Anne. "He had to be punished."

"I like him best of them all," said unreasonable Diana.

"Well, he's dead, and he'll have to stay dead," said Anne, rather resentfully. "If I had let him live he'd have gone on persecuting *Averil* and *Perceval*."

"Yes—unless you had reformed him."

"That wouldn't have been romantic, and, besides, it would have made the story too long."

"Well, anyway, it's a perfectly elegant story, Anne, and will make you famous, of that I'm sure. Have you got a title for it?"

"Oh, I decided on the title long ago. I call it *Averil's Atonement*. Doesn't that sound nice and alliterative? Now, Diana, tell me candidly, do you see any faults in my story?"

"Well," hesitated Diana, "that part where *Averil* makes the cake doesn't seem to me quite romantic enough to match the rest. It's just what anybody might do. Heroines shouldn't do cooking, *I* think."

"Why, that is where the humor comes in, and it's one of the best parts of the whole story," said Anne. And it may be stated that in this she was quite right.

Diana prudently refrained from any further criticism, but Mr. Harrison was much harder to please. First he told her there was entirely too much description in the story.

"Cut out all those flowery passages," he said unfeelingly.

Anne had an uncomfortable conviction that Mr. Harrison was right, and she forced herself to expunge most of her beloved descriptions, though it took three rewritings before the story could be pruned down to please the fastidious Mr. Harrison.

"I've left out *all* the descriptions but the sunset," she said at last. "I simply *couldn't* let it go. It was the best of them all."

"It hasn't anything to do with the story," said Mr. Harrison, "and you shouldn't have laid the scene among rich city people. What do you know of them? Why didn't you lay it right here in Avonlea—changing the name, of course, or else Mrs. Rachel Lynde would probably think she was the heroine."

"Oh, that would never have done," protested Anne. "Avonlea is the dearest place in the world, but it isn't quite romantic enough for the scene of a story."

"I daresay there's been many a romance in Avonlea—and many a tragedy, too," said Mr. Harrison drily. "But your folks ain't like real folks anywhere. They talk too much and use too high-flown language. There's one place where that *Dalrymple* chap talks even on for two pages, and never lets the girl get a word in edgewise. If he'd done that in real life she'd have pitched him."

"I don't believe it," said Anne flatly. In her secret soul she thought that the beautiful, poetical things said to *Averil* would win any girl's heart completely. Besides, it was gruesome to hear of *Averil*, the stately queen-like *Averil*, "pitching" any one. *Averil* "declined her suitors."

"Anyhow," resumed the merciless Mr. Harrison, "I don't see why *Maurice Lennox* didn't get her. He was twice the man the other is. He did bad things, but he *did* them. *Perceval* hadn't time for anything but mooning."

"Mooning." That was even worse than "pitching!"

"*Maurice Lennox* was the villain," said Anne indignantly. "I don't see why every one likes him better than *Perceval*."

"Perceval is too good. He's aggravating. Next time you write about a hero put a little spice of human nature in him."

"*Averil* couldn't have married *Maurice*. He was bad."

"She'd have reformed him. You *can* reform a man; you can't reform a jelly-fish, of course. Your story isn't bad—it's kind of interesting, I'll admit. But you're too young to write a story that would be worth while. Wait ten years."

Anne made up her mind that the next time she wrote a story she wouldn't ask anybody to criticize it. It was too discouraging. She would not read the story to Gilbert, although she told him about it.

"If it is a success you'll see it when it is published, Gilbert, but if it is a failure nobody shall ever see it."

Marilla knew nothing about the venture. In imagination Anne saw herself reading a story out of a magazine to Marilla, entrapping her into praise of it—for in imagination all things are possible—and then triumphantly announcing herself the author.

One day Anne took to the Post Office a long, bulky envelope, addressed, with the delightful confidence of youth and inexperience, to the very biggest of the "big" magazines. Diana was as excited over it as Anne herself.

"How long do you suppose it will be before you hear from it?" she asked.

"It shouldn't be longer than a fortnight. Oh, how happy and proud I shall be if it is accepted!"

"Of course it will be accepted, and they will likely ask you to send them more. You may be as famous as Mrs. Morgan some day, Anne, and then how proud I'll be of knowing you," said Diana, who possessed, at least, the striking merit of an unselfish admiration of the gifts and graces of her friends.

A week of delightful dreaming followed, and then came a bitter awakening. One evening Diana found Anne in the porch gable, with suspicious-looking eyes. On the table lay a long envelope and a crumpled manuscript.

"Anne, your story hasn't come back?" cried Diana incredulously.

"Yes, it has," said Anne shortly.

"Well, that editor must be crazy. What reason did he give?"

"No reason at all. There is just a printed slip saying that it wasn't found available."

"I never thought much of that magazine, anyway," said Diana hotly. "The stories in it are not half as interesting as those in the *Canadian Woman*, although it costs so much more. I suppose the editor is prejudiced against any one who isn't a Yankee. Don't be discouraged, Anne. Remember how Mrs. Morgan's stories came back. Send yours to the *Canadian Woman*."

"I believe I will," said Anne, plucking up heart. "And if it is published I'll send that American editor a marked copy. But I'll cut the sunset out. I believe Mr. Harrison was right."

Out came the sunset; but in spite of this heroic mutilation the editor of the *Canadian Woman* sent *Averil's Atonement* back so promptly that the indignant Diana declared that it couldn't have been read at all, and vowed she was going to stop her subscription immediately. Anne took this second rejection with the calmness of despair. She locked the story away in the garret trunk where the old Story Club tales reposed; but first she yielded to Diana's entreaties and gave her a copy.

"This is the end of my literary ambitions," she said bitterly.

She never mentioned the matter to Mr. Harrison, but one evening he asked her bluntly if her story had been accepted.

"No, the editor wouldn't take it," she answered briefly.

Mr. Harrison looked sidewise at the flushed, delicate profile.

"Well, I suppose you'll keep on writing them," he said encouragingly.

"No, I shall never try to write a story again," declared Anne, with the hopeless finality of nineteen when a door is shut in its face.

"I wouldn't give up altogether," said Mr. Harrison reflectively. "I'd write a story once in a while, but I wouldn't pester editors with it. I'd write of people and places I knew, and I'd make my characters talk every-day English; and I'd let the sun rise and set in the usual quiet way without much fuss over the fact. If I had to have villains at all, I'd give them a chance, Anne—I'd give them a chance. There *are* some terrible bad men in the world, I suppose, but you'd have to go a long piece to find them—though Mrs. Lynde believes we're all bad. But most of us have got a little decency somewhere in us. Keep on writing, Anne."

"No. It was very foolish of me to attempt it. When I'm through Redmond I'll stick to teaching. I *can* teach. I can't write stories."

"It'll be time for you to be getting a husband when you're through Redmond," said Mr. Harrison. "I don't believe in putting marrying off too long—like I did."

Anne got up and marched home. There were times when Mr. Harrison was really intolerable. "Pitching," "mooning," and "getting a husband." Ow!!

13

THE WAY OF TRANSGRESSORS

Davy and Dora were ready for Sunday School. They were going alone, which did not often happen, for Mrs. Lynde always attended Sunday School. But Mrs. Lynde had twisted her ankle and was lame, so she was staying home this morning. The twins were also to represent the family at church, for Anne had gone away the evening before to spend Sunday with friends in Carmody, and Marilla had one of her headaches.

Davy came downstairs slowly. Dora was waiting in the hall for him, having been made ready by Mrs. Lynde. Davy had attended to his own preparations. He had a cent in his pocket for Sunday School collection, and a five-cent piece for the church collection; he carried his Bible in one hand and his Sunday School quarterly in the other; he knew his lesson and his Golden Text and his catechism question perfectly. Had he not studied them—per-force—in Mrs. Lynde's kitchen, all last Sunday afternoon? Davy, therefore, should have been in a placid frame of mind. As a matter of fact, despite text and catechism, he was inwardly as a ravening wolf.

Mrs. Lynde limped out of her kitchen as he joined Dora.

"Are you clean?" she demanded severely.

"Yes—all of me that shows," Davy answered with a defiant scowl.

Mrs. Rachel sighed. She had her suspicions about Davy's neck and ears. But she knew that if she attempted to make a personal examination Davy would likely take to his heels and she could not pursue him today.

"Well, be sure you behave yourselves," she warned them. "Don't walk in the dust. Don't stop in the porch to talk to the other children. Don't squirm or wriggle in your places. Don't forget the Golden Text. Don't lose your collection or forget to put it in. Don't whisper at prayer time, and don't forget to pay attention to the sermon."

Davy deigned no response. He marched away down the lane, followed by the meek Dora. But his soul seethed within him. Davy had suffered, or thought he had suffered, many things at the hands and tongue of Mrs. Rachel Lynde since she had come to Green Gables, for Mrs. Lynde could not live with anybody, whether they were nine or ninety, without trying to bring them up properly. And it was only the preceding afternoon that she had interfered to influence Marilla against allowing Davy to go fishing with the Timothy Cottons. Davy was still boiling over this.

As soon as he was out of the lane Davy stopped and twisted his countenance into such an unearthly and terrific contortion that Dora, although she knew his gifts in that respect, was honestly alarmed lest he should never in the world be able to get it straightened out again.

"Darn her," exploded Davy.

"Oh, Davy, don't swear," gasped Dora in dismay.

"'Darn' isn't swearing—not real swearing. And I don't care if it is," retorted Davy recklessly.

"Well, if you *must* say dreadful words don't say them on Sunday," pleaded Dora.

Davy was as yet far from repentance, but in his secret soul he felt that, perhaps, he had gone a little too far.

"I'm going to invent a swear word of my own," he declared.

"God will punish you if you do," said Dora solemnly.

"Then I think God is a mean old scamp," retorted Davy. "Doesn't He know a fellow must have some way of 'spressing his feelings?"

"Davy!!!" said Dora. She expected that Davy would be struck down dead on the spot. But nothing happened.

"Anyway, I ain't going to stand any more of Mrs. Lynde's bossing," spluttered Davy. "Anne and Marilla may have the right to boss me, but *she* hasn't. I'm going to do every single thing she told me not to do. You watch me."

In grim, deliberate silence, while Dora watched him with the fascination of horror, Davy stepped off the green grass of the roadside, ankle deep into the fine dust which four weeks of rainless weather had made on the road, and marched along in it, shuffling his feet viciously until he was enveloped in a hazy cloud.

"That's the beginning," he announced triumphantly. "And I'm going to stop in the porch and talk as long as there's anybody there to talk to. I'm going to squirm and wriggle and whisper, and I'm going to say I don't know the Golden Text. And I'm going to throw away both of my collections *right now*."

And Davy hurled cent and nickel over Mr. Barry's fence with fierce delight.

"Satan made you do that," said Dora reproachfully.

"He didn't," cried Davy indignantly. "I just thought it out for myself. And I've thought of something else. I'm not going to Sunday School or church at all. I'm going to play with the Cottons.

They told me yesterday they weren't going to Sunday School today, 'cause their mother was away and there was nobody to make them. Come along, Dora, we'll have a great time."

"I don't want to go," protested Dora.

"You've got to," said Davy. "If you don't come I'll tell Marilla that Frank Bell kissed you in school last Monday."

"I couldn't help it. I didn't know he was going to," cried Dora, blushing scarlet.

"Well, you didn't slap him or seem a bit cross," retorted Davy. "I'll tell her *that*, too, if you don't come. We'll take the short cut up this field."

"I'm afraid of those cows," protested poor Dora, seeing a prospect of escape.

"The very idea of your being scared of those cows," scoffed Davy. "Why, they're both younger than you."

"They're bigger," said Dora.

"They won't hurt you. Come along, now. This is great. When I grow up I ain't going to bother going to church at all. I believe I can get to heaven by myself."

"You'll go to the other place if you break the Sabbath day," said unhappy Dora, following him sorely against her will.

But Davy was not scared—yet. Hell was very far off, and the delights of a fishing expedition with the Cottons were very near. He wished Dora had more spunk. She kept looking back as if she were going to cry every minute, and that spoiled a fellow's fun. Hang girls, anyway. Davy did not say "darn" this time, even in thought. He was not sorry—yet—that he had said it once, but it might be as well not to tempt the Unknown Powers too far on one day.

The small Cottons were playing in their back yard, and hailed Davy's appearance with whoops of delight. Pete, Tommy, Adolphus, and Mirabel Cotton were all alone. Their mother and older sisters were away. Dora was thankful Mirabel was there, at least. She had been afraid she would be alone in a crowd of boys. Mirabel was almost as bad as a boy—she was so noisy and sunburned and reckless. But at least she wore dresses.

"We've come to go fishing," announced Davy.

"Whoop," yelled the Cottons. They rushed away to dig worms at once, Mirabel leading the van with a tin can. Dora could have sat down and cried. Oh, if only that hateful Frank Bell had never kissed her! Then she could have defied Davy, and gone to her beloved Sunday School.

They dared not, of course, go fishing on the pond, where they would be seen by people going to church. They had to resort to the brook in the woods behind the Cotton house. But it was full of trout, and they had a glorious time that morning—at least the Cottons certainly had, and Davy seemed to have it. Not being entirely bereft of prudence, he had discarded boots and stockings and borrowed Tommy Cotton's overalls. Thus accoutered, bog and marsh and undergrowth had no terrors for him. Dora was frankly and manifestly miserable. She followed the others in their peregrinations from pool to pool, clasping her Bible and quarterly tightly and thinking with bitterness of soul of her beloved class where she should be sitting that very moment, before a teacher she adored. Instead, here she was roaming the woods with those half-wild Cottons, trying to keep her boots clean and her pretty white dress free from rents and stains. Mirabel had offered the loan of an apron but Dora had scornfully refused.

The trout bit as they always do on Sundays. In an hour the transgressors had all the fish they wanted, so they returned to the house, much to Dora's relief. She sat primly on a hencoop in the yard while the others played an uproarious game of tag; and then they all climbed to the top of the pig-house roof and cut their initials on the saddle-board. The flat-roofed henhouse and a pile of straw beneath gave Davy another inspiration. They spent a splendid half hour climbing on the roof and diving off into the straw with whoops and yells.

But even unlawful pleasures must come to an end. When the rumble of wheels over the pond bridge told that people were going home from church Davy knew they must go. He discarded Tommy's overalls, resumed his own rightful attire, and turned away from his string of trout with a sigh. No use to think of taking them home.

"Well, hadn't we a splendid time?" he demanded defiantly, as they went down the hill field.

"I hadn't," said Dora flatly. "And I don't believe you had— really—either," she added, with a flash of insight that was not to be expected of her.

"I had so," cried Davy, but in the voice of one who doth protest too much. "No wonder *you* hadn't—just sitting there like a—like a mule."

"I ain't going to 'sociate with the Cottons," said Dora loftily.

"The Cottons are all right," retorted Davy. "And they have far better times than we have. They do just as they please and say just what they like before everybody. I'm going to do that, too, after this."

"There are lots of things you wouldn't dare say before everybody," averred Dora.

"No, there isn't."

"There is, too. Would you," demanded Dora gravely, "would you say 'tomcat' before the minister?"

This was a staggerer. Davy was not prepared for such a concrete example of the freedom of speech. But one did not have to be consistent with Dora.

"Of course not," he admitted sulkily. "'Tomcat' isn't a holy word. I wouldn't mention such an animal before a minister at all."

"But if you had to?" persisted Dora.

"I'd call it a Thomas pussy," said Davy.

"*I* think 'gentleman cat' would be more polite," reflected Dora.

"*You* thinking!" retorted Davy with withering scorn.

Davy was not feeling comfortable, though he would have died before he admitted it to Dora. Now that the exhilaration of truant delights had died away, his conscience was beginning to give him salutary twinges. After all, perhaps it would have been better to have gone to Sunday School and church. Mrs. Lynde might be

bossy; but there was always a box of cookies in her kitchen cupboard and she was not stingy. At this inconvenient moment Davy
remembered that when he had torn his new school pants the
week before, Mrs. Lynde had mended them beautifully and never
said a word to Marilla about them.

But Davy's cup of iniquity was not yet full. He was to discover
that one sin demands another to cover it. They had dinner with
Mrs. Lynde that day, and the first thing she asked Davy was,

"Were all your class in Sunday School today?"

"Yes'm," said Davy with a gulp. "All were there—'cept one."

"Did you say your Golden Text and catechism?"

"Yes'm."

"Did you put your collection in?"

"Yes'm.

"Was Mrs. Malcolm MacPherson in church?"

"I don't know." This, at least, was the truth, thought wretched
Davy.

"Was the Ladies' Aid announced for next week?"

"Yes'm"—quakingly.

"Was prayer-meeting?"

"I—I don't know."

"You *should* know. You should listen more attentively to the
announcements. What was Mr. Harvey's text?"

Davy took a frantic gulp of water and swallowed it and the last
protest of conscience together. He glibly recited an old Golden
Text learned several weeks ago. Fortunately Mrs. Lynde now
stopped questioning him; but Davy did not enjoy his dinner. He
could only eat one helping of pudding.

"What's the matter with you?" demanded justly astonished
Mrs. Lynde. "Are you sick?"

"No," muttered Davy.

"You look pale. You'd better keep out of the sun this afternoon," admonished Mrs. Lynde.

"Do you know how many lies you told Mrs. Lynde?" asked
Dora reproachfully, as soon as they were alone after dinner.

Davy, goaded to desperation, turned fiercely.

"I don't know and I don't care," he said. "You just shut up, Dora Keith."

Then poor Davy betook himself to a secluded retreat behind the wood-pile to think over the way of transgressors.

Green Gables was wrapped in darkness and silence when Anne reached home. She lost no time going to bed, for she was very tired and sleepy. There had been several Avonlea jollifications the preceding week, involving rather late hours. Anne's head was hardly on her pillow before she was half asleep; but just then her door was softly opened and a pleading voice said, "Anne."

Anne sat up drowsily.

"Davy, is that you? What is the matter?"

A white-clad figure flung itself across the floor and on to the bed.

"Anne," sobbed Davy, getting his arms about her neck. "I'm awful glad you're home. I couldn't go to sleep till I'd told somebody."

"Told somebody what?"

"How mis'rubul I am."

"Why are you miserable, dear?"

"'Cause I was so bad today, Anne. Oh, I was awful bad—badder'n I've ever been yet."

"What did you do?"

"Oh, I'm afraid to tell you. You'll never like me again, Anne. I couldn't say my prayers tonight. I couldn't tell God what I'd done. I was 'shamed to have Him know."

"But He knew anyway, Davy."

"That's what Dora said. But I thought p'raps He mightn't have noticed just at the time. Anyway, I'd rather tell you first."

"*What* is it you did?"

Out it all came in a rush.

"I run away from Sunday School—and went fishing with the Cottons—and I told ever so many whoppers to Mrs. Lynde—oh!

'most half a dozen—and—and—I—I said a swear word, Anne—a pretty near swear word, anyhow—and I called God names."

There was a silence. Davy didn't know what to make of it. Was Anne so shocked that she never would speak to him again?

"Anne, what are you going to do to me?" he whispered.

"Nothing, dear. You've been punished already, I think."

"No, I haven't. Nothing's been done to me."

"You've been very unhappy ever since you did wrong, haven't you?"

"You bet!" said Davy emphatically.

"That was your conscience punishing you, Davy."

"What's my conscience? I want to know."

"It's something in you, Davy, that always tells you when you are doing wrong and makes you unhappy if you persist in doing it. Haven't you noticed that?"

"Yes, but I didn't know what it was. I wish I didn't have it. I'd have lots more fun. Where is my conscience, Anne? I want to know. Is it in my stomach?"

"No, it's in your soul," answered Anne, thankful for the darkness, since gravity must be preserved in serious matters.

"I s'pose I can't get clear of it then," said Davy with a sigh. "Are you going to tell Marilla and Mrs. Lynde on me, Anne?"

"No, dear, I'm not going to tell any one. You are sorry you were naughty, aren't you?"

"You bet!"

"And you'll never be bad like that again."

"No, but—" added Davy cautiously, "I might be bad some other way."

"You won't say naughty words, or run away on Sundays, or tell falsehoods to cover up your sins?"

"No. It doesn't pay," said Davy.

"Well, Davy, just tell God you are sorry and ask Him to forgive you."

"Have *you* forgive me, Anne?"

"Yes, dear."

"Then," said Davy joyously, "I don't care much whether God does or not."

"Davy!"

"Oh—I'll ask Him—I'll ask Him," said Davy quickly, scrambling off the bed, convinced by Anne's tone that he must have said something dreadful. "I don't mind asking Him, Anne.—Please, God, I'm awful sorry I behaved bad today and I'll try to be good on Sundays always and please forgive me.—There now, Anne."

"Well, now, run off to bed like a good boy."

"All right. Say, I don't feel mis'rubul any more. I feel fine. Good-night."

Anne slipped down on her pillows with a sigh of relief. Oh— how sleepy—she was! In another second—

"Anne!"

Davy was back again by her bed. Anne dragged her eyes open.

"What is it now, dear?" she asked, trying to keep a note of impatience out of her voice.

"Anne, have you ever noticed how Mr. Harrison spits? Do you s'pose, if I practice hard, I can learn to spit just like him?"

Anne sat up.

"Davy Keith," she said, "go straight to your bed and don't let me catch you out of it again tonight! Go, now!"

Davy went, and stood not upon the order of his going.

14

THE SUMMONS

Anne was sitting with Ruby Gillis in the Gillis' garden after the day had crept lingeringly through it and was gone. It had been a warm, smoky summer afternoon. The world was in a splendor of out-flowering. The idle valleys were full of hazes. The wood-ways were pranked with shadows and the fields with the purple of the asters.

Anne had given up a moonlight drive to the White Sands beach that she might spend the evening with Ruby. She had so spent many evenings that summer, although she often wondered what good it did any one, and sometimes went home deciding that she could not go again.

Ruby grew paler as the summer waned; the White Sands school was given up—"her father thought it better that she shouldn't teach till New Year's"—and the fancy work she loved oftener and oftener fell from hands grown too weary for it. But she was always gay, always hopeful, always chattering and whispering of her beaux, and their rivalries and despairs. It was this that made Anne's visits hard for her. What had once been silly or amusing was gruesome now; it was death peering through a wilful mask of life. Yet Ruby seemed to cling to her, and never let her go until she had promised to come again soon. Mrs. Lynde grumbled about Anne's frequent visits, and declared she would catch consumption; even Marilla was dubious.

"Every time you go to see Ruby you come home looking tired out," she said.

"It's so very sad and dreadful," said Anne in a low tone. "Ruby doesn't seem to realize her condition in the least. And yet I somehow feel she needs help—craves it—and I want to give it to her and can't. All the time I'm with her I feel as if I were watching her struggle with an invisible foe—trying to push it back with such feeble resistance as she has. That is why I come home tired."

But tonight Anne did not feel this so keenly. Ruby was strangely quiet. She said not a word about parties and drives and dresses and "fellows." She lay in the hammock, with her untouched work beside her, and a white shawl wrapped about her thin shoulders. Her long yellow braids of hair—how Anne had envied those beautiful braids in old schooldays!—lay on either side of her. She had taken the pins out—they made her head ache, she said. The hectic flush was gone for the time, leaving her pale and childlike.

The moon rose in the silvery sky, empearling the clouds

around her. Below, the pond shimmered in its hazy radiance. Just beyond the Gillis homestead was the church, with the old graveyard beside it. The moonlight shone on the white stones, bringing them out in clear-cut relief against the dark trees behind.

"How strange the graveyard looks by moonlight!" said Ruby suddenly. "How ghostly!" she shuddered. "Anne, it won't be long now before I'll be lying over there. You and Diana and all the rest will be going about, full of life—and I'll be there—in the old graveyard—dead!"

The surprise of it bewildered Anne. For a few moments she could not speak.

"You know it's so, don't you?" said Ruby insistently.

"Yes, I know," answered Anne in a low tone. "Dear Ruby, I know."

"Everybody knows it," said Ruby bitterly. "I know it—I've known it all summer, though I wouldn't give in. Anne, oh, Anne"—she reached out and caught Anne's hand pleadingly, impulsively—"I don't want to die. I'm *afraid* to die."

"Why should you be afraid, Ruby?" asked Anne quietly.

"Because—because—oh, I'm not afraid but that I'll go to heaven, Anne. I'm a church member. But—it'll be all so different. I think—and think—and I get so frightened—and—and—home-sick. Heaven must be very beautiful, of course, the Bible says so—but, Anne, *it won't be what I've been used to.*"

Through Anne's mind drifted an intrusive recollection of a funny story she had heard Philippa Gordon tell—the story of some old man who had said very much the same thing about the world to come. It *had* sounded funny then—she remembered how she and Priscilla had laughed over it. But it did not seem in the least humorous now, coming from Ruby's pale, trembling lips. It was sad, tragic—and *true*! Heaven could not be what Ruby had been used to. There had been nothing in her gay, frivolous life, her shallow ideals and aspirations, to fit her for that great change, or make the life to come seem to her anything but alien and unreal and undesirable. Anne wondered helplessly what she could say that would help her. Could she say anything? "I think, Ruby," she began hesitatingly—for it was difficult for Anne to speak to any one of the deepest thoughts of her heart, or the new ideas that had vaguely begun to shape themselves in her mind, concerning the great mysteries of life here and hereafter, super-seding her old childish conceptions, and it was hardest of all to speak of them to such as Ruby Gillis—"I think, perhaps, we have very mistaken ideas about heaven—what it is and what it holds for us. I don't think it can be so very different from life here as most people seem to think. I believe we'll just go on living, a good deal as we live here—and be *ourselves* just the same—only it will be easier to be good and to—follow the highest. All the hindrances and perplexities will be taken away, and we shall see clearly. Don't be afraid, Ruby."

"I can't help it," said Ruby pitifully. "Even if what you say about heaven is true—and you can't be sure—it may be only that imagination of yours—it won't be *just* the same. It *can't* be. I want to go on living *here*. I'm so young, Anne. I haven't had my life. I've fought so hard to live—and it isn't any use—I have to die—and leave *everything* I care for."

Anne sat in a pain that was almost intolerable. She could not tell comforting falsehoods; and all that Ruby said was so horribly true. She *was* leaving everything she cared for. She had laid up her treasures on earth only; she had lived solely for the little things of life,—the things that pass,—forgetting the great things that go onward into eternity, bridging the gulf between the two lives and making of death a mere passing from one dwelling to the other—from twilight to unclouded day. God would take care of her there—Anne believed—she would learn—but now it was no wonder her soul clung, in blind helplessness, to the only things she knew and loved.

Ruby raised herself on her arm and lifted up her bright, beau-tiful blue eyes to the moonlit skies.

"I want to live," she said, in a trembling voice. "I want to live like other girls. I—I want to be married, Anne—and—and—have little children. You know I always loved babies, Anne. I couldn't say this to any one but you. I know you understand. And then poor Herb—he—he loves me and I love him, Anne. The others meant nothing to me, but *he* does—and if I could live I would be his wife and be so happy. Oh, Anne, it's hard."

Ruby sank back on her pillows and sobbed convulsively. Anne pressed her hand in an agony of sympathy—silent sympathy, which perhaps helped Ruby more than broken, imperfect words could have done; for presently she grew calmer and her sobs ceased.

"I'm glad I've told you this, Anne," she whispered. "It has helped me just to say it all out. I've wanted to all summer—every time you came I wanted to talk it over with you—but I *couldn't*. It seemed as if it would make death so *sure* if I *said* I was going to die, or if any one else said it or hinted it. I wouldn't say it, or even think it. In the daytime, when people were around me and everything was cheerful, it wasn't so hard to keep from thinking of it. But in the night, when I couldn't sleep—it was so dreadful, Anne. I couldn't get away from it then. Death just came and stared me in the face, until I got so frightened I could have screamed."

"But you won't be frightened any more, Ruby, will you? You'll be brave, and believe that all is going to be well with you."

"I'll try. I'll think over what you have said, and try to believe it. And you'll come up as often as you can, won't you, Anne?"

"Yes, dear."

"It—it won't be very long now, Anne. I feel sure of that. And I'd rather have you than any one else. I always liked you best of all the girls I went to school with. You were never jealous, or mean, like some of them were. Poor Em White was up to see me yesterday. You remember Em and I were such chums for three years when we went to school? And then we quarrelled the time of the school concert. We've never spoken to each other since. Wasn't it silly! Anything like that seems silly *now*. But Em and I made up the old quarrel yesterday. She said she'd have spoken years ago, only she thought I wouldn't. And I never spoke to her because I was sure she wouldn't speak to me. Isn't it strange how people misunderstand each other, Anne?"

"Most of the trouble in life comes from misunderstanding, I think," said Anne. "I must go now, Ruby. It's getting late—and you shouldn't be out in the damp."

"You'll come up soon again."

"Yes, very soon. And if there's anything I can do to help you I'll be so glad."

"I know. You *have* helped me already. Nothing seems quite so dreadful now. Good-night, Anne."

"Good-night, dear."

Anne walked home very slowly in the moonlight. The evening had changed something for her. Life held a different meaning, a deeper purpose. On the surface it would go on just the same; but the deeps had been stirred. It must not be with her as with poor butterfly Ruby. When she came to the end of one life it must not be to face the next with the shrinking terror of something wholly different—something for which accustomed thought and ideal and aspiration had unfitted her. The little things of life, sweet and excellent in their place, must not be the things lived for; the highest must be sought and followed; the life of heaven must be begun here on earth.

That good-night in the garden was for all time. Anne never saw Ruby in life again. The next night the A.V.I.S. gave a farewell party to Jane Andrews before her departure for the West. And, while light feet danced and bright eyes laughed and merry tongues chattered, there came a summons to a soul in Avonlea that might not be disregarded or evaded. The next morning the word went from house to house that Ruby Gillis was dead. She had died in her sleep, painlessly and calmly, and on her face was a smile—as if, after all, death had come as a kindly friend to lead her over the threshold, instead of the grisly phantom she had dreaded.

Mrs. Rachel Lynde said emphatically after the funeral that Ruby Gillis was the handsomest corpse she ever laid eyes on. Her loveliness, as she lay, white-clad, among the delicate flowers that Anne had placed about her, was remembered and talked of for years in Avonlea. Ruby had always been beautiful; but her beauty had been of the earth, earthy; it had had a certain insolent quality in it, as if it flaunted itself in the beholder's eye; spirit had never shone through it, intellect had never refined it. But death had touched it and consecrated it, bringing out delicate modellings and purity of outline never seen before—doing what life and love and great sorrow and deep womanhood joys might have done for Ruby. Anne, looking down through a mist of tears, at her old playfellow, thought she saw the face God had meant Ruby to have, and remembered it so always.

Mrs. Gillis called Anne aside into a vacant room before the funeral procession left the house, and gave her a small packet.

"I want you to have this," she sobbed. "Ruby would have liked you to have it. It's the embroidered centerpiece she was working at. It isn't quite finished—the needle is sticking in it just where her poor little fingers put it the last time she laid it down, the afternoon before she died."

"There's always a piece of unfinished work left," said Mrs. Lynde, with tears in her eyes. "But I suppose there's always some one to finish it."

"How difficult it is to realize that one we have always known can really be dead," said Anne, as she and Diana walked home. "Ruby is the first of our schoolmates to go. One by one, sooner or later, all the rest of us must follow."

"Yes, I suppose so," said Diana uncomfortably. She did not want to talk of that. She would have preferred to have discussed the details of the funeral—the splendid white velvet casket Mr. Gillis had insisted on having for Ruby—"the Gillises must always make a splurge, even at funerals," quoth Mrs. Rachel Lynde—Herb Spencer's sad face, the uncontrolled, hysteric grief of one of Ruby's sisters—but Anne would not talk of these things. She seemed wrapped in a reverie in which Diana felt lonesomely that she had neither lot nor part.

"Ruby Gillis was a great girl to laugh," said Davy suddenly. "Will she laugh as much in heaven as she did in Avonlea, Anne? I want to know."

"Yes, I think she will," said Anne.

"Oh, Anne," protested Diana, with a rather shocked smile.

"Well, why not, Diana? asked Anne seriously. "Do you think we'll never laugh in heaven?"

"Oh—I—I don't know," floundered Diana. "It doesn't seem just right, somehow. You know it's rather dreadful to laugh in church."

"But heaven won't be like church—all the time," said Anne.

"I hope it ain't," said Davy emphatically. "If it is I don't want to go. Church is awful dull. Anyway, I don't mean to go for ever so long. I mean to live to be a hundred years old, like Mr. Thomas Blewett of White Sands. He says he's lived so long 'cause he always smoked tobacco and it killed all the germs. Can I smoke tobacco pretty soon, Anne?"

"No, Davy, I hope you'll never use tobacco," said Anne absently.

"What'll you feel like if the germs kill me then?"demanded Davy.

15
A DREAM TURNED UPSIDE DOWN

"Just one more week and we go back to Redmond," said Anne. She was happy at the thought of returning to work, classes and Redmond friends. Pleasing visions were also being woven around Patty's Place. There was a warm pleasant sense of home in the thought of it, even though she had never lived there.

But the summer had been a very happy one, too—a time of glad living with summer suns and skies, a time of keen delight on wholesome things; a time of renewing and deepening of old friendships; a time in which she had learned to live more nobly, to work more patiently, to play more heartily.

"All life lessons are not learned at college," she thought. "Life teaches them everywhere.

But alas, the final week of that pleasant vacation was spoiled for Anne, by one of those impish happenings which are like a dream turned upside down.

"Been writing any more stories lately?" inquired Mr. Harrison genially one evening when Anne was taking tea with him and Mrs. Harrison.

"No," answered Anne, rather crisply.

"Well, no offence meant. Mrs. Hiram Sloane told me the other day that a big envelope addressed to the Rollings Reliable Baking Powder Company of Montreal had been dropped into the post office box a month ago, and she suspicioned that somebody was trying for the prize they'd offered for the best story that introduced the name of their baking powder. She said it wasn't addressed in your writing, but I thought maybe it was you."

"Indeed, no! I saw the prize offer, but I'd never dream of competing for it. I think it would be perfectly disgraceful to write a story to advertise a baking powder. It would be almost as bad as Judson Parker's patent medicine fence."

So spake Anne loftily, little dreaming of the valley of humiliation awaiting her. That very evening Diana popped into the porch gable, bright-eyed and rosy cheeked, carrying a letter.

"Oh, Anne, here's a letter for you. I was at the office, so I thought I'd bring it along. Do open it quick. If it is what I believe it is I shall just be wild with delight."

Anne, puzzled, opened the letter and glanced over the typewritten contents.

"Miss Anne Shirley,
        "Green Gables,
      "Avonlea, P. E. Island.

"DEAR MADAM: We have much pleasure in informing you that your charming story 'Averil's Atonement' has won the prize of twenty-five dollars offered in our recent competition. We enclose the check herewith. We are arranging for the publication of the story in several prominent Canadian newspapers, and we also intend to have it printed in pamphlet form for distribution among our patrons. Thanking you for the interest you have shown in our enterprise,   "We remain,

"Yours very truly,

"THE ROLLINGS RELIABLE BAKING POWDER CO."

"I don't understand," said Anne, blankly.

Diana clapped her hands.

"Oh, I *knew* it would win the prize—I was sure of it. *I* sent your story into the competition, Anne."

"Diana—Barry!"

"Yes, I did," said Diana gleefully, perching herself on the bed. "When I saw the offer I thought of your story in a minute, and at first I thought I'd ask you to send it in. But then I was afraid you wouldn't—you had so little faith left in it. So I just decided I'd send the copy you gave me, and say nothing about it. Then, if it didn't win the prize, you'd never know and you wouldn't feel badly over it, because the stories that failed were not to be returned, and if it did you'd have such a delightful surprise."

Diana was not the most discerning of mortals, but just at this moment it struck her that Anne was not looking exactly over-joyed. The surprise was there, beyond doubt—but where was the delight?

"Why, Anne, you don't seem a bit pleased!" she exclaimed.

Anne instantly manufactured a smile and put it on.

"Of course I couldn't be anything but pleased over your unselfish wish to give me pleasure," she said slowly. "But you know—I'm so amazed—I can't realize it—and I don't understand. There wasn't a word in my story about—about—" Anne choked a little over the word—"baking powder."

"Oh, *I* put that in," said Diana, reassured. "It was as easy as wink—and of course my experience in our old Story Club helped me. You know the scene where Averil makes the cake? Well, I just stated that she used the Rollings Reliable in it, and that was why it turned out so well; and then, in the last paragraph where *Perceval* clasps *Averil* in his arms and says, 'Sweetheart, the beautiful coming years will bring us the fulfilment of our home of dreams,' I added 'in which we will never use any baking powder except Rollings Reliable.'"

"Oh," gasped poor Anne, as if some one had dashed cold water on her.

"And you've won the twenty-five dollars," continued Diana jubilantly. "Why, I heard Priscilla say once that the *Canadian Woman* only pays five dollars for a story!"

Anne held out the hateful pink slip in shaking fingers.

"I can't take it—it's yours by right, Diana. You sent the story in and made the alterations. I—I would certainly never have sent it. So you must take the check."

"I'd like to see myself," said Diana scornfully. "Why, what I did wasn't any trouble. The honor of being a friend of the prize-winner is enough for me. Well, I must go. I should have gone straight home from the post office for we have company. But I simply had to come and hear the news. I'm *so* glad for your sake, Anne."

Anne suddenly bent forward, put her arms about Diana, and kissed her cheek.

"I think you are the sweetest and truest friend in the world, Diana," she said, with a little tremble in her voice, "and I assure you I appreciate the motive of what you've done."

Diana, pleased and embarrassed, got herself away, and poor Anne, after flinging the innocent check into her bureau drawer as if it were blood-money, cast herself on her bed and wept tears of shame and outraged sensibility. Oh, she could never live this down—never!

Gilbert arrived at dusk, brimming over with congratulations, for he had called at Orchard Slope and heard the news. But his congratulations died on his lips at sight of Anne's face.

"Why, Anne, what is the matter? I expected to find you radiant over winning Rollings Reliable prize. Good for you!"

"Oh, Gilbert, not you," implored Anne, in an *et-tu Brute* tone. "I thought *you* would understand. Can't you see how awful it is?"

"I must confess I can't. *What* is wrong?"

"Everything," moaned Anne. "I feel as if I were disgraced forever. What do you think a mother would feel like if she found her child tattooed over with a baking powder advertisement? I feel just the same. I loved my poor little story, and I wrote it out of the best that was in me. And it is *sacrilege* to have it degraded to the level of a baking powder advertisement. Don't you remember what Professor Hamilton used to tell us in the literature class at Queen's? He said we were never to write a word for a low or unworthy motive, but always to cling to the very highest ideals. What will he think when he hears I've written a story to advertise Rollings Reliable? And, oh, when it gets out at Redmond! Think how I'll be teased and laughed at!"

"That you won't," said Gilbert, wondering uneasily if it were that confounded Junior's opinion in particular over which Anne was worried. "The Reds will think just as I thought—that you, being like nine out of ten of us, not over-burdened with worldly wealth, had taken this way of earning an honest penny to help yourself through the year. I don't see that there's anything low or unworthy about that, or anything ridiculous either. One would rather write masterpieces of literature no doubt—but meanwhile board and tuition fees have to be paid."

This common-sense, matter-of-fact view of the case cheered Anne a little. At least it removed her dread of being laughed at, though the deeper hurt of an outraged ideal remained.

16
ADJUSTED RELATIONSHIPS

"It's the homiest spot I ever saw—it's homier than home," avowed Philippa Gordon, looking about her with delighted eyes. They were all assembled at twilight in the big living room at Patty's Place—Anne and Priscilla, Phil and Stella, Aunt Jamesina, Rusty, Joseph, the Sarah-Cat, and Gog and Magog. The firelight shadows were dancing over the walls; the cats were purring; and a huge bowl of hot-house chrysanthemums, sent to Phil by one of the victims, shone through the golden gloom like creamy moons.

It was three weeks since they had considered themselves settled, and already all believed the experiment would be a success. The first fortnight after their return had been a pleasantly exciting one; they had been busy setting up their household goods, organizing their little establishment, and adjusting different opinions.

Anne was not over-sorry to leave Avonlea when the time came to return to college. The last few days of her vacation had not been pleasant. Her prize story had been published in the Island papers; and Mr. William Blair had, upon the counter of his store, a huge pile of pink, green and yellow pamphlets, containing it, one of which he gave to every customer. He sent a complimentary bundle to Anne, who promptly dropped them all in the kitchen stove. Her humiliation was the consequence of her own ideals only, for Avonlea folks thought it quite splendid that she should have won the prize. Her many friends regarded her with honest admiration; her few foes with scornful envy. Josie Pye said she believed Anne Shirley had just copied the story; she was sure she remembered reading it in a paper years before. The Sloanes, who had found out or guessed that Charlie had been "turned down," said they didn't think it was much to be proud of; almost any one could have done it, if she tried. Aunt Atossa told Anne she was very sorry to hear she had taken to writing novels; nobody born and bred in Avonlea would do it; that was what came of adopting orphans from goodness knew where, with goodness knew what kind of parents. Even Mrs. Rachel Lynde was darkly dubious about the propriety of writing fiction, though she was almost reconciled to it by that twenty-five dollar check.

"It is perfectly amazing, the price they pay for such lies, that's what," she said, half-proudly, half-severely.

All things considered, it was a relief when going-away time came. And it was very jolly to be back at Redmond, a wise, experienced Soph with hosts of friends to greet on the merry opening day. Pris and Stella and Gilbert were there, Charlie Sloane, looking more important than ever Sophomore looked before, Phil, with the Alec-and-Alonzo question still unsettled, and Moody Spurgeon MacPherson. Moody Spurgeon had been teaching school ever since leaving Queen's, but his mother had concluded it was high time he gave it up and turned his attention to learning how to be a minister. Poor Moody Spurgeon fell on hard luck at the very beginning of his college career. Half a dozen ruthless Sophs, who were among his fellow-boarders, swooped down upon him one night and shaved half of his head. In this guise the luckless Moody Spurgeon had to go about until his hair grew again. He told Anne bitterly that there were times when he had his doubts as to whether he was really called to be a minister.

Aunt Jamesina did not come until the girls had Patty's Place ready for her. Miss Patty had sent the key to Anne, with a letter in which she said Gog and Magog were packed in a box under the spare-room bed, but might be taken out when wanted; in a post-script she added that she hoped the girls would be careful about putting up pictures. The living room had been newly papered five years before and she and Miss Maria did not want any more holes made in that new paper than was absolutely necessary. For the rest she trusted everything to Anne.

How those girls enjoyed putting their nest in order! As Phil said, it was almost as good as getting married. You had the fun of home-making without the bother of a husband. All brought something with them to adorn or make comfortable the little house. Pris and Phil and Stella had nick-nacks and pictures galore, which later they proceeded to hang according to taste, in reckless disregard of Miss Patty's new paper.

"We'll putty the holes up when we leave, dear—she'll never know," they said to protesting Anne.

Diana had given Anne a pine needle cushion and Miss Ada had given both her and Priscilla a fearfully and wonderfully embroidered one. Marilla had sent a big box of preserves, and darkly hinted at a hamper for Thanksgiving, and Mrs. Lynde gave Anne a patch work quilt and loaned her five more.

"You take them," she said authoritatively. "They might as well be in use as packed away in that trunk in the garret for moths to gnaw."

No moths would ever have ventured near those quilts, for they reeked of moth-balls to such an extent that they had to be hung in the orchard of Patty's Place for a full fortnight before they could be endured indoors. Verily, aristocratic Spofford Avenue had rarely beheld such a display. The gruff old millionaire who lived "next door" came over and wanted to buy the gorgeous red and yellow "tulip-pattern" one which Mrs. Rachel had given Anne. He said his mother used to make quilts like that, and by Jove, he wanted one to remind him of her. Anne would not sell it, much to his disappointment, but she wrote all about it to Mrs. Lynde. That highly-gratified lady sent word back that she had one just like it to spare, so the tobacco king got his quilt after all, and insisted on having it spread on his bed, to the disgust of his fashionable wife.

Mrs. Lynde's quilts served a very useful purpose that winter. Patty's Place for all its many virtues, had its faults also. It was really a rather cold house; and when the frosty nights came the girls were very glad to snuggle down under Mrs. Lynde's quilts, and hoped that the loan of them might be accounted unto her for righteousness. Anne had the blue room she had coveted at sight. Priscilla and Stella had the large one. Phil was blissfully content with the little one over the kitchen; and Aunt Jamesina was to have the downstairs one off the living room. Rusty at first slept on the doorstep.

Anne, walking home from Redmond a few days after her return, became aware that the people that she met surveyed her with a covert, indulgent smile. Anne wondered uneasily what was the matter with her. Was her hat crooked? Was her belt loose? Craning her head to investigate, Anne, for the first time, saw Rusty.

Trotting along behind her, close to her heels, was quite the most forlorn specimen of the cat-tribe she had ever beheld. The animal was well past kittenhood, lank, thin, disreputable-looking. Pieces of both ears were lacking, one eye was temporarily out of repair, and one jowl ludicrously swollen. As for color, if a once black cat had been well and thoroughly singed the result would have resembled the hue of this waif's thin, draggled, unsightly fur.

Anne "shooed," but the cat would not "shoo." As long as she stood he sat back on his haunches and gazed at her reproachfully out of his one good eye; when she resumed her walk he followed. Anne resigned herself to his company until she reached the gate of Patty's Place, which she coldly shut in his face, fondly supposing she had seen the last of him. But when, fifteen minutes later, Phil opened the door, there sat the rusty-brown cat on the step. More, he promptly darted in and sprang upon Anne's lap with a half-pleading, half-triumphant "miaow."

"Anne," said Stella severely, "do you own that animal?"

"No, I do *not*," protested Anne. "The creature followed me home from somewhere. I couldn't get rid of him. Ugh, get down. I like decent cats reasonably well; but I don't like beasties of your complexion."

Pussy, however, refused to get down. He coolly curled up in Anne's lap and began to purr.

"He has evidently adopted you," laughed Priscilla.

"I won't *be* adopted," said Anne stubbornly.

"The poor creature is starving," said Phil pityingly. "Why, his bones are almost coming through his skin."

"Well, I'll give him a square meal and then he must return to whence he came," said Anne resolutely.

The cat was fed and put out. In the morning he was still on the doorstep. On the doorstep he continued to sit, bolting in whenever the door was opened. No coolness of welcome had the least effect on him; of nobody save Anne did he take the least notice. Out of compassion the girls fed him; but when a week had passed they decided that something must be done. The cat's appearance had improved. His eye and cheek had resumed their normal appearance; he was not quite so thin; and he had been seen washing his face.

"But for all that we can't keep him," said Stella. "Aunt Jimsie is coming next week and she will bring the Sarah-cat with her. We can't keep two cats; and if we did this Rusty Coat would fight all the time with the Sarah-cat. He's a fighter by nature. He had a pitched battle last evening with the tobacco-king's cat and routed him, horse, foot and artillery."

"We must get rid of him," agreed Anne, looking darkly at the subject of their discussion, who was purring on the hearth-rug with an air of lamb-like meekness. "But the question is—how? How can four unprotected females get rid of a cat who won't be got rid of?"

"We must chloroform him," said Phil briskly. "That is the most humane way."

"Who of us knows anything about chloroforming a cat?" demanded Anne gloomily.

"I do, honey. It's one of my few—sadly few—useful accomplishments. I've disposed of several at home. You take the cat in the morning and give him a good breakfast. Then you take an old burlap bag—there's one in the back porch—put the cat on it and turn over him a wooden box. Then take a two-ounce bottle of chloroform, uncork it, and slip it under the edge of the box. Put a heavy weight on top of the box and leave it till evening. The cat will be dead, curled up peacefully as if he were asleep. No pain— no struggle.

"It sounds easy," said Anne dubiously.

"It *is* easy. Just leave it to me. I'll see to it," said Phil reassuringly.

Accordingly the chloroform was procured, and the next morning Rusty was lured to his doom. He ate his breakfast, licked his
chops, and climbed into Anne's lap. Anne's heart misgave her.
This poor creature loved her—trusted her. How could she be a
party to his destruction?

"Here, take him," she said hastily to Phil. "I feel like a murderess."

"He won't suffer, you know," comforted Phil, but Anne had fled.

The fatal deed was done in the back porch. Nobody went near
it that day. But at dusk Phil declared that Rusty must be buried.

"Pris and Stella must dig his grave in the orchard," decreed
Phil, "and Anne must come with me to lift the box off. That's the
part I always hate."

The two conspirators tip-toed reluctantly to the back porch.
Phil gingerly lifted the stone she had put on the box. Suddenly,
faint but distinct, sounded an unmistakable mew under the box.

"He—he isn't dead," gasped Anne, sitting blankly down on
the kitchen door-step.

"He must be," said Phil incredulously.

Another tiny mew proved that he wasn't. The two girls stared
at each other.

"What will we do?" questioned Anne.

"Why in the world don't you come?" demanded Stella,
appearing in the doorway. "We've got the grave ready. 'What,
silent still and silent all?'" she quoted teasingly.

"'Oh, no, the voices of the dead
Sound like the distant torrent's fall'"
promptly counter-quoted Anne, pointing solemnly to the box.

A burst of laughter broke the tension.

"We must leave him here till morning," said Phil, replacing
the stone. "He hasn't mewed for five minutes. Perhaps the mews
we heard were his dying groan. Or perhaps we merely imagined
them, under the strain of our guilty consciences."

But, when the box was lifted in the morning, Rusty bounded

at one gay leap to Anne's shoulder where he began to lick her face
affectionately. Never was there a cat more decidedly alive.

"Here's a knothole in the box," groaned Phil. "I never saw it.
That's why he didn't die. Now, we've got to do it all over again."

"No, we haven't," declared Anne suddenly. "Rusty isn't going
to be killed again. He's my cat—and you've just got to make the
best of it."

"Oh, well, if you'll settle with Aunt Jimsie and the Sarah-cat,"
said Stella, with the air of one washing her hands of the
whole affair.

From that time Rusty was one of the family. He slept o' nights
on the scrubbing cushion in the back porch and lived on the fat
of the land. By the time Aunt Jamesina came he was plump and
glossy and tolerably respectable. But, like Kipling's cat, he
"walked by himself." His paw was against every cat, and every
cat's paw against him. One by one he vanquished the aristocratic
felines of Spofford Avenue. As for human beings, he loved Anne
and Anne alone. Nobody else even dared stroke him. An angry
spit and something that sounded much like very improper language greeted any one who did.

"The airs that cat puts on are perfectly intolerable," declared Stella.

"Him was a nice old pussens, him was," vowed Anne, cuddling her pet defiantly.

"Well, I don't know how he and the Sarah-cat will ever make
out to live together," said Stella pessimistically. "Cat-fights in the
orchard o' nights are bad enough. But cat-fights here in the living
room are unthinkable."

In due time Aunt Jamesina arrived. Anne and Priscilla and
Phil had awaited her advent rather dubiously; but when Aunt
Jamesina was enthroned in the rocking chair before the open fire
they figuratively bowed down and worshipped her.

Aunt Jamesina was a tiny old woman with a little, softly-
triangular face, and large, soft blue eyes that were alight with
unquenchable youth, and as full of hopes as a girl's. She had pink

cheeks and snow-white hair which she wore in quaint little puffs over her ears.

"It's a very old-fashioned way," she said, knitting industriously at something as dainty and pink as a sunset cloud. "But *I* am old-fashioned. My clothes are, and it stands to reason my opinions are, too. I don't say they're any the better of that, mind you. In fact, I daresay they're a good deal the worse. But they've worn nice and easy. New shoes are smarter than old ones, but the old ones are more comfortable. I'm old enough to indulge myself in the matter of shoes and opinions. I mean to take it real easy here. I know you expect me to look after you and keep you proper, but I'm not going to do it. You're old enough to know how to behave if you're ever going to be. So, as far as I am concerned," concluded Aunt Jamesina, with a twinkle in her young eyes, "you can all go to destruction in your own way."

"Oh, will somebody separate those cats?" pleaded Stella, shudderingly.

Aunt Jamesina had brought with her not only the Sarah-cat but Joseph. Joseph, she explained, had belonged to a dear friend of hers who had gone to live in Vancouver.

"She couldn't take Joseph with her so she begged me to take him. I really couldn't refuse. He's a beautiful cat—that is, his disposition is beautiful. She called him Joseph because his coat is of many colors."

It certainly was. Joseph, as the disgusted Stella said, looked like a walking rag-bag. It was impossible to say what his ground color was. His legs were white with black spots on them. His back was gray with a huge patch of yellow on one side and a black patch on the other. His tail was yellow with a gray tip. One ear was black and one yellow. A black patch over one eye gave him a fearfully rakish look. In reality he was meek and inoffensive, of a sociable disposition. In one respect, if in no other, Joseph was like a lily of the field. He toiled not neither did he spin or catch mice. Yet Solomon in all his glory slept not on softer cushions, or feasted more fully on fat things.

Joseph and the Sarah-cat arrived by express in separate boxes. After they had been released and fed, Joseph selected the cushion and corner which appealed to him, and the Sarah-cat gravely sat her down before the fire and proceeded to wash her face. She was a large, sleek, gray-and-white cat, with an enormous dignity which was not at all impaired by any consciousness of her plebeian origin. She had been given to Aunt Jamesina by her washerwoman.

"Her name was Sarah, so my husband always called puss the Sarah-cat," explained Aunt Jamesina. "She is eight years old, and a remarkable mouser. Don't worry, Stella. The Sarah-cat *never* fights and Joseph rarely."

"They'll have to fight here in self-defense," said Stella.

At this juncture Rusty arrived on the scene. He bounded joyously half way across the room before he saw the intruders. Then he stopped short; his tail expanded until it was as big as three tails. The fur on his back rose up in a defiant arch; Rusty lowered his head, uttered a fearful shriek of hatred and defiance, and launched himself at the Sarah-cat.

That stately animal had stopped washing her face and was looking at him curiously. She met his onslaught with one contemptuous sweep of her capable paw. Rusty went rolling helplessly over on the rug; he picked himself up dazedly. What sort of a cat was this who had boxed his ears? He looked dubiously at the Sarah-cat. Would he or would he not? The Sarah-cat deliberately turned her back on him and resumed her toilet operations. Rusty decided that he would not. He never did. From that time on the Sarah-cat ruled the roost. Rusty never again interfered with her.

But Joseph rashly sat up and yawned. Rusty, burning to avenge his disgrace, swooped down upon him. Joseph, pacific by nature, could fight upon occasion and fight well. The result was a series of drawn battles. Every day Rusty and Joseph fought at sight. Anne took Rusty's part and detested Joseph. Stella was in despair. But Aunt Jamesina only laughed.

"Let them fight it out," she said tolerantly. "They'll make

friends after a bit. Joseph needs some exercise—he was getting too fat. And Rusty has to learn he isn't the only cat in the world."

Eventually Joseph and Rusty accepted the situation and from sworn enemies became sworn friends. They slept on the same cushion with their paws about each other, and gravely washed each other's faces.

"We've all got used to each other," said Phil. "And I've learned how to wash dishes and sweep a floor."

"But you needn't try to make us believe you can chloroform a cat," laughed Anne.

"It was all the fault of the knothole," protested Phil.

"It was a good thing the knothole was there," said Aunt Jamesina rather severely. "Kittens *have* to be drowned, I admit, or the world would be over-run. But no decent, grown-up cat should be done to death—unless he sucks eggs."

"You wouldn't have thought Rusty very decent if you'd seen him when he came here," said Stella. "He positively looked like the Old Nick."

"I don't believe Old Nick can be so very ugly," said Aunt Jamesina reflectively. "He wouldn't do so much harm if he was. *I* always think of him as a rather handsome gentleman."

17
A LETTER FROM DAVY

"It's beginning to snow, girls," said Phil, coming in one November evening, "and there are the loveliest little stars and crosses all over the garden walk. I never noticed before what exquisite things snowflakes really are. One has time to notice things like that in the simple life. Bless you all for permitting me to live it. It's really delightful to feel worried because butter has gone up five cents a pound."

"Has it?" demanded Stella, who kept the household accounts.

"It has—and here's your butter. I'm getting quite expert at marketing. It's better fun than flirting," concluded Phil gravely.

"Everything is going up scandalously," sighed Stella.

"Never mind. Thank goodness air and salvation are still free," said Aunt Jamesina.

"And so is laughter," added Anne. "There's no tax on it yet and that is well, because you're all going to laugh presently. I'm going to read you Davy's letter. His spelling has improved immensely this past year, though he is not strong on apostrophes, and he certainly possesses the gift of writing an interesting letter. Listen and laugh, before we settle down to the evening's study-grind."

"Dear Anne," ran Davy's letter, "I take my pen to tell you that we are all pretty well and hope this will find you the same. It's snowing some today and Marilla says the old woman in the sky is shaking her feather beds. Is the old woman in the sky God's wife, Anne? I want to know.

"Mrs. Lynde has been real sick but she is better now. She fell down the cellar stairs last week. When she fell she grabbed hold of the shelf with all the milk pails and stewpans on it, and it gave way and went down with her and made a splendid crash. Marilla thought it was an earthquake at first. One of the stewpans was all dinged up and Mrs. Lynde straned her ribs. The doctor come and give her medicine to rub on her ribs but she didn't understand him and took it all inside instead. The doctor said it was a wonder it dident kill her but it dident and it cured her ribs and Mrs. Lynde says doctors dont know much anyhow. But we couldent fix up the stewpan. Marilla had to throw it out. Thanksgiving was last week. There was no school and we had a great dinner. I et mince pie and rost turkey and frut cake and donuts and cheese and jam and choklut cake. Marilla said Id die but I dident. Dora had earake after it, only it wasent in her ears it was in her stummick. I dident have earake anywhere.

"Our new teacher is a man. He does things for jokes. Last

week he made all us third-class boys write a composishun on what kind of a wife we'd like to have and the girls what kind of a husband. He laughed fit to kill when he read them. This was mine. I thought youd like to see it.

"'The kind of a wife Id like to Have.

"'She must have good manners and get my meals on time and do what I tell her and always be very polite to me. She must be fifteen years old. She must be good to the poor and keep her house tidy and be good tempered and go to church reglarly. She must be very handsome and have curly hair. If I get a wife that is just what I like Ill be an awful good husband to her. I think a woman ought to be awful good to her husband. Some poor women havent any husbands.

"'THE END.'

"I was at Mrs. Isaac Wrights funeral at White Sands last week. The husband of the corpse felt real sorry. Mrs. Lynde says Mrs. Wrights grandfather stole a sheep but Marilla says we mustent speak ill of the dead. Why mustent we, Anne? I want to know. It's pretty safe, ain't it?

"Mrs. Lynde was awful mad the other day because I asked her if she was alive in Noah's time. I dident mean to hurt her feelings. I just wanted to know. Was she, Anne?

"Mr. Harrison wanted to get rid of his dog. So he hunged him once but he come to life and scooted for the barn while Mr. Harrison was digging the grave, so he hunged him again and he stayed dead that time. Mr. Harrison has a new man working for him. He's awful okward. Mr. Harrison says he is left handed in both his feet. Mr. Barry's hired man is lazy. Mrs. Barry says that but Mr. Barry says he aint lazy exactly only he thinks it easier to pray for things than to work for them.

"Mrs. Harmon Andrews prize pig that she talked so much of died in a fit. Mrs. Lynde says it was a judgment on her for pride. But I think it was hard on the pig. Milty Boulter has been sick. The doctor gave him medecine and it tasted horrid. I offered to take it for him for a quarter but the Boulters are so mean. Milty says he'd rather take it himself and save his money. I asked Mrs. Boulter how a person would go about catching a man and she got awful mad and said she dident know, shed never chased men.

"The A.V.I.S. is going to paint the hall again. They're tired of having it blue.

"The new minister was here to tea last night. He took three pieces of pie. If I did that Mrs. Lynde would call me piggy. And he et fast and took big bites and Marilla is always telling me not to do that. Why can ministers do what boys can't? I want to know.

"I havent any more news. Here are six kisses. xxxxxx. Dora sends one. Heres hers. x.

"Your loving friend
"DAVID KEITH"

"P.S. Anne, who was the devils father? I want to know."

18
MISS JOSEPHINE REMEMBERS THE ANNE-GIRL

When Christmas holidays came the girls of Patty's Place scattered to their respective homes, but Aunt Jamesina elected to stay where she was.

"I couldn't go any of the places I've been invited and take those three cats," she said. "And I'm not going to leave the poor creatures here alone for nearly three weeks. If we had any decent neighbors who would feed them I might, but there's nothing except millionaires on this street. So I'll stay here and keep Patty's Place warm for you."

Anne went home with the usual joyous anticipations—which were not wholly fulfilled. She found Avonlea in the grip of such an early, cold, and stormy winter as even the "oldest inhabitant" could not recall. Green Gables was literally hemmed in by huge drifts. Almost every day of that ill-starred vacation it stormed fiercely; and even on fine days it drifted unceasingly. No sooner were the roads broken than they filled in again. It was almost impossible to stir out. The A.V.I.S. tried on three evenings, to have a party in honor of the college students, and on each evening the storm was so wild that nobody could go, so they gave up the attempt in despair. Anne, despite her love of and loyalty to Green Gables, could not help thinking longingly of Patty's Place, its cosy open fire, Aunt Jamesina's mirthful eyes, the three cats, the merry chatter of the girls, the pleasantness of Friday evenings when college friends dropped in to talk of grave and gay.

Anne was lonely; Diana, during the whole of the holidays, was imprisoned at home with a bad attack of bronchitis. She could not come to Green Gables and it was rarely Anne could get to Orchard Slope, for the old way through the Haunted Wood was impassable with drifts, and the long way over the frozen Lake of Shining Waters was almost as bad. Ruby Gillis was sleeping in the white-heaped graveyard; Jane Andrews was teaching a school on western prairies. Gilbert, to be sure, was still faithful, and waded up to Green Gables every possible evening. But Gilbert's visits were not what they once were. Anne almost dreaded them. It was very disconcerting to look up in the midst of a sudden silence and find Gilbert's hazel eyes fixed upon her with a quite unmistakable expression in their grave depths; and it was still more disconcerting to find herself blushing hotly and uncomfortably under his gaze, just as if—just as if—well, it was very embarrassing. Anne wished herself back at Patty's Place, where there was always somebody else about to take the edge off a delicate situation. At Green Gables Marilla went promptly to Mrs. Lynde's domain when Gilbert came and insisted on taking the twins with her. The significance of this was unmistakable and Anne was in a helpless fury over it.

Davy, however, was perfectly happy. He revelled in getting out in the morning and shovelling out the paths to the well and henhouse. He gloried in the Christmas-tide delicacies which Marilla and Mrs. Lynde vied with each other in preparing for Anne, and he was reading an enthralling tale, in a school library book, of a wonderful hero who seemed blessed with a miraculous faculty for getting into scrapes from which he was usually delivered by an earthquake or a volcanic explosion, which blew him high and dry out of his troubles, landed him in a fortune, and closed the story with proper *éclat*.

"I tell you it's a bully story, Anne," he said ecstatically. "I'd ever so much rather read it than the Bible."

"Would you?" smiled Anne.

Davy peered curiously at her.

"You don't seem a bit shocked, Anne. Mrs. Lynde was awful shocked when I said it to her."

"No, I'm not shocked, Davy. I think it's quite natural that a nine-year-old boy would sooner read an adventure story than the Bible. But when you are older I hope and think that you will realize what a wonderful book the Bible is."

"Oh, I think some parts of it are fine," conceded Davy. "That story about Joseph now—it's bully. But if I'd been Joseph *I* wouldn't have forgive the brothers. No, siree, Anne. I'd have cut all their heads off. Mrs. Lynde was awful mad when I said that and shut the Bible up and said she'd never read me any more of it if I talked like that. So I don't talk now when she reads it Sunday afternoons; I just think things and say them to Milty Boulter next day in school. I told Milty the story about Elisha and the bears and it scared him so he's never made fun of Mr. Harrison's bald head since. Are there any bears on P. E. Island, Anne? I want to know."

"Not nowadays," said Anne, absently, as the wind blew a scud of snow against the window. "Oh, dear, will it ever stop storming."

"God knows," said Davy airily, preparing to resume his reading. Anne *was* shocked this time.

"Davy!" she exclaimed reproachfully.

"Mrs. Lynde says that," protested Davy. "One night last week Marilla said 'Will Ludovic Speed and Theodora Dix *ever* get married,' and Mrs. Lynde said, 'God knows'—just like that."

"Well, it wasn't right for her to say it," said Anne, promptly deciding upon which horn of this dilemma to empale herself. "It isn't right for anybody to take that name in vain or speak it lightly, Davy. Don't ever do it again."

"Not if I say it slow and solemn, like the minister?" queried Davy gravely.

"No, not even then."

"Well, I won't. Ludovic Speed and Theodora Dix live in Middle Grafton and Mrs. Rachel says he has been courting her for a hundred years. Won't they soon be too old to get married, Anne? I hope Gilbert won't court *you* that long. When are you going to be married, Anne? Mrs. Lynde says it's a sure thing."

"Mrs. Lynde is a—" began Anne hotly; then stopped.

"Awful old gossip," completed Davy calmly. "That's what every one calls her. But *is* it a sure thing, Anne? I want to know."

"You're a very silly little boy, Davy," said Anne, stalking haughtily out of the room. The kitchen was deserted and she sat down by the window in the fast falling wintry twilight. The sun had set and the wind had died down. A pale chilly moon looked out behind a bank of purple clouds in the west. The sky faded out, but the strip of yellow along the western horizon grew brighter and fiercer, as if all the stray gleams of light were concentrating on one spot; the distant hills, rimmed with priest-like firs, stood out in dark distinctness against it. Anne looked across the still, white fields, cold and lifeless in the harsh light of that grim sunset, and sighed. She was very lonely; and she was sad at heart; for she was wondering if she would be able to return to Redmond next year. It did not seem likely. The only scholarship possible in the Sophomore year was a very small affair. She would not take Marilla's money; and there seemed little prospect of being able to earn enough in the summer vacation.

"I suppose I'll just have to drop out next year," she thought drearily, "and teach a district school again until I earn enough to finish my course. And by that time all my old class will have graduated and Patty's Place will be out of the question. But there!

I'm not going to be a coward. I'm thankful I can earn my way through if necessary."

"Here's Mr. Harrison wading up the lane," announced Davy, running out. "I hope he's brought the mail. It's three days since we got it. I want to see what them pesky Grits are doing. I'm a Coservative, Anne. And I tell you, you have to keep your eye on them Grits."

Mr. Harrison had brought the mail, and merry letters from Stella and Priscilla and Phil soon dissipated Anne's blues. Aunt Jamesina, too, had written, saying that she was keeping the hearth-fire alight, and that the cats were all well, and the house plants doing fine.

"The weather has been real cold," she wrote, "so I let the cats sleep in the house—Rusty and Joseph on the sofa in the living room, and the Sarah-cat on the foot of my bed. It's real company to hear her purring when I wake up in the night and think of my poor daughter in the foreign field. If it was anywhere but in India I wouldn't worry, but they say the snakes out there are terrible. It takes all the Sarah-cat's purring to drive away the thought of those snakes. I have enough faith for everything but the snakes. I can't think why Providence ever made them. Sometimes I don't think He did. I'm inclined to believe the Old Harry had a hand in making *them*."

Anne had left a thin, typewritten communication till the last, thinking it unimportant. When she had read it she sat very still, with tears in her eyes.

"What is the matter, Anne?" asked Marilla.

"Miss Josephine Barry is dead," said Anne, in a low tone.

"So she has gone at last," said Marilla. "Well, she has been sick for over a year, and the Barrys have been expecting to hear of her death any time. It is well she is at rest for she has suffered dreadfully, Anne. She was always kind to you."

"She has been kind to the last, Marilla. This letter is from her lawyer. She has left me a thousand dollars in her will."

"Gracious, ain't that an awful lot of money," exclaimed Davy.

"She's the woman you and Diana lit on when you jumped into the spare room bed, ain't she? Diana told me that story. Is that why she left you so much?"

"Hush, Davy," said Anne gently. She slipped away to the porch gable with a full heart, leaving Marilla and Mrs. Lynde to talk over the news to their hearts' content.

"Do you s'pose Anne will ever get married now?" speculated Davy anxiously. "When Dorcas Sloane got married last summer she said if she'd had enough money to live on she'd never have been bothered with a man, but even a widower with eight children was better'n living with a sister-in-law."

"Davy Keith, do hold your tongue," said Mrs. Rachel severely. "The way you talk is scandalous for a small boy, that's what."

19

AN INTERLUDE

"To think that this is my twentieth birthday, and that I've left my teens behind me forever," said Anne, who was curled up on the hearth-rug with Rusty in her lap, to Aunt Jamesina who was reading in her pet chair. They were alone in the living room. Stella and Priscilla had gone to a committee meeting and Phil was upstairs adorning herself for a party.

"I suppose you feel kind of sorry," said Aunt Jamesina. "The teens are such a nice part of life. I'm glad I've never gone out of them myself."

Anne laughed.

"You never will, Aunty. You'll be eighteen when you should be a hundred. Yes, I'm sorry, and a little dissatisfied as well. Miss Stacy told me long ago that by the time I was twenty my character would be formed, for good or evil. I don't feel that it's what it should be. It's full of flaws."

"So's everybody's," said Aunt Jamesina cheerfully. "Mine's

cracked in a hundred places. Your Miss Stacy likely meant that when you were twenty your character would have got its permanent bent in one direction or 'tother, and would go on developing in that line. Don't worry over it, Anne. Do your duty by God and your neighbor and yourself, and have a good time. That's my philosophy and it's always worked pretty well. Where's Phil off to tonight?"

"She's going to a dance, and she's got the sweetest dress for it—creamy yellow silk and cobwebby lace. It just suits those brown tints of hers."

"There's magic in the words 'silk' and 'lace,' isn't there?" said Aunt Jamesina. "The very sound of them makes me feel like skipping off to a dance. And *yellow* silk. It makes one think of a dress of sunshine. I always wanted a yellow silk dress, but first my mother and then my husband wouldn't hear of it. The very first thing I'm going to do when I get to heaven is to get a yellow silk dress."

Amid Anne's peal of laughter Phil came downstairs, trailing clouds of glory, and surveyed herself in the long oval mirror on the wall.

"A flattering looking-glass is a promoter of amiability," she said. "The one in my room does certainly make me green. Do I look pretty nice, Anne?"

"Do you really know how pretty you are, Phil?" asked Anne, in honest admiration.

"Of course I do. What are looking-glasses and men for? That wasn't what I meant. Are all my ends tucked in? Is my skirt straight? And would this rose look better lower down? I'm afraid it's too high—it will make me look lop-sided. But I hate things tickling my ears."

"Everything is just right, and that southwest dimple of yours is lovely."

"Anne, there's one thing in particular I like about you,—you are so ungrudging. There isn't a particle of envy in you."

"Why should she be envious?" demanded Aunt Jamesina.

"She's not quite as good-looking as you, maybe, but she's got a far handsomer nose."

"I know it," conceded Phil.

"My nose always has been a great comfort to me," confessed Anne.

"And I love the way your hair grows on your forehead, Anne. And that one wee curl, always looking as if it were going to drop, but never dropping, is delicious. But as for noses, mine is a dreadful worry to me. I know by the time I'm forty it will be Byrney. What do you think I'll look like when I'm forty, Anne?"

"Like an old, matronly, married woman," teased Anne.

"I won't," said Phil, sitting down comfortably to wait for her escort. "Joseph, you calico beastie, don't you dare jump on my lap. I won't go to a dance all over cat-hairs. No, Anne, I *won't* look matronly. But no doubt I'll be married."

"To Alec or Alonzo?" asked Anne.

"To one of them, I suppose," sighed Phil, "if I can ever decide which."

"It shouldn't be hard to decide," scolded Aunt Jamesina.

"I was born a see-saw, Aunty, and nothing can ever prevent me from teetering."

"You ought to be more level-headed, Philippa."

"It's best to be level-headed, of course," agreed Philippa, "but you miss lots of fun. As for Alec and Alonzo, if you knew them you'd understand why it's difficult to choose between them. They're equally nice."

"Then take somebody who is nicer," suggested Aunt Jamesina. "There's that Senior who is so devoted to you—Will Leslie. He has such nice, large, mild eyes."

"They're a little bit too large and too mild—like a cow's," said Phil cruelly.

"What do you say about George Parker?"

"There's nothing to say about him except that he always looks as if he had just been starched and ironed."

"Marr Holworthy then. You can't find a fault with him."

"No, he would do if he wasn't poor. I must marry a rich man, Aunt Jamesina. That—and good looks—is an indispensable qualification. I'd marry Gilbert Blythe if he were rich."

"Oh, would you?" said Anne, rather viciously.

"We don't like that idea a little bit, although we don't want Gilbert ourselves, oh, no," mocked Phil. "But don't let's talk of disagreeable subjects. I'll have to marry sometime, I suppose, but I shall put off the evil day as long as I can."

"You mustn't marry anybody you don't love, Phil, when all's said and done," said Aunt Jamesina.

> "'Oh, hearts that loved in the good old way,
>   Have been out o' the fashion this many a day,'"

trilled Phil mockingly. "There's the carriage. I fly—Bi-bi, you two old-fashioned darlings."

When Phil had gone Aunt Jamesina looked solemnly at Anne.

"That girl is pretty and sweet and good-hearted, but do you think she is quite right in her mind, by spells, Anne?"

"Oh, I don't think there's anything the matter with Phil's mind," said Anne, hiding a smile. "It's just her way of talking."

Aunt Jamesina shook her head.

"Well, I hope so, Anne. I do hope so, because I love her. But I can't understand her—she beats me. She isn't like any of the girls I ever knew, or any of the girls I was myself."

"How many girls were you, Aunt Jimsie?"

"About half a dozen, my dear."

20
GILBERT SPEAKS

"This has been a dull, prosy day," yawned Phil, stretching herself idly on the sofa, having previously dispossessed two exceedingly indignant cats.

Anne looked up from *Pickwick Papers*. Now that spring examinations were over she was treating herself to Dickens.

"It has been a prosy day for us," she said thoughtfully, "but to some people it has been a wonderful day. Some one has been rapturously happy in it. Perhaps a great deed has been done somewhere today—or a great poem written—or a great man born. And some heart has been broken, Phil."

"Why did you spoil your pretty thought by tagging that last sentence on, honey?" grumbled Phil. "I don't like to think of broken hearts—or anything unpleasant."

"Do you think you'll be able to shirk unpleasant things all your life, Phil?"

"Dear me, no. Am I not up against them now? You don't call Alec and Alonzo pleasant things, do you, when they simply plague my life out?"

"You never take anything seriously, Phil."

"Why should I? There are enough folks who do. The world needs people like me, Anne, just to amuse it. It would be a terrible place if *everybody* were intellectual and serious and in deep, deadly earnest. *My* mission is, as *Josiah Allen* says, 'to charm and allure.' Confess now. Hasn't life at Patty's Place been really much brighter and pleasanter this past winter because I've been here to leaven you?"

"Yes, it has," owned Anne.

"And you all love me—even Aunt Jamesina, who thinks I'm stark mad. So why should I try to be different? Oh, dear, I'm so sleepy. I was awake until one last night, reading a harrowing ghost story. I read it in bed, and after I had finished it do you suppose I could get out of bed to put the light out? No! And if Stella had not fortunately come in late that lamp would have burned good and bright till morning. When I heard Stella I called her in, explained my predicament, and got her to put out the light. If I had got out myself to do it I knew something would grab me by the feet when I was getting in again. By the way, Anne, has Aunt Jamesina decided what to do this summer?"

"Yes, she's going to stay here. I know she's doing it for the sake of those blessed cats, although she says it's too much trouble to open her own house, and she hates visiting."

"What are you reading?"

"*Pickwick.*"

"That's a book that always makes me hungry," said Phil. "There's so much good eating in it. The characters seem always to be revelling on ham and eggs and milk punch. I generally go on a cupboard rummage after reading *Pickwick*. The mere thought reminds me that I'm starving. Is there any tidbit in the pantry, Queen Anne?"

"I made a lemon pie this morning. You may have a piece of it."

Phil dashed out to the pantry and Anne betook herself to the orchard in company with Rusty. It was a moist, pleasantly-odorous night in early spring. The snow was not quite all gone from the park; a little dingy bank of it yet lay under the pines of the harbor road, screened from the influence of April suns. It kept the harbor road muddy, and chilled the evening air. But grass was growing green in sheltered spots and Gilbert had found some pale, sweet arbutus in a hidden corner. He came up from the park, his hands full of it.

Anne was sitting on the big gray boulder in the orchard look-ing at the poem of a bare, birchen bough hanging against the pale red sunset with the very perfection of grace. She was building a castle in air—a wondrous mansion whose sunlit courts and state-ly halls were steeped in Araby's perfume, and where she reigned queen and chatelaine. She frowned as she saw Gilbert coming through the orchard. Of late she had managed not to be left alone with Gilbert. But he had caught her fairly now; and even Rusty had deserted her.

Gilbert sat down beside her on the boulder and held out his Mayflowers.

"Don't these remind you of home and our old school-day picnics, Anne?"

Anne took them and buried her face in them.

"I'm in Mr. Silas Sloane's barrens this very minute," she said rapturously.

"I suppose you will be there in reality in a few days?"

"No, not for a fortnight. I'm going to visit with Phil in Bolingbroke before I go home. You'll be in Avonlea before I will."

"No, I shall not be in Avonlea at all this summer, Anne. I've been offered a job in the *Daily News* office and I'm going to take it."

"Oh," said Anne vaguely. She wondered what a whole Avonlea summer would be like without Gilbert. Somehow she did not like the prospect. "Well," she concluded flatly, "it is a good thing for you, of course."

"Yes, I've been hoping I would get it. It will help me out next year."

"You mustn't work *too* hard," said Anne, without any very clear idea of what she was saying. She wished desperately that Phil would come out. "You've studied very constantly this winter. Isn't this a delightful evening? Do you know, I found a cluster of white violets under that old twisted tree over there today? I felt as if I had discovered a gold mine."

"You are always discovering gold mines," said Gilbert—also absently.

"Let us go and see if we can find some more," suggested Anne eagerly. "I'll call Phil and—"

"Never mind Phil and the violets just now, Anne," said Gilbert quietly, taking her hand in a clasp from which she could not free it. "There is something I want to say to you."

"Oh, don't say it," cried Anne, pleadingly. "Don't—*please*, Gilbert."

"I must. Things can't go on like this any longer. Anne, I love you. You know I do. I—I can't tell you how much. Will you promise me that some day you'll be my wife?"

"I—I can't," said Anne miserably. "Oh, Gilbert—you—you've spoiled everything."

"Don't you care for me at all?" Gilbert asked after a very dreadful pause, during which Anne had not dared to look up.

"Not—not in that way. I do care a great deal for you as a friend. But I don't love you, Gilbert."

"But can't you give me some hope that you will—yet?"

"No, I can't," exclaimed Anne desperately. "I never, never can love you—in that way—Gilbert. You must never speak of this to me again."

There was another pause—so long and so dreadful that Anne was driven at last to look up. Gilbert's face was white to the lips. And his eyes—but Anne shuddered and looked away. There was nothing romantic about this. Must proposals be either grotesque or—horrible? Could she ever forget Gilbert's face?

"Is there anybody else?" he asked at last in a low voice.

"No—no," said Anne eagerly. "I don't care for any one like *that*—and I *like* you better than anybody else in the world, Gilbert. And we must—we *must* go on being friends, Gilbert."

Gilbert gave a bitter little laugh.

"Friends! Your friendship can't satisfy me, Anne. I want your love—and you tell me I can never have that."

"I'm sorry. Forgive me, Gilbert," was all Anne could say. Where, oh, where were all the gracious and graceful speeches wherewith, in imagination, she had been wont to dismiss rejected suitors?

Gilbert released her hand gently.

"There isn't anything to forgive. There have been times when I thought you did care. I've deceived myself, that's all. Good-bye, Anne."

Anne got herself to her room, sat down on her window seat behind the pines, and cried bitterly. She felt as if something incalculably precious had gone out of her life. It was Gilbert's friendship, of course. Oh, why must she lose it after this fashion?

"What is the matter, honey?" asked Phil, coming in through the moonlit gloom.

Anne did not answer. At that moment she wished Phil were a thousand miles away.

"I suppose you've gone and refused Gilbert Blythe. You are an idiot, Anne Shirley!"

"Do you call it idiotic to refuse to marry a man I don't love?" said Anne coldly, goaded to reply.

"You don't know love when you see it. You've tricked something out with your imagination that you think love, and you expect the real thing to look like that. There, that's the first sensible thing I've ever said in my life. I wonder how I managed it?"

"Phil," pleaded Anne, "please go away and leave me alone for a little while. My world has tumbled into pieces. I want to reconstruct it."

"Without any Gilbert in it?" said Phil, going.

A world without any Gilbert in it! Anne repeated the words drearily. Would it not be a very lonely, forlorn place? Well, it was all Gilbert's fault. He had spoiled their beautiful comradeship. She must just learn to live without it.

21
ROSES OF YESTERDAY

The fortnight Anne spent in Bolingbroke was a very pleasant one, with a little undercurrent of vague pain and dissatisfaction running through it whenever she thought about Gilbert. There was not, however, much time to think about him. "Mount Holly," the beautiful old Gordon homestead, was a very gay place, overrun by Phil's friends of both sexes. There was quite a bewildering succession of drives, dances, picnics and boating parties, all expressively lumped together by Phil under the head of "jamborees"; Alec and Alonzo were so constantly on hand that Anne wondered if they ever did anything but dance attendance on that will-o'-the-wisp of a Phil. They were both nice, manly fellows, but Anne would not be drawn into any opinion as to which was the nicer.

"And I depended so on you to help me make up my mind which of them I should promise to marry," mourned Phil.

"You must do that for yourself. You are quite expert at making up your mind as to whom other people should marry," retorted Anne, rather caustically.

"Oh, that's a very different thing," said Phil truly.

But the sweetest incident of Anne's sojourn in Bolingbroke was the visit to her birthplace—the little shabby yellow house in an out-of-the-way street she had so often dreamed about. She looked at it with delighted eyes, as she and Phil turned in at the gate.

"It's almost exactly as I've pictured it," she said. "There is no honeysuckle over the windows, but there *is* a lilac tree by the gate, and—yes, there are the muslin curtains in the windows. How glad I am it is still painted yellow."

A very tall, very thin woman opened the door.

"Yes, the Shirleys lived here twenty years ago," she said, in answer to Anne's question. "They had it rented. I remember 'em. They both died of fever at onct. It was turrible sad. They left a baby. I guess it's dead long ago. It was a sickly thing. Old Thomas and his wife took it—as if they hadn't enough of their own."

"It didn't die," said Anne, smiling. "I was that baby."

"You don't say so! Why, you *have* grown," exclaimed the woman, as if she were much surprised that Anne was not still a baby. "Come to look at you, I see the resemblance. You're complected like your pa. He had red hair. But you favor your ma in your eyes and mouth. She was a nice little thing. My darter went to school to her and was nigh crazy about her. They was buried in the one grave and the School Board put up a tombstone to them as a reward for faithful service. Will you come in?"

"Will you let me go all over the house?" asked Anne eagerly.

"Laws, yes, you can if you like. 'Twon't take you long—there ain't much of it. I keep at my man to build a new kitchen, but he ain't one of your hustlers. The parlor's in there and there's two rooms upstairs. Just prowl about yourselves. I've got to see to the baby. The east room was the one you were born in. I remember your ma saying she loved to see the sunrise; and I mind hearing that you was born just as the sun was rising and its light on your face was the first thing your ma saw."

Anne went up the narrow stairs and into that little east room with a full heart. It was as a shrine to her. Here her mother had dreamed the exquisite, happy dreams of anticipated motherhood; here that red sunrise light had fallen over them both in the sacred hour of birth; here her mother had died. Anne looked about her reverently, her eyes dim with tears. It was for her one of the jewelled hours of life that gleam out radiantly forever in memory.

"Just to think of it—mother was younger than I am now when I was born," she whispered.

When Anne went downstairs the lady of the house met her in the hall. She held out a dusty little packet tied with faded blue ribbon.

"Here's a bundle of old letters I found in that closet upstairs when I came here," she said. "I dunno what they are—I never bothered to look in 'em, but the address on the top one is 'Miss Bertha Willis,' and that was your ma's maiden name. You can take 'em if you'd keer to have 'em."

"Oh, thank you—thank you," cried Anne, clasping the packet rapturously.

"That was all that was in the house," said her hostess. "The furniture was all sold to pay the doctor bills, and Mrs. Thomas got your ma's clothes and little things. I reckon they didn't last long among that drove of Thomas youngsters. They was destructive young animals, as I mind 'em."

"I haven't one thing that belonged to my mother," said Anne, chokily. "I—I can never thank you enough for these letters."

"You're quite welcome. Law's, but your eyes is like your ma's. She could just about talk with hers. Your father was sorter homely but awful nice. I mind hearing folks say when they was married that there never was two people more in love with each other—Pore creetures, they didn't live much longer; but they was awful happy while they was alive, and I s'pose that counts for a good deal."

Anne longed to get home to read her precious letters; but she made one little pilgrimage first. She went alone to the green corner of the "old" Bolingbroke cemetery where her father and mother were buried, and left on their grave the white flowers she carried. Then she hastened back to Mount Holly, shut herself up in her room, and read the letters. Some were written by her father, some by her mother. There were not many—only a dozen in all—for Walter and Bertha Shirley had not been often separated during their courtship. The letters were yellow and faded and dim, blurred with the touch of passing years. No profound words of wisdom were traced on the stained and wrinkled pages, but only lines of love and trust. The sweetness of forgotten things clung to them—the far-off, fond imaginings of those long-dead lovers. Bertha Shirley had possessed the gift of writing letters which embodied the charming personality of the writer in words and thoughts that retained their beauty and fragrance after the lapse of time. The letters were tender, intimate, sacred. To Anne, the sweetest of all was the one written after her birth to the father on a brief absence. It was full of a proud young mother's accounts of "baby"—her cleverness, her brightness, her thousand sweetnesses.

"I love her best when she is asleep and better still when she is awake," Bertha Shirley had written in the postscript. Probably it was the last sentence she had ever penned. The end was very near for her.

"This has been the most beautiful day of my life," Anne said to Phil that night. "I've *found* my father and mother. Those letters have made them *real* to me. I'm not an orphan any longer. I feel as if I had opened a book and found roses of yesterday, sweet and beloved, between its leaves."

22
SPRING AND ANNE RETURN TO GREEN GABLES

The firelight shadows were dancing over the kitchen walls at Green Gables, for the spring evening was chilly; through the open east window drifted in the subtly sweet voices of the night. Marilla was sitting by the fire—at least, in body. In spirit she was roaming olden ways, with feet grown young. Of late Marilla had thus spent many an hour, when she thought she should have been knitting for the twins.

"I suppose I'm growing old," she said.

Yet Marilla had changed but little in the past nine years, save to grow something thinner, and even more angular; there was a little more gray in the hair that was still twisted up in the same hard knot, with two hairpins—*were* they the same hairpins?— still stuck through it. But her expression was very different; the something about the mouth which had hinted at a sense of humor had developed wonderfully; her eyes were gentler and milder, her smile more frequent and tender.

Marilla was thinking of her whole past life, her cramped but not unhappy childhood, the jealously hidden dreams and the blighted hopes of her girlhood, the long, gray, narrow, monotonous years of dull middle life that followed. And the coming of Anne—the vivid, imaginative, impetuous child with her heart of love, and her world of fancy, bringing with her color and warmth and radiance, until the wilderness of existence had blossomed like the rose. Marilla felt that out of her sixty years she had *lived* only the nine that had followed the advent of Anne. And Anne would be home tomorrow night.

The kitchen door opened. Marilla looked up expecting to see Mrs. Lynde. Anne stood before her, tall and starry-eyed, with her hands full of Mayflowers and violets.

"Anne Shirley!" exclaimed Marilla. For once in her life she was surprised out of her reserve; she caught her girl in her arms and crushed her and her flowers against her heart, kissing the bright hair and sweet face warmly. "I never looked for you till tomorrow night. How did you get from Carmody?"

"Walked, dearest of Marillas. Haven't I done it a score of times in the Queen's days? The mailman is to bring my trunk tomorrow; I just got homesick all at once, and came a day earlier. And oh! I've had such a lovely walk in the May twilight; I stopped by the barrens and picked these Mayflowers; I came through Violet-Vale; it's just a big bowlful of violets now—the dear, sky-tinted things. Smell them, Marilla—drink them in."

Marilla sniffed obligingly, but she was more interested in Anne than in drinking violets.

"Sit down, child. You must be real tired. I'm going to get you some supper."

"There's a darling moonrise behind the hills tonight, Marilla, and oh, how the frogs sang me home from Carmody! I do love the music of the frogs. It seems bound up with all my happiest recollections of old spring evenings. And it always reminds me of the night I came here first. Do you remember it, Marilla?"

"Well, yes," said Marilla with emphasis. "I'm not likely to forget it ever."

"They used to sing so madly in the marsh and brook that year. I would listen to them at my window in the dusk, and wonder how they could seem so glad and so sad at the same time. Oh, but it's good to be home again! Redmond was splendid and Bolingbroke delightful—but Green Gables is *home*."

"Gilbert isn't coming home this summer, I hear," said Marilla.

"No." Something in Anne's tone made Marilla glance at her sharply, but Anne was apparently absorbed in arranging her violets in a bowl. "See, aren't they sweet?" she went on hurriedly. "The year is a book, isn't it, Marilla? Spring's pages are written in Mayflowers and violets, summer's in roses, autumn's in red maple leaves, and winter in holly and evergreen."

"Did Gilbert do well in his examinations?" persisted Marilla.

"Excellently well. He led his class. But where are the twins and Mrs. Lynde?"

"Rachel and Dora are over at Mr. Harrison's. Davy is down at Boulters'. I think I hear him coming now."

Davy burst in, saw Anne, stopped, and then hurled himself upon her with a joyful yell.

"Oh, Anne, ain't I glad to see you! Say, Anne, I've grown two inches since last fall. Mrs. Lynde measured me with her tape today, and say, Anne, see my front tooth. It's gone. Mrs. Lynde tied one end of a string to it and the other end to the door, and then shut the door. I sold it to Milty for two cents. Milty's collecting teeth."

"What in the world does he want teeth for?" asked Marilla.

"To make a necklace for playing Indian Chief," explained Davy, climbing upon Anne's lap. "He's got fifteen already, and everybody else's promised, so there's no use in the rest of us starting to collect, too. I tell you the Boulters are great business people."

"Were you a good boy at Mrs. Boulter's?" asked Marilla severely.

"Yes; but say, Marilla, I'm tired of being good."

"You'd get tired of being bad much sooner, Davy-boy," said Anne.

"Well, it'd be fun while it lasted, wouldn't it?" persisted Davy. "I could be sorry for it afterwards, couldn't I?"

"Being sorry wouldn't do away with the consequences of being bad, Davy. Don't you remember the Sunday last summer when you ran away from Sunday School? You told me then that being bad wasn't worth while. What were you and Milty doing today?"

"Oh, we fished and chased the cat, and hunted for eggs, and yelled at the echo. There's a great echo in the bush behind the Boulter barn. Say, what is an echo, Anne; I want to know."

"Echo is a beautiful nymph, Davy, living far away in the woods, and laughing at the world from among the hills."

"What does she look like?"

"Her hair and eyes are dark, but her neck and arms are white as snow. No mortal can ever see how fair she is. She is fleeter than a deer, and that mocking voice of hers is all we can know of her. You can hear her calling at night; you can hear her laughing under the stars. But you can never see her. She flies afar if you follow her, and laughs at you always just over the next hill."

"Is that all true, Anne? Or is it a whopper?" demanded Davy staring.

"Davy," said Anne despairingly, "haven't you sense enough to distinguish between a fairy-tale and a falsehood?"

"Then *what* is it that sasses back from the Boulter bush? I want to know," insisted Davy.

"When you are a little older, Davy, I'll explain it all to you."

The mention of age evidently gave a new turn to Davy's thoughts for after a few moments of reflection, he whispered solemnly:

"Anne, I'm going to be married."

"When?" asked Anne with equal solemnity.

"Oh, not until I'm grown-up, of course."

"Well, that's a relief, Davy. Who is the lady?"

"Stella Fletcher; she's in my class at school. And say, Anne, she's the prettiest girl you ever saw. If I die before I grow up you'll keep an eye on her, won't you?"

"Davy Keith, do stop talking such nonsense," said Marilla severely.

"'Tisn't nonsense," protested Davy in an injured tone. "She's my promised wife, and if I was to die she'd be my promised widow, wouldn't she? And she hasn't got a soul to look after her except her old grandmother."

"Come and have your supper, Anne," said Marilla, "and don't encourage that child in his absurd talk."

23
PAUL CANNOT FIND THE ROCK PEOPLE

Life was very pleasant in Avonlea that summer, although Anne, amid all her vacation joys, was haunted by a sense of "something gone which should be there." She would not admit, even in her inmost reflections, that this was caused by Gilbert's absence. But when she had to walk home alone from prayer meetings and A.V.I.S. pow-wows, while Diana and Fred, and many other gay couples, loitered along the dusky, starlit country roads, there was a queer, lonely ache in her heart which she could not explain away. Gilbert did not even write to her, as she thought he might have done. She knew he wrote to Diana occasionally, but she would not inquire about him; and Diana, supposing that Anne heard from him, volunteered no information. Gilbert's mother, who was a gay, frank, light-hearted lady, but not over-burdened with tact, had a very embarrassing habit of asking Anne, always in the presence of a crowd, if she had heard from Gilbert lately. Poor Anne could only blush horribly and murmur, "not very lately," which was taken by all, Mrs. Blythe included, to be merely a maidenly evasion.

Apart from this, Anne enjoyed her summer. Priscilla came for a merry visit in June; and when she had gone, Mr. and Mrs. Irving, Paul and Charlotta the Fourth came "home" for July and August.

Echo Lodge was the scene of gaieties once more, and the echoes over the river were kept busy mimicking the laughter that rang in the old garden behind the spruces.

"Miss Lavendar" had not changed, except to grow even sweeter and prettier. Paul adored her, and the companionship between them was beautiful to see.

"But I don't call her 'mother' just by itself," he explained to Anne. "You see, *that* name belongs just to my own little mother, and I can't give it to any one else. *You* know, teacher. But I call her 'Mother Lavendar' and I love her next best to father. I—I even love her a *little* better than you, teacher."

"Which is just as it ought to be," answered Anne.

Paul was thirteen now and very tall for his years. His face and eyes were as beautiful as ever, and his fancy was still like a prism, separating everything that fell upon it into rainbows. He and Anne had delightful rambles to wood and field and shore. Never were there two more thoroughly "kindred spirits."

Charlotta the Fourth had blossomed out into young ladyhood. She wore her hair now in an enormous pompadour and had discarded the blue ribbon bows of auld land syne, but her face was as freckled, her nose as snubbed, and her mouth and smiles as wide as ever.

"You don't think I talk with a Yankee accent, do you, Miss Shirley, ma'am?" she demanded anxiously.

"I don't notice it, Charlotta."

"I'm real glad of that. They said I did at home but I thought likely they just wanted to aggravate me. I don't want no Yankee accent. Not that I've a word to say against the Yankees, Miss Shirley, ma'am. They're real civilized. But give me old P. E. Island every time."

Paul spent his first fortnight with his grandmother Irving in Avonlea. Anne was there to meet him when he came, and found him wild with eagerness to get to the shore—Nora and the Golden Lady and the Twin Sailors would be there. He could hardly wait to eat his supper. Could he not see Nora's elfin face peering around the point, watching for him wistfully? But it was a very sober Paul who came back from the shore in the twilight.

"Didn't you find your Rock People?" asked Anne.

Paul shook his chestnut curls sorrowfully.

"The Twin Sailors and the Golden Lady never came at all," he said. "Nora was there—but Nora is not the same, teacher. She is changed."

"Oh, Paul, it is you who are changed," said Anne. "You have grown too old for the Rock People. They like only children for playfellows. I am afraid the Twin Sailors will never again come to you in the pearly, enchanted boat with the sail of moonshine;

and the Golden Lady will play no more for you on her golden harp. Even Nora will not meet you much longer. You must pay the penalty of growing-up, Paul. You must leave fairyland behind you."

"You two talk as much foolishness as ever you did," said old Mrs. Irving, half-indulgently, half-reprovingly.

"Oh, no, we don't," said Anne, shaking her head gravely. "We are getting very, very wise, and it is such a pity. We are never half so interesting when we have learned that language is given us to enable us to conceal our thoughts."

"But it isn't—it is given us to exchange our thoughts," said Mrs. Irving seriously. She had never heard of Tallyrand and did not understand epigrams.

Anne spent a fortnight of halcyon days at Echo Lodge in the golden prime of August. While there she incidentally contrived to hurry Ludovic Speed in his leisurely courting of Theodora Dix, as related duly in another chronicle of her history.[1] Arnold Sherman, an elderly friend of the Irvings, was there at the same time, and added not a little to the general pleasantness of life.

"What a nice play-time this has been," said Anne. "I feel like a giant refreshed. And it's only a fortnight more till I go back to Kingsport, and Redmond and Patty's Place. Patty's Place is the dearest spot, Miss Lavendar. I feel as if I had two homes—one at Green Gables and one at Patty's Place. But where has the summer gone? It doesn't seem a day since I came home that spring evening with the Mayflowers. When I was little I couldn't see from one end of summer to the other. It stretched before me like an unending season. Now 'tis a handbreadth, 'tis a tale.'"

"Anne, are you and Gilbert Blythe as good friends as you used to be?" asked Miss Lavendar quietly.

"I am just as much Gilbert's friend as ever I was, Miss Lavendar." Miss Lavendar shook her head.

"I see something's gone wrong, Anne. I'm going to be impertinent and ask what. Have you quarrelled?"

1. *Chronicles of Avonlea.* The Page Company.

"No; it's only that Gilbert wants more than friendship and I can't give him more."

"Are you sure of that, Anne?"

"Perfectly sure."

"I'm very, very sorry."

"I wonder why everybody seems to think I ought to marry Gilbert Blythe," said Anne petulantly.

"Because you were made and meant for each other, Anne— that is why. You needn't toss that young head of yours. It's a fact."

24
ENTER JONAS

"PROSPECT POINT,

"August 20th.

"Dear Anne—spelled—with—an—E," wrote Phil, "I must prop my eyelids open long enough to write you. I've neglected you shamefully this summer, honey, but all my other correspondents have been neglected, too. I have a huge pile of letters to answer, so I must gird up the loins of my mind and hoe in. Excuse my mixed metaphors. I'm fearfully sleepy. Last night Cousin Emily and I were calling at a neighbor's. There were several other callers there, and, as soon as those unfortunate creatures left, our hostess and her three daughters picked them all to pieces. I knew they would begin on Cousin Emily and me as soon as the door shut behind us. When we came home Mrs. Lilly informed us that the aforesaid neighbor's hired boy was supposed to be down with scarlet fever. You can always trust Mrs. Lilly to tell you cheerful things like that. I have a horror of scarlet fever. I couldn't sleep when I went to bed for thinking of it. I tossed and tumbled about, dreaming fearful dreams when I did snooze for a minute; and at three I wakened up with a high fever, a sore throat, and a raging headache. I knew I had scarlet fever; I got up in a panic and hunted up Cousin Emily's 'doctor book' to read up the symptoms. Anne, I had them all. So I went back to bed, and knowing the worst, slept like a top the rest of the night. Though why a top should sleep sounder than anything else I never could understand. But this morning I was quite well, so it couldn't have been the fever. I suppose if I did catch it last night it couldn't have developed so soon. I can remember that in day-time, but at three o'clock at night I never can be logical.

"I suppose you wonder what I'm doing at Prospect Point. Well, I always like to spend a month of summer at the shore, and father insists that I come to his second-cousin Emily's 'select boarding-house' at Prospect Point. So a fortnight ago I came as usual. And as usual old 'Uncle Mark Miller' brought me from the station with his ancient buggy and what he calls his 'generous purpose' horse. He is a nice old man and gave me a handful of pink peppermints. Peppermints always seem to me such a religious sort of candy.—I suppose because when I was a little girl Grandmother Gordon always gave them to me in church. Once I asked, referring to the smell of peppermints, 'Is that the odor of sanctity?' I didn't like to eat Uncle Mark's peppermints because he just fished them loose out of his pocket, and had to pick some rusty nails and other things from among them before he gave them to me. But I wouldn't hurt his dear old feelings for anything, so I carefully sowed them along the road at intervals. When the last one was gone, Uncle Mark said, a little rebukingly, 'Ye shouldn't a'et all them candies at onct, Miss Phil. You'll likely have the stummick-ache.'

"Cousin Emily has only five boarders besides myself,—four old ladies and one young man. My right-hand neighbor is Mrs. Lilly. She is one of those people who seem to take a gruesome pleasure in detailing all their many aches and pains and sicknesses. You cannot mention any ailment but she says, shaking her head, 'Ah, I know too well what that is'—and then you get all the details. Jonas declares he once spoke of locomotor ataxia in her hearing and she said she knew too well what that was. She suffered from it for ten years and was finally cured by a travelling doctor.

"Who is Jonas? Just wait, Anne Shirley. You'll hear all about Jonas in the proper time and place. He is not to be mixed up with estimable old ladies.

"My left-hand neighbor at the table is Mrs. Phinney. She always speaks with a wailing, dolorous voice—you are nervously expecting her to burst into tears every moment. She gives you the impression that life to her is indeed a vale of tears, and that a smile, never to speak of a laugh, is a frivolity truly reprehensible. She has a worse opinion of me than Aunt Jamesina, and she doesn't love me hard to atone for it, as Aunty J. does, either.

"Miss Maria Grimsby sits cati-corner from me. The first day I came I remarked to Miss Maria that it looked a little like rain— and Miss Maria laughed. I said the road from the station was very pretty—and Miss Maria laughed. I said there seemed to be a few mosquitoes left yet—and Miss Maria laughed. I said that Prospect Point was as beautiful as ever—and Miss Maria laughed. If I were to say to Miss Maria, 'My father has hanged himself, my mother has taken poison, my brother is in the penitentiary, and I am in the last stages of consumption,' Miss Maria would laugh. She can't help it—she was born so; but it's very sad and awful.

"The fifth old lady is Mrs. Grant. She is a sweet old thing; but she never says anything but good of anybody and so she is a very uninteresting conversationalist.

"And now for Jonas, Anne.

"That first day I came I saw a young man sitting opposite to me at the table, smiling at me as if he had known me from the cradle. I knew, for Uncle Mark had told me, that his name was Jonas Blake, that he was a Theological Student from St. Columba, and that he had taken charge of the Point Prospect Mission Church for the summer.

"He is a very ugly young man—really, the ugliest young man I've ever seen. He has a big, loose-jointed figure with absurdly long legs. His hair is tow-color and lank, his eyes are green, and his mouth is big, and his ears—but I never think about his ears if I can help it.

"He has a lovely voice—if you shut your eyes he is adorable—and he certainly has a beautiful soul and disposition.

"We were good chums right away. Of course he is a graduate of Redmond, and that is a link between us. We fished and boated together; and we walked on the sands by moonlight. He didn't look so homely by moonlight and oh, he was nice. Niceness fairly exhaled from him. The old ladies—except Mrs. Grant—don't approve of Jonas, because he laughs and jokes—and because he evidently likes the society of frivolous me better than theirs.

"Somehow, Anne, I don't want him to think me frivolous. This is ridiculous. Why should I care what a tow-haired person called Jonas, whom I never saw before, thinks of me?

"Last Sunday Jonas preached in the village church. I went, of course, but I couldn't realize that Jonas was going to preach. The fact that he was a minister—or going to be one—persisted in seeming a huge joke to me.

"Well, Jonas preached. And, by the time he had preached ten minutes, I felt so small and insignificant that I thought I must be invisible to the naked eye. Jonas never said a word about women and he never looked at me. But I realized then and there what a pitiful, frivolous, small-souled little butterfly I was, and how horribly different I must be from Jonas' ideal woman. *She* would be grand and strong and noble. He was so earnest and tender and true. He was everything a minister ought to be. I wondered how I could ever have thought him ugly—but he really is!—with those inspired eyes and that intellectual brow which the roughly-falling hair hid on week days.

"It was a splendid sermon and I could have listened to it forever, and it made me feel utterly wretched. Oh, I wish I was like *you*, Anne.

"He caught up with me on the road home, and grinned as cheerfully as usual. But his grin could never deceive me again. I had seen the *real* Jonas. I wondered if he could ever see the *real* Phil—whom *nobody*, not even you, Anne, has ever seen yet.

"'Jonas,' I said—I forgot to call him Mr. Blake. Wasn't it dreadful? But there are times when things like that don't matter —'Jonas, you were born to be a minister. You *couldn't* be anything else.'

"'No, I couldn't,' he said soberly. 'I tried to be something else for a long time—I didn't want to be a minister. But I came to see at last that it was the work given me to do—and God helping me, I shall try to do it.'

"His voice was low and reverent. I thought that he would do his work and do it well and nobly; and happy the woman fitted by nature and training to help him do it. *She* would be no feather, blown about by every fickle wind of fancy. *She* would always know what hat to put on. Probably she would have only one. Ministers never have much money. But she wouldn't mind having one hat or none at all, because she would have Jonas.

"Anne Shirley, don't you dare to say or hint or think that I've fallen in love with Mr. Blake Could *I* care for a lank, poor, ugly theologue—named Jonas? As Uncle Mark says, 'It's impossible, and what's more it's improbable.'

"Good-night,

"PHIL."

"P. S. It is impossible—but I am horribly afraid it's true. I'm happy and wretched and scared. *He* can *never* care for me, I know. Do you think I could ever develop into a passable minister's wife, Anne? And *would* they expect me to lead in prayer? P.G."

25
ENTER PRINCE CHARMING

"I'm contrasting the claims of indoors and out," said Anne, looking from the window of Patty's Place to the distant pines of the park.

"I've an afternoon to spend in sweet doing nothing, Aunt

Jimsie. Shall I spend it here where there is a cosy fire, a plateful of delicious russets, three purring and harmonious cats, and two impeccable china dogs with green noses? Or shall I go to the park, where there is the lure of gray woods and of gray water lapping on the harbor rocks?"

"If I was as young as you, I'd decide in favor of the park," said Aunt Jamesina, tickling Joseph's yellow ear with a knitting needle.

"I thought that you claimed to be as young as any of us, Aunty," teased Anne.

"Yes, in my soul. But I'll admit my legs aren't as young as yours. You go and get some fresh air, Anne. You look pale lately."

"I think I will go to the park," said Anne restlessly. "I don't feel like tame domestic joys today. I want to feel alone and free and wild. The park will be empty, for every one will be at the football match."

"Why didn't you go to it?"

"'Nobody axed me, sir, she said,'—at least, nobody but that horrid little Dan Ranger. I wouldn't go anywhere with him; but rather than hurt his poor little tender feelings I said I wasn't going to the game at all. I don't mind. I'm not in the mood for football today somehow."

"You go and get some fresh air," repeated Aunt Jamesina, "but take your umbrella, for I believe it's going to rain. I've rheumatism in my leg."

"Only old people should have rheumatism, Aunty."

"Anybody is liable to rheumatism in her legs, Anne. It's only old people who should have rheumatism in their souls, though. Thank goodness, I never have. When you get rheumatism in your soul you might as well go and pick out your coffin."

It was November—the month of crimson sunsets, parting birds, deep, sad hymns of the sea, passionate wind-songs in the pines. Anne roamed through the pineland alleys in the park and, as she said, let that great sweeping wind blow the fogs out of her soul. Anne was not wont to be troubled with soul fog. But, somehow, since her return to Redmond for this third year, life had not mirrored her spirit back to her with its old, perfect, sparkling clearness.

Outwardly, existence at Patty's Place, was the same pleasant round of work and study and recreation that it had always been. On Friday evenings the big, fire-lighted living room was crowded by callers and echoed to endless jest and laughter, while Aunt Jamesina smiled beamingly on them all. The "Jonas" of Phil's letter came often, running up from St. Columba on the early train and departing on the late. He was a general favorite at Patty's Place, though Aunt Jamesina shook her head and opined that divinity students were not what they used to be.

"He's *very* nice, my dear," she told Phil, "but ministers ought to be graver and more dignified."

"Can't a man laugh and laugh and be a Christian still?" demanded Phil.

"Oh, *men*—yes. But I was speaking of *ministers*, my dear," said Aunt Jamesina rebukingly. "And you shouldn't flirt so with Mr. Blake—you really shouldn't."

"I'm not flirting with him," protested Phil.

Nobody believed her, except Anne. The others thought she was amusing herself as usual, and told her roundly that she was behaving very badly.

"Mr. Blake isn't of the Alec-and-Alonzo type, Phil," said Stella severely. "He takes things seriously. You may break his heart."

"Do you really think I could?" asked Phil. "I'd love to think so."

"Philippa Gordon! I never thought you were utterly unfeeling. The idea of you saying you'd love to break a man's heart!"

"I didn't say so, honey. Quote me correctly. I said I'd like to think I *could* break it. I would like to know I had the *power* to do it."

"I don't understand you, Phil. You are leading that man on deliberately—and you know you don't mean anything by it."

"I mean to make him ask me to marry him if I can," said Phil calmly.

"I give you up," said Stella hopelessly.

Gilbert came occasionally on Friday evenings. He seemed always in good spirits, and held his own in the jests and repartee that flew about. He neither sought nor avoided Anne. When circumstances brought them in contact he talked to her pleasantly and courteously, as to any newly-made acquaintance. The old camaraderie was gone entirely. Anne felt it keenly; but she told herself she was very glad and thankful that Gilbert had got so completely over his disappointment in regard to her. She had really been afraid, that April evening in the orchard, that she had hurt him terribly and that the wound would be long in healing. Now she saw that she need not have worried. Men have died and the worms have eaten them but not for love. Gilbert evidently was in no danger of immediate dissolution. He was enjoying life, and he was full of ambition and zest. For him there was to be no wasting in despair because a woman was fair and cold. Anne, as she listened to the ceaseless badinage that went on between him and Phil, wondered if she had only imagined that look in his eyes when she had told him she could never care for him.

There were not lacking those who would gladly have stepped into Gilbert's vacant place. But Anne snubbed them without fear and without reproach. If the real Prince Charming was never to come she would none of a substitute. So she sternly told herself that gray day in the windy park.

Suddenly the rain of Aunt Jamesina's prophecy came with a swish and rush. Anne put up her umbrella and hurried down the slope. As she turned out on the harbor road a savage gust of wind tore along it. Instantly her umbrella turned wrong side out. Anne clutched at it in despair. And then—there came a voice close to her:

"Pardon me—may I offer you the shelter of my umbrella?"

Anne looked up. Tall and handsome and distinguished-looking—dark, melancholy, inscrutable eyes—melting, musical, sympathetic voice—yes, the very hero of her dreams stood before her in the flesh. He could not have more closely resembled her ideal if he had been made to order.

"Thank you," she said confusedly.

"We'd better hurry over to that little pavilion on the point," suggested the unknown. "We can wait there until this shower is over. It is not likely to rain so heavily very long."

The words were very commonplace, but oh, the tone! And the smile which accompanied them! Anne felt her heart beating strangely.

Together they scurried to the pavilion and sat breathlessly down under its friendly roof. Anne laughingly held up her false umbrella.

"It is when my umbrella turns inside out that I am convinced of the total depravity of inanimate things," she said gaily.

The rain drops sparkled on her shining hair; its loosened rings curled around her neck and forehead. Her cheeks were flushed, her eyes big and starry. Her companion looked down at her admiringly. She felt herself blushing under his gaze. Who could he be? Why, there was a bit of the Redmond white and scarlet pinned to his coat-lapel. Yet she had thought she knew, by sight at least, all the Redmond students except the Freshmen. And this courtly youth surely was no Freshman.

"We are schoolmates, I see," he said, smiling at Anne's colors. "That ought to be sufficient introduction. My name is Royal Gardner. And you are the Miss Shirley who read the Tennyson paper at the Philomathic the other evening, aren't you?"

"Yes; but I cannot place you at all," said Anne, frankly. "Please, where *do* you belong?"

"*I* feel as if I didn't belong anywhere yet. I put in my Freshman and Sophomore years at Redmond two years ago. I've been in Europe ever since. Now I've come back to finish my Arts course."

"This is my Junior year, too," said Anne.

"So we are classmates as well as college-mates. I am reconciled to the loss of the years that the locust has eaten," said her companion, with a world of meaning in those wonderful eyes of his.

The rain came steadily down for the best part of an hour. But the time seemed really very short. When the clouds parted and a burst of pale November sunshine fell athwart the harbor and the pines Anne and her companion walked home together. By the time they had reached the gate of Patty's Place he had asked permission to call, and had received it. Anne went in with cheeks of flame and her heart beating to her finger-tips. Rusty, who climbed into her lap and tried to kiss her, found a very absent welcome. Anne, with her soul full of romantic thrills, had no attention to spare just then for a crop-eared pussy cat.

That evening a parcel was left at Patty's Place for Miss Shirley. It was a box containing a dozen magnificent roses. Phil pounced impertinently on the card that fell from it, read the name and the poetical quotation written on the back.

"Royal Gardner!" she exclaimed. "Why, Anne, I didn't know you were acquainted with Roy Gardner!"

"I met him in the park this afternoon in the rain," explained Anne hurriedly. "My umbrella turned inside out and he came to my rescue with his."

"Oh!" Phil peered curiously at Anne. "And is that exceedingly common-place incident any reason why he should send us long-stemmed roses by the dozen, with a very sentimental rhyme? Or why we should blush divinest rosy-red when we look at his card? Anne, thy face betrayeth thee."

"Don't talk nonsense, Phil. Do you know Mr. Gardner?"

"I've met his two sisters, and I know of him. So does everybody worth while in Kingsport. The Gardners are among the richest, bluest, of Bluenoses. Roy is adorably handsome and clever. Two years ago his mother's health failed and he had to leave college and go abroad with her—his father is dead. He must have been greatly disappointed to have to give up his class, but they say he was perfectly sweet about it. Fee—fi—fo—fum, Anne. I smell romance. Almost do I envy you, but not quite. After all, Roy Gardner isn't Jonas."

"You goose!" said Anne loftily. But she lay long awake that night, nor did she wish for sleep. Her waking fancies were more alluring than any vision of dreamland. Had the real Prince come at last? Recalling those glorious dark eyes which had gazed so deeply into her own, Anne was very strongly inclined to think he had.

26
ENTER CHRISTINE

The girls at Patty's Place were dressing for the reception which the Juniors were giving for the Seniors in February. Anne surveyed herself in the mirror of the blue room with girlish satisfaction. She had a particularly pretty gown on. Originally it had been only a simple little slip of cream silk with a chiffon over-dress. But Phil had insisted on taking it home with her in the Christmas holidays and embroidering tiny rosebuds all over the chiffon. Phil's fingers were deft, and the result was a dress which was the envy of every Redmond girl. Even Allie Boone, whose frocks came from Paris, was wont to look with longing eyes on that rosebud concoction as Anne trailed up the main staircase at Redmond in it.

Anne was trying the effect of a white orchid in her hair. Roy Gardner had sent her white orchids for the reception, and she knew no other Redmond girl would have them that night—when Phil came in with admiring gaze.

"Anne, this is certainly your night for looking handsome. Nine nights out of ten I can easily outshine you. The tenth you blossom out suddenly into something that eclipses me altogether. How do you manage it?"

"It's the dress, dear. Fine feathers."

"'Tisn't. The last evening you flamed out into beauty you wore your old blue flannel shirtwaist that Mrs. Lynde made you. If Roy hadn't already lost head and heart about you he certainly would tonight. But I don't like orchids on you, Anne. No; it isn't jealousy. Orchids don't seem to *belong* to you. They're too exotic—too tropical—too insolent. Don't put them in your hair, anyway."

"Well, I won't. I admit I'm not fond of orchids myself. I don't think they're related to me. Roy doesn't often send them—he knows I like flowers I can live with. Orchids are only things you can visit with."

"Jonas sent me some dear pink rosebuds for the evening—but—he isn't coming himself. He said he had to lead a prayer-meeting in the slums! I don't believe he wanted to come. Anne, I'm horribly afraid Jonas doesn't really care anything about me. And I'm trying to decide whether I'll pine away and die, or go on and get my B.A. and be sensible and useful."

"You couldn't possibly be sensible and useful, Phil, so you'd better pine away and die," said Anne cruelly.

"Heartless Anne!"

"Silly Phil! You know quite well that Jonas loves you."

"But—he won't *tell* me so. And I can't *make* him. He *looks* it, I'll admit. But speak-to-me-only-with-thine-eyes isn't a really reliable reason for embroidering doilies and hemstitching table-cloths. I don't want to begin such work until I'm really engaged. It would be tempting Fate."

"Mr. Blake is afraid to ask you to marry him, Phil. He is poor and can't offer you a home such as you've always had. You know that is the only reason he hasn't spoken long ago."

"I suppose so," agreed Phil dolefully. "Well"—brightening up—"if he *won't* ask me to marry him I'll ask him, that's all. So it's bound to come right. I won't worry. By the way, Gilbert Blythe is going about constantly with Christine Stuart. Did you know?"

Anne was trying to fasten a little gold chain about her throat. She suddenly found the clasp difficult to manage. *What* was the matter with it—or with her fingers?

"No," she said carelessly. "Who is Christine Stuart?"

"Ronald Stuart's sister. She's in Kingsport this winter studying music. I haven't seen her, but they say she's very pretty and that Gilbert is quite crazy over her. How angry I was when you refused Gilbert, Anne. But Roy Gardner was fore-ordained for you. I can see that now. You were right, after all."

Anne did not blush, as she usually did when the girls assumed that her eventual marriage to Roy Gardner was a settled thing. All at once she felt rather dull. Phil's chatter seemed trivial and the reception a bore. She boxed poor Rusty's ears.

"Get off that cushion instantly, you cat, you! Why don't you stay down where you belong?"

Anne picked up her orchids and went downstairs, where Aunt Jamesina was presiding over a row of coats hung before the fire to warm. Roy Gardner was waiting for Anne and teasing the Sarah-cat while he waited. The Sarah-cat did not approve of him. She always turned her back on him. But everybody else at Patty's Place liked him very much. Aunt Jamesina, carried away by his unfailing and deferential courtesy, and the pleading tones of his delightful voice, declared he was the nicest young man she ever knew, and that Anne was a very fortunate girl. Such remarks made Anne restive. Roy's wooing had certainly been as romantic as a girlish heart could desire, but—she wished Aunt Jamesina and the girls would not take things so for granted. When Roy murmured a poetical compliment as he helped her on with her coat, she did not blush and thrill as usual; and he found her rather silent in their brief walk to Redmond. He thought she looked a little pale when she come out of the co-eds' dressing-room; but as they entered the reception-room her color and sparkle suddenly returned to her. She turned to Roy with her gayest expression. He smiled back at her with what Phil called "his deep, black, velvety smile." Yet she really did not see Roy at all. She was acutely conscious that Gilbert was standing under the palms just across the room talking to a girl who must be Christine Stuart.

She was very handsome, in the stately style destined to become rather massive in middle life. A tall girl, with large dark-blue eyes, ivory outlines, and a gloss of darkness on her smooth hair.

"She looks just as I've always wanted to look," thought Anne miserably. "Rose-leaf complexion—starry violet eyes—raven hair—yes, she has them all. It's a wonder her name isn't Cordelia Fitzgerald into the bargain! But I don't believe her figure is as good as mine, and her nose certainly isn't."

Anne felt a little comforted by this conclusion.

27
MUTUAL CONFIDENCES

March came in that winter like the meekest and mildest of lambs, bringing days that were crisp and golden and tingling, each followed by a frosty pink twilight which gradually lost itself in an elfland of moonshine.

Over the girls at Patty's Place was falling the shadow of April examinations. They were studying hard; even Phil had settled down to text and notebooks with a doggedness not to be expected of her.

"I'm going to take the Johnson Scholarship in Mathematics," she announced calmly. "I could take the one in Greek easily, but I'd rather take the mathematical one because I want to prove to Jonas that I'm really enormously clever."

"Jonas likes you better for your big brown eyes and your crooked smile than for all the brains you carry under your curls," said Anne.

"When I was a girl it wasn't considered lady-like to know anything about Mathematics," said Aunt Jamesina. "But times have changed. I don't know that it's all for the better. Can you cook, Phil?"

"No, I never cooked anything in my life except a ginger-bread and it was a failure—flat in the middle and hilly round the edges. You know the kind. But, Aunty, when I begin in good earnest to learn to cook don't you think the brains that enable me to win a

mathematical scholarship will also enable me to learn cooking
just as well?"

"Maybe," said Aunt Jamesina cautiously. "I am not decrying
the higher education of women. My daughter is an M.A. She can
cook, too. But I taught her to cook *before* I let a college professor
teach her Mathematics."

In mid-March came a letter from Miss Patty Spofford, saying
that she and Miss Maria had decided to remain abroad for another year.

"So you may have Patty's Place next winter, too," she wrote.
"Maria and I are going to run over Egypt. I want to see the
Sphinx once before I die."

"Fancy those two dames 'running over Egypt'! I wonder if
they'll look up at the Sphinx and knit," laughed Priscilla.

"I'm so glad we can keep Patty's Place for another year," said
Stella. "I was afraid they'd come back. And then our jolly little
nest here would be broken up—and we poor callow nestlings
thrown out on the cruel world of boarding-houses again."

"I'm off for a tramp in the park," announced Phil, tossing her
book aside. "I think when I am eighty I'll be glad I went for a
walk in the park tonight."

"What do you mean?" asked Anne.

"Come with me and I'll tell you, honey."

They captured in their ramble all the mysteries and magics of
a March evening. Very still and mild it was, wrapped in a great,
white, brooding silence—a silence which was yet threaded
through with many little silvery sounds which you could hear if
you hearkened as much with your soul as your ears. The girls
wandered down a long pineland aisle that seemed to lead right
out into the heart of a deep-red, overflowing winter sunset.

"I'd go home and write a poem this blessed minute if I only
knew how," declared Phil, pausing in an open space where a rosy
light was staining the green tips of the pines. "It's all so wonderful
here—this great, white stillness, and those dark trees that always
seem to be thinking."

"'The woods were God's first temples,'" quoted Anne softly. "One can't help feeling reverent and adoring in such a place. I always feel so near Him when I walk among the pines."

"Anne, I'm the happiest girl in the world," confessed Phil suddenly.

"So Mr. Blake has asked you to marry him at last?" said Anne calmly.

"Yes. And I sneezed three times while he was asking me. Wasn't that horrid? But I said 'yes' almost before he finished—I was so afraid he might change his mind and stop. I'm besottedly happy. I couldn't really believe before that Jonas would ever care for frivolous me."

"Phil, you're not really frivolous," said Anne gravely. "'Way down underneath that frivolous exterior of yours you've got a dear, loyal, womanly little soul. Why do you hide it so?"

"I can't help it, Queen Anne. You are right—I'm not frivolous at heart. But there's a sort of frivolous skin over my soul and I can't take it off. As *Mrs. Poyser* says, I'd have to be hatched over again and hatched different before I could change it. But Jonas knows the real me and loves me, frivolity and all. And I love him. I never was so surprised in my life as I was when I found out I loved him. I'd never thought it possible to fall in love with an ugly man. Fancy me coming down to one solitary beau. And one named Jonas! But I mean to call him Jo. That's such a nice, crisp little name. I couldn't nickname Alonzo."

"What about Alec and Alonzo?"

"Oh, I told them at Christmas that I never could marry either of them. It seems so funny now to remember that I ever thought it possible that I might. They felt so badly I just cried over both of them—howled. But I knew there was only one man in the world I could ever marry. I had made up my own mind for once and it was real easy, too. It's very delightful to feel so sure, and know it's your own sureness and not somebody else's."

"Do you suppose you'll be able to keep it up?"

"Making up my mind, you mean? I don't know, but Jo has given me a splendid rule. He says, when I'm perplexed, just to do what I would wish I had done when I shall be eighty. Anyhow, Jo can make up his mind quickly enough, and it would be uncomfortable to have too much mind in the same house."

"What will your father and mother say?"

"Father won't say much. He thinks everything I do right. But mother *will* talk. Oh, her tongue will be as Byrney as her nose. But in the end it will be all right."

"You'll have to give up a good many things you've always had, when you marry Mr. Blake, Phil."

"But I'll have *him*. I won't miss the other things. We're to be married a year from next June. Jo graduates from St. Columba this spring, you know. Then he's going to take a little mission church down on Patterson Street in the slums. Fancy me in the slums! But I'd go there or to Greenland's icy mountains with him."

"And this is the girl who would *never* marry a man who wasn't rich," commented Anne to a young pine tree.

"Oh, don't cast up the follies of my youth to me. I shall be poor as gaily as I've been rich. You'll see. I'm going to learn how to cook and make over dresses. I've learned how to market since I've lived at Patty's Place; and once I taught a Sunday School class for a whole summer. Aunt Jamesina says I'll ruin Jo's career if I marry him. But I won't. I know I haven't much sense or sobriety, but I've got what is ever so much better—the knack of making people like me. There is a man in Bolingbroke who lisps and always testifies in prayer-meeting. He says, 'If you can't thine like an electric thtar thine like a candlethtick.' I'll be Jo's little candlestick."

"Phil, you're incorrigible. Well, I love you so much that I can't make nice, light, congratulatory little speeches. But I'm heart-glad of your happiness."

"I know. Those big gray eyes of yours are brimming over with real friendship, Anne. Some day I'll look the same way at you. You're going to marry Roy, aren't you, Anne?"

"My dear Philippa, did you ever hear of the famous Betty Baxter, who 'refused a man before he'd axed her'? I am not going to emulate that celebrated lady by either refusing or accepting any one before he 'axes' me."

"All Redmond knows that Roy is crazy about you," said Phil candidly. "And you *do* love him, don't you, Anne?"

"I—I suppose so," said Anne reluctantly. She felt that she ought to be blushing while making such a confession; but she was not; on the other hand, she always blushed hotly when any one said anything about Gilbert Blythe or Christine Stuart in her hearing. Gilbert Blythe and Christine Stuart were nothing to her—absolutely nothing. But Anne had given up trying to analyze the reason of her blushes. As for Roy, of course she was in love with him—madly so. How could she help it? Was he not her ideal? Who could resist those glorious dark eyes, and that pleading voice? Were not half the Redmond girls wildly envious? And what a charming sonnet he had sent her, with a box of violets, on her birthday! Anne knew every word of it by heart. It was very good stuff of its kind, too. Not exactly up to the level of Keats or Shakespeare—even Anne was not so deeply in love as to think that. But it was very tolerable magazine verse. And it was addressed to *her*—not to Laura or Beatrice or the Maid of Athens, but to her, Anne Shirley. To be told in rhythmical cadences that her eyes were stars of the morning—that her cheek had the flush it stole from the sunrise—that her lips were redder than the roses of Paradise, was thrillingly romantic. Gilbert would never have dreamed of writing a sonnet to her eyebrows. But then, Gilbert could see a joke. She had once told Roy a funny story—and he had not seen the point of it. She recalled the chummy laugh she and Gilbert had had together over it, and wondered uneasily if life with a man who had no sense of humor might not be somewhat uninteresting in the long run. But who could expect a melancholy, inscrutable hero to see the humorous side of things? It would be flatly unreasonable.

28
A JUNE EVENING

"I wonder what it would be like to live in a world where it was always June," said Anne, as she came through the spice and bloom of the twilit orchard to the front-door steps, where Marilla and Mrs. Rachel were sitting, talking over Mrs. Samson Coates' funeral, which they had attended that day. Dora sat between them, diligently studying her lessons; but Davy was sitting tailor-fashion on the grass, looking as gloomy and depressed as his single dimple would let him.

"You'd get tired of it," said Marilla, with a sigh.

"I daresay; but just now I feel that it would take me a long time to get tired of it, if it were all as charming as today. Everything loves June. Davy-boy, why this melancholy November face in blossom-time?"

"I'm just sick and tired of living," said the youthful pessimist.

"At ten years? Dear me, how sad!"

"I'm not making fun," said Davy with dignity. "I'm dis—dis—discouraged"— bringing out the big word with a valiant effort.

"Why and wherefore?" asked Anne, sitting down beside him.

"'Cause the new teacher that come when Mr. Holmes got sick give me ten sums to do for Monday. It'll take me all day tomorrow to do them. It isn't fair to have to work Saturdays. Milty Boulter said he wouldn't do them, but Marilla says I've got to. I don't like Miss Carson a bit."

"Don't talk like that about your teacher, Davy Keith," said Mrs. Rachel severely. "Miss Carson is a very fine girl. There is no nonsense about her."

"That doesn't sound very attractive," laughed Anne. "I like people to have a little nonsense about them. But I'm inclined to have a better opinion of Miss Carson than you have. I saw her in prayer-meeting last night, and she has a pair of eyes that can't always look sensible. Now, Davy-boy, take heart of grace. 'Tomorrow will bring another day' and I'll help you with the sums as far as in me lies. Don't waste this lovely hour 'twixt light and dark worrying over arithmetic."

"Well, I won't," said Davy, brightening up. "If you help me with the sums I'll have 'em done in time to go fishing with Milty. I wish old Aunt Atossa's funeral was tomorrow instead of today. I wanted to go to it 'cause Milty said his mother said Aunt Atossa would be sure to rise up in her coffin and say sarcastic things to the folks that come to see her buried. But Marilla said she didn't."

"Poor Atossa laid in her coffin peaceful enough," said Mrs. Lynde solemnly. "I never saw her look so pleasant before, that's what. Well, there weren't many tears shed over her, poor old soul. The Elisha Wrights are thankful to be rid of her, and I can't say I blame them a mite."

"It seems to me a most dreadful thing to go out of the world and not leave one person behind you who is sorry you are gone," said Anne, shuddering.

"Nobody except her parents ever loved poor Atossa, that's certain, not even her husband," averred Mrs. Lynde. "She was his fourth wife. He'd sort of got into the habit of marrying. He only lived a few years after he married her. The doctor said he died of dyspepsia, but I shall always maintain that he died of Atossa's tongue, that's what. Poor soul, she always knew everything about her neighbors, but she never was very well acquainted with herself. Well, she's gone anyhow; and I suppose the next excitement will be Diana's wedding."

"It seems so funny and horrible to think of Diana's being married," sighed Anne, hugging her knees and looking through the gap in the Haunted Wood to the light that was shining in Diana's room.

"I don't see what's horrible about it, when she's doing so well," said Mrs. Lynde emphatically. "Fred Wright has a fine farm and he is a model young man."

"He certainly isn't the wild, dashing, wicked, young man

Diana once wanted to marry," smiled Anne. "Fred is extremely good."

"That's just what he ought to be. Would you want Diana to marry a wicked man? Or marry one yourself?"

"Oh, no. I wouldn't want to marry anybody who was wicked, but I think I'd like it if he *could* be wicked and *wouldn't*. Now, Fred is *hopelessly* good."

"You'll have more sense some day, I hope," said Marilla.

Marilla spoke rather bitterly. She was grievously disappointed. She knew Anne had refused Gilbert Blythe. Avonlea gossip buzzed over the fact, which had leaked out, nobody knew how. Perhaps Charlie Sloane had guessed and told his guesses for truth. Perhaps Diana had betrayed it to Fred and Fred had been indiscreet. At all events it was known; Mrs. Blythe no longer asked Anne, in public or private, if she had heard lately from Gilbert, but passed her by with a frosty bow. Anne, who had always liked Gilbert's merry, young-hearted mother, was grieved in secret over this. Marilla said nothing; but Mrs. Lynde gave Anne many exasperated digs about it, until fresh gossip reached that worthy lady, through the medium of Moody Spurgeon MacPherson's mother, that Anne had another "beau" at college, who was rich and handsome and good all in one. After that Mrs. Rachel held her tongue, though she still wished in her inmost heart that Anne had accepted Gilbert. Riches were all very well; but even Mrs. Rachel, practical soul though she was, did not consider them the one essential. If Anne "liked" the Handsome Unknown better than Gilbert there was nothing more to be said; but Mrs. Rachel was dreadfully afraid that Anne was going to make the mistake of marrying for money. Marilla knew Anne too well to fear this; but she felt that something in the universal scheme of things had gone sadly awry.

"What is to be, will be," said Mrs. Rachel gloomily, "and what isn't to be happens sometimes. I can't help believing it's going to happen in Anne's case, if Providence doesn't interfere, that's what."

Mrs. Rachel sighed. She was afraid Providence wouldn't interfere; and she didn't dare to.

Anne had wandered down to the Dryad's Bubble and was
curled up among the ferns at the root of the big white birch
where she and Gilbert had so often sat in summers gone by. He
had gone into the newspaper office again when college closed,
and Avonlea seemed very dull without him. He never wrote to
her, and Anne missed the letters that never came. To be sure, Roy
wrote twice a week; his letters were exquisite compositions
which would have read beautifully in a memoir or biography.
Anne felt herself more deeply in love with him than ever when
she read them; but her heart never gave the queer, quick, painful
bound at sight of his letters which it had given one day when
Mrs. Hiram Sloane had handed her out an envelope addressed in
Gilbert's black, upright handwriting. Anne had hurried home to
the east-gable and opened it eagerly—to find a typewritten copy
of some college society report—"only that and nothing more."
Anne flung the harmless screed across her room and sat down to
write an especially nice epistle to Roy.

Diana was to be married in five more days. The gray house at
Orchard Slope was in a turmoil of baking and brewing and boiling and stewing, for there was to be a big, old-timey wedding.
Anne, of course, was to be bridesmaid, as had been arranged
when they were twelve years old, and Gilbert was coming from
Kingsport to be best-man. Anne was enjoying the excitement of
the various preparations, but under it all she carried a little
heartache. She was, in a sense, losing her dear old chum; Diana's
new home would be two miles from Green Gables, and the old
constant companionship could never be theirs again. Anne
looked up at Diana's light and thought how it had beaconed to
her for many years; but soon it would shine through the summer twilights no more. Two big, painful tears welled up in her
gray eyes.

"Oh," she thought, "how horrible it is that people have to
grow up—and marry—and *change*!"

29
DIANA'S WEDDING

"After all, the only real roses are the pink ones," said Anne, as she tied white ribbon around Diana's bouquet in the westward-looking gable at Orchard Slope. "They are the flowers of love and faith."

Diana was standing nervously in the middle of the room, arrayed in her bridal white, her black curls frosted over with the film of her wedding veil. Anne had draped that veil, in accordance with the sentimental compact of years before.

"It's all pretty much as I used to imagine it long ago, when I wept over your inevitable marriage and our consequent parting," she laughed. "You are the bride of my dreams, Diana, with the 'lovely misty veil'; and I am your bridesmaid. But, alas! I haven't the puffed sleeves—though these short lace ones are even prettier. Neither is my heart wholly breaking nor do I exactly hate Fred."

"We are not really parting, Anne," protested Diana. "I'm not going far away. We'll love each other just as much as ever. We've always kept that 'oath' of friendship we swore long ago, haven't we?"

"Yes. We've kept it faithfully. We've had a beautiful friendship, Diana. We've never marred it by one quarrel or coolness or unkind word; and I hope it will always be so. But things can't be quite the same after this. You'll have other interests. I'll just be on the outside. But 'such is life' as Mrs. Rachel says. Mrs. Rachel has given you one of her beloved knitted quilts of the 'tobacco stripe' pattern, and she says when I am married she'll give me one, too."

"The mean thing about your getting married is that I won't be able to be *your* bridesmaid," lamented Diana.

"I'm to be Phil's bridesmaid next June, when she marries Mr. Blake, and then I must stop, for you know the proverb 'three times a bridesmaid, never a bride,'" said Anne, peeping through the window over the pink and snow of the blossoming orchard beneath. "Here comes the minister, Diana."

"Oh, Anne," gasped Diana, suddenly turning very pale and beginning to tremble. "Oh, Anne—I'm so nervous—I can't go through with it—Anne, I know I'm going to faint."

"If you do I'll drag you down to the rain-water hogshead and drop you in," said Anne unsympathetically. "Cheer up, dearest. Getting married can't be so very terrible when so many people survive the ceremony. See how cool and composed *I* am, and take courage."

"Wait till your turn comes, Miss Anne. Oh, Anne, I hear father coming upstairs. Give me my bouquet. Is my veil right? Am I very pale?"

"You look just lovely. Di, darling, kiss me good-bye for the last time. Diana Barry will never kiss me again."

"Diana Wright will, though. There, mother's calling. Come."

Following the simple, old-fashioned way in vogue then, Anne went down to the parlor on Gilbert's arm. They met at the top of the stairs for the first time since they had left Kingsport, for Gilbert had arrived only that day. Gilbert shook hands courteously. He was looking very well, though, as Anne instantly noted, rather thin. He was not pale; there was a flush on his cheek that had burned into it as Anne came along the dim hall towards him, in her soft, white dress with the lilies-of-the-valley in the shining masses of her hair. As they entered the crowded parlor together a little murmur of admiration ran around the room. "What a fine-looking pair they are," whispered the impressible Mrs. Rachel to Marilla.

Fred ambled in alone, with a very red face, and then Diana swept in on her father's arm. She did not faint, and nothing untoward occurred to interrupt the ceremony. Feasting and merry-making followed; then, as the evening waned, Fred and Diana drove away through the moonlight to their new home, and Gilbert walked with Anne to Green Gables.

Something of their old comradeship had returned during the

informal mirth of the evening. Oh, it was nice to be walking over
that well-known road with Gilbert again!

The night was so very still that one should have been able to
hear the whisper of roses in blossom—the laughter of daisies—
the piping of grasses—many sweet sounds, all tangled up
together. The beauty of moonlight on familiar fields irradiated
the world.

"Can't we take a ramble up Lovers' Lane before you go in?"
asked Gilbert as they crossed the bridge over the Lake of Shining
Waters, in which the moon lay like a great, drowned blossom
of gold.

Anne assented readily. Lovers' Lane was a veritable path in
fairyland that night—a shimmering, mysterious place, full of wizardry in the white-woven enchantment of moonlight. There had
been a time when such a walk with Gilbert through Lovers' Lane
would have been far too dangerous. But Roy and Christine had
made it very safe now. Anne found herself thinking a good deal
about Christine as she chatted lightly to Gilbert. She had met her
several times before leaving Kingsport, and had been charmingly
sweet to her. Christine had also been charmingly sweet. Indeed,
they were a most cordial pair. But for all that, their acquaintance
had not ripened into friendship. Evidently Christine was not a
kindred spirit.

"Are you going to be in Avonlea all summer?" asked Gilbert.

"No. I'm going down east to Valley Road next week. Esther
Haythorne wants me to teach for her through July and August.
They have a summer term in that school, and Esther isn't feeling
well. So I'm going to substitute for her. In one way I don't mind.
Do you know, I'm beginning to feel a little bit like a stranger in
Avonlea now? It makes me sorry—but it's true. It's quite
appalling to see the number of children who have shot up into
big boys and girls—really young men and women—these past
two years. Half of my pupils are grown up. It makes me feel
awfully old to see them in the places you and I and our mates
used to fill."

Anne laughed and sighed. She felt very old and mature and wise—which showed how young she was. She told herself that she longed greatly to go back to those dear merry days when life was seen through a rosy mist of hope and illusion, and possessed an indefinable something that had passed away forever. Where was it now—the glory and the dream?

"'So wags the world away,'" quoted Gilbert practically, and a trifle absently. Anne wondered if he were thinking of Christine. Oh, Avonlea was going to be so lonely now—with Diana gone!

30
MRS. SKINNER'S ROMANCE

Anne stepped off the train at Valley Road station and looked about to see if any one had come to meet her. She was to board with a certain Miss Janet Sweet, but she saw no one who answered in the least to her preconception of that lady, as formed from Esther's letter. The only person in sight was an elderly woman, sitting in a wagon with mail bags piled around her. Two hundred would have been a charitable guess at her weight; her face was as round and red as a harvest-moon and almost as featureless. She wore a tight, black, cashmere dress, made in the fashion of ten years ago, a little dusty black straw hat trimmed with bows of yellow ribbon, and faded black lace mits.

"Here, you," she called, waving her whip at Anne. "Are you the new Valley Road schoolma'am?"

"Yes."

"Well, I thought so. Valley Road is noted for its good-looking schoolma'ams, just as Millersville is noted for its humly ones. Janet Sweet asked me this morning if I could bring you out. I said, 'Sartin I kin, if she don't mind being scrunched up some. This rig of mine's kinder small for the mail bags and I'm some heftier than Thomas!' Just wait, miss, till I shift these bags a bit and I'll tuck you in somehow. It's only two miles to Janet's. Her next-door neighbor's hired boy is coming for your trunk tonight. My name is Skinner—Amelia Skinner."

Anne was eventually tucked in, exchanging amused smiles with herself during the process.

"Jog along, black mare," commanded Mrs. Skinner, gathering up the reins in her pudgy hands. "This is my first trip on the mail rowte. Thomas wanted to hoe his turnips today so he asked me to come. So I jest sot down and took a standing-up snack and started. I sorter like it. O' course it's rather tejus. Part of the time I sits and thinks and the rest I jest sits. Jog along, black mare. I want to git home airly. Thomas is terrible lonesome when I'm away. You see, we haven't been married very long."

"Oh!" said Anne politely.

"Just a month. Thomas courted me for quite a spell, though. It was real romantic."

Anne tried to picture Mrs. Skinner on speaking terms with romance and failed.

"Oh?" she said again.

"Yes. Y'see, there was another man after me. Jog along, black mare. I'd been a widder so long folks had given up expecting me to marry again. But when my darter—she's a schoolma'am like you—went out West to teach I felt real lonesome and wasn't nowise sot against the idea. Bime-by Thomas began to come up and so did the other feller—William Obadiah Seaman, *his* name was. For a long time I couldn't make up my mind which of them to take, and they kep' coming and coming, and I kep' worrying. Y'see, W. O. was rich—he had a fine place and carried considerable style. He was by far the best match. Jog along, black mare."

"Why didn't you marry him?" asked Anne.

"Well, y'see, he didn't love me," answered Mrs. Skinner, solemnly.

Anne opened her eyes widely and looked at Mrs. Skinner. But there was not a glint of humor on that lady's face. Evidently Mrs. Skinner saw nothing amusing in her own case.

"He'd been a widder-man for three years, and his sister kept house for him. Then she got married and he just wanted some one to look after his house. It was worth looking after, too, mind you that. It's a handsome house. Jog along, black mare. As for Thomas, he was poor, and if his house didn't leak in dry weather it was about all that could be said for it, though it looks kind of pictureaskew. But, y'see, I loved Thomas, and I didn't care one red cent for W. O. So I argued it out with myself. 'Sarah Crowe,' says I—my first was a Crowe—'you can marry your rich man if you like but you won't be happy. Folks can't get along together in this world without a little bit of love. You'd just better tie up to Thomas, for he loves you and you love him and nothing else ain't going to do you.' Jog along, black mare. So I told Thomas I'd take him. All the time I was getting ready I never dared drive past W. O.'s place for fear the sight of that fine house of his would put me in the swithers again. But now I never think of it at all, and I'm just that comfortable and happy with Thomas. Jog along, black mare."

"How did William Obadiah take it?" queried Anne.

"Oh, he rumpussed a bit. But he's going to see a skinny old maid in Millersville now, and I guess she'll take him fast enough. She'll make him a better wife than his first did. W. O. never wanted to marry *her*. He just asked her to marry him 'cause his father wanted him to, never dreaming but that she'd say 'no.' But mind you, she said 'yes.' There was a predicament for you. Jog along, black mare. She was a great housekeeper, but most awful mean. She wore the same bonnet for eighteen years. Then she got a new one and W. O. met her on the road and didn't know her. Jog along, black mare. I feel that I'd a narrer escape. I might have married him and been most awful miserable, like my poor cousin, Jane Ann. Jane Ann married a rich man she didn't care anything about, and she hasn't the life of a dog. She come to see me last week and says, says she, 'Sarah Skinner, I envy you. I'd rather live in a little hut on the side of the road with a man I was fond of than in my big house with the one I've got.' Jane Ann's

man ain't such a bad sort, nuther, though he's so contrary that he
wears his fur coat when the thermometer's at ninety. The only
way to git him to do anything is to coax him to do the opposite.
But there ain't any love to smooth things down and it's a poor
way of living. Jog along, black mare. There's Janet's place in the
hollow—'Wayside,' she calls it. Quite pictureaskew, ain't it? I
guess you'll be glad to git out of this, with all them mail bags jam-
ming round you."

"Yes, but I have enjoyed my drive with you very much," said
Anne sincerely.

"Git away now!" said Mrs. Skinner, highly flattered. "Wait till
I tell Thomas that. He always feels dretful tickled when I git a
compliment. Jog along, black mare. Well, here we are. I hope
you'll git on well in the school, miss. There's a short cut to it
through the ma'sh back of Janet's. If you take that way be awful
keerful. If you once got stuck in that black mud you'd be sucked
right down and never seen or heard tell of again till the day of
judgment, like Adam Palmer's cow. Jog along, black mare."

31
ANNE TO PHILIPPA

"Anne Shirley to Philippa Gordon, greeting.

"Well-beloved, it's high time I was writing you. Here am I,
installed once more as a country 'schoolma'am' at Valley Road,
boarding at 'Wayside,' the home of Miss Janet Sweet. Janet is a
dear soul and very nice-looking; tall, but not over-tall; stoutish,
yet with a certain restraint of outline suggestive of a thrifty soul
who is not going to be over-lavish even in the matter of avoirdu-
pois. She has a knot of soft, crimpy, brown hair with a thread of
gray in it, a sunny face with rosy cheeks, and big, kind eyes as
blue as forget-me-nots. Moreover, she is one of those delightful,

old-fashioned cooks who don't care a bit if they ruin your diges-
tion as long as they can give you feasts of fat things.

"I like her; and she likes me—principally, it seems, because
she had a sister named Anne who died young.

"'I'm real glad to see you,' she said briskly, when I landed in her
yard. 'My, you don't look a mite like I expected. I was sure you'd
be dark—my sister Anne was dark. And here you're red-headed!'

"For a few minutes I thought I wasn't going to like Janet as
much as I had expected at first sight. Then I reminded myself
that I really must be more sensible than to be prejudiced against
any one simply because she called my hair red. Probably the
word 'auburn' was not in Janet's vocabulary at all.

"'Wayside' is a dear sort of little spot. The house is small and
white, set down in a delightful little hollow that drops away from
the road. Between road and house is an orchard and flower-gar-
den all mixed up together. The front door walk is bordered with
quahog clam-shells—'cow-hawks,' Janet calls them; there is Vir-
ginia Creeper over the porch and moss on the roof. My room is a
neat little spot 'off the parlor'—just big enough for the bed and
me. Over the head of my bed there is a picture of Robby Burns
standing at Highland Mary's grave, shadowed by an enormous
weeping willow tree. Robby's face is so lugubrious that it is no
wonder I have bad dreams. Why, the first night I was here I
dreamed I *couldn't laugh*.

"The parlor is tiny and neat. Its one window is so shaded by a
huge willow that the room has a grotto-like effect of emerald
gloom. There are wonderful tidies on the chairs, and gay mats on
the floor, and books and cards carefully arranged on a round
table, and vases of dried grass on the mantel-piece. Between the
vases is a cheerful decoration of preserved coffin plates—five in
all, pertaining respectively to Janet's father and mother, a brother,
her sister Anne, and a hired man who died here once! If I go suddenly insane some of these days 'know all men by these presents'
that those coffin-plates have caused it.

"But it's all delightful and I said so. Janet loved me for it, just as she detested poor Esther because Esther had said so much shade was unhygienic and had objected to sleeping on a feather bed. Now, I glory in feather-beds, and the more unhygienic and feathery they are the more I glory. Janet says it is such a comfort to see me eat; she had been so afraid I would be like Miss Haythorne, who wouldn't eat anything but fruit and hot water for breakfast and tried to make Janet give up frying things. Esther is really a dear girl, but she is rather given to fads. The trouble is that she hasn't enough imagination and *has* a tendency to indigestion.

"Janet told me I could have the use of the parlor when any young men called! I don't think there are many to call. I haven't seen a young man in Valley Road yet, except the next-door hired boy—Sam Tolliver, a very tall, lank, tow-haired youth. He came over one evening recently and sat for an hour on the garden fence, near the front porch where Janet and I were doing fancy-work. The only remarks he volunteered in all that time were, 'Hev a peppermint, miss! *Dew* now—fine thing for ca*tarrh*, peppermints,' and 'Powerful lot o' jump-grasses round here ter-night. Yep.'

"But there *is* a love affair going on here. It seems to be my for-tune to be mixed up, more of less actively, with elderly love affairs. Mr. and Mrs. Irving always say that I brought about their marriage. Mrs. Stephen Clark of Carmody persists in being most grateful to me for a suggestion which somebody else would prob-ably have made if I hadn't. I do really think, though, that Ludovic Speed would never have got any further along than placid courtship if I had not helped him and Theodora Dix out.

"In the present affair I am only a passive spectator. I've tried once to help things along and made an awful mess of it. So I shall not meddle again. I'll tell you all about it when we meet."

32
TEA WITH MRS. DOUGLAS

On the first Thursday night of Anne's sojourn in Valley Road Janet asked her to go to prayer-meeting. Janet blossomed out like a rose to attend that prayer-meeting. She wore a pale-blue, pansy-sprinkled muslin dress with more ruffles than one would ever have supposed economical Janet could be guilty of, and a white leghorn hat with pink roses and three ostrich feathers on it. Anne felt quite amazed. Later on she found out Janet's motive in so arraying herself—a motive as old as Eden.

Valley Road prayer-meetings seemed to be essentially femi-nine. There were thirty-two women present, two half-grown boys, and one solitary man, beside the minister. Anne found her-self studying this man. He was not handsome or young or graceful; he had remarkably long legs—so long that he had to keep them coiled up under his chair to dispose of them—and he was stoop-shouldered. His hands were big, his hair wanted bar-bering, and his moustache was unkempt. But Anne thought she liked his face; it was kind and honest and tender; there was something else in it, too—just what, Anne found it hard to define. She finally concluded that this man had suffered and been strong, and it had been made manifest in his face. There was a sort of patient, humorous endurance in his expression which indicated that he would go to the stake if need be, but would keep on looking pleasant until he really had to begin squirming.

When prayer-meeting was over this man came up to Janet and said,

"May I see you home, Janet?"

Janet took his arm—"as primly and shyly as if she were no more than sixteen, having her first escort home," Anne told the girls at Patty's Place later on.

"Miss Shirley, permit me to introduce Mr. Douglas," she said stiffly.

Mr. Douglas nodded and said,

"I was looking at you in prayer-meeting, miss, and thinking what a nice little girl you were."

Such a speech from ninety-nine people out of a hundred would have annoyed Anne bitterly; but the way in which Mr. Douglas said it made her feel that she had received a very real and pleasing compliment. She smiled appreciatively at him and dropped obligingly behind on the moonlit road.

So Janet had a beau! Anne was delighted. Janet would make a paragon of a wife—cheery, economical, tolerant, and a very queen of cooks. It would be a flagrant waste on Nature's part to keep her a permanent old maid.

"John Douglas asked me to take you up to see his mother," said Janet the next day. "She's bed-rid a lot of the time and never goes out of the house. But she's powerful fond of company and always wants to see my boarders. Can you go up this evening?"

Anne assented; but later in the day Mr. Douglas called on his mother's behalf to invite them up to tea on Saturday evening.

"Oh, why didn't you put on your pretty pansy dress?" asked Anne, when they left home. It was a hot day, and poor Janet, between her excitement and her heavy black cashmere dress, looked as if she were being broiled alive.

"Old Mrs. Douglas would think it terrible frivolous and unsuitable, I'm afraid. John likes that dress, though," she added wistfully.

The old Douglas homestead was half a mile from "Wayside" cresting a windy hill. The house itself was large and comfortable, old enough to be dignified, and girdled with maple groves and orchards. There were big, trim barns behind it, and everything bespoke prosperity. Whatever the patient endurance in Mr. Douglas' face had meant it hadn't, so Anne reflected, meant debts and duns.

John Douglas met them at the door and took them into the sitting-room, where his mother was enthroned in an arm-chair.

Anne had expected old Mrs. Douglas to be tall and thin, because Mr. Douglas was. Instead, she was a tiny scrap of a woman, with soft pink cheeks, mild blue eyes, and a mouth like a baby's. Dressed in a beautiful, fashionably-made black silk dress, with a fluffy white shawl over her shoulders, and her snowy hair surmounted by a dainty lace cap, she might have posed as a grandmother doll.

"How do you do, Janet dear?" she said sweetly. "I am *so* glad to see you again, dear." She put up her pretty old face to be kissed. "And this is our new teacher. I'm delighted to meet you. My son has been singing your praises until I'm half jealous, and I'm sure Janet ought to be wholly so."

Poor Janet blushed, Anne said something polite and conventional, and then everybody sat down and made talk. It was hard work, even for Anne, for nobody seemed at ease except old Mrs. Douglas, who certainly did not find any difficulty in talking. She made Janet sit by her and stroked her hand occasionally. Janet sat and smiled, looking horribly uncomfortable in her hideous dress, and John Douglas sat without smiling.

At the tea-table Mrs. Douglas gracefully asked Janet to pour the tea. Janet turned redder than ever but did it. Anne wrote a description of that meal to Stella.

"We had cold tongue and chicken and strawberry preserves, lemon pie and tarts and chocolate cake and raisin cookies and pound cake and fruit cake—and a few other things, including more pie—caramel pie, I think it was. After I had eaten twice as much as was good for me, Mrs. Douglas sighed and said she feared she had nothing to tempt my appetite.

"'I'm afraid dear Janet's cooking has spoiled you for any other,' she said sweetly. 'Of course nobody in Valley Road aspires to rival *her*. Won't you have another piece of pie, Miss Shirley? You haven't eaten *anything*.'

"Stella, I had eaten a helping of tongue and one of chicken, three biscuits, a generous allowance of preserves, a piece of pie, a tart, and a square of chocolate cake!"

After tea Mrs. Douglas smiled benevolently and told John to take "dear Janet" out into the garden and get her some roses.

"Miss Shirley will keep me company while you are out—won't you?" she said plaintively. She settled down in her arm-chair with a sigh.

"I am a very frail old woman, Miss Shirley. For over twenty years I've been a great sufferer. For twenty long, weary years I've been dying by inches."

"How painful!" said Anne, trying to be sympathetic and succeeding only in feeling idiotic.

"There have been scores of nights when they've thought I could never live to see the dawn," went on Mrs. Douglas solemnly. "Nobody knows what I've gone through—nobody can know but myself. Well, it can't last very much longer now. My weary pilgrimage will soon be over, Miss Shirley. It is a great comfort to me that John will have such a good wife to look after him when his mother is gone—a great comfort, Miss Shirley."

"Janet is a lovely woman," said Anne warmly.

"Lovely! A beautiful character," assented Mrs. Douglas. "And a perfect housekeeper—something I never was. My health would not permit it, Miss Shirley. I am indeed thankful that John has made such a wise choice. I hope and believe that he will be happy. He is my only son, Miss Shirley, and his happiness lies very near my heart."

"Of course," said Anne stupidly. For the first time in her life she was stupid. Yet she could not imagine why. She seemed to have absolutely nothing to say to this sweet, smiling, angelic old lady who was patting her hand so kindly.

"Come and see me soon again, dear Janet," said Mrs. Douglas lovingly, when they left. "You don't come half often enough. But then I suppose John will be bringing you here to stay all the time one of these days."

Anne, happening to glance at John Douglas, as his mother spoke, gave a positive start of dismay. He looked as a tortured man might look when his tormentors gave the rack the last turn of possible endurance. She felt sure he must be ill and hurried poor blushing Janet away.

"Isn't old Mrs. Douglas a sweet woman?" asked Janet, as they went down the road.

"M—m," answered Anne absently. She was wondering why John Douglas had looked so.

"She's been a terrible sufferer," said Janet feelingly. "She takes terrible spells. It keeps John all worried up. He's scared to leave home for fear his mother will take a spell and nobody there but the hired girl."

33
"HE JUST KEPT COMING AND COMING"

Three days later Anne came home from school and found Janet crying. Tears and Janet seemed so incongruous that Anne was honestly alarmed.

"Oh, what is the matter?" she cried anxiously.

"I'm—I'm forty today," sobbed Janet.

"Well, you were nearly that yesterday and it didn't hurt," comforted Anne, trying not to smile.

"But—but," went on Janet with a big gulp, "John Douglas won't ask me to marry him."

"Oh, but he will," said Anne lamely. "You must give him time, Janet."

"Time!" said Janet with indescribable scorn. "He has had twenty years. How much more time does he want?"

"Do you mean that John Douglas has been coming to see you for twenty years?"

"He has. And he has never so much as mentioned marriage to me. And I don't believe he ever will now. I've never said a word to a mortal about it, but it seems to me I've just got to talk it out with some one at last or go crazy. John Douglas begun to go with me twenty years ago, before mother died. Well, he kept coming and coming, and after a spell I begun making quilts and things; but he never said anything about getting married, only just kept coming and coming. There wasn't anything I could do. Mother died when we'd been going together for eight years. I thought he maybe would speak out then, seeing as I was left alone in the world. He was real kind and feeling, and did everything he could for me, but he never said marry. And that's the way it has been going on ever since. People blame *me* for it. They say I won't marry him because his mother is so sickly and I don't want the bother of waiting on her. Why, I'd *love* to wait on John's mother! But I let them think so. I'd rather they'd blame me than pity me! It's so dreadful humiliating that John won't ask me. And *why* won't he? Seems to me if I only knew his reason I wouldn't mind it so much."

"Perhaps his mother doesn't want him to marry anybody," suggested Anne.

"Oh, she does. She's told me time and again that she'd love to see John settled before her time comes. She's always giving him hints—you heard her yourself the other day. I thought I'd ha' gone through the floor."

"It's beyond me," said Anne helplessly. She thought of Ludovic Speed. But the cases were not parallel. John Douglas was not a man of Ludovic's type.

"You should show more spirit, Janet," she went on resolutely. "Why didn't you send him about his business long ago?"

"I couldn't," said poor Janet pathetically. "You see, Anne, I've always been awful fond of John. He might just as well keep coming as not, for there was never anybody else I'd want, so it didn't matter."

"But it might have made him speak out like a man," urged Anne.

Janet shook her head.

"No, I guess not. I was afraid to try, anyway, for fear he'd think I meant it and just go. I suppose I'm a poor-spirited creature, but that is how I feel. And I can't help it."

"Oh, you *could* help it, Janet. It isn't too late yet. Take a firm stand. Let that man know you are not going to endure his shilly-shallying any longer. I'll back you up."

"I dunno," said Janet hopelessly. "I dunno if I could ever get up enough spunk. Things have drifted so long. But I'll think it over."

Anne felt that she was disappointed in John Douglas. She had liked him so well, and she had not thought him the sort of man who would play fast and loose with a woman's feelings for twenty years. He certainly should be taught a lesson, and Anne felt vindictively that she would enjoy seeing the process. Therefore she was delighted when Janet told her, as they were going to prayer-meeting the next night, that she meant to show some "sperrit."

"I'll let John Douglas see I'm not going to be trodden on any longer."

"You are perfectly right," said Anne emphatically.

When prayer-meeting was over John Douglas came up with his usual request. Janet looked frightened but resolute.

"No, thank you," she said icily. "I know the road home pretty well alone. I ought to, seeing I've been travelling it for forty years. So you needn't trouble yourself, Mr. Douglas."

Anne was looking at John Douglas; and, in that brilliant moonlight, she saw the last twist of the rack again. Without a word he turned and strode down the road.

"Stop! Stop!" Anne called wildly after him, not caring in the least for the other dumbfounded onlookers. "Mr. Douglas, stop! Come back."

John Douglas stopped but he did not come back. Anne flew down the road, caught his arm and fairly dragged him back to Janet.

"You must come back," she said imploringly. "It's all a mistake, Mr. Douglas—all my fault. I made Janet do it. She didn't want to—but it's all right now, isn't it, Janet?"

Without a word Janet took his arm and walked away. Anne followed them meekly home and slipped in by the back door.

"Well, you are a nice person to back one up," said Janet sarcastically.

"I couldn't help it, Janet," said Anne repentantly. "I just felt as if I had stood by and seen murder done. I *had* to run after him."

"Oh, I'm just as glad you did. When I saw John Douglas making off down that road I just felt as if every little bit of joy and happiness that was left in my life was going with him. It was an awful feeling."

"Did he ask you why you did it?" asked Anne.

"No, he never said a word about it," replied Janet dully.

34
JOHN DOUGLAS SPEAKS AT LAST

Anne was not without a feeble hope that something might come of it after all. But nothing did. John Douglas came and took Janet driving, and walked home from prayer-meeting with her, as he had been doing for twenty years, and as he seemed likely to do for twenty years more. The summer waned. Anne taught her school and wrote letters and studied a little. Her walks to and from school were pleasant. She always went by way of the swamp; it was a lovely place—a boggy soil, green with the greenest of mossy hillocks; a silvery brook meandered through it and spruces stood erectly, their boughs a-trail with gray-green mosses, their roots overgrown with all sorts of woodland lovelinesses.

Nevertheless, Anne found life in Valley Road a little monotonous. To be sure, there was one diverting incident.

She had not seen the lank, tow-headed Samuel of the peppermints since the evening of his call, save for chance meetings on the road. But one warm August night he appeared, and solemnly seated himself on the rustic bench by the porch. He wore his usual working habiliments, consisting of vari-patched trousers, a blue jean shirt, out at the elbows, and a ragged straw hat. He was chewing a straw and he kept on chewing it while he looked solemnly at Anne. Anne laid her book aside with a sigh and took up her doily. Conversation with Sam was really out of the question.

After a long silence Sam suddenly spoke.

"I'm leaving over there," he said abruptly, waving his straw in the direction of the neighboring house.

"Oh, are you?" said Anne politely.

"Yep."

"And where are you going now?"

"Wall, I've been thinking some of gitting a place of my own. There's one that'd suit me over at Millersville. But ef I rents it I'll want a woman."

"I suppose so," said Anne vaguely.

"Yep."

There was another long silence. Finally Sam removed his straw again and said,

"Will yeh hev me?"

"Wh—a—t!" gasped Anne.

"Will yeh hev me?"

"Do you mean—*marry* you?" queried poor Anne feebly.

"Yep."

"Why, I'm hardly acquainted with you," cried Anne indignantly.

"But yeh'd git acquainted with me after we was married," said Sam.

Anne gathered up her poor dignity.

"Certainly I won't marry you," she said haughtily.

"Wall, yeh might do worse," expostulated Sam. "I'm a good worker and I've got some money in the bank."

"Don't speak of this to me again. Whatever put such an idea into your head?" said Anne, her sense of humor getting the better of her wrath. It was such an absurd situation.

"Yeh're a likely-looking girl and hev a right-smart way o' stepping," said Sam. "I don't want no lazy woman. Think it over. I won't change my mind yit awhile. Wall, I must be gitting. Gotter milk the cows."

Anne's illusions concerning proposals had suffered so much of late years that there were few of them left. So she could laugh whole-heartedly over this one, not feeling any secret sting. She mimicked poor Sam to Janet that night, and both of them laughed immoderately over his plunge into sentiment.

One afternoon, when Anne's sojourn in Valley Road was drawing to a close, Alec Ward came driving down to "Wayside" in hot haste for Janet.

"They want you at the Douglas place quick," he said. "I really believe old Mrs. Douglas is going to die at last, after pretending to do it for twenty years."

Janet ran to get her hat. Anne asked if Mrs. Douglas was worse than usual.

"She's not half as bad," said Alec solemnly, "and that's what makes me think it's serious. Other times she'd be screaming and throwing herself all over the place. This time she's lying still and mum. When Mrs. Douglas is mum she is pretty sick, you bet."

"You don't like old Mrs. Douglas?" said Anne curiously.

"I like cats as is cats. I don't like cats as is women," was Alec's cryptic reply.

Janet came home in the twilight.

"Mrs. Douglas is dead," she said wearily. "She died soon after I got there. She just spoke to me once—'I suppose you'll marry John now?' she said. It cut me to the heart, Anne. To think John's own mother thought I wouldn't marry him because of her! I couldn't say a word either—there were other women there. I was thankful John had gone out."

Janet began to cry drearily. But Anne brewed her a hot drink of ginger tea to her comforting. To be sure, Anne discovered later on that she had used white pepper instead of ginger; but Janet never knew the difference.

The evening after the funeral Janet and Anne were sitting on the front porch steps at sunset. The wind had fallen asleep in the pinelands and lurid sheets of heat-lightning flickered across the northern skies. Janet wore her ugly black dress and looked her very worst, her eyes and nose red from crying. They talked little, for Janet seemed faintly to resent Anne's efforts to cheer her up. She plainly preferred to be miserable.

Suddenly the gate-latch clicked and John Douglas strode into the garden. He walked towards them straight over the geranium bed. Janet stood up. So did Anne. Anne was a tall girl and wore a white dress; but John Douglas did not see her.

"Janet," he said, "will you marry me?"

The words burst out as if they had been wanting to be said for twenty years and *must* be uttered now, before anything else.

Janet's face was so red from crying that it couldn't turn any redder, so it turned a most unbecoming purple.

"Why didn't you ask me before?" she said slowly.

"I couldn't. She made me promise not to—mother made me promise not to. Nineteen years ago she took a terrible spell. We thought she couldn't live through it. She implored me to promise not to ask you to marry me while she was alive. I didn't want to promise such a thing, even though we all thought she couldn't live very long—the doctor only gave her six months. But she begged it on her knees, sick and suffering. I had to promise."

"What had your mother against me?" cried Janet.

"Nothing—nothing. She just didn't want another woman— *any* woman—there while she was living. She said if I didn't promise she'd die right there and I'd have killed her. So I promised. And she's held me to that promise ever since, though I've gone on my knees to her in my turn to beg her to let me off."

"Why didn't you tell me this?" asked Janet chokingly. "If I'd only *known*! Why didn't you just tell me?"

"She made me promise I wouldn't tell a soul," said John hoarsely. "She swore me to it on the Bible; Janet, I'd never have done it if I'd dreamed it was to be for so long. Janet, you'll never know what I've suffered these nineteen years. I know I've made you suffer, too, but you'll marry me for all, won't you, Janet? Oh, Janet, won't you? I've come as soon as I could to ask you."

At this moment the stupified Anne came to her senses and realized that she had no business to be there. She slipped away and did not see Janet until the next morning, when the latter told her the rest of the story.

"That cruel, relentless, deceitful old woman!" cried Anne.

"Hush—she's dead," said Janet solemnly. "If she wasn't—but she *is*. So we mustn't speak evil of her. But I'm happy at last, Anne. And I wouldn't have minded waiting so long a bit if I'd only known why."

"When are you to be married?"

"Next month. Of course it will be very quiet. I suppose people will talk terrible. They'll say I made enough haste to snap John up as soon as his poor mother was out of the way. John wanted to let them know the truth but I said, 'No, John; after all she was your mother, and we'll keep the secret between us, and not cast any shadow on her memory. I don't mind what people say, now that I know the truth myself. It don't matter a mite. Let it all be buried with the dead,' says I to him. So I coaxed him round to agree with me."

"You're much more forgiving than I could ever be," Anne said, rather crossly.

"You'll feel differently about a good many things when you get to be my age," said Janet tolerantly. "That's one of the things we learn as we grow older—how to forgive. It comes easier at forty than it did at twenty."

<h1 style="text-align:center">35</h1>

THE LAST REDMOND YEAR OPENS

"Here we are, all back again, nicely sunburned and rejoicing as a strong man to run a race," said Phil, sitting down on a suitcase with a sigh of pleasure. "Isn't it jolly to see this dear old Patty's Place again—and Aunty—and the cats? Rusty has lost another piece of ear, hasn't he?"

"Rusty would be the nicest cat in the world if he had no ears at all," declared Anne loyally from her trunk, while Rusty writhed about her lap in a frenzy of welcome.

"Aren't you glad to see us back, Aunty?" demanded Phil.

"Yes. But I wish you'd tidy things up," said Aunt Jamesina plaintively, looking at the wilderness of trunks and suitcases by which the four laughing, chattering girls were surrounded. "You can talk just as well later on. Work first and then play used to be my motto when I was a girl."

"Oh, we've just reversed that in this generation, Aunty. *Our* motto is play your play and then dig in. You can do your work so much better if you've had a good bout of play first."

"If you are going to marry a minister," said Aunt Jamesina, picking up Joseph and her knitting and resigning herself to the inevitable with the charming grace that made her the queen of house-mothers, "you will have to give up such expressions as 'dig in.'"

"Why?" moaned Phil. "Oh, why must a minister's wife be supposed to utter only prunes and prisms? I shan't. Everybody on Patterson Street uses slang—that is to say, metaphorical language—and if I didn't they would think me insufferably proud and stuck up."

"Have you broken the news to your family?" asked Priscilla, feeding the Sarah-cat bits from her lunch-basket.

Phil nodded.

"How did they take it?"

"Oh, mother rampaged. But I stood rock-firm—even I, Philippa Gordon, who never before could hold fast to anything. Father was calmer. Father's own daddy was a minister, so you see he has a soft spot in his heart for the cloth. I had Jo up to Mount Holly, after mother grew calm, and they both loved him. But mother gave him some frightful hints in every conversation regarding what she had hoped for me. Oh, my vacation pathway hasn't been exactly strewn with roses, girls dear. But—I've won out and I've got Jo. Nothing else matters."

"To you," said Aunt Jamesina darkly.

"Nor to Jo, either," retorted Phil. "You keep on pitying him. Why, pray? *I* think he's to be envied. He's getting brains, beauty, and a heart of gold in *ME*."

"It's well we know how to take your speeches," said Aunt Jamesina patiently. "I hope you don't talk like that before strangers. What would they think?"

"Oh, I don't want to know what they think. *I* don't want to see myself as others see me. I'm sure it would be horribly uncomfortable most of the time. I don't believe Burns was really sincere in that prayer, either."

"Oh, I daresay we all pray for some things that we really don't want, if we were only honest enough to look into our hearts," owned Aunt Jamesina candidly. "I've a notion that such prayers don't rise very far. *I* used to pray that I might be enabled to forgive a certain person, but I know now I really didn't want to forgive her. When I finally got that I *did* want to I forgave her without having to pray about it."

"I can't picture you as being unforgiving for long," said Stella.

"Oh, I used to be. But holding spite doesn't seem worth while when you get along in years."

"That reminds me," said Anne, and told the tale of John and Janet.

"And now tell us about that romantic scene you hinted so darkly at in one of your letters," demanded Phil.

Anne acted out Samuel's proposal with great spirit. The girls shrieked with laughter and Aunt Jamesina smiled.

"It isn't in good taste to make fun of your beaux," she said severely; "but," she added calmly, "I always did it myself."

"Tell us about your beaux, Aunty," entreated Phil. "You must have had any number of them."

"They're not in the past tense," retorted Aunt Jamesina. "I've got them yet. There are three old widowers at home who have been casting sheep's eyes at me for some time. You children needn't think you own all the romance in the world."

"Widowers and sheep's eyes don't sound very romantic, Aunty."

"Well, no; but young folks aren't always romantic either. Some of my beaux certainly weren't. I used to laugh at them scandalous, poor boys. There was Jim Elwood—he was always in a sort of day-dream—never seemed to sense what was going on. He didn't wake up to the fact that I'd said 'no' till a year after I'd said it. When he did get married his wife fell out of the sleigh one night when they were driving home from church and he never missed her. Then there was Dan Winston. He knew too much. He knew everything in this world and most of what is in the next. He could give you an answer to any question, even if you asked him when the Judgment Day was to be. Milton Edwards was real nice and I liked him but I didn't marry him. For one thing, he took a week to get a joke through his head, and for another he never asked me. Horatio Reeve was the most interesting beau I ever had. But when he told a story he dressed it up so that you couldn't see it for frills. I never could decide whether he was lying or just letting his imagination run loose."

"And what about the others, Aunty?"

"Go away and unpack," said Aunt Jamesina, waving Joseph at them by mistake for a needle. "The others were too nice to make fun of. I shall respect their memory. There's a box of flowers in your room, Anne. They came about an hour ago."

After the first week the girls of Patty's Place settled down to a steady grind of study; for this was their last year at Redmond and graduation honors must be fought for persistently. Anne devoted herself to English, Priscilla pored over classics, and Philippa pounded away at Mathematics. Sometimes they grew tired, sometimes they felt discouraged, sometimes nothing seemed worth the struggle for it. In one such mood Stella wandered up to the blue room one rainy November evening. Anne sat on the floor in a little circle of light cast by the lamp beside her, amid a surrounding snow of crumpled manuscript.

"What in the world are you doing?"

"Just looking over some old Story Club yarns. I wanted something to cheer *and* inebriate. I'd studied until the world seemed azure. So I came up here and dug these out of my trunk. They are so drenched in tears and tragedy that they are excruciatingly funny."

"I'm blue and discouraged myself," said Stella, throwing herself on the couch. "Nothing seems worth while. My very thoughts are old. I've thought them all before. What is the use of living after all, Anne?"

"Honey, it's just brain fag that makes us feel that way, and the weather. A pouring rainy night like this, coming after a hard day's grind, would squelch any one but a *Mark Tapley*. You know it *is* worth while to live."

"Oh, I suppose so. But I can't prove it to myself just now."

"Just think of all the great and noble souls who have lived and worked in the world," said Anne dreamily. "Isn't it worth while to come after them and inherit what they won and taught? And think of all the great people in the world today! Isn't it worth while to think we can share their inspiration? And then, all the great souls that will come in the future? Isn't it worth while to work a little and prepare the way for them—make just one step in their path easier?"

"Oh, my mind agrees with you, Anne. But my soul remains doleful and uninspired. I'm always grubby and dingy on rainy nights."

"Some nights I like the rain—I like to lie in bed and hear it pattering on the roof and drifting through the pines."

"I like it when it stays on the roof," said Stella. "It doesn't always. I spent a gruesome night in an old country farmhouse last summer. The roof leaked and the rain came pattering down on my bed. There was no poetry in *that*. I had to get up in the 'mirk midnight' and chivy round to pull the bedstead out of the drip—and it was one of those solid, old-fashioned beds that weigh a ton—more or less. And then that drip-drop, drip-drop kept up all night until my nerves just went to pieces. You've no idea what an eerie noise a great drop of rain falling with a mushy thud on a bare floor makes in the night. It sounds like ghostly footsteps and all that sort of thing. What are you laughing over, Anne?"

"These stories. As Phil would say they are killing—in more senses than one, for everybody died in them. What dazzlingly lovely heroines we had—and how we dressed them! Silks—satins—velvets—jewels—laces—they never wore anything else. Here is one of Jane Andrews' stories depicting her heroine as sleeping in a beautiful white satin night-dress trimmed with seed pearls."

"Go on," said Stella. "I begin to feel that life *is* worth living as long as there's a laugh in it."

"Here's one I wrote. My heroine is disporting herself at a ball 'glittering from head to foot with large diamonds of the first water.' But what booted beauty or rich attire? 'The paths of glory lead but to the grave.' They must either be murdered or die of a broken heart. There was no escape for them."

"Let me read some of your stories."

"Well, here's my masterpiece. Note its cheerful title—*'My Graves.'* I shed quarts of tears while writing it, and the other girls shed gallons while I read it. Jane Andrews' mother scolded her frightfully because she had so many handkerchiefs in the wash that week. It's a harrowing tale of the wanderings of a Methodist minister's wife. I made her a Methodist because it was necessary that she should wander. She buried a child every place she lived in. There were nine of them and their graves were severed far apart, ranging from Newfoundland to Vancouver. I described the children, pictured their several death beds, and detailed their tombstones and epitaphs. I had intended to bury the whole nine but when I had disposed of eight my invention of horrors gave out and I permitted the ninth to live as a hopeless cripple."

While Stella read *My Graves*, punctuating its tragic paragraphs with chuckles, and Rusty slept the sleep of a just cat who has been out all night curled up on a Jane-Andrews tale of a beautiful maiden of fifteen who went to nurse in a leper colony—of course dying of the loathsome disease finally—Anne glanced over the other manuscripts and recalled the old days at Avonlea school when the members of the Story Club, sitting under the spruce trees or down among the ferns by the brook, had written them. What fun they had had! How the sunshine and mirth of those olden summers returned as she read. Not all the glory that was Greece or the grandeur that was Rome could weave such wizardry as those funny, tearful tales of the Story Club. Among the manuscripts Anne found one written on sheets of wrapping paper. A wave of laughter filled her gray eyes as she recalled the time and place of its genesis. It was the sketch she had written the day she fell through the roof of the Cobb duckhouse on the Tory Road.

Anne glanced over it, then fell to reading it intently. It was a little dialogue between asters and sweet-peas, wild canaries in the lilac bush, and the guardian spirit of the garden. After she had read it, she sat, staring into space; and when Stella had gone she smoothed out the crumpled manuscript.

"I believe I will," she said resolutely.

36
THE GARDNERS' CALL

"Here is a letter with an Indian stamp for you, Aunt Jimsie," said Phil. "Here are three for Stella, and two for Pris, and a glorious fat one for me from Jo. There's nothing for you, Anne, except a circular."

Nobody noticed Anne's flush as she took the thin letter Phil tossed her carelessly. But a few minutes later Phil looked up to see a transfigured Anne.

"Honey, what good thing has happened?"

"The *Youth's Friend* has accepted a little sketch I sent them a fortnight ago," said Anne, trying hard to speak as if she were accustomed to having sketches accepted every mail, but not quite succeeding.

"Anne Shirley! How glorious! What was it? When is it to be published? Did they pay you for it?"

"Yes; they've sent a check for ten dollars, and the editor writes that he would like to see more of my work. Dear man, he shall. It was an old sketch I found in my box. I rewrote it and sent it in—but I never really thought it could be accepted because it had no plot," said Anne, recalling the bitter experiences of *Averil's Atonement*.

"What are you going to do with that ten dollars, Anne? Let's all go up town and get drunk," suggested Phil.

"I *am* going to squander it in a wild soulless revel of some sort," declared Anne gaily. "At all events it isn't tainted money— like the check I got for that horrible Reliable Baking Powder story. I spent *it* usefully on clothes and hated them every time I put them on."

"Think of having a real live author at Patty's Place," said Priscilla.

"It's a great responsibility," said Aunt Jamesina solemnly.

"Indeed it is," agreed Pris with equal solemnity. "Authors are kittle cattle. You never know when or how they will break out. Anne may make copy of *us*."

"I meant that the ability to write for the Press was a great responsibility," said Aunt Jamesina severely; "and I hope Anne realizes it. My daughter used to write stories before she went to the foreign field, but now she has turned her attention to higher things. She used to say her motto was 'Never write a line you would be ashamed to read at your own funeral.' You'd better take that for yours, Anne, if you are going to embark in literature. Though, to be sure," added Aunt Jamesina perplexedly, "Elizabeth always used to laugh when she said it. She always laughed so much that I don't know how she ever came to decide on being

a missionary. I'm thankful she did—I prayed that she might—
but—I wish she hadn't."

Then Aunt Jamesina wondered why those giddy girls all
laughed.

Anne's eyes shone all that day; literary ambitions sprouted and
budded in her brain; their exhilaration accompanied her to Jennie Cooper's walking party, and not even the sight of Gilbert and
Christine, walking just ahead of her and Roy, could quite subdue
the sparkle of her starry hopes. Nevertheless, she was not so rapt
from things of earth as to be unable to notice that Christine's
walk was decidedly ungraceful.

"But I suppose Gilbert looks only at her face. So like a man,"
thought Anne scornfully.

"Shall you be home Saturday afternoon?" asked Roy.

"Yes."

"My mother and sisters are coming to call on you," said Roy
quietly.

Something went over Anne which might be described as a
thrill, but it was hardly a pleasant one. She had never met any of
Roy's family; she realized the significance of his statement; and it
had, somehow, an irrevocableness about it that chilled her.

"I shall be glad to see them," she said flatly; and then wondered if she really would be glad. She ought to be, of course. But
would it not be something of an ordeal? Gossip had filtered to
Anne regarding the light in which the Gardners viewed the
"infatuation" of son and brother. Roy must have brought pressure
to bear in the matter of this call. Anne knew she would be
weighed in the balance. From the fact that they had consented to
call she understood that, willingly or unwillingly, they regarded
her as a possible member of their clan.

"I shall just be myself. I shall not *try* to make a good impression," thought Anne loftily. But she was wondering what dress
she would better wear Saturday afternoon, and if the new style
of high hair-dressing would suit her better than the old; and
the walking party was rather spoiled for her. By night she had

decided that she would wear her brown chiffon on Saturday, but would do her hair low.

Friday afternoon none of the girls had classes at Redmond. Stella took the opportunity to write a paper for the Philomathic Society, and was sitting at the table in the corner of the living room with an untidy litter of notes and manuscript on the floor around her. Stella always vowed she never could write anything unless she threw each sheet down as she completed it. Anne, in her flannel blouse and serge skirt, with her hair rather blown from her windy walk home, was sitting squarely in the middle of the floor, teasing the Sarah-cat with a wish-bone. Joseph and Rusty were both curled up in her lap. A warm plummy odor filled the whole house, for Priscilla was cooking in the kitchen. Presently she came in, enshrouded in a huge work-apron, with a smudge of flour on her nose, to show Aunt Jamesina the chocolate cake she had just iced.

At this auspicious moment the knocker sounded. Nobody paid any attention to it save Phil, who sprang up and opened it, expecting a boy with the hat she had bought that morning. On the doorstep stood Mrs. Gardner and her daughters.

Anne scrambled to her feet somehow, emptying two indignant cats out of her lap as she did so, and mechanically shifting her wish-bone from her right hand to her left. Priscilla, who would have had to cross the room to reach the kitchen door, lost her head, wildly plunged the chocolate cake under a cushion on the ingle-nook sofa, and dashed up-stairs. Stella began feverishly gathering up her manuscript. Only Aunt Jamesina and Phil remained normal. Thanks to them, everybody was soon sitting at ease, even Anne. Priscilla came down, apronless and smudgeless, Stella reduced her corner to decency, and Phil saved the situation by a stream of ready small talk.

Mrs. Gardner was tall and thin and handsome, exquisitely gowned, cordial with a cordiality that seemed a trifle forced. Aline Gardner was a younger edition of her mother, lacking the cordiality. She endeavored to be nice, but succeeded only in being haughty and patronizing. Dorothy Gardner was slim and jolly and rather tomboyish. Anne knew she was Roy's favorite sister and warmed to her. She would have looked very much like Roy if she had had dreamy dark eyes instead of roguish hazel ones. Thanks to her and Phil, the call really went off very well, except for a slight sense of strain in the atmosphere and two rather untoward incidents. Rusty and Joseph, left to themselves, began a game of chase, and sprang madly into Mrs. Gardner's silken lap and out of it in their wild career. Mrs. Gardner lifted her lorgnette and gazed after their flying forms as if she had never seen cats before, and Anne, choking back slightly nervous laughter, apologized as best she could.

"You are fond of cats?" said Mrs. Gardner, with a slight intonation of tolerant wonder.

Anne, despite her affection for Rusty, was *not* especially fond of cats, but Mrs. Gardner's tone annoyed her. Inconsequently she remembered that Mrs. John Blythe was so fond of cats that she kept as many as her husband would allow.

"They *are* adorable animals, aren't they?" she said wickedly.

"I have never liked cats," said Mrs. Gardner remotely.

"I love them," said Dorothy. "They are so nice and selfish. Dogs are *too* good and unselfish. They make me feel uncomfortable. But cats are gloriously human."

"You have two delightful old china dogs there. May I look at them closely?" said Aline, crossing the room towards the fireplace and thereby becoming the unconscious cause of the other accident. Picking up Magog, she sat down on the cushion under which was secreted Priscilla's chocolate cake. Priscilla and Anne exchanged agonized glances but could do nothing. The stately Aline continued to sit on the cushion and discuss china dogs until the time of departure.

Dorothy lingered behind a moment to squeeze Anne's hand and whisper impulsively.

"I *know* you and I are going to be chums. Oh, Roy has told me all about you. I'm the only one of the family he tells things to, poor boy—nobody *could* confide in mamma and Aline, you know. What glorious times you girls must have here! Won't you let me come often and have a share in them?"

"Come as often as you like," Anne responded heartily, thankful that one of Roy's sisters was likable. She would never like Aline, so much was certain; and Aline would never like her, though Mrs. Gardner might be won. Altogether, Anne sighed with relief when the ordeal was over.

> "'Of all sad words of tongue or pen
> The saddest are it might have been,'"

quoted Priscilla tragically, lifting the cushion. "This cake is now what you might call a flat failure. And the cushion is likewise ruined. Never tell me that Friday isn't unlucky."

"People who send word they are coming on Saturday shouldn't come on Friday," said Aunt Jamesina.

"I fancy it was Roy's mistake," said Phil. "That boy isn't really responsible for what he says when he talks to Anne. Where *is* Anne?"

Anne had gone upstairs. She felt oddly like crying. But she made herself laugh instead. Rusty and Joseph had been *too* awful! And Dorothy *was* a dear.

37
FULL-FLEDGED B.A.'S

"I wish I were dead, or that it were tomorrow night," groaned Phil.

"If you live long enough both wishes will come true," said Anne calmly.

"It's easy for you to be serene. You're at home in Philosophy. I'm not—and when I think of that horrible paper tomorrow I quail. If I should fail in it what would Jo say?"

"You won't fail. How did you get on in Greek today?"

"I don't know. Perhaps it was a good paper and perhaps it was bad enough to make Homer turn over in his grave. I've studied and mulled over notebooks until I'm incapable of forming an opinion of anything. How thankful little Phil will be when all this examinating is over."

"Examinating? I never heard such a word."

"Well, haven't I as good a right to make a word as any one else?" demanded Phil.

"Words aren't made—they grow," said Anne.

"Never mind—I begin faintly to discern clear water ahead where no examination breakers loom. Girls, do you—can you realize that our Redmond life is almost over?"

"I can't," said Anne, sorrowfully. "it seems just yesterday that Pris and I were alone in that crowd of Freshmen at Redmond. And now we are Seniors in our final examinations."

"'Potent, wise, and reverend Seniors,'" quoted Phil. "Do you suppose we really are any wiser than when we came to Redmond?"

"You don't act as if you were by times," said Aunt Jamesina severely.

"Oh, Aunt Jimsie, haven't we been pretty good girls, take us by and large, these three winters you've mothered us?" pleaded Phil.

"You've been four of the dearest, sweetest, goodest girls that ever went together through college," averred Aunt Jamesina, who never spoiled a compliment by misplaced economy. "But I mistrust you haven't any too much sense yet. It's not to be expected, of course. Experience teaches sense. You can't learn it in a college course. You've been to college four years and I never was, but I know heaps more than you do, young ladies."

> "'There are lots of things that never go by rule,
> There's a powerful pile o' knowledge
> That you never get at college,
> There are heaps of things you never learn at school,'"

quoted Stella.

"Have you learned anything at Redmond except dead languages and geometry and such trash?" queried Aunt Jamesina.

"Oh, yes. I think we have, Aunty," protested Anne.

"We've learned the truth of what Professor Woodleigh told us last Philomathic," said Phil. "He said, 'Humor is the spiciest condiment in the feast of existence. Laugh at your mistakes but learn from them, joke over your troubles but gather strength from them, make a jest of your difficulties but overcome them.' Isn't that worth learning, Aunt Jimsie?"

"Yes, it is, dearie. When you've learned to laugh at the things that should be laughed at, and *not* to laugh at those that shouldn't, you've got wisdom and understanding."

"What have you got out of your Redmond course, Anne?" murmured Priscilla aside.

"I think," said Anne slowly, "that I really have learned to look upon each little hindrance as a jest and each great one as the fore-shadowing of victory. Summing up, I think that is what Redmond has given me."

"I shall have to fall back on another Professor Woodleigh quo-tation to express what it has done for me," said Priscilla. "You remember that he said in his address, 'There is so much in the world for us all if we only have the eyes to see it, and the heart to love it, and the hand to gather it to ourselves—so much in men and women, so much in art and literature, so much everywhere in which to delight, and for which to be thankful.' I think Red-mond has taught me that in some measure, Anne."

"Judging from what you all say," remarked Aunt Jamesina, "the sum and substance is that you can learn—if you've got nat-ural gumption enough—in four years at college what it would take about twenty years of living to teach you. Well, that justifies higher education in my opinion. It's a matter I was always dubi-ous about before."

"But what about people who haven't natural gumption, Aunt Jimsie?"

"People who haven't natural gumption *never* learn," retorted Aunt Jamesina, "neither in college or life. If they live to be a hun-dred they really don't know anything more than when they were born. It's their misfortune not their fault, poor souls. But those of us who have some gumption should duly thank the Lord for it."

"Will you please define what gumption is, Aunt Jimsie?" asked Phil.

"No, I won't, young woman. Any one who has gumption knows what it is, and any one who hasn't can never know what it is. So there is no need of defining it."

The busy days flew by and examinations were over. Anne took High Honors in English. Priscilla took Honors in Classics, and Phil in Mathematics. Stella obtained a good all-round showing. Then came Convocation.

"This is what I would once have called an epoch in my life," said Anne, as she took Roy's violets out of their box and gazed at them thoughtfully. She meant to carry them, of course, but her eyes wandered to another box on her table. It was filled with lilies-of-the-valley, as fresh and fragrant as those which bloomed in the Green Gables yard when June came to Avonlea. Gilbert Blythe's card lay beside it.

Anne wondered why Gilbert should have sent her flowers for Convocation. She had seen very little of him during the past winter. He had come to Patty's Place only one Friday evening since the Christmas holidays, and they rarely met elsewhere. She knew he was studying very hard, aiming at High Honors and the Cooper Prize, and he took little part in the social doings of Redmond. Anne's own winter had been quite gay socially. She had seen a good deal of the Gardners; she and Dorothy were very intimate; college circles expected the announcement of her engagement to Roy any day. Anne expected it herself. Yet just before she left Patty's Place for Convocation she flung Roy's violets aside and put Gilbert's lilies-of-the-valley in their place. She could not have told why she did it. Somehow, old Avonlea days and dreams and friendships seemed very close to her in this attainment of her long-cherished ambitions. She and Gilbert had once pictured out merrily the day on which they should be capped and gowned graduates in Arts. The wonderful day had come and Roy's violets

had no place in it. Only her old friend's flowers seemed to belong to this fruition of old-blossoming hopes which he had
once shared.

For years this day had beckoned and allured to her; but when
it came the one single, keen, abiding memory it left with her was
not that of the breathless moment when the stately president of
Redmond gave her cap and diploma and hailed her B.A.; it was
not of the flash in Gilbert's eyes when he saw her lilies, nor the
puzzled pained glance Roy gave her as he passed her on the
platform. It was not of Aline Gardner's condescending congratulations, or Dorothy's ardent, impulsive good wishes. It was of one
strange, unaccountable pang that spoiled this long-expected
day for her and left in it a certain faint but enduring flavor of
bitterness.

The Arts graduates gave a graduation dance that night. When
Anne dressed for it she tossed aside the pearl beads she usually
wore and took from her trunk the small box that had come to
Green Gables on Christmas day. In it was a thread-like gold chain
with a tiny pink enamel heart as a pendant. On the accompany-
ing card was written, "With all good wishes from your old chum,
Gilbert." Anne, laughing over the memory the enamel heart con-
jured up of the fatal day when Gilbert had called her "Carrots"
and vainly tried to make his peace with a pink candy heart, had
written him a nice little note of thanks. But she had never worn
the trinket. Tonight she fastened it about her white throat with a
dreamy smile.

She and Phil walked to Redmond together. Anne walked in
silence; Phil chattered of many things. Suddenly she said,

"I heard today that Gilbert Blythe's engagement to Christine
Stuart was to be announced as soon as Convocation was over.
Did you hear anything of it?"

"No," said Anne.

"I think it's true," said Phil lightly.

Anne did not speak. In the darkness she felt her face burning.
She slipped her hand inside her collar and caught at the gold

chain. One energetic twist and it gave way. Anne thrust the broken trinket into her pocket. Her hands were trembling and her eyes were smarting.

But she was the gayest of all the gay revellers that night, and told Gilbert unregretfully that her card was full when he came to ask her for a dance. Afterwards, when she sat with the girls before the dying embers at Patty's Place, removing the spring chilliness from their satin skins, none chatted more blithely than she of the day's events.

"Moody Spurgeon MacPherson called here tonight after you left," said Aunt Jamesina, who had sat up to keep the fire on. "He didn't know about the graduation dance. That boy ought to sleep with a rubber band around his head to train his ears not to stick out. I had a beau once who did that and it improved him immensely. It was I who suggested it to him and he took my advice, but he never forgave me for it."

"Moody Spurgeon is a very serious young man," yawned Priscilla. "He is concerned with graver matters than his ears. He is going to be a minister, you know."

"Well, I suppose the Lord doesn't regard the ears of a man," said Aunt Jamesina gravely, dropping all further criticism of Moody Spurgeon. Aunt Jamesina had a proper respect for the cloth even in the case of an unfledged parson.

38
FALSE DAWN

"Just imagine—this night week I'll be in Avonlea—delightful thought!" said Anne, bending over the box in which she was packing Mrs. Rachel Lynde's quilts. "But just imagine—this night week I'll be gone forever from Patty's Place—horrible thought!"

"I wonder if the ghost of all our laughter will echo through the maiden dreams of Miss Patty and Miss Maria," speculated Phil.

Miss Patty and Miss Maria were coming home, after having trotted over most of the habitable globe.

"We'll be back the second week in May," wrote Miss Patty. "I expect Patty's Place will seem rather small after the Hall of the Kings in Karnak, but I never did like big places to live in. And I'll be glad enough to be home again. When you start travelling late in life you're apt to do too much of it because you know you haven't much time left, and it's a thing that grows on you. I'm afraid Maria will never be contented again."

"I shall leave here my fancies and dreams to bless the next comer," said Anne, looking around the blue room wistfully—her pretty blue room where she had spent three such happy years. She had knelt at its window to pray and had bent from it to watch the sunset behind the pines. She had heard the autumn raindrops beating against it and had welcomed the spring robins at its sill. She wondered if old dreams could haunt rooms—if, when one left forever the room where she had joyed and suffered and laughed and wept, something of her, intangible and invisible, yet none the less real, did not remain behind like a voiceful memory.

"I think," said Phil, "that a room where one dreams and grieves and rejoices and *lives* becomes inseparably connected with those processes and acquires a personality of its own. I am sure if I came into this room fifty years from now it would say 'Anne, Anne' to me. What nice times we've had here, honey! What chats and jokes and good chummy jamborees! Oh, dear me! I'm to marry Jo in June and I know I will be rapturously happy. But just now I feel as if I wanted this lovely Redmond life to go on forever."

"I'm unreasonable enough just now to wish that, too," admitted Anne. "No matter what deeper joys may come to us later on we'll never again have just the same delightful, irresponsible existence we've had here. It's over forever, Phil."

"What are you going to do with Rusty?" asked Phil, as that privileged pussy padded into the room.

"*I* am going to take him home with me and Joseph and the Sarah-cat," announced Aunt Jamesina, following Rusty. "It would be a shame to separate those cats now that they have learned to live together. It's a hard lesson for cats and humans to learn."

"I'm sorry to part with Rusty," said Anne regretfully, "but it would be no use to take him to Green Gables. Marilla detests cats, and Davy would tease his life out. Besides, I don't suppose I'll be home very long. I've been offered the principalship of the Summerside High School."

"Are you going to accept it?" asked Phil.

"I—I haven't decided yet," answered Anne, with a confused flush.

Phil nodded understandingly. Naturally Anne's plans could not be settled until Roy had spoken. He would soon—there was no doubt of that. And there was no doubt that Anne would say "yes" when he said "Will you, please?" Anne herself regarded the state of affairs with a seldom-ruffled complacency. She was deeply in love with Roy. True, it was not just what she had imagined love to be. But was anything in life, Anne asked herself wearily, like one's imagination of it? It was the old diamond disillusion of childhood repeated—the same disappointment she had felt when she had first seen the chill sparkle instead of the purple splendor she had anticipated. "That's not my idea of a diamond," she had said. But Roy was a dear fellow and they would be very happy together, even if some indefinable zest was missing out of life. When Roy came down that evening and asked Anne to walk in the park every one at Patty's Place knew what he had come to say; and every one knew, or thought they knew, what Anne's answer would be.

"Anne is a very fortunate girl," said Aunt Jamesina.

"I suppose so," said Stella, shrugging her shoulders. "Roy is a nice fellow and all that. But there's really nothing in him."

"That sounds very like a jealous remark, Stella Maynard," said Aunt Jamesina rebukingly.

"It does—but I am not jealous," said Stella calmly. "I love

Anne and I like Roy. Everybody says she is making a brilliant match, and even Mrs. Gardner thinks her charming now. It all sounds as if it were made in heaven, but I have my doubts. Make the most of that, Aunt Jamesina."

Roy asked Anne to marry him in the little pavilion on the harbor shore where they had talked on the rainy day of their first meeting. Anne thought it very romantic that he should have chosen that spot. And his proposal was as beautifully worded as if he had copied it, as one of Ruby Gillis' lovers had done, out of a Deportment of Courtship and Marriage. The whole effect was quite flawless. And it was also sincere. There was no doubt that Roy meant what he said. There was no false note to jar the symphony. Anne felt that she ought to be thrilling from head to foot. But she wasn't; she was horribly cool. When Roy paused for his answer she opened her lips to say her fateful yes.

And then—she found herself trembling as if she were reeling back from a precipice. To her came one of those moments when we realize, as by a blinding flash of illumination, more than all our previous years have taught us. She pulled her hand from Roy's.

"Oh, I can't marry you—I can't—I can't," she cried, wildly.

Roy turned pale—and also looked rather foolish. He had—small blame to him—felt very sure.

"What do you mean?" he stammered.

"I mean that I can't marry you," repeated Anne desperately. "I thought I could—but I can't."

"Why can't you?" Roy asked more calmly.

"Because—I don't care enough for you."

A crimson streak came into Roy's face.

"So you've just been amusing yourself these two years?" he said slowly.

"No, no, I haven't," gasped poor Anne. Oh, how could she explain? She *couldn't* explain. There are some things that cannot be explained. "I did think I cared—truly I did—but I know now I don't."

"You have ruined my life," said Roy bitterly.

"Forgive me," pleaded Anne miserably, with hot cheeks and stinging eyes.

Roy turned away and stood for a few minutes looking out seaward. When he came back to Anne, he was very pale again.

"You can give me no hope?" he said.

Anne shook her head mutely.

"Then—good-bye," said Roy. "I can't understand it—I can't believe you are not the woman I've believed you to be. But reproaches are idle between us. You are the only woman I can ever love. I thank you for your friendship, at least. Good-bye, Anne."

"Good-bye," faltered Anne. When Roy had gone she sat for a long time in the pavilion, watching a white mist creeping subtly and remorselessly landward up the harbor. It was her hour of humiliation and self-contempt and shame. Their waves went over her. And yet, underneath it all, was a queer sense of recovered freedom.

She slipped into Patty's Place in the dusk and escaped to her room. But Phil was there on the window seat.

"Wait," said Anne, flushing to anticipate the scene. "Wait till you hear what I have to say. Phil, Roy asked me to marry him—and I refused."

"You—you *refused* him?" said Phil blankly.

"Yes."

"Anne Shirley, are you in your senses?"

"I think so," said Anne wearily. "Oh, Phil, don't scold me. You don't understand."

"I certainly don't understand. You've encouraged Roy Gardner in every way for two years—and now you tell me you've refused him. Then you've just been flirting scandalously with him. Anne, I couldn't have believed it of *you*."

"I *wasn't* flirting with him—I honestly thought I cared up to the last minute—and then—well, I just knew I *never* could marry him."

"I suppose," said Phil cruelly, "that you intended to marry him for his money, and then your better self rose up and prevented you."

"I *didn't*. I never thought about his money. Oh, I can't explain it to you any more than I could to him."

"Well, I certainly think you have treated Roy shamefully," said Phil in exasperation. "He's handsome and clever and rich and good. What more do you want?"

"I want some one who *belongs* in my life. He doesn't. I was swept off my feet at first by his good looks and knack of paying romantic compliments; and later on I thought I *must* be in love because he was my dark-eyed ideal."

"I am bad enough for not knowing my own mind, but you are worse," said Phil.

"*I do* know my own mind," protested Anne. "The trouble is, my mind changes and then I have to get acquainted with it all over again."

"Well, I suppose there is no use in saying anything to you."

"There is no need, Phil. I'm in the dust. This has spoiled everything backwards. I can never think of Redmond days without recalling the humiliation of this evening. Roy despises me— and you despise me—and I despise myself."

"You poor darling," said Phil, melting. "Just come here and let me comfort you. I've no right to scold you. I'd have married Alec or Alonzo if I hadn't met Jo. Oh, Anne, things are so mixed-up in real life. They aren't clear-cut and trimmed off, as they are in novels."

"I hope that *no* one will ever again ask me to marry his as long as I live," sobbed poor Anne, devoutly believing that she meant it.

39

DEALS WITH WEDDINGS

Anne felt that life partook of the nature of an anticlimax dur-ing the first few weeks after her return to Green Gables. She missed the merry comradeship of Patty's Place. She had dreamed some brilliant dreams during the past winter and now they lay in the dust around her. In her present mood of self-disgust, she could not immediately begin dreaming again. And she discovered that, while solitude with dreams is glorious, solitude without them has few charms.

She had not seen Roy again after their painful parting in the park pavilion; but Dorothy came to see her before she left Kingsport.

"I'm awfully sorry you won't marry Roy," she said. "I did want you for a sister. But you are quite right. He would bore you to death. I love him, and he is a dear sweet boy, but really he isn't a bit interesting. He looks as if he ought to be, but he isn't."

"This won't spoil *our* friendship, will it, Dorothy?" Anne had asked wistfully.

"No, indeed. You're too good to lose. If I can't have you for a sister I mean to keep you as a chum anyway. And don't fret over Roy. He *is* feeling terribly just now—I have to listen to his outpourings every day—but he'll get over it. He always does."

"Oh—*always*?" said Anne with a slight change of voice. "So he has 'got over it' before?"

"Dear me, yes," said Dorothy frankly. "Twice before. And he raved to me just the same both times. Not that the others actually refused him—they simply announced their engagements to some one else. Of course, when he met you he vowed to me that he had never really loved before—that the previous affairs had been merely boyish fancies. But I don't think you need worry."

Anne decided not to worry. Her feelings were a mixture of relief and resentment. Roy had certainly told her she was the only one he had ever loved. No doubt he believed it. But it was a comfort to feel that she had not, in all likelihood, ruined his life. There were other goddesses, and Roy, according to Dorothy, must needs be worshipping at some shrine. Nevertheless, life was stripped of several more illusions, and Anne began to think drearily that it seemed rather bare.

She came down from the porch gable on the evening of her return with a sorrowful face.

"What has happened to the old Snow Queen, Marilla?"

"Oh, I knew you'd feel bad over that," said Marilla. "I felt bad myself. That tree was there ever since I was a young girl. It blew down in the big gale we had in March. It was rotten at the core."

"I'll miss it so," grieved Anne. "The porch gable doesn't seem the same room without it. I'll never look from its window again without a sense of loss. And, oh, I never came home to Green Gables before that Diana wasn't here to welcome me."

"Diana has something else to think of just now," said Mrs. Lynde significantly.

"Well, tell me all the Avonlea news," said Anne, sitting down on the porch steps, where the evening sunshine fell over her hair in a fine golden rain.

"There isn't much news except what we've wrote you," said Mrs. Lynde. "I suppose you haven't heard that Simon Fletcher broke his leg last week. It's a great thing for his family. They're getting a hundred things done that they've always wanted to do but couldn't as long as he was about, the old crank."

"He came of an aggravating family," remarked Marilla.

"Aggravating? Well, rather! His mother used to get up in prayer-meeting and tell all her children's shortcomings and ask prayers for them. 'Course it made them mad, and worse than ever."

"You haven't told Anne the news about Jane," suggested Marilla.

"Oh, Jane," sniffed Mrs. Lynde. "Well," she conceded grudgingly, "Jane Andrews is home from the West—came last week—and she's going to be married to a Winnipeg millionaire. You may be sure Mrs. Harmon lost no time in telling it far and wide."

"Dear old Jane—I'm so glad," said Anne heartily. "She deserves the good things of life."

"Oh, I ain't saying anything against Jane. She's a nice enough girl. But she isn't in the millionaire class, and you'll find there's not much to recommend that man but his money, that's what. Mrs. Harmon says he's an Englishman who has made money in mines but *I* believe he'll turn out to be a Yankee. He certainly must have money, for he has just showered Jane with jewelry. Her engagement ring is a diamond cluster so big that it looks like a plaster on Jane's fat paw."

Mrs. Lynde could not keep some bitterness out of her tone. Here was Jane Andrews, that plain little plodder, engaged to a millionaire, while Anne, it seemed, was not yet bespoken by any one, rich or poor. And Mrs. Harmon Andrews did brag insufferably.

"What has Gilbert Blythe been doing to himself at college?" asked Marilla. "I saw him when he came home last week, and he is so pale and thin I hardly knew him."

"He studied very hard last winter," said Anne. "You know he took High Honors in Classics and the Cooper Prize. It hasn't been taken for five years! So I think he's rather run down. We're all a little tired."

"Anyway, you're a B.A. and Jane Andrews isn't and never will be," said Mrs. Lynde, with gloomy satisfaction.

A few evenings later Anne went down to see Jane, but the latter was away in Charlottetown—"getting sewing done," Mrs. Harmon informed Anne proudly. "Of course an Avonlea dressmaker wouldn't do for Jane under the circumstances."

"I've heard something very nice about Jane," said Anne.

"Yes, Jane has done pretty well, even if she isn't a B.A.," said Mrs. Harmon, with a slight toss of her head. "Mr. Inglis is worth millions, and they're going to Europe on their wedding tower. When they come back they'll live in a perfect mansion of marble in Winnipeg. Jane has only one trouble—she can cook so well and her husband won't let her cook. He is so rich he hires his cooking done. They're going to keep a cook and two other maids and a coachman and a man-of-all-work. But what about *you*, Anne? I don't hear anything of your being married, after all your college-going."

"Oh," laughed Anne. "I am going to be an old maid. I really can't find any one to suit me."

It was rather wicked of her. She deliberately meant to remind Mrs. Andrews that if she became an old maid it was not because she had not had at least one chance of marriage. But Mrs. Harmon took swift revenge.

"Well, the over-particular girls generally get left, I notice. And what's this I hear about Gilbert Blythe being engaged to a Miss Stuart? Charlie Sloane tells me she is perfectly beautiful. Is it true?"

"I don't know if it is true that he is engaged to Miss Stuart," replied Anne, with Spartan composure, "but it is certainly true that she is very lovely."

"I once thought you and Gilbert would have made a match of it," said Mrs. Harmon. "If you don't take care, Anne, all your beaux will slip through your fingers."

Anne decided not to continue her duel with Mrs. Harmon. You could not fence with an antagonist who met rapier thrust with blow of battle axe.

"Since Jane is away," she said, rising haughtily, "I don't think I can stay longer this morning. I'll come down when she comes home."

"Do," said Mrs. Harmon effusively. "Jane isn't a bit proud. She just means to associate with her old friends the same as ever. She'll be real glad to see you."

Jane's millionaire arrived the last of May and carried her off in a blaze of splendor. Mrs. Lynde was spitefully gratified to find that Mr. Inglis was every day of forty, and short and thin and grayish. Mrs. Lynde did not spare him in her enumeration of his shortcomings, you may be sure.

"It will take all his gold to gild a pill like him, that's what," said Mrs. Rachel solemnly.

"He looks kind and good-hearted," said Anne loyally, "and I'm sure he thinks the world of Jane."

"Humph!" said Mrs. Rachel.

Phil Gordon was married the next week and Anne went over to Bolingbroke to be her bridesmaid. Phil made a dainty fairy of a bride, and the Rev. Jo was so radiant in his happiness that nobody thought him plain.

"We're going for a lovers' saunter through the land of Evangeline," said Phil, "and then we'll settle down on Patterson Street.

Mother thinks it is terrible—she thinks Jo might at least take a church in a decent place. But the wilderness of the Patterson slums will blossom like the rose for me if Jo is there. Oh, Anne, I'm so happy my heart aches with it."

Anne was always glad in the happiness of her friends; but it is sometimes a little lonely to be surrounded everywhere by a happiness that is not your own. And it was just the same when she went back to Avonlea. This time it was Diana who was bathed in the wonderful glory that comes to a woman when her first-born is laid beside her. Anne looked at the white young mother with a certain awe that had never entered into her feelings for Diana before. Could this pale woman with the rapture in her eyes be the little black-curled, rosy-cheeked Diana she had played with in vanished schooldays? It gave her a queer desolate feeling that she herself somehow belonged only in those past years and had no business in the present at all.

"Isn't he perfectly beautiful?" said Diana proudly.

The little fat fellow was absurdly like Fred—just as round, just as red. Anne really could not say conscientiously that she thought him beautiful, but she vowed sincerely that he was sweet and kissable and altogether delightful.

"Before he came I wanted a girl, so that I could call her *Anne*," said Diana. "But now that little Fred is here I wouldn't exchange him for a million girls. He just *couldn't* have been anything but his own precious self."

"'Every little baby is the sweetest and the best,'" quoted Mrs. Allan gaily. "If little Anne *had* come you'd have felt just the same about her."

Mrs. Allan was visiting in Avonlea, for the first time since leaving it. She was as gay and sweet and sympathetic as ever. Her old girl friends had welcomed her back rapturously. The reigning minister's wife was an estimable lady, but she was not exactly a kindred spirit.

"I can hardly wait till he gets old enough to talk," sighed Diana. "I just long to hear him say 'mother.' And oh, I'm determined that his first memory of me shall be a nice one. The first memory I have of my mother is of her slapping me for something I had done. I am sure I deserved it, and mother was always a good mother and I love her dearly. But I do wish my first memory of her was nicer."

"I have just one memory of my mother and it is the sweetest of all my memories," said Mrs. Allan. "I was five years old, and I had been allowed to go to school one day with my two older sisters. When school came out my sisters went home in different groups, each supposing I was with the other. Instead I had run off with a little girl I had played with at recess. We went to her home, which was near the school, and began making mud pies. We were having a glorious time when my older sister arrived, breathless and angry.

"'You naughty girl,' she cried, snatching my reluctant hand and dragging me along with her. 'Come home this minute. Oh, you're going to catch it! Mother is awful cross. She is going to give you a good whipping.'

"I had never been whipped. Dread and terror filled my poor little heart. I have never been so miserable in my life as I was on that walk home. I had not meant to be naughty. Phemy Cameron had asked me to go home with her and I had not known it was wrong to go. And now I was to be whipped for it. When we got home my sister dragged me into the kitchen where mother was sitting by the fire in the twilight. My poor wee legs were trembling so that I could hardly stand. And mother—mother just took me up in her arms, without one word of rebuke or harshness, kissed me and held me close to her heart. 'I was so frightened you were lost, darling,' she said tenderly. I could see the love shining in her eyes as she looked down on me. She never scolded or reproached me for what I had done—only told me I must never go away again without asking permission. She died very soon afterwards. That is the only memory I have of her. Isn't it a beautiful one?"

Anne felt lonelier than ever as she walked home, going by way of the Birch Path and Willowmere. She had not walked that way for many moons. It was a darkly-purple bloomy night. The air was heavy with blossom fragrance—almost too heavy. The cloyed senses recoiled from it as from an overfull cup. The birches of the path had grown from the fairy saplings of old to big trees. Everything had changed. Anne felt that she would be glad when the summer was over and she was away at work again. Perhaps life would not seem so empty then.

> "'I've tried the world—it wears no more
> The coloring of romance it wore,'"

sighed Anne—and was straightway much comforted by the romance in the idea of the world being denuded of romance!

40
A BOOK OF REVELATION

The Irvings came back to Echo Lodge for the summer, and Anne spent a happy three weeks there in July. Miss Lavendar had not changed; Charlotta the Fourth was a very grown-up young lady now, but still adored Anne sincerely.

"When all's said and done, Miss Shirley, ma'am, I haven't seen any one in Boston that's equal to you," she said frankly.

Paul was almost grown-up, too. He was sixteen, his chestnut curls had given place to close-cropped brown locks, and he was more interested in football than fairies. But the bond between him and his old teacher still held. Kindred spirits alone do not change with changing years.

It was a wet, bleak, cruel evening in July when Anne came back to Green Gables. One of the fierce summer storms which sometimes sweep over the gulf was ravaging the sea. As Anne come in the first raindrops dashed against the panes.

"Was that Paul who brought you home?" asked Marilla.

"Why didn't you make him stay all night? It's going to be a wild evening."

"He'll reach Echo Lodge before the rain gets very heavy, I think. Anyway, he wanted to go back tonight. Well, I've had a splendid visit, but I'm glad to see you dear folks again. 'East, west, hame's best.' Davy, have you been growing again lately?"

"I've growed a whole inch since you left," said Davy proudly. "I'm as tall as Milty Boulter now. Ain't I glad. He'll have to stop crowing about being bigger. Say, Anne, did you know that Gilbert Blythe is dying?"

Anne stood quite silent and motionless, looking at Davy. Her face had gone so white that Marilla thought she was going to faint.

"Davy, hold your tongue," said Mrs. Rachel angrily. "Anne, don't look like that—*don't look like that*! We didn't mean to tell you so suddenly."

"Is—it—true?" asked Anne in a voice that was not hers.

"Gilbert is very ill," said Mrs. Lynde gravely. "He took down with typhoid fever just after you left for Echo Lodge. Did you never hear of it?"

"No," said that unknown voice.

"It was a very bad case from the start. The doctor said he'd been terribly run down. They've a trained nurse and everything's been done. *Don't* look like that, Anne. While there's life there's hope."

"Mr. Harrison was here this evening and he said they had no hope of him," reiterated Davy.

Marilla, looking old and worn and tired, got up and marched Davy grimly out of the kitchen.

"Oh, *don't* look so, dear," said Mrs. Rachel, putting her kind old arms about the pallid girl. "I haven't given up hope, indeed I haven't. He's got the Blythe constitution in his favor, that's what."

Anne gently put Mrs. Lynde's arms away from her, walked blindly across the kitchen, through the hall, up the stairs to her old room. At its window she knelt down, staring out unseeingly.

It was very dark. The rain was beating down over the shivering fields. The Haunted Wood was full of the groans of mighty trees wrung in the tempest, and the air throbbed with the thunderous crash of billows on the distant shore. And Gilbert was dying!

There is a book of Revelation in every one's life, as there is in the Bible. Anne read hers that bitter night, as she kept her agonized vigil through the hours of storm and darkness. She loved Gilbert—had always loved him! She knew that now. She knew that she could no more cast him out of her life without agony than she could have cut off her right hand and cast it from her. And the knowledge had come too late—too late even for the bitter solace of being with him at the last. If she had not been so blind—so foolish—she would have had the right to go to him now. But he would never know that she loved him—he would go away from this life thinking that she did not care. Oh, the black years of emptiness stretching before her! She could not live through them—she could not! She cowered down by her window and wished, for the first time in her gay young life, that she could die, too. If Gilbert went away from her, without one word or sign or message, she could not live. Nothing was of any value without him. She belonged to him and he to her. In her hour of supreme agony she had no doubt of that. He did not love Christine Stuart—never had loved Christine Stuart. Oh, what a fool she had been not to realize what the bond was that had held her to Gilbert—to think that the flattered fancy she had felt for Roy Gardner had been love. And now she must pay for her folly as for a crime.

Mrs. Lynde and Marilla crept to her door before they went to bed, shook their heads doubtfully at each other over the silence, and went away. The storm raged all night, but when the dawn came it was spent. Anne saw a fairy fringe of light on the skirts of darkness. Soon the eastern hill-tops had a fire-shot ruby rim. The clouds rolled themselves away into great, soft, white masses on the horizon; the sky gleamed blue and silvery. A hush fell over the world.

Anne rose from her knees and crept downstairs. The freshness of the rain-wind blew against her white face as she went out into the yard, and cooled her dry, burning eyes. A merry rollicking whistle was lilting up the lane. A moment later Pacifique Buote came in sight.

Anne's physical strength suddenly failed her. If she had not clutched at a low willow bough she would have fallen. Pacifique was George Fletcher's hired man, and George Fletcher lived next door to the Blythes. Mrs. Fletcher was Gilbert's aunt. Pacifique would know if—if—Pacifique would know what there was to be known.

Pacifique strode sturdily on along the red lane, whistling. He did not see Anne. She made three futile attempts to call him. He was almost past before she succeeded in making her quivering lips call, "Pacifique!"

Pacifique turned with a grin and a cheerful good-morning.

"Pacifique," said Anne faintly, "did you come from George Fletcher's this morning?"

"Sure," said Pacifique amiably. "I got de word las' night dat my fader, he was seeck. It was so stormy dat I couldn't go den, so I start vair early dis mornin'. I'm goin' troo do woods for short cut."

"Did you hear how Gilbert Blythe was this morning?"

Anne's desperation drove her to the question. Even the worst would be more endurable than this hideous suspense.

"He's better," said Pacifique. "He got de turn las' night. De doctor say he'll be all right now dis soon while. Had close shave, dough! Dat boy, he jus' keel himself at colloge. Well, I mus' hurry. De old man, he'll be in hurry to see me."

Pacifique resumed his walk and his whistle. Anne gazed after him with eyes where joy was driving out the strained anguish of the night. He was a very lank, very ragged, very homely youth. But in her sight he was as beautiful as those who bring good tidings on the mountains. Never, as long as she lived, would Anne see Pacifique's brown, round, black-eyed face without a warm remembrance of the moment when he had given to her the oil of joy for mourning.

Long after Pacifique's gay whistle had faded into the phantom of music and then into silence far up under the maples of Lovers' Lane Anne stood under the willows, tasting the poignant sweetness of life when some great dread has been removed from it. The morning was a cup filled with mist and glamor. In the corner near her was a rich surprise of new-blown, crystal-dewed roses. The trills and trickles of song from the birds in the big tree above her seemed in perfect accord with her mood. A sentence from a very old, very true, very wonderful Book came to her lips,

"Weeping may endure for a night but joy cometh in the morning."

41
LOVE TAKES UP THE GLASS OF TIME

"I've come up to ask you to go for one of our old-time rambles through September woods and 'over hills where spices grow,' this afternoon," said Gilbert, coming suddenly around the porch corner. "Suppose we visit Hester Gray's garden."

Anne, sitting on the stone step with her lap full of a pale, filmy, green stuff, looked up rather blankly.

"Oh, I wish I could," she said slowly, "but I really can't, Gilbert. I'm going to Alice Penhallow's wedding this evening, you know. I've got to do something to this dress, and by the time it's finished I'll have to get ready. I'm so sorry. I'd love to go."

"Well, can you go tomorrow afternoon, then?" asked Gilbert apparently not much disappointed.

"Yes, I think so."

"In that case I shall hie me home at once to do something I should otherwise have to do tomorrow. So Alice Penhallow is to be married tonight. Three weddings for you in one summer,

Anne—Phil's, Alice's and Jane's. I'll never forgive Jane for not inviting me to her wedding."

"You really can't blame her when you think of the tremendous Andrews connection who had to be invited. The house could hardly hold them all. I was only bidden by grace of being Jane's old chum—at least on Jane's part. I think Mrs. Harmon's motive for inviting me was to let me see Jane's surpassing gorgeousness."

"Is it true that she wore so many diamonds that you couldn't tell where the diamonds left off and Jane began?"

Anne laughed.

"She certainly wore a good many. What with all the diamonds and white satin and tulle and lace and roses and orange-blossoms, prim little Jane was almost lost to sight. But she was *very* happy, and so was Mr. Inglis—and so was Mrs. Harmon."

"Is that the dress you're going to wear tonight?" asked Gilbert, looking down at the fluffs and frills.

"Yes. Isn't it pretty? And I shall wear starflowers in my hair. The Haunted Wood is full of them this summer."

Gilbert had a sudden vision of Anne, arrayed in a frilly green gown, with the virginal curves of arms and throat slipping out of it, and white stars shining against the coils of her ruddy hair. The vision made him catch his breath. But he turned lightly away.

"Well, I'll be up tomorrow. Hope you'll have a nice time tonight."

Anne looked after him as he strode away, and sighed. Gilbert was friendly—very friendly—far too friendly. He had come quite often to Green Gables after his recovery, and something of their old comradeship had returned. But Anne no longer found it satisfying. The rose of love made the blossom of friendship pale and scentless by contrast. And Anne had again begun to doubt if Gilbert now felt anything for her but friendship. In the common light of common day her radiant certainty of that rapt morning had faded. She was haunted by a miserable fear that her mistake could never be rectified. It was quite likely that it was Christine whom Gilbert loved after all. Perhaps he was even engaged to her. Anne tried to put all unsettling hopes out of her heart, and reconcile herself to a future where work and ambition must take the place of love. She could do good, if not noble, work as a teacher; and the success her little sketches were beginning to meet with in certain editorial sanctums augured well for her budding literary dreams. But—but—Anne picked up her green dress and sighed again.

When Gilbert came the next afternoon he found Anne waiting for him, fresh as the dawn and fair as a star, after all the gaiety of the preceding night. She wore a green dress—not the one she had worn to the wedding, but an old one which Gilbert had told her at a Redmond reception he liked especially. It was just the shade of green that brought out the rich tints of her hair, and the starry gray of her eyes and the iris-like delicacy of her skin. Gilbert, glancing at her sideways as they walked along a shadowy wood-path, thought she had never looked so lovely. Anne, glancing sideways at Gilbert, now and then, thought how much older he looked since his illness. It was as if he had put boyhood behind him forever.

The day was beautiful and the way was beautiful. Anne was almost sorry when they reached Hester Gray's garden, and sat down on the old bench. But it was beautiful there, too—as beautiful as it had been on the far-away day of the Golden Picnic, when Diana and Jane and Priscilla and she had found it. Then it had been lovely with narcissus and violets; now goldenrod had kindled its fairy torches in the corners and asters dotted it bluely. The call of the brook came up through the woods from the valley of birches with all its old allurement; the mellow air was full of the purr of the sea; beyond were fields rimmed by fences bleached silvery gray in the suns of many summers, and long hills scarfed with the shadows of autumnal clouds; with the blowing of the west wind old dreams returned.

"I think," said Anne softly, "that 'the land where dreams come true' is in the blue haze yonder, over that little valley."

"Have you any unfulfilled dreams, Anne?" asked Gilbert.

Something in his tone—something she had not heard since

that miserable evening in the orchard at Patty's Place—made Anne's heart beat wildly. But she made answer lightly.

"Of course. Everybody has. It wouldn't do for us to have all our dreams fulfilled. We would be as good as dead if we had nothing left to dream about. What a delicious aroma that low-descending sun is extracting from the asters and ferns. I wish we could *see* perfumes as well as smell them. I'm sure they would be very beautiful."

Gilbert was not to be thus side-tracked.

"I have a dream," he said slowly. "I persist in dreaming it, although it has often seemed to me that it could never come true. I dream of a home with a hearth-fire in it, a cat and dog, the foot-steps of friends,—and *you*!"

Anne wanted to speak but she could find no words. Happiness was breaking over her like a wave. It almost frightened her.

"I asked you a question over two years ago, Anne. If I ask it again today will you give me a different answer?"

Still Anne could not speak. But she lifted her eyes, shining with all the love-rapture of countless generations, and looked into his for a moment. He wanted no other answer.

They lingered in the old garden until twilight, sweet as dusk in Eden must have been, crept over it. There was so much to talk over and recall—things said and done and heard and thought and felt and misunderstood.

"I thought you loved Christine Stuart," Anne told him, as reproachfully as if she had not given him every reason to suppose that she loved Roy Gardner.

Gilbert laughed boyishly.

"Christine was engaged to somebody in her home town. I knew it and she knew I knew it. When her brother graduated he told me his sister was coming to Kingsport the next winter to take music, and asked me if I would look after her a bit, as she knew no one and would be very lonely. So I did. And then I liked Christine for her own sake. She is one of the nicest girls I've ever known. I knew college gossip credited us with being in love with each other. I didn't care. Nothing mattered much to me for a time there, after you told me you could never love me, Anne. There was nobody else—there never could be anybody else for me but you. I've loved you ever since that day you broke your slate over my head in school."

"I don't see how you could keep on loving me when I was such a little fool," said Anne.

"Well, I tried to stop," said Gilbert frankly, "not because I thought you what you call yourself, but because I felt sure there was no chance for me after Gardner came on the scene. But I couldn't—and I can't tell you, either, what it's meant to me these two years to believe you were going to marry him, and be told every week by some busybody that your engagement was on the point of being announced. I believed it until one blessed day when I was sitting up after the fever. I got a letter from Phil Gordon—Phil Blake, rather—in which she told me there was really nothing between you and Roy, and advised me to 'try again.' Well, the doctor was amazed at my rapid recovery after that."

Anne laughed—then shivered.

"I can never forget the night I thought you were dying, Gilbert. Oh, I knew—I *knew* then—and I thought it was too late."

"But it wasn't, sweetheart. Oh, Anne, this makes up for everything, doesn't it? Let's resolve to keep this day sacred to perfect beauty all our lives for the gift it has given us."

"It's the birthday of our happiness," said Anne softly. "I've always loved this old garden of Hester Gray's and now it will be dearer than ever."

"But I'll have to ask you to wait a long time, Anne," said Gilbert sadly. "It will be three years before I'll finish my medical course. And even then there will be no diamond sunbursts and marble halls."

Anne laughed.

"I don't want sunbursts and marble halls. I just want *you*. You see I'm quite as shameless as Phil about it. Sunbursts and marble halls may be all very well, but there is more 'scope for imagination' without them. And as for the waiting, that doesn't matter. We'll just be happy, waiting and working for each other—and dreaming. Oh, dreams will be very sweet now."

Gilbert drew her close to him and kissed her. Then they walked home together in the dusk, crowned king and queen in the bridal realm of love, along winding paths fringed with the sweetest flowers that ever bloomed, and over haunted meadows where winds of hope and memory blew.

. . .

LUCY MAUD MONTGOMERY

ANNE'S HOUSE OF DREAMS

1
IN THE GARRET OF GREEN GABLES

"Thanks be, I'm done with geometry, learning or teaching it," said Anne Shirley, a trifle vindictively, as she thumped a somewhat battered volume of Euclid into a big chest of books, banged the lid in triumph, and sat down upon it, looking at Diana Wright across the Green Gables garret, with gray eyes that were like a morning sky.

The garret was a shadowy, suggestive, delightful place, as all garrets should be. Through the open window, by which Anne sat, blew the sweet, scented, sun-warm air of the August afternoon; outside, poplar boughs rustled and tossed in the wind; beyond them were the woods, where Lover's Lane wound its enchanted path, and the old apple orchard which still bore its rosy harvests munificently. And, over all, was a great mountain range of snowy clouds in the blue southern sky. Through the other window was glimpsed a distant, white-capped, blue sea—the beautiful St. Lawrence Gulf, on which floats, like a jewel, Abegweit, whose softer, sweeter Indian name has long been forsaken for the more prosaic one of Prince Edward Island.

Diana Wright, three years older than when we last saw her, had grown somewhat matronly in the intervening time. But her eyes were as black and brilliant, her cheeks as rosy, and her dimples as enchanting, as in the long-ago days when she and Anne

Shirley had vowed eternal friendship in the garden at Orchard Slope. In her arms she held a small, sleeping, black-curled creature, who for two happy years had been known to the world of Avonlea as "Small Anne Cordelia." Avonlea folks knew why Diana had called her Anne, of course, but Avonlea folks were puzzled by the Cordelia. There had never been a Cordelia in the Wright or Barry connections. Mrs. Harmon Andrews said she supposed Diana had found the name in some trashy novel, and wondered that Fred hadn't more sense than to allow it. But Diana and Anne smiled at each other. They knew how Small Anne Cordelia had come by her name.

"You always hated geometry," said Diana with a retrospective smile. "I should think you'd be real glad to be through with teaching, anyhow."

"Oh, I've always liked teaching, apart from geometry. These past three years in Summerside have been very pleasant ones. Mrs. Harmon Andrews told me when I came home that I wouldn't likely find married life as much better than teaching as I expected. Evidently Mrs. Harmon is of Hamlet's opinion that it may be better to bear the ills that we have than fly to others that we know not of."

Anne's laugh, as blithe and irresistible as of yore, with an added note of sweetness and maturity, rang through the garret. Marilla in the kitchen below, compounding blue plum preserve, heard it and smiled; then sighed to think how seldom that dear laugh would echo through Green Gables in the years to come. Nothing in her life had ever given Marilla so much happiness as the knowledge that Anne was going to marry Gilbert Blythe; but every joy must bring with it its little shadow of sorrow. During the three Summerside years Anne had been home often for vacations and week-ends; but, after this, a bi-annual visit would be as much as could be hoped for.

"You needn't let what Mrs. Harmon says worry you," said Diana, with the calm assurance of the four-years matron. "Married life has its ups and downs, of course. You mustn't expect that everything will always go smoothly. But I can assure you, Anne, that's a happy life, when you're married to the right man."

Anne smothered a smile. Diana's airs of vast experience always amused her a little.

"I daresay I'll be putting them on too, when I've been married four years," she thought. "Surely my sense of humor will pre-serve me from it, though."

"Is it settled yet where you are going to live?" asked Diana, cuddling Small Anne Cordelia with the inimitable gesture of motherhood which always sent through Anne's heart, filled with sweet, unuttered dreams and hopes, a thrill that was half pure pleasure and half a strange, ethereal pain.

"Yes. That was what I wanted to tell you when I 'phoned to you to come down today. By the way, I can't realize that we really have telephones in Avonlea now. It sounds so preposterously up-to-date and modernish for this darling, leisurely old place."

"We can thank the A.V.I.S. for them," said Diana. "We should never have got the line if they hadn't taken the matter up and car-ried it through. There was enough cold water thrown to discourage any society. But they stuck to it, nevertheless. You did a splendid thing for Avonlea when you founded that society, Anne. What fun we did have at our meetings! Will you ever for-get the blue hall and Judson Parker's scheme for painting medicine advertisements on his fence?"

"I don't know that I'm wholly grateful to the A.V.I.S. in the matter of the telephone," said Anne. "Oh, I know it's most con-venient—even more so than our old device of signalling to each other by flashes of candlelight! And, as Mrs. Rachel says, 'Avon-lea must keep up with the procession, that's what.' But somehow I feel as if I didn't want Avonlea spoiled by what Mr. Harrison, when he wants to be witty, calls 'modern inconveniences.' I should like to have it kept always just as it was in the dear old years. That's foolish—and sentimental—and impossible. So I shall immediately become wise and practical and possible. The telephone, as Mr. Harrison concedes, is 'a buster of a good

thing'—even if you do know that probably half a dozen interested people are listening along the line."

"That's the worst of it," sighed Diana. "It's so annoying to hear
the receivers going down whenever you ring anyone up. They
say Mrs. Harmon Andrews insisted that their 'phone should be
put in their kitchen just so that she could listen whenever it rang
and keep an eye on the dinner at the same time. Today, when you
called me, I distinctly heard that queer clock of the Pyes' striking.
So no doubt Josie or Gertie was listening."

"Oh, so that is why you said, 'You've got a new clock at Green
Gables, haven't you?' I couldn't imagine what you meant. I heard
a vicious click as soon as you had spoken. I suppose it was the
Pye receiver being hung up with profane energy. Well, never
mind the Pyes. As Mrs. Rachel says, 'Pyes they always were and
Pyes they always will be, world without end, amen.' I want to
talk of pleasanter things. It's all settled as to where my new home
shall be."

"Oh, Anne, where? I do hope it's near here."

"No-o-o, that's the drawback. Gilbert is going to settle at Four
Winds Harbor—sixty miles from here."

"Sixty! It might as well be six hundred," sighed Diana. "I
never can get further from home now than Charlottetown."

"You'll have to come to Four Winds. It's the most beautiful
harbor on the Island. There's a little village called Glen St. Mary
at its head, and Dr. David Blythe has been practicing there for
fifty years. He is Gilbert's great-uncle, you know. He is going to
retire, and Gilbert is to take over his practice. Dr. Blythe is going
to keep his house, though, so we shall have to find a habitation
for ourselves. I don't know yet what it is, or where it will be in
reality, but I have a little house o' dreams all furnished in my
imagination—a tiny, delightful castle in Spain."

"Where are you going for your wedding tour?" asked Diana.

"Nowhere. Don't look horrified, Diana dearest. You suggest
Mrs. Harmon Andrews. She, no doubt, will remark condescendingly that people who can't afford wedding 'towers' are real

sensible not to take them; and then she'll remind me that Jane went to Europe for hers. I want to spend *my* honeymoon at Four Winds in my own dear house of dreams."

"And you've decided not to have any bridesmaid?"

"There isn't any one to have. You and Phil and Priscilla and Jane all stole a march on me in the matter of marriage; and Stella is teaching in Vancouver. I have no other 'kindred soul' and I won't have a bridesmaid who isn't."

"But you are going to wear a veil, aren't you?" asked Diana, anxiously.

"Yes, indeedy. I shouldn't feel like a bride without one. I remember telling Matthew, that evening when he brought me to Green Gables, that I never expected to be a bride because I was so homely no one would ever want to marry me—unless some foreign missionary did. I had an idea then that foreign missionaries couldn't afford to be finicky in the matter of looks if they wanted a girl to risk her life among cannibals. You should have seen the foreign missionary Priscilla married. He was as handsome and inscrutable as those day-dreams we once planned to marry ourselves, Diana; he was the best dressed man I ever met, and he raved over Priscilla's 'ethereal, golden beauty.' But of course there are no cannibals in Japan."

"Your wedding dress is a dream, anyhow," sighed Diana rapturously. "You'll look like a perfect queen in it—you're so tall and slender. How *do* you keep so slim, Anne? I'm fatter than ever— I'll soon have no waist at all."

"Stoutness and slimness seem to be matters of predestination," said Anne. "At all events, Mrs. Harmon Andrews can't say to you what she said to me when I came home from Summerside, 'Well, Anne, you're just about as skinny as ever.' It sounds quite romantic to be 'slender,' but 'skinny' has a very different tang."

"Mrs. Harmon has been talking about your trousseau. She admits it's as nice as Jane's, although she says Jane married a millionaire and you are only marrying a 'poor young doctor without a cent to his name.'"

Anne laughed.

"My dresses *are* nice. I love pretty things. I remember the first pretty dress I ever had—the brown gloria Matthew gave me for our school concert. Before that everything I had was so ugly. It seemed to me that I stepped into a new world that night."

"That was the night Gilbert recited 'Bingen on the Rhine,' and looked at you when he said, 'There's another, *not* a sister.' And you were so furious because he put your pink tissue rose in his breast pocket! You didn't much imagine then that you would ever marry him."

"Oh, well, that's another instance of predestination," laughed Anne, as they went down the garret stairs.

2

THE HOUSE OF DREAMS

There was more excitement in the air of Green Gables than there had ever been before in all its history. Even Marilla was so excited that she couldn't help showing it—which was little short of being phenomenal.

"There's never been a wedding in this house," she said, half apologetically, to Mrs. Rachel Lynde. "When I was a child I heard an old minister say that a house was not a real home until it had been consecrated by a birth, a wedding and a death. We've had deaths here—my father and mother died here as well as Matthew; and we've even had a birth here. Long ago, just after we moved into this house, we had a married hired man for a little while, and his wife had a baby here. But there's never been a wedding before. It does seem so strange to think of Anne being married. In a way she just seems to me the little girl Matthew brought home here fourteen years ago. I can't realize that she's grown up. I shall never forget what I felt when I saw Matthew bringing in a *girl*. I wonder what became of the boy we would have got if there hadn't been a mistake. I wonder what *his* fate was."

"Well, it was a fortunate mistake," said Mrs. Rachel Lynde, "though, mind you, there was a time I didn't think so—that evening I came up to see Anne and she treated us to such a scene. Many things have changed since then, that's what."

Mrs. Rachel sighed, and then brisked up again. When weddings were in order Mrs. Rachel was ready to let the dead past bury its dead.

"I'm going to give Anne two of my cotton warp spreads," she resumed. "A tobacco-stripe one and an apple-leaf one. She tells me they're getting to be real fashionable again. Well, fashion or no fashion, I don't believe there's anything prettier for a spare-room bed than a nice apple-leaf spread, that's what. I must see about getting them bleached. I've had them sewed up in cotton bags ever since Thomas died, and no doubt they're an awful color. But there's a month yet, and dew-bleaching will work wonders."

Only a month! Marilla sighed and then said proudly:

"I'm giving Anne that half dozen braided rugs I have in the garret. I never supposed she'd want them—they're so old-fashioned, and nobody seems to want anything but hooked mats now. But she asked me for them—said she'd rather have them than anything else for her floors. They *are* pretty. I made them of the nicest rags, and braided them in stripes. It was such company these last few winters. And I'll make her enough blue plum preserve to stock her jam closet for a year. It seems real strange. Those blue plum trees hadn't even a blossom for three years, and I thought they might as well be cut down. And this last spring they were white, and such a crop of plums I never remember at Green Gables."

"Well, thank goodness that Anne and Gilbert really are going to be married after all. It's what I've always prayed for," said Mrs. Rachel, in the tone of one who is comfortably sure that her prayers have availed much. "It was a great relief to find out that she really didn't mean to take the Kingsport man. He was rich, to be sure, and Gilbert is poor—at least, to begin with; but then he's an Island boy."

"He's Gilbert Blythe," said Marilla contentedly. Marilla would have died the death before she would have put into words the thought that was always in the background of her mind whenever she had looked at Gilbert from his childhood up—the thought that, had it not been for her own wilful pride long, long ago, he might have been *her* son. Marilla felt that, in some strange way, his marriage with Anne would put right that old mistake. Good had come out of the evil of the ancient bitterness.

As for Anne herself, she was so happy that she almost felt frightened. The gods, so says the old superstition, do not like to behold too happy mortals. It is certain, at least, that some human beings do not. Two of that ilk descended upon Anne one violet dusk and proceeded to do what in them lay to prick the rainbow bubble of her satisfaction. If she thought she was getting any particular prize in young Dr. Blythe, or if she imagined that he was still as infatuated with her as he might have been in his salad days, it was surely their duty to put the matter before her in another light. Yet these two worthy ladies were not enemies of Anne; on the contrary, they were really quite fond of her, and would have defended her as their own young had anyone else attacked her. Human nature is not obliged to be consistent.

Mrs. Inglis—*neé* Jane Andrews, to quote from the *Daily Enterprise*—came with her mother and Mrs. Jasper Bell. But in Jane the milk of human kindness had not been curdled by years of matrimonial bickerings. Her lines had fallen in pleasant places. In spite of the fact—as Mrs. Rachel Lynde would say—that she had married a millionaire, her marriage had been happy. Wealth had not spoiled her. She was still the placid, amiable, pink-cheeked Jane of the old quartette, sympathizing with her old chum's happiness and as keenly interested in all the dainty details of Anne's trousseau as if it could rival her own silken and bejewelled splendors. Jane was not brilliant, and had probably never made a remark worth listening to in her life; but she never said anything that would hurt anyone's feelings—which may be a negative talent but is likewise a rare and enviable one.

"So Gilbert didn't go back on you after all," said Mrs. Harmon Andrews, contriving to convey an expression of surprise in her tone. "Well, the Blythes generally keep their word when they've once passed it, no matter what happens. Let me see—you're twenty-five, aren't you, Anne? When I was a girl twenty-five was the first corner. But you look quite young. Red-headed people always do."

"Red hair is very fashionable now," said Anne, trying to smile, but speaking rather coldly. Life had developed in her a sense of humor which helped her over many difficulties; but as yet nothing had availed to steel her against a reference to her hair.

"So it is—so it is," conceded Mrs. Harmon. "There's no telling what queer freaks fashion will take. Well, Anne, your things are very pretty, and very suitable to your position in life, aren't they, Jane? I hope you'll be very happy. You have my best wishes, I'm sure. A long engagement doesn't often turn out well. But, of course, in your case it couldn't be helped."

"Gilbert looks very young for a doctor. I'm afraid people won't have much confidence in him," said Mrs. Jasper Bell gloomily. Then she shut her mouth tightly, as if she had said what she considered it her duty to say and held her conscience clear. She belonged to the type which always has a stringy black feather in its hat and straggling locks of hair on its neck.

Anne's surface pleasure in her pretty bridal things was temporarily shadowed; but the deeps of happiness below could not thus be disturbed; and the little stings of Mesdames Bell and Andrews were forgotten when Gilbert came later, and they wandered down to the birches of the brook, which had been saplings when Anne had come to Green Gables, but were now tall, ivory columns in a fairy palace of twilight and stars. In their shadows Anne and Gilbert talked in lover-fashion of their new home and their new life together.

"I've found a nest for us, Anne."

"Oh, where? Not right in the village, I hope. I wouldn't like that altogether."

"No. There was no house to be had in the village. This is a little white house on the harbor shore, half way between Glen St. Mary and Four Winds Point. It's a little out of the way, but when we get a 'phone in that won't matter so much. The situation is beautiful. It looks to the sunset and has the great blue harbor before it. The sand-dunes aren't very far away—the sea-winds blow over them and the sea spray drenches them."

"But the house itself, Gilbert,—*our* first home? What is it like?"

"Not very large, but large enough for us. There's a splendid living room with a fireplace in it downstairs, and a dining room that looks out on the harbor, and a little room that will do for my office. It is about sixty years old—the oldest house in Four Winds. But it has been kept in pretty good repair, and was all done over about fifteen years ago—shingled, plastered and re-floored. It was well built to begin with. I understand that there was some romantic story connected with its building, but the man I rented it from didn't know it. He said Captain Jim was the only one who could spin that old yarn now."

"Who is Captain Jim?"

"The keeper of the lighthouse on Four Winds Point. You'll love that Four Winds light, Anne. It's a revolving one, and it flashes like a magnificent star through the twilights. We can see it from our living room windows and our front door."

"Who owns the house?"

"Well, it's the property of the Glen St. Mary Presbyterian Church now, and I rented it from the trustees. But it belonged until lately to a very old lady, Miss Elizabeth Russell. She died last spring, and as she had no near relatives she left her property to the Glen St. Mary Church. Her furniture is still in the house, and I bought most of it—for a mere song you might say, because it was all so old-fashioned that the trustees despaired of selling it. Glen St. Mary folks prefer plush brocade and sideboards with mirrors and ornamentations, I fancy. But Miss Russell's furniture is very good and I feel sure you'll like it, Anne."

"So far, good," said Anne, nodding cautious approval. "But, Gilbert, people cannot live by furniture alone. You haven't yet mentioned one very important thing. Are there *trees* about this house?"

"Heaps of them, oh, dryad! There is a big grove of fir trees behind it, two rows of Lombardy poplars down the lane, and a ring of white birches around a very delightful garden. Our front door opens right into the garden, but there is another entrance— a little gate hung between two firs. The hinges are on one trunk and the catch on the other. Their boughs form an arch overhead."

"Oh, I'm so glad! I couldn't live where there were no trees— something vital in me would starve. Well, after that, there's no use asking you if there's a brook anywhere near. *That* would be expecting too much."

"But there *is* a brook—and it actually cuts across one corner of the garden."

"Then," said Anne, with a long sigh of supreme satisfaction, "this house you have found *is* my house of dreams and none other."

3
THE LAND OF DREAMS AMONG

"Have you made up your mind who you're going to have to the wedding, Anne?" asked Mrs. Rachel Lynde, as she hemstitched table napkins industriously. "It's time your invitations were sent, even if they are to be only informal ones."

"I don't mean to have very many," said Anne. "We just want those we love best to see us married. Gilbert's people, and Mr. and Mrs. Allan, and Mr. and Mrs. Harrison."

"There was a time when you'd hardly have numbered Mr. Harrison among your dearest friends," said Marilla drily.

"Well, I wasn't *very* strongly attracted to him at our first meeting," acknowledged Anne, with a laugh over the recollection.

"But Mr. Harrison has improved on acquaintance, and Mrs. Harrison is really a dear. Then, of course, there are Miss Lavendar and Paul."

"Have they decided to come to the Island this summer? I thought they were going to Europe."

"They changed their minds when I wrote them I was going to be married. I had a letter from Paul today. He says he *must* come to my wedding, no matter what happens to Europe."

"That child always idolized you," remarked Mrs. Rachel.

"That 'child' is a young man of nineteen now, Mrs. Lynde."

"How time does fly!" was Mrs. Lynde's brilliant and original response.

"Charlotta the Fourth may come with them. She sent word by Paul that she would come if her husband would let her. I wonder if she still wears those enormous blue bows, and whether her husband calls her Charlotta or Leonora. I should love to have Charlotta at my wedding. Charlotta and I were at a wedding long syne. They expect to be at Echo Lodge next week. Then there are Phil and the Reverend Jo——"

"It sounds awful to hear you speaking of a minister like that, Anne," said Mrs. Rachel severely.

"His wife calls him that."

"She should have more respect for his holy office, then," retorted Mrs. Rachel.

"I've heard you criticize ministers pretty sharply yourself," teased Anne.

"Yes, but I do it reverently," protested Mrs. Lynde. "You never heard me *nickname* a minister."

Anne smothered a smile.

"Well, there are Diana and Fred and little Fred and Small Anne Cordelia—and Jane Andrews. I wish I could have Miss Stacey and Aunt Jamesina and Priscilla and Stella. But Stella is in Vancouver, and Pris is in Japan, and Miss Stacey is married in California, and Aunt Jamesina has gone to India to explore her daughter's mission field, in spite of her horror of snakes.

It's really dreadful—the way people get scattered over the globe."

"The Lord never intended it, that's what," said Mrs. Rachel authoritatively. "In my young days people grew up and married and settled down where they were born, or pretty near it. Thank goodness you've stuck to the Island, Anne. I was afraid Gilbert would insist on rushing off to the ends of the earth when he got through college, and dragging you with him."

"If everybody stayed where he was born places would soon be filled up, Mrs. Lynde."

"Oh, I'm not going to argue with you, Anne. *I* am not a B.A. What time of the day is the ceremony to be?"

"We have decided on noon—high noon, as the society reporters say. That will give us time to catch the evening train to Glen St. Mary."

"And you'll be married in the parlor?"

"No—not unless it rains. We mean to be married in the orchard—with the blue sky over us and the sunshine around us. Do you know when and where I'd like to be married, if I could? It would be at dawn—a June dawn, with a glorious sunrise, and roses blooming in the gardens; and I would slip down and meet Gilbert and we would go together to the heart of the beech woods,—and there, under the green arches that would be like a splendid cathedral, we would be married."

Marilla sniffed scornfully and Mrs. Lynde looked shocked.

"But that would be terrible queer, Anne. Why, it wouldn't really seem legal. And what would Mrs. Harmon Andrews say?"

"Ah, there's the rub," sighed Anne. "There are so many things in life we cannot do because of the fear of what Mrs. Harmon Andrews would say. ''Tis true, 'tis pity, and pity 'tis, 'tis true.' What delightful things we might do were it not for Mrs. Harmon Andrews!"

"By times, Anne, I don't feel quite sure that I understand you altogether," complained Mrs. Lynde.

"Anne was always romantic, you know," said Marilla apologetically.

"Well, married life will most likely cure her of that," Mrs. Rachel responded comfortingly.

Anne laughed and slipped away to Lover's Lane, where Gilbert found her; and neither of them seemed to entertain much fear, or hope, that their married life would cure them of romance.

The Echo Lodge people came over the next week, and Green Gables buzzed with the delight of them. Miss Lavendar had changed so little that the three years since her last Island visit might have been a watch in the night; but Anne gasped with amazement over Paul. Could this splendid six feet of manhood be the little Paul of Avonlea schooldays?

"You really make me feel old, Paul," said Anne. "Why, I have to look up to you!"

"You'll never grow old, Teacher," said Paul. "You are one of the fortunate mortals who have found and drunk from the Fountain of Youth,—you and Mother Lavendar. See here! When you're married I *won't* call you Mrs. Blythe. To me you'll always be 'Teacher'—the teacher of the best lessons I ever learned. I want to show you something."

The "something" was a pocketbook full of poems. Paul had put some of his beautiful fancies into verse, and magazine editors had not been as unappreciative as they are sometimes supposed to be. Anne read Paul's poems with real delight. They were full of charm and promise.

"You'll be famous yet, Paul. I always dreamed of having one famous pupil. He was to be a college president—but a great poet would be even better. Some day I'll be able to boast that I whipped the distinguished Paul Irving. But then I never did whip you, did I, Paul? What an opportunity lost! I think I kept you in at recess, however."

"You may be famous yourself, Teacher. I've seen a good deal of your work these last three years."

"No. I know what I can do. I can write pretty, fanciful little sketches that children love and editors send welcome cheques for. But I can do nothing big. My only chance for earthly immortality is a corner in your Memoirs."

Charlotta the Fourth had discarded the blue bows but her freckles were not noticeably less.

"I never did think I'd come down to marrying a Yankee, Miss Shirley, ma'am," she said. "But you never know what's before you, and it isn't his fault. He was born that way."

"You're a Yankee yourself, Charlotta, since you've married one."

"Miss Shirley, ma'am, I'm *not*! And I wouldn't be if I was to marry a dozen Yankees! Tom's kind of nice. And besides, I thought I'd better not be too hard to please, for I mightn't get another chance. Tom don't drink and he don't growl because he has to work between meals, and when all's said and done I'm satisfied, Miss Shirley, ma'am."

"Does he call you Leonora?" asked Anne.

"Goodness, no, Miss Shirley, ma'am. I wouldn't know who he meant if he did. Of course, when we got married he had to say, 'I take thee, Leonora,' and I declare to you, Miss Shirley, ma'am, I've had the most dreadful feeling ever since that it wasn't me he was talking to and I haven't been rightly married at all. And so you're going to be married yourself, Miss Shirley, ma'am? I always thought I'd like to marry a doctor. It would be so handy when the children had measles and croup. Tom is only a bricklayer, but he's real good-tempered. When I said to him, says I, 'Tom, can I go to Miss Shirley's wedding? I mean to go anyhow, but I'd like to have your consent,' he just says, 'Suit yourself, Charlotta, and you'll suit me.' That's a real pleasant kind of husband to have, Miss Shirley, ma'am."

Philippa and her Reverend Jo arrived at Green Gables the day before the wedding. Anne and Phil had a rapturous meeting which presently simmered down to a cozy, confidential chat over all that had been and was about to be.

"Queen Anne, you're as queenly as ever. I've got fearfully thin since the babies came. I'm not half so good-looking; but I think

Jo likes it. There's not such a contrast between us, you see. And oh, it's perfectly magnificent that you're going to marry Gilbert. Roy Gardner wouldn't have done at all, at all. I can see that now, though I was horribly disappointed at the time. You know, Anne, you did treat Roy very badly."

"He has recovered, I understand," smiled Anne.

"Oh, yes. He is married and his wife is a sweet little thing and they're perfectly happy. Everything works together for good. Jo and the Bible say that, and they are pretty good authorities."

"Are Alec and Alonzo married yet?"

"Alec is, but Alonzo isn't. How those dear old days at Patty's Place come back when I'm talking to you, Anne! What fun we had!"

"Have you been to Patty's Place lately?"

"Oh, yes, I go often. Miss Patty and Miss Maria still sit by the fireplace and knit. And that reminds me—we've brought you a wedding gift from them, Anne. Guess what it is."

"I never could. How did they know I was going to be married?"

"Oh, I told them. I was there last week. And they were so interested. Two days ago Miss Patty wrote me a note asking me to call; and then she asked if I would take her gift to you. What would you wish most from Patty's Place, Anne?"

"You can't mean that Miss Patty has sent me her china dogs?"

"Go up head. They're in my trunk this very moment. And I've a letter for you. Wait a moment and I'll get it."

"Dear Miss Shirley," Miss Patty had written, "Maria and I were very much interested in hearing of your approaching nuptials. We send you our best wishes. Maria and I have never married, but we have no objection to other people doing so. We are sending you the china dogs. I intended to leave them to you in my will, because you seemed to have a sincere affection for them. But Maria and I expect to live a good while yet (D.V.), so I have decided to give you the dogs while you are young. You will not have forgotten that Gog looks to the right and Magog to the left."

"Just fancy those lovely old dogs sitting by the fireplace in my house of dreams," said Anne rapturously. "I never expected anything so delightful."

That evening Green Gables hummed with preparations for the following day; but in the twilight Anne slipped away. She had a little pilgrimage to make on this last day of her girlhood and she must make it alone. She went to Matthew's grave, in the little poplar-shaded Avonlea graveyard, and there kept a silent tryst with old memories and immortal loves.

"How glad Matthew would be tomorrow if he were here," she whispered. "But I believe he does know and is glad of it—somewhere else. I've read somewhere that 'our dead are never dead until we have forgotten them.' Matthew will never be dead to me, for I can never forget him."

She left on his grave the flowers she had brought and walked slowly down the long hill. It was a gracious evening, full of delectable lights and shadows. In the west was a sky of mackerel clouds—crimson and amber-tinted, with long strips of apple-green sky between. Beyond was the glimmering radiance of a sunset sea, and the ceaseless voice of many waters came up from the tawny shore. All around her, lying in the fine, beautiful country silence, were the hills and fields and woods she had known and loved so long.

"History repeats itself," said Gilbert, joining her as she passed the Blythe gate. "Do you remember our first walk down this hill, Anne—our first walk together anywhere, for that matter?"

"I was coming home in the twilight from Matthew's grave—and you came out of the gate; and I swallowed the pride of years and spoke to you."

"And all heaven opened before me," supplemented Gilbert. "From that moment I looked forward to tomorrow. When I left you at your gate that night and walked home I was the happiest boy in the world. Anne had forgiven me."

"I think you had the most to forgive. I was an ungrateful little wretch—and after you had really saved my life that day on the pond, too. How I loathed that load of obligation at first! I don't deserve the happiness that has come to me."

Gilbert laughed and clasped tighter the girlish hand that wore his ring. Anne's engagement ring was a circlet of pearls. She had refused to wear a diamond.

"I've never really liked diamonds since I found out they weren't the lovely purple I had dreamed. They will always suggest my old disappointment."

"But pearls are for tears, the old legend says," Gilbert had objected.

"I'm not afraid of that. And tears can be happy as well as sad. My very happiest moments have been when I had tears in my eyes—when Marilla told me I might stay at Green Gables—when Matthew gave me the first pretty dress I ever had—when I heard that you were going to recover from the fever. So give me pearls for our troth ring, Gilbert, and I'll willingly accept the sorrow of life with its joy."

But tonight our lovers thought only of joy and never of sorrow. For the morrow was their wedding day, and their house of dreams awaited them on the misty, purple shore of Four Winds Harbor.

4

THE FIRST BRIDE OF GREEN GABLES

Anne wakened on the morning of her wedding day to find the sunshine winking in at the window of the little porch gable and a September breeze frolicking with her curtains.

"I'm so glad the sun will shine on me," she thought happily.

She recalled the first morning she had wakened in that little porch room, when the sunshine had crept in on her through the blossom-drift of the old Snow Queen. That had not been a happy wakening, for it brought with it the bitter disappointment of the preceding night. But since then the little room had been endeared and consecrated by years of happy childhood dreams and maiden visions. To it she had come back joyfully after all her absences; at its window she had knelt through that night of bitter agony when she believed Gilbert dying, and by it she had sat in speechless happiness the night of her betrothal. Many vigils of joy and some of sorrow had been kept there; and today she must leave it forever. Henceforth it would be hers no more; fifteen-year-old Dora was to inherit it when she had gone. Nor did Anne wish it otherwise; the little room was sacred to youth and girlhood—to the past that was to close today before the chapter of wifehood opened.

Green Gables was a busy and joyous house that forenoon. Diana arrived early, with little Fred and Small Anne Cordelia, to lend a hand. Davy and Dora, the Green Gables twins, whisked the babies off to the garden.

"Don't let Small Anne Cordelia spoil her clothes," warned Diana anxiously.

"You needn't be afraid to trust her with Dora," said Marilla. "That child is more sensible and careful than most of the mothers I've known. She's really a wonder in some ways. Not much like that other harum-scarum I brought up."

Marilla smiled across her chicken salad at Anne. It might even be suspected that she liked the harum-scarum best after all.

"Those twins are real nice children," said Mrs. Rachel, when she was sure they were out of earshot. "Dora is so womanly and helpful, and Davy is developing into a very smart boy. He isn't the holy terror for mischief he used to be."

"I never was so distracted in my life as I was the first six months he was here," acknowledged Marilla. "After that I suppose I got used to him. He's taken a great notion to farming lately, and wants me to let him try running the farm next year. I may, for Mr. Barry doesn't think he'll want to rent it much longer, and some new arrangement will have to be made."

"Well, you certainly have a lovely day for your wedding, Anne," said Diana, as she slipped a voluminous apron over her silken array. "You couldn't have had a finer one if you'd ordered it from Eaton's."

"Indeed, there's too much money going out of this Island to that same Eaton's," said Mrs. Lynde indignantly. She had strong views on the subject of octopus-like department stores, and never lost an opportunity of airing them. "And as for those catalogues of theirs, they're the Avonlea girls' Bible now, that's what. They pore over them on Sundays instead of studying the Holy Scriptures."

"Well, they're splendid to amuse children with," said Diana. "Fred and Small Anne look at the pictures by the hour."

"I amused ten children without the aid of Eaton's catalogue," said Mrs. Rachel severely.

"Come, you two, don't quarrel over Eaton's catalogue," said Anne gaily. "This is my day of days, you know. I'm so happy I want every one else to be happy, too."

"I'm sure I hope your happiness will last, child," sighed Mrs. Rachel. She did hope it truly, and believed it, but she was afraid it was in the nature of a challenge to Providence to flaunt your happiness too openly. Anne, for her own good, must be toned down a trifle.

But it was a happy and beautiful bride who came down the old, homespun-carpeted stairs that September noon—the first bride of Green Gables, slender and shining-eyed, in the mist of her maiden veil, with her arms full of roses. Gilbert, waiting for her in the hall below, looked up at her with adoring eyes. She was his at last, this evasive, long-sought Anne, won after years of patient waiting. It was to him she was coming in the sweet surrender of the bride. Was he worthy of her? Could he make her as happy as he hoped? If he failed her—if he could not measure up to her standard of manhood—then, as she held out her hand, their eyes met and all doubt was swept away in a glad certainty. They belonged to each other; and, no matter what life might hold for them, it could never alter that. Their happiness was in each other's keeping and both were unafraid.

They were married in the sunshine of the old orchard, circled by the loving and kindly faces of long-familiar friends. Mr. Allan married them, and the Reverend Jo made what Mrs. Rachel Lynde afterwards pronounced to be the "most beautiful wedding prayer" she had ever heard. Birds do not often sing in September, but one sang sweetly from some hidden bough while Gilbert and Anne repeated their deathless vows. Anne heard it and thrilled to it; Gilbert heard it, and wondered only that all the birds in the world had not burst into jubilant song; Paul heard it and later wrote a lyric about it which was one of the most admired in his first volume of verse; Charlotta the Fourth heard it and was blissfully sure it meant good luck for her adored Miss Shirley. The bird sang until the ceremony was ended and then it wound up with one mad little, glad little trill. Never had the old gray-green house among its enfolding orchards known a blither, merrier afternoon. All the old jests and quips that must have done duty at weddings since Eden were served up, and seemed as new and brilliant and mirth-provoking as if they had never been uttered before. Laughter and joy had their way; and when Anne and Gilbert left to catch the Carmody train, with Paul as driver, the twins were ready with rice and old shoes, in the throwing of which Charlotta the Fourth and Mr. Harrison bore a valiant part. Marilla stood at the gate and watched the carriage out of sight down the long lane with its banks of goldenrod. Anne turned at its end to wave her last good-bye. She was gone—Green Gables was her home no more; Marilla's face looked very gray and old as she turned to the house which Anne had filled for fourteen years, and even in her absence, with light and life.

But Diana and her small fry, the Echo Lodge people and the Allans, had stayed to help the two old ladies over the loneliness of the first evening; and they contrived to have a quietly pleasant little supper time, sitting long around the table and chatting over all the details of the day. While they were sitting there Anne and Gilbert were alighting from the train at Glen St. Mary.

5
THE HOME COMING

Dr. David Blythe had sent his horse and buggy to meet them, and the urchin who had brought it slipped away with a sympathetic grin, leaving them to the delight of driving alone to their new home through the radiant evening.

Anne never forgot the loveliness of the view that broke upon them when they had driven over the hill behind the village. Her new home could not yet be seen; but before her lay Four Winds Harbor like a great, shining mirror of rose and silver. Far down, she saw its entrance between the bar of sand-dunes on one side and a steep, high, grim, red-sandstone cliff on the other. Beyond the bar the sea, calm and austere, dreamed in the afterlight. The little fishing village, nestled in the cove where the sand-dunes met the harbor shore, looked like a great opal in the haze. The sky over them was like a jewelled cup from which the dusk was pouring; the air was crisp with the compelling tang of the sea, and the whole landscape was infused with the subtleties of a sea evening. A few dim sails drifted along the darkening, fir-clad harbor shores. A bell was ringing from the tower of a little white church on the far side; mellowly and dreamily sweet, the chime floated across the water blent with the moan of the sea. The great revolving light on the cliff at the channel flashed warm and golden against the clear northern sky, a trembling, quivering star of good hope. Far out along the horizon was the crinkled gray ribbon of a passing steamer's smoke.

"Oh, beautiful, beautiful," murmured Anne. "I shall love Four Winds, Gilbert. Where is our house?"

"We can't see it yet—the belt of birch running up from that little cove hides it. It's about two miles from Glen St. Mary, and there's another mile between it and the lighthouse. We won't have many neighbors, Anne. There's only one house near us and I don't know who lives in it. Shall you be lonely when I'm away?"

"Not with that light and that loveliness for company. Who lives in that house, Gilbert?"

"I don't know. It doesn't look—exactly—as if the occupants would be kindred spirits, Anne, does it?"

The house was a large, substantial affair, painted such a vivid green that the landscape seemed quite faded by contrast. There was an orchard behind it, and a nicely kept lawn before it, but, somehow, there was a certain bareness about it. Perhaps its neatness was responsible for this; the whole establishment, house, barns, orchard, garden, lawn and lane, was so starkly neat.

"It doesn't seem probable that anyone with that taste in paint could be *very* kindred," acknowledged Anne, "unless it were an accident—like our blue hall. I feel certain there are no children there, at least. It's even neater than the old Copp place on the Tory road, and I never expected to see anything neater than that."

They had not met anybody on the moist, red road that wound along the harbor shore. But just before they came to the belt of birch which hid their home, Anne saw a girl who was driving a flock of snow-white geese along the crest of a velvety green hill on the right. Great, scattered firs grew along it. Between their trunks one saw glimpses of yellow harvest fields, gleams of golden sand-hills, and bits of blue sea. The girl was tall and wore a dress of pale blue print. She walked with a certain springiness of step and erectness of bearing. She and her geese came out of the gate at the foot of the hill as Anne and Gilbert passed. She stood with her hand on the fastening of the gate, and looked steadily at them, with an expression that hardly attained to interest, but did not descend to curiosity. It seemed to Anne, for a fleeting moment, that there was even a veiled hint of hostility in it. But it was the girl's beauty which made Anne give a little gasp—a beauty so marked that it must have attracted attention anywhere. She was hatless, but heavy braids of burnished hair, the hue of ripe wheat, were twisted about her head like a coronet; her eyes were blue and star-like; her figure, in its plain print gown, was magnificent; and her lips were as crimson as the bunch of blood-red poppies she wore at her belt.

"Gilbert, who is the girl we have just passed?" asked Anne, in a low voice.

"I didn't notice any girl," said Gilbert, who had eyes only for his bride.

"She was standing by that gate—no, don't look back. She is still watching us. I never saw such a beautiful face."

"I don't remember seeing any very handsome girls while I was here. There are some pretty girls up at the Glen, but I hardly think they could be called beautiful."

"This girl is. You can't have seen her, or you would remember her. Nobody could forget her. I never saw such a face except in pictures. And her hair! It made me think of Browning's 'cord of gold' and 'gorgeous snake'!"

"Probably she's some visitor in Four Winds—likely some one from that big summer hotel over the harbor."

"She wore a white apron and she was driving geese."

"She might do that for amusement. Look, Anne—there's our house."

Anne looked and forgot for a time the girl with the splendid, resentful eyes. The first glimpse of her new home was a delight to eye and spirit—it looked so like a big, creamy seashell stranded on the harbor shore. The rows of tall Lombardy poplars down its lane stood out in stately, purple silhouette against the sky. Behind it, sheltering its garden from the too keen breath of sea winds, was a cloudy fir wood, in which the winds might make all kinds of weird and haunting music. Like all woods, it seemed to be holding and enfolding secrets in its recesses,—secrets whose charm is only to be won by entering in and patiently seeking. Outwardly, dark green arms keep them inviolate from curious or indifferent eyes.

The night winds were beginning their wild dances beyond the bar and the fishing hamlet across the harbor was gemmed with lights as Anne and Gilbert drove up the poplar lane. The door of the little house opened, and a warm glow of firelight flickered out into the dusk. Gilbert lifted Anne from the buggy and led her into the garden, through the little gate between the ruddy-tipped firs, up the trim, red path to the sandstone step.

"Welcome home," he whispered, and hand in hand they stepped over the threshold of their house of dreams.

6
CAPTAIN JIM

"Old Doctor Dave" and "Mrs. Doctor Dave" had come down to the little house to greet the bride and groom. Doctor Dave was a big, jolly, white-whiskered old fellow, and Mrs. Doctor was a trim, rosy-cheeked, silver-haired little lady who took Anne at once to her heart, literally and figuratively.

"I'm so glad to see you, dear. You must be real tired. We've got a bite of supper ready, and Captain Jim brought up some trout for you. Captain Jim—where are you? Oh, he's slipped out to see to the horse, I suppose. Come upstairs and take your things off."

Anne looked about her with bright, appreciative eyes as she followed Mrs. Doctor Dave upstairs. She liked the appearance of her new home very much. It seemed to have the atmosphere of Green Gables and the flavor of her old traditions.

"I think I would have found Miss Elizabeth Russell a 'kindred spirit,'" she murmured when she was alone in her room. There were two windows in it; the dormer one looked out on the lower harbor and the sand-bar and the Four Winds light.

> "'A magic casement opening on the foam
> Of perilous seas in fairy lands forlorn,'"

quoted Anne softly. The gable window gave a view of a little harvest-hued valley through which a brook ran. Half a mile up the brook was the only house in sight—an old, rambling, gray one surrounded by huge willows through which its windows peered, like shy, seeking eyes, into the dusk. Anne wondered who lived there; they would be her nearest neighbors and she hoped they would be nice. She suddenly found herself thinking of the beautiful girl with the white geese.

"Gilbert thought she didn't belong here," mused Anne, "but I feel sure she does. There was something about her that made her part of the sea and the sky and the harbor. Four Winds is in her blood."

When Anne went downstairs Gilbert was standing before the fireplace talking to a stranger. Both turned as Anne entered.

"Anne, this is Captain Boyd. Captain Boyd, my wife."

It was the first time Gilbert had said "my wife" to anybody but Anne, and he narrowly escaped bursting with the pride of it. The old captain held out a sinewy hand to Anne; they smiled at each other and were friends from that moment. Kindred spirit flashed recognition to kindred spirit.

"I'm right down pleased to meet you, Mistress Blythe; and I hope you'll be as happy as the first bride was who came here. I can't wish you no better than *that*. But your husband doesn't introduce me jest exactly right. 'Captain Jim' is my week-a-day name and you might as well begin as you're sartain to end up— calling me that. You sartainly are a nice little bride, Mistress Blythe. Looking at you sorter makes me feel that I've jest been married myself."

Amid the laughter that followed Mrs. Doctor Dave urged Captain Jim to stay and have supper with them.

"Thank you kindly. 'Twill be a real treat, Mistress Doctor. I mostly has to eat my meals alone, with the reflection of my ugly old phiz in a looking-glass opposite for company. 'Tisn't often I have a chance to sit down with two such sweet, purty ladies."

Captain Jim's compliments may look very bald on paper, but he paid them with such a gracious, gentle deference of tone and look that the woman upon whom they were bestowed felt that she was being offered a queen's tribute in a kingly fashion.

Captain Jim was a high-souled, simple-minded old man, with

eternal youth in his eyes and heart. He had a tall, rather ungainly figure, somewhat stooped, yet suggestive of great strength and endurance; a clean-shaven face deeply lined and bronzed; a thick mane of iron-gray hair falling quite to his shoulders, and a pair of remarkably blue, deep-set eyes, which sometimes twinkled and sometimes dreamed, and sometimes looked out seaward with a wistful quest in them, as of one seeking something precious and lost. Anne was to learn one day what it was for which Captain Jim looked.

It could not be denied that Captain Jim was a homely man. His spare jaws, rugged mouth, and square brow were not fashioned on the lines of beauty; and he had passed through many hardships and sorrows which had marked his body as well as his soul; but though at first sight Anne thought him plain she never thought anything more about it—the spirit shining through that rugged tenement beautified it so wholly.

They gathered gaily around the supper table. The hearth fire banished the chill of the September evening, but the window of the dining room was open and sea breezes entered at their own sweet will. The view was magnificent, taking in the harbor and the sweep of low, purple hills beyond. The table was heaped with Mrs. Doctor's delicacies but the *pièce de resistance* was undoubtedly the big platter of sea-trout.

"Thought they'd be sorter tasty after travelling," said Captain Jim. "They're fresh as trout can be, Mistress Blythe. Two hours ago they were swimming in the Glen Pond."

"Who is attending to the light tonight, Captain Jim?" asked Doctor Dave.

"Nephew Alec. He understands it as well as I do. Well, now, I'm real glad you asked me to stay to supper. I'm proper hungry—didn't have much of a dinner today."

"I believe you half starve yourself most of the time down at that light," said Mrs. Doctor Dave severely. "You won't take the trouble to get up a decent meal."

"Oh, I do, Mistress Doctor, I do," protested Captain Jim.

"Why, I live like a king gen'rally. Last night I was up to the Glen and took home two pounds of steak. I meant to have a spanking good dinner today."

"And what happened to the steak?" asked Mrs. Doctor Dave. "Did you lose it on the way home?"

"No." Captain Jim looked sheepish. "Just at bedtime a poor, ornery sort of dog came along and asked for a night's lodging. Guess he belonged to some of the fishermen 'long shore. I couldn't turn the poor cur out—he had a sore foot. So I shut him in the porch, with an old bag to lie on, and went to bed. But somehow I couldn't sleep. Come to think it over, I sorter remembered that the dog looked hungry."

"And you got up and gave him that steak—*all* that steak," said Mrs. Doctor Dave, with a kind of triumphant reproof.

"Well, there wasn't anything else *to* give him," said Captain Jim deprecatingly. "Nothing a dog'd care for, that is. I reckon he *was* hungry, for he made about two bites of it. I had a fine sleep the rest of the night but my dinner had to be sorter scanty—potatoes and point, as you might say. The dog, he lit out for home this morning. I reckon *he* weren't a vegetarian."

"The idea of starving yourself for a worthless dog!" sniffed Mrs. Doctor.

"You don't know but he may be worth a lot to somebody," protested Captain Jim. "He didn't *look* of much account, but you can't go by looks in jedging a dog. Like meself, he might be a real beauty inside. The First Mate didn't approve of him, I'll allow. His language was right down forcible. But the First Mate is prejudiced. No use in taking a cat's opinion of a dog. 'Tennyrate, I lost my dinner, so this nice spread in this dee-lightful company is real pleasant. It's a great thing to have good neighbors."

"Who lives in the house among the willows up the brook?" asked Anne.

"Mrs. Dick Moore," said Captain Jim—"and her husband," he added, as if by way of an afterthought.

Anne smiled, and deduced a mental picture of Mrs. Dick

Moore from Captain Jim's way of putting it; evidently a second Mrs. Rachel Lynde.

"You haven't many neighbors, Mistress Blythe," Captain Jim went on. "This side of the harbor is mighty thinly settled. Most of the land belongs to Mr. Howard up yander past the Glen, and he rents it out for pasture. The other side of the harbor, now, is thick with folks—'specially MacAllisters. There's a whole colony of MacAllisters—you can't throw a stone but you hit one. I was talking to old Leon Blacquiere the other day. He's been working on the harbor all summer. 'They're nearly all MacAllisters over thar,' he told me. 'Dare's Neil MacAllister and Sandy MacAllister and William MacAllister and Alec MacAllister and Angus MacAllister—and I believe dare's de Devil MacAllister.'"

"There are nearly as many Elliotts and Crawfords," said Doctor Dave, after the laughter had subsided. "You know, Gilbert, we folk from this side of Four Winds have an old saying—'From the conceit of the Elliotts, the pride of the MacAllisters, and the vainglory of the Crawfords, good Lord deliver us.'"

"There's a plenty of fine people among them, though," said Captain Jim. "I sailed with William Crawford for many a year, and for courage and endurance and truth that man hadn't an equal. They've got brains over on that side of Four Winds. Mebbe that's why this side is sorter inclined to pick on 'em. Strange, ain't it, how folks seem to resent anyone being born a mite cleverer than they be."

Doctor Dave, who had a forty years' feud with the over-harbor people, laughed and subsided.

"Who lives in that brilliant emerald house about half a mile up the road?" asked Gilbert.

Captain Jim smiled delightedly.

"Miss Cornelia Bryant. She'll likely be over to see you soon, seeing you're Presbyterians. If you were Methodists she wouldn't come at all. Cornelia has a holy horror of Methodists."

"She's quite a character," chuckled Doctor Dave. "A most inveterate man-hater!"

"Sour grapes?" queried Gilbert, laughing.

"No, 'tisn't sour grapes," answered Captain Jim seriously. "Cornelia could have had her pick when she was young. Even yet she's only to say the word to see the old widowers jump. She jest seems to have been born with a sort of chronic spite agin men and Methodists. She's got the bitterest tongue and the kindest heart in Four Winds. Wherever there's any trouble, that woman is there, doing everything to help in the tenderest way. She never says a harsh word about another woman, and if she likes to card us poor scalawags of men down I reckon our tough old hides can stand it."

"She always speaks well of you, Captain Jim," said Mrs. Doctor.

"Yes, I'm afraid so. I don't half like it. It makes me feel as if there must be something sorter unnatteral about me."

7
THE SCHOOLMASTER'S BRIDE

"Who was the first bride who came to this house, Captain Jim?" Anne asked, as they sat around the fireplace after supper.

"Was she a part of the story I've heard was connected with this house?" asked Gilbert. "Somebody told me you could tell it, Captain Jim."

"Well, yes, I know it. I reckon I'm the only person living in Four Winds now that can remember the schoolmaster's bride as she was when she come to the Island. She's been dead this thirty year, but she was one of them women you never forget."

"Tell us the story," pleaded Anne. "I want to find out all about the women who have lived in this house before me."

"Well, there's jest been three—Elizabeth Russell, and Mrs. Ned Russell, and the schoolmaster's bride. Elizabeth Russell was a nice, clever little critter, and Mrs. Ned was a nice woman, too. But they weren't ever like the schoolmaster's bride.

"The schoolmaster's name was John Selwyn. He came out from the Old Country to teach school at the Glen when I was a boy of sixteen. He wasn't much like the usual run of derelicts who used to come out to P. E. I. to teach school in them days. Most of them were clever, drunken critters who taught the children the three R's when they were sober, and lambasted them when they wasn't. But John Selwyn was a fine, handsome young fellow. He boarded at my father's, and he and me were cronies, though he was ten years older'n me. We read and walked and talked a heap together. He knew about all the poetry that was ever written, I reckon, and he used to quote it to me along shore in the evenings. Dad thought it an awful waste of time, but he sorter endured it, hoping it'd put me off the notion of going to sea. Well, nothing could do *that*—mother come of a race of sea-going folk and it was born in me. But I loved to hear John read and recite. It's almost sixty years ago, but I could repeat yards of poetry I learned from him. Nearly sixty years!"

Captain Jim was silent for a space, gazing into the glowing fire in a quest of the bygones. Then, with a sigh, he resumed his story.

"I remember one spring evening I met him on the sand-hills. He looked sorter uplifted—jest like you did, Dr. Blythe, when you brought Mistress Blythe in tonight. I thought of him the minute I seen you. And he told me that he had a sweetheart back home and that she was coming out to him. I wasn't more'n half pleased, orney young lump of selfishness that I was; I thought he wouldn't be as much my friend after she came. But I'd enough decency not to let him see it. He told me all about her. Her name was Persis Leigh, and she would have come out with him if it hadn't been for her old uncle. He was sick, and he'd looked after her when her parents died and she wouldn't leave him. And now he was dead and she was coming out to marry John Selwyn. 'Twasn't no easy journey for a woman in them days. There weren't no steamers, you must ricollect."

"'When do you expect her?' says I.

"'She sails on the *Royal William*, the 20th of June,' says he, 'and so she should be here by mid-July. I must set Carpenter Johnson to building me a home for her. Her letter come today. I know before I opened it that it had good news for me. I saw her a few nights ago.'

"I didn't understand him, and then he explained—though I didn't understand *that* much better. He said he had a gift—or a curse. Them was his words, Mistress Blythe—a gift or a curse. He didn't know which it was. He said a great-great-grandmother of his had had it, and they burned her for a witch on account of it. He said queer spells—trances, I think was the name he give 'em— come over him now and again. Are there such things, Doctor?"

"There are people who are certainly subject to trances," answered Gilbert. "The matter is more in the line of psychical research than medical. What were the trances of this John Selwyn like?"

"Like dreams," said the old Doctor skeptically.

"He said he could see things in them," said Captain Jim slowly. "Mind you, I'm telling you jest what *he* said—things that were happening—things that were *going* to happen. He said they were sometimes a comfort to him and sometimes a horror. Four nights before this he'd been in one—went into it while he was sitting looking at the fire. And he saw an old room he knew well in England, and Persis Leigh in it, holding out her hands to him and looking glad and happy. So he knew he was going to hear good news of her."

"A dream—a dream," scoffed the old Doctor.

"Likely—likely," conceded Captain Jim. "That's what *I* said to him at the time. It was a vast more comfortable to think so. I didn't like the idea of him seeing things like that—it was real uncanny.

"'No,' says he, 'I didn't dream it. But we won't talk of this again. You won't be so much my friend if you think much about it.'

"I told him nothing could make me any less his friend. But he jest shook his head and says, says he:

"'Lad, I know. I've lost friends before because of this. I don't blame them. There are times when I feel hardly friendly to myself because of it. Such a power has a bit of divinity in it—whether of a good or an evil divinity who shall say? And we mortals all shrink from too close contact with God or devil.'

"Them was his words. I remember them as if 'twas yesterday, though I didn't know jest what he meant. What do you s'pose he *did* mean, doctor?"

"I doubt if he knew what he meant himself," said Doctor Dave testily.

"I think I understand," whispered Anne. She was listening in her old attitude of clasped lips and shining eyes. Captain Jim treated himself to an admiring smile before he went on with his story.

"Well, purty soon all the Glen and Four Winds people knew the schoolmaster's bride was coming, and they were all glad because they thought so much of him. And everybody took an interest in his new house—*this* house. He picked this site for it, because you could see the harbor and hear the sea from it. He made the garden out there for his bride, but he didn't plant the Lombardies. Mrs. Ned Russell planted *them*. But there's a double row of rose-bushes in the garden that the little girls who went to the Glen school set out there for the schoolmaster's bride. He said they were pink for her cheeks and white for her brow and red for her lips. He'd quoted poetry so much that he sorter got into the habit of talking it, too, I reckon.

"Almost everybody sent him some little present to help out the furnishing of the house. When the Russells came into it they were well-to-do and furnished it real handsome, as you can see; but the first furniture that went into it was plain enough. This little house was rich in love, though. The women sent in quilts and table-cloths and towels, and one man made a chest for her, and another a table and so on. Even blind old Aunt Margaret Boyd wove a little basket for her out of the sweet-scented sand-hill grass. The schoolmaster's wife used it for years to keep her handkerchiefs in.

"Well, at last everything was ready—even to the logs in the big fireplace ready for lighting. 'Twasn't exactly *this* fireplace, though 'twas in the same place. Miss Elizabeth had this put in when she made the house over fifteen years ago. It was a big, old-fashioned fireplace where you could have roasted an ox. Many's the time I've sat here and spun yarns, same's I'm doing tonight."

Again there was a silence, while Captain Jim kept a passing tryst with visitants Anne and Gilbert could not see—the folks who had sat with him around that fireplace in the vanished years, with mirth and bridal joy shining in eyes long since closed forever under churchyard sod or heaving leagues of sea. Here on olden nights children had tossed laughter lightly to and fro. Here on winter evenings friends had gathered. Dance and music and jest had been here. Here youths and maidens had dreamed. For Captain Jim the little house was tenanted with shapes entreating remembrance.

"It was the first of July when the house was finished. The schoolmaster began to count the days then. We used to see him walking along the shore, and we'd say to each other, 'She'll soon be with him now.'

"She was expected the middle of July, but she didn't come then. Nobody felt anxious. Vessels were often delayed for days and mebbe weeks. The *Royal William* was a week overdue—and then two—and then three. And at last we began to be frightened, and it got worse and worse. Fin'lly I couldn't bear to look into John Selwyn's eyes. D'ye know, Mistress Blythe"—Captain Jim lowered his voice—"I used to think that they looked just like what his old great-great-grandmother's must have been when they were burning her to death. He never said much but he taught school like a man in a dream and then hurried to the shore. Many a night he walked there from dark to dawn. People said he was losing his mind. Everybody had given up hope—the *Royal William* was eight weeks overdue. It was the middle of September and the schoolmaster's bride hadn't come—never would come, we thought.

"There was a big storm then that lasted three days, and on the evening after it died away I went to the shore. I found the schoolmaster there, leaning with his arms folded against a big rock, gazing out to sea.

"I spoke to him but he didn't answer. His eyes seemed to be looking at something I couldn't see. His face was set, like a dead man's.

"'John—John,' I called out—jest like that—jest like a frightened child, 'wake up—wake up.'

"That strange, awful look seemed to sorter fade out of his eyes. He turned his head and looked at me. I've never forgot his face—never will forget it till I ships for my last voyage.

"'All is well, lad,' he says. 'I've seen the *Royal William* coming around East Point. She will be here by dawn. Tomorrow night I shall sit with my bride by my own hearth-fire.'

"Do you think he did see it?" demanded Captain Jim abruptly.

"God knows," said Gilbert softly. "Great love and great pain might compass we know not what marvels."

"I am sure he did see it," said Anne earnestly.

"Fol-de-rol," said Doctor Dave, but he spoke with less conviction than usual.

"Because, you know," said Captain Jim solemnly, "the *Royal William* came into Four Winds Harbor at daylight the next morning. Every soul in the Glen and along the shore was at the old wharf to meet her. The schoolmaster had been watching there all night. How we cheered as she sailed up the channel."

Captain Jim's eyes were shining. They were looking at the Four Winds Harbor of sixty years agone, with a battered old ship sailing through the sunrise splendor.

"And Persis Leigh was on board?" asked Anne.

"Yes—her and the captain's wife. They'd had an awful passage—storm after storm—and their provisions give out, too. But there they were at last. When Persis Leigh stepped onto the old wharf John Selwyn took her in his arms—and folks stopped cheering and begun to cry. I cried myself, though 'twas years, mind you, afore I'd admit it. Ain't it funny how ashamed boys are of tears?"

"Was Persis Leigh beautiful?" asked Anne.

"Well, I don't know that you'd call her beautiful exactly—I—don't—know," said Captain Jim slowly. "Somehow, you never got so far along as to wonder if she was handsome or not. It jest didn't matter. There was something so sweet and winsome about her that you had to love her, that was all. But she was pleasant to look at—big, clear, hazel eyes and heaps of glossy brown hair, and an English skin. John and her were married at our house that night at early candle-lighting; everybody from far and near was there to see it and we all brought them down here afterwards. Mistress Selwyn lighted the fire, and we went away and left them sitting here, jest as John had seen in that vision of his. A strange thing—a strange thing! But I've seen a turrible lot of strange things in my time."

Captain Jim shook his head sagely.

"It's a dear story," said Anne, feeling that for once she had got enough romance to satisfy her. "How long did they live here?"

"Fifteen years. I ran off to sea soon after they were married, like the young scalawag I was. But every time I come back from a voyage I'd head for here, even before I went home, and tell Mistress Selwyn all about it. Fifteen happy years! They had a sort of talent for happiness, them two. Some folks are like that, if you've noticed. They *couldn't* be unhappy for long, no matter what happened. They quarrelled once or twice, for they was both high-spirited. But Mistress Selwyn says to me once, says she, laughing in that pretty way of hers, 'I felt dreadful when John and I quarrelled, but underneath it all I was very happy because I had such a nice husband to quarrel with and make it up with.' Then they moved to Charlottetown, and Ned Russell bought this house and brought his bride here. They were a gay young pair, as I remember them. Miss Elizabeth Russell was Alec's sister. She came to live with them a year or so later, and she was a creature of mirth, too. The walls of this house must be sorter *soaked* with laughing and good times. You're the third bride I've seen come here, Mistress Blythe—and the handsomest."

Captain Jim contrived to give his sunflower compliment the delicacy of a violet, and Anne wore it proudly. She was looking her best that night, with the bridal rose on her cheeks and the love-light in her eyes; even gruff old Doctor Dave gave her an approving glance, and told his wife, as they drove home together, that that red-headed wife of the boy's was something of a beauty.

"I must be getting back to the light," announced Captain Jim. "I've enj'yed this evening something tremenjus."

"You must come often to see us," said Anne.

"I wonder if you'd give that invitation if you knew how likely I'll be to accept it," Captain Jim remarked whimsically.

"Which is another way of saying you wonder if I mean it," smiled Anne. "I do, 'cross my heart,' as we used to say at school."

"Then I'll come. You're likely to be pestered with me at any hour. And I'll be proud to have you drop down and visit me now and then, too. Gin'rally I haven't anyone to talk to but the First Mate, bless his sociable heart. He's a mighty good listener, and has forgot more'n any MacAllister of them all ever knew, but he isn't much of a conversationalist. You're young and I'm old, but our souls are about the same age, I reckon. We both belong to the race that knows Joseph, as Cornelia Bryant would say."

"'The race that knows Joseph'?" puzzled Anne.

"Yes. Cornelia divides all the folks in the world into two kinds—the race that knows Joseph and the race that don't. If a person sorter sees eye to eye with you, and has pretty much the same ideas about things, and the same taste in jokes—why, then he belongs to the race that knows Joseph."

"Oh, I understand," exclaimed Anne, light breaking in upon her. "It's what I used to call—and still call in quotation marks—'kindred spirits.'"

"Jest so—jest so," agreed Captain Jim. "We're *it*, whatever it is. When you come in tonight, Mistress Blythe, I says to myself, says

I, 'Yes, she's of the race that knows Joseph.' And mighty glad I was, for if it wasn't so we couldn't have had any real satisfaction in each other's company. The race that knows Joseph is the salt of the airth, I reckon."

The moon had just risen when Anne and Gilbert went to the door with their guests. Four Winds Harbor was beginning to be a thing of dream and glamor and enchantment—a spellbound haven where no tempest might ever ravin. The Lombardies down the lane, tall and sombre as the priestly forms of some mystic band, were tipped with silver.

"Always liked Lombardies," said Captain Jim, waving a long arm at them. "They're the trees of princesses. They're out of fashion now. Folks complain that they die at the top and get ragged-looking. So they do—so they do, if you don't risk your neck every spring climbing up a light ladder to trim them out. I always did it for Miss Elizabeth, so her Lombardies never got out-at-elbows. She was especially fond of them. She liked their dignity and stand-offishness. *They* don't hobnob with every Tom, Dick and Harry. If it's maples for company, Mistress Blythe, it's Lombardies for society."

"What a beautiful night," said Mrs. Doctor Dave, as she climbed into the Doctor's buggy.

"Most nights are beautiful," said Captain Jim. "But I 'low that moonlight over Four Winds makes me sorter wonder what's left for heaven. The moon's a great friend or mine, Mistress Blythe. I've loved her ever since I can remember. When I was a little chap of eight I fell asleep in the garden one evening and wasn't missed. I woke up along in the night and I was most scared to death. What shadows and queer noises there was! I dursn't move. Jest crouched there quaking, poor small mite. Seemed 'sif there weren't anyone in the world but meself and it was mighty big. Then all at once I saw the moon looking down at me through the apple boughs, jest like an old friend. I was comforted right off. Got up and walked to the house as brave as a lion, looking at her. Many's the night I've watched her from the deck of my vessel, on seas far away from here. Why don't you folks tell me to take in the slack of my jaw and go home?"

The laughter of the good-nights died away. Anne and Gilbert walked hand in hand around their garden. The brook that ran across the corner dimpled pellucidly in the shadows of the birches. The poppies along its banks were like shallow cups of moonlight. Flowers that had been planted by the hands of the schoolmaster's bride flung their sweetness on the shadowy air, like the beauty and blessing of sacred yesterdays. Anne paused in the gloom to gather a spray.

"I love to smell flowers in the dark," she said. "You get hold of their soul then. Oh, Gilbert, this little house is all I've dreamed it. And I'm so glad that we are not the first who have kept bridal tryst here!"

8

MISS CORNELIA BRYANT COMES TO CALL

That September was a month of golden mists and purple hazes at Four Winds Harbor—a month of sun-steeped days and of nights that were swimming in moonlight, or pulsating with stars. No storm marred it, no rough wind blew. Anne and Gilbert put their nest in order, rambled on the shores, sailed on the harbor, drove about Four Winds and the Glen, or through the ferny, sequestered roads of the woods around the harbor head; in short, had such a honeymoon as any lovers in the world might have envied them.

"If life were to stop short just now it would still have been richly worth while, just for the sake of these past four weeks, wouldn't it?" said Anne. "I don't suppose we will ever have four such perfect weeks again—but we've *had* them. Everything— wind, weather, folks, house of dreams—has conspired to make our honeymoon delightful. There hasn't even been a rainy day since we came here."

"And we haven't quarrelled once," teased Gilbert.

"Well, 'that's a pleasure all the greater for being deferred,'" quoted Anne. "I'm so glad we decided to spend our honeymoon here. Our memories of it will always belong here, in our house of dreams, instead of being scattered about in strange places."

There was a certain tang of romance and adventure in the atmosphere of their new home which Anne had never found in Avonlea. There, although she had lived in sight of the sea, it had not entered intimately into her life. In Four Winds it surrounded her and called to her constantly. From every window of her new home she saw some varying aspect of it. Its haunting murmur was ever in her ears. Vessels sailed up the harbor every day to the wharf at the Glen, or sailed out again through the sunset, bound for ports that might be half way round the globe. Fishing boats went white-winged down the channel in the mornings, and returned laden in the evenings. Sailors and fisher-folk travelled the red, winding harbor roads, light-hearted and content. There was always a certain sense of things going to happen—of adventures and farings-forth. The ways of Four Winds were less staid and settled and grooved than those of Avonlea; winds of change blew over them; the sea called ever to the dwellers on shore, and even those who might not answer its call felt the thrill and unrest and mystery and possibilities of it.

"I understand now why some men must go to sea," said Anne. "That desire which comes to us all at times—'to sail beyond the bourne of sunset'—must be very imperious when it is born in you. I don't wonder Captain Jim ran away because of it. I never see a ship sailing out of the channel, or a gull soaring over the sand-bar, without wishing I were on board the ship or had wings, not like a dove 'to fly away and be at rest,' but like a gull, to sweep out into the very heart of a storm."

"You'll stay right here with me, Anne-girl," said Gilbert lazily. "I won't have you flying away from me into the hearts of storms."

They were sitting on their red sand-stone doorstep in the late afternoon. Great tranquillities were all about them in land and sea and sky. Silvery gulls were soaring over them. The horizons were laced with long trails of frail, pinkish clouds. The hushed air was threaded with a murmurous refrain of minstrel winds and waves. Pale asters were blowing in the sere and misty meadows between them and the harbor.

"Doctors who have to be up all night waiting on sick folk don't feel very adventurous, I suppose," Anne said indulgently. "If you had had a good sleep last night, Gilbert, you'd be as ready as I am for a flight of imagination."

"I did good work last night, Anne," said Gilbert quietly. "Under God, I saved a life. This is the first time I could ever really claim that. In other cases I may have helped; but, Anne, if I had not stayed at Allonby's last night and fought death hand to hand, that woman would have died before morning. I tried an experiment that was certainly never tried in Four Winds before. I doubt if it was ever tried anywhere before outside of a hospital. It was a new thing in Kingsport hospital last winter. I could never have dared try it here if I had not been absolutely certain that there was no other chance. I risked it—and it succeeded. As a result, a good wife and mother is saved for long years of happiness and usefulness. As I drove home this morning, while the sun was rising over the harbor, I thanked God that I had chosen the profession I did. I had fought a good fight and won—think of it, Anne, *won*, against the Great Destroyer. It's what I dreamed of doing long ago when we talked together of what we wanted to do in life. That dream of mine came true this morning."

"Was that the only one of your dreams that has come true?" asked Anne, who knew perfectly well what the substance of his answer would be, but wanted to hear it again.

"*You* know, Anne-girl," said Gilbert, smiling into her eyes. At that moment there were certainly two perfectly happy people sitting on the doorstep of a little white house on the Four Winds Harbor shore.

Presently Gilbert said, with a change of tone, "Do I or do I not see a full-rigged ship sailing up our lane?"

Anne looked and sprang up.

"That must be either Miss Cornelia Bryant or Mrs. Moore coming to call," she said.

"I'm going into the office, and if it is Miss Cornelia I warn you that I'll eavesdrop," said Gilbert. "From all I've heard regarding Miss Cornelia I conclude that her conversation will not be dull, to say the least."

"It may be Mrs. Moore."

"I don't think Mrs. Moore is built on those lines. I saw her working in her garden the other day, and, though I was too far away to see clearly, I thought she was rather slender. She doesn't seem very socially inclined when she has never called on you yet, although she's your nearest neighbor."

"She can't be like Mrs. Lynde, after all, or curiosity would have brought her," said Anne. "This caller is, I think, Miss Cornelia."

Miss Cornelia it was; moreover, Miss Cornelia had not come to make any brief and fashionable wedding call. She had her work under her arm in a substantial parcel, and when Anne asked her to stay she promptly took off her capacious sun-hat, which had been held on her head, despite irreverent September breezes, by a tight elastic band under her hard little knob of fair hair. No hat pins for Miss Cornelia, an it please ye! Elastic bands had been good enough for her mother and they were good enough for *her*. She had a fresh, round, pink-and-white face, and jolly brown eyes. She did not look in the least like the traditional old maid, and there was something in her expression which won Anne instantly. With her old instinctive quickness to discern kindred spirits she knew she was going to like Miss Cornelia, in spite of uncertain oddities of opinion, and certain oddities of attire.

Nobody but Miss Cornelia would have come to make a call arrayed in a striped blue-and-white apron and a wrapper of chocolate print, with a design of huge, pink roses scattered over it. And nobody but Miss Cornelia could have looked dignified and suitably garbed in it. Had Miss Cornelia been entering a palace to call on a prince's bride, she would have been just as dignified and just as wholly mistress of the situation. She would have trailed her rose-spattered flounce over the marble floors just as unconcernedly, and she would have proceeded just as calmly to disabuse the mind of the princess of any idea that the possession of a mere man, be he prince or peasant, was anything to brag of.

"I've brought my work, Mrs. Blythe, dearie," she remarked, unrolling some dainty material. "I'm in a hurry to get this done, and there isn't any time to lose."

Anne looked in some surprise at the white garment spread over Miss Cornelia's ample lap. It was certainly a baby's dress, and it was most beautifully made, with tiny frills and tucks. Miss Cornelia adjusted her glasses and fell to embroidering with exquisite stitches.

"This is for Mrs. Fred Proctor up at the Glen," she announced. "She's expecting her eighth baby any day now, and not a stitch has she ready for it. The other seven have wore out all she made for the first, and she's never had time or strength or spirit to make any more. The woman is a martyr, Mrs. Blythe, believe me. When she married Fred Proctor I knew how it would turn out. He was one of your wicked, fascinating men. After he got married he left off being fascinating and just kept on being wicked. He drinks and he neglects his family. Isn't that like a man? I don't know how Mrs. Proctor would ever keep her children decently clothed if her neighbors didn't help her out."

As Anne was afterwards to learn, Miss Cornelia was the only neighbor who troubled herself much about the decency of the young Proctors.

"When I heard this eighth baby was coming I decided to make some things for it," Miss Cornelia went on. "This is the last and I want to finish it today."

"It's certainly very pretty," said Anne. "I'll get my sewing and we'll have a little thimble party of two. You are a beautiful sewer, Miss Bryant."

"Yes, I'm the best sewer in these parts," said Miss Cornelia in a matter-of-fact tone. "I ought to be! Lord, I've done more of it than if I'd had a hundred children of my own, believe *me*! I s'pose I'm a fool, to be putting hand embroidery on this dress for an eighth baby. But, Lord, Mrs. Blythe, dearie, it isn't to blame for being the eighth, and I kind of wished it to have one real pretty dress, just as if it *was* wanted. Nobody's wanting the poor mite—so I put some extra fuss on its little things just on that account."

"Any baby might be proud of that dress," said Anne, feeling still more strongly that she was going to like Miss Cornelia.

"I s'pose you've been thinking I was never coming to call on you," resumed Miss Cornelia. "But this is harvest month, you know, and I've been busy—and a lot of extra hands hanging round, eating more'n they work, just like the men. I'd have come yesterday, but I went to Mrs. Roderick MacAllister's funeral. At first I thought my head was aching so badly I couldn't enjoy myself if I did go. But she was a hundred years old, and I'd always promised myself that I'd go to her funeral."

"Was it a successful function?" asked Anne, noticing that the office door was ajar.

"What's that? Oh, yes, it was a tremendous funeral. She had a very large connection. There was over one hundred and twenty carriages in the procession. There was one or two funny things happened. I thought that die I would to see old Joe Bradshaw, who is an infidel and never darkens the door of a church, singing 'Safe in the Arms of Jesus' with great gusto and fervor. He glories in singing—that's why he never misses a funeral. Poor Mrs. Bradshaw didn't look much like singing—all wore out slaving. Old Joe starts out once in a while to buy her a present and brings home some new kind of farm machinery. Isn't that like a man? But what else would you expect of a man who never goes to church, even a Methodist one? I was real thankful to see you and the young Doctor in the Presbyterian church your first Sunday. No doctor for me who isn't a Presbyterian."

"We were in the Methodist church last Sunday evening," said Anne wickedly.

"Oh, I s'pose Dr. Blythe has to go to the Methodist church once in a while or he wouldn't get the Methodist practice."

"We liked the sermon very much," declared Anne boldly. "And I thought the Methodist minister's prayer was one of the most beautiful I ever heard."

"Oh, I've no doubt he can pray. I never heard anyone make more beautiful prayers than old Simon Bentley, who was always drunk, or hoping to be, and the drunker he was the better he prayed."

"The Methodist minister is very fine looking," said Anne, for the benefit of the office door.

"Yes, he's quite ornamental," agreed Miss Cornelia. "Oh, and *very* ladylike. And he thinks that every girl who looks at him falls in love with him—as if a Methodist minister, wandering about like any Jew, was such a prize! If you and the young doctor take *my* advice, you won't have much to do with the Methodists. My motto is—if you *are* a Presbyterian, *be* a Presbyterian."

"Don't you think that Methodists go to heaven as well as Presbyterians?" asked Anne smilelessly.

"That isn't for *us* to decide. It's in higher hands than ours," said Miss Cornelia solemnly. "But I ain't going to associate with them on earth whatever I may have to do in heaven. *This* Methodist minister isn't married. The last one they had was, and his wife was the silliest, flightiest little thing I ever saw. I told her husband once that he should have waited till she was grown up before he married her. He said he wanted to have the training of her. Wasn't that like a man?"

"It's rather hard to decide just when people *are* grown up," laughed Anne.

"That's a true word, dearie. Some are grown up when they're born, and others ain't grown up when they're eighty, believe *me*. That same Mrs. Roderick I was speaking of never grew up. She was as foolish when she was a hundred as when she was ten."

"Perhaps that was why she lived so long," suggested Anne.

"Maybe 'twas. I'd rather live fifty sensible years than a hundred foolish ones."

"But just think what a dull world it would be if everyone was sensible," pleaded Anne.

Miss Cornelia disdained any skirmish of flippant epigram.

"Mrs. Roderick was a Milgrave, and the Milgraves never had much sense. Her nephew, Ebenezer Milgrave, used to be insane for years. He believed he was dead and used to rage at his wife because she wouldn't bury him. I'd a-done it."

Miss Cornelia looked so grimly determined that Anne could almost see her with a spade in her hand.

"Don't you know *any* good husbands, Miss Bryant?"

"Oh, yes, lots of them—over yonder," said Miss Cornelia, waving her hand through the open window towards the little graveyard of the church across the harbor.

"But living—going about in the flesh?" persisted Anne.

"Oh, there's a few, just to show that with God all things are possible," acknowledged Miss Cornelia reluctantly. "I don't deny that an odd man here and there, if he's caught young and trained up proper, and if his mother has spanked him well beforehand, may turn out a decent being. *Your* husband, now, isn't so bad, as men go, from all I hear. I s'pose"—Miss Cornelia looked sharply at Anne over her glasses—"you think there's nobody like him in the world."

"There isn't," said Anne promptly.

"Ah, well, I heard another bride say that once," sighed Miss Cornelia. "Jennie Dean thought when she married that there wasn't anybody like *her* husband in the world. And she was right—there wasn't! And a good thing, too, believe *me*! He led her an awful life—and he was courting his second wife while Jennie was dying. Wasn't that like a man? However, I hope *your* confidence will be better justified, dearie. The young doctor is taking real well. I was afraid at first he mightn't, for folks hereabouts have always thought old Doctor Dave the only doctor in the world. Doctor Dave hadn't much tact, to be sure—he was always talking of ropes in houses where someone had hanged himself. But folks forgot their hurt feelings when they had a pain in their stomachs. If he'd been a minister instead of a doctor they'd never have forgiven him. Soul-ache doesn't worry folks near as much as stomach-ache. Seeing as we're both Presbyterians and no Methodists around, will you tell me your candid opinion of *our* minister?"

"Why—really—I—well," hesitated Anne.

Miss Cornelia nodded.

"Exactly. I agree with you, dearie. We made a mistake when we called *him*. His face just looks like one of those long, narrow stones in the graveyard, doesn't it? 'Sacred to the memory' ought to be written on his forehead. I shall never forget the first sermon he preached after he came. It was on the subject of everyone doing what they were best fitted for—a very good subject, of course; but such illustrations as he used! He said, 'If you had a cow and an apple tree, and if you tied the apple tree in your stable and planted the cow in your orchard, with her legs up, how much milk would you get from the apple tree, or how many apples from the cow?' Did you ever hear the like in your born days, dearie? I was so thankful there were no Methodists there that day—they'd never have been done hooting over it. But what I dislike most in him is his habit of agreeing with everybody, no matter what is said. If you said to him, 'You're a scoundrel,' he'd say, with that smooth smile of his, 'Yes, that's so.' A minister should have more backbone. The long and the short of it is, I consider him a reverend jackass. But, of course, this is just between you and me. When there are Methodists in hearing I praise him to the skies. Some folks think his wife dresses too gay, but *I* say when she has to live with a face like that she needs something to cheer her up. You'll never hear *me* condemning a woman for her dress. I'm only too thankful when her husband isn't too mean and miserly to allow it. Not that I bother much with dress myself. Women just dress to please the men, and I'd never stoop to *that*. I have had a real placid, comfortable life, dearie, and it's just because I never cared a cent what the men thought."

"Why do you hate the men so, Miss Bryant?"

"Lord, dearie, I don't hate them. They aren't worth it. I just sort of despise them. I think I'll like *your* husband if he keeps on as he has begun. But apart from him, about the only men in the world I've much use for are the old doctor and Captain Jim."

"Captain Jim is certainly splendid," agreed Anne cordially.

"Captain Jim is a good man, but he's kind of vexing in one way. You *can't* make him mad. I've tried for twenty years and he just keeps on being placid. It does sort of rile me. And I s'pose the woman he should have married got a man who went into tantrums twice a day."

"Who was she?"

"Oh, I don't know, dearie. I never remember of Captain Jim making up to anybody. He was edging on old as far as my memory goes. He's seventy-six, you know. I never heard any reason for his staying a bachelor, but there must be one, believe *me*. He sailed all his life till five years ago, and there's no corner of the earth he hasn't poked his nose into. He and Elizabeth Russell were great cronies, all their lives, but they never had any notion of sweet-hearting. Elizabeth never married, though she had plenty of chances. She was a great beauty when she was young. The year the Prince of Wales came to the Island she was visiting her uncle in Charlottetown and he was a Government official, and so she got invited to the great ball. She was the prettiest girl there, and the Prince danced with her, and all the other women he didn't dance with were furious about it, because their social standing was higher than hers and they said he shouldn't have passed them over. Elizabeth was always very proud of that dance. Mean folks said that was why she never married—she couldn't put up with an ordinary man after dancing with a prince. But that wasn't so. She told me the reason once—it was because she had such a temper that she was afraid she couldn't live peaceably with any man. She *had* an awful temper—she used to have to go upstairs and bite pieces out of her bureau to keep it down by times. But I told her that wasn't any reason for not marrying if she wanted to. There's no reason why we should let the men have a monopoly of temper, is there, Mrs. Blythe, dearie?"

"I've a bit of temper myself," sighed Anne.

"It's well you have, dearie. You won't be half so likely to be trodden on, believe *me!* My, how that golden glow of yours is blooming! Your garden looks fine. Poor Elizabeth always took such care of it."

"I love it," said Anne. "I'm glad it's so full of old-fashioned flowers. Speaking of gardening, we want to get a man to dig up that little lot beyond the fir grove and set it out with strawberry plants for us. Gilbert is so busy he will never get time for it this fall. Do you know anyone we can get?"

"Well, Henry Hammond up at the Glen goes out doing jobs like that. He'll do, maybe. He's always a heap more interested in his wages than in his work, just like a man, and he's so slow in the uptake that he stands still for five minutes before it dawns on him that he's stopped. His father threw a stump at him when he was small. Nice gentle missile, wasn't it? So like a man! Course, the boy never got over it. But he's the only one I can recommend at all. He painted my house for me last spring. It looks real nice now, don't you think?"

Anne was saved by the clock striking five.

"Lord, is it that late?" exclaimed Miss Cornelia. "How time does slip by when you're enjoying yourself! Well, I must betake myself home."

"No, indeed! You are going to stay and have tea with us," said Anne eagerly.

"Are you asking me because you think you ought to, or because you really want to?" demanded Miss Cornelia.

"Because I really want to."

"Then I'll stay. *You* belong to the race that knows Joseph."

"I know we are going to be friends," said Anne, with the smile that only they of the household of faith ever saw.

"Yes, we are, dearie. Thank goodness, we can choose our friends. We have to take our relatives as they are, and be thankful if there are no penitentiary birds among them. Not that I've many—none nearer than second cousins. I'm a kind of lonely soul, Mrs. Blythe."

There was a wistful note in Miss Cornelia's voice.

"I wish you would call me Anne," exclaimed Anne impulsively. "It would seem more *homey*. Everyone in Four Winds, except my husband, calls me Mrs. Blythe, and it makes me feel like a stranger. Do you know that your name is very near being the one I yearned after when I was a child. I hated 'Anne' and I called myself 'Cordelia' in imagination."

"I like Anne. It was my mother's name. Old-fashioned names are the best and sweetest in my opinion. If you're going to get tea you might send the young doctor to talk to me. He's been lying on the sofa in that office ever since I came, laughing fit to kill over what I've been saying."

"How did you know?" cried Anne, too aghast at this instance of Miss Cornelia's uncanny prescience to make a polite denial.

"I saw him sitting beside you when I came up the lane, and I know men's tricks," retorted Miss Cornelia. "There, I've finished my little dress, dearie, and the eighth baby can come as soon as it pleases."

9

AN EVENING AT FOUR WINDS POINT

It was late September when Anne and Gilbert were able to pay Four Winds light their promised visit. They had often planned to go, but something always occurred to prevent them. Captain Jim had "dropped in" several times at the little house.

"I don't stand on ceremony, Mistress Blythe," he told Anne. "It's a real pleasure to me to come here, and I'm not going to deny myself jest because you haven't got down to see me. There

oughtn't to be no bargaining like that among the race that knows
Joseph. I'll come when I can, and you come when you can, and
so long's we have our pleasant little chat it don't matter a mite
what roof's over us."

Captain Jim took a great fancy to Gog and Magog, who were
presiding over the destinies of the hearth in the little house with
as much dignity and aplomb as they had done at Patty's Place.

"Aren't they the cutest little cusses?" he would say delightedly;
and he bade them greeting and farewell as gravely and invariably
as he did his host and hostess. Captain Jim was not going to
offend household deities by any lack of reverence and ceremony.

"You've made this little house just about perfect," he told
Anne. "It never was so nice before. Mistress Selwyn had your
taste and she did wonders; but folks in those days didn't have the
pretty little curtains and pictures and nicknacks you have. As for
Elizabeth, she lived in the past. You've kinder brought the future
into it, so to speak. I'd be real happy even if we couldn't talk at
all, when I come here—jest to sit and look at you and your
pictures and your flowers would be enough of a treat. It's beautiful—beautiful."

Captain Jim was a passionate worshipper of beauty. Every
lovely thing heard or seen gave him a deep, subtle, inner joy that
irradiated his life. He was quite keenly aware of his own lack of
outward comeliness and lamented it.

"Folks say I'm good," he remarked whimsically upon one
occasion, "but I sometimes wish the Lord had made me only half
as good and put the rest of it into looks. But there, I reckon He
knew what He was about, as a good Captain should. Some of us
have to be homely, or the purty ones—like Mistress Blythe
here—wouldn't show up so well."

One evening Anne and Gilbert finally walked down to the
Four Winds light. The day had begun sombrely in gray cloud and
mist, but it had ended in a pomp of scarlet and gold. Over the
western hills beyond the harbor were amber deeps and crystalline
shallows, with the fire of sunset below. The north was a mackerel

sky of little, fiery golden clouds. The red light flamed on the white sails of a vessel gliding down the channel, bound to a southern port in a land of palms. Beyond her, it smote upon and incarnadined the shining, white, grassless faces of the sand-dunes. To the right, it fell on the old house among the willows up the brook, and gave it for a fleeting space casements more splendid than those of an old cathedral. They glowed out of its quiet and grayness like the throbbing, blood-red thoughts of a vivid soul imprisoned in a dull husk of environment.

"That old house up the brook always seems so lonely," said Anne. "I never see visitors there. Of course, its lane opens on the upper road—but I don't think there's much coming and going. It seems odd we've never met the Moores yet, when they live within fifteen minutes' walk of us. I may have seen them in church, of course, but if so I didn't know them. I'm sorry they are so unsociable, when they are our only near neighbors."

"Evidently they don't belong to the race that knows Joseph," laughed Gilbert. "Have you ever found out who that girl was whom you thought so beautiful?"

"No. Somehow I have never remembered to ask about her. But I've never seen her anywhere, so I suppose she must have been a stranger. Oh, the sun has just vanished—and there's the light."

As the dusk deepened, the great beacon cut swathes of light through it, sweeping in a circle over the fields and the harbor, the sandbar and the gulf.

"I feel as if it might catch me and whisk me leagues out to sea," said Anne, as one drenched them with radiance; and she felt rather relieved when they got so near the Point that they were inside the range of those dazzling, recurrent flashes.

As they turned into the little lane that led across the fields to the Point they met a man coming out of it—a man of such extraordinary appearance that for a moment they both frankly stared. He was a decidedly fine-looking person—tall, broad-shouldered, well-featured, with a Roman nose and frank gray eyes; he was dressed in a prosperous farmer's Sunday best; in so far he might have been any inhabitant of Four Winds or the Glen. But, flowing over his breast nearly to his knees, was a river of crinkly brown beard; and adown his back, beneath his commonplace felt hat, was a corresponding cascade of thick, wavy, brown hair.

"Anne," murmured Gilbert, when they were out of earshot, "you didn't put what Uncle Dave calls 'a little of the Scott Act' in that lemonade you gave me just before we left home, did you?"

"No, I didn't," said Anne, stifling her laughter, lest the retreating enigma should hear her. "Who in the world can he be?"

"I don't know; but if Captain Jim keeps apparitions like that down at this Point I'm going to carry cold iron in my pocket when I come here. He wasn't a sailor, or one might pardon his eccentricity of appearance; he must belong to the over-harbor clans. Uncle Dave says they have several freaks over there."

"Uncle Dave is a little prejudiced, I think. You know all the over-harbor people who come to the Glen Church seem very nice. Oh, Gilbert, isn't this beautiful?"

The Four Winds light was built on a spur of red sand-stone cliff jutting out into the gulf. On one side, across the channel, stretched the silvery sand shore of the bar; on the other, extended a long, curving beach of red cliffs, rising steeply from the pebbled coves. It was a shore that knew the magic and mystery of storm and star. There is a great solitude about such a shore. The woods are never solitary—they are full of whispering, beckoning, friendly life. But the sea is a mighty soul, forever moaning of some great, unshareable sorrow, which shuts it up into itself for all eternity. We can never pierce its infinite mystery—we may only wander, awed and spell-bound, on the outer fringe of it. The woods call to us with a hundred voices, but the sea has one only—a mighty voice that drowns our souls in its majestic music. The woods are human, but the sea is of the company of the archangels.

Anne and Gilbert found Uncle Jim sitting on a bench outside the lighthouse, putting the finishing touches to a wonderful, full-rigged, toy schooner. He rose and welcomed them to his abode with the gentle, unconscious courtesy that became him so well.

"This has been a purty nice day all through, Mistress Blythe, and now, right at the last, it's brought its best. Would you like to sit down here outside a bit, while the light lasts? I've just finished this bit of a plaything for my little grand-nephew, Joe, up at the Glen. After I promised to make it for him I was kinder sorry, for his mother was vexed. She's afraid he'll be wanting to go to sea later on and she doesn't want the notion encouraged in him. But what could I do, Mistress Blythe? I'd *promised* him, and I think it's sorter real dastardly to break a promise you make to a child. Come, sit down. It won't take long to stay an hour."

The wind was off shore, and only broke the sea's surface into long, silvery ripples, and sent sheeny shadows flying out across it, from every point and headland, like transparent wings. The dusk was hanging a curtain of violet gloom over the sand-dunes and the headlands where gulls were huddling. The sky was faintly filmed over with scarfs of silken vapor. Cloud fleets rode at anchor along the horizons. An evening star was watching over the bar.

"Isn't that a view worth looking at?" said Captain Jim, with a loving, proprietary pride. "Nice and far from the market-place, ain't it? No buying and selling and getting gain. You don't have to pay anything—all that sea and sky free—'without money and without price.' There's going to be a moonrise purty soon, too— I'm never tired of finding out what a moonrise can be over them rocks and sea and harbor. There's a surprise in it every time."

They had their moonrise, and watched its marvel and magic in a silence that asked nothing of the world or each other. Then they went up into the tower, and Captain Jim showed and explained the mechanism of the great light. Finally they found themselves in the dining room, where a fire of driftwood was weaving flames of wavering, elusive, sea-born hues in the open fireplace.

"I put this fireplace in myself," remarked Captain Jim. "The

Government don't give lighthouse keepers such luxuries. Look at the colors that wood makes. If you'd like some driftwood for your fire, Mistress Blythe, I'll bring you up a load some day. Sit down. I'm going to make you a cup of tea."

Captain Jim placed a chair for Anne, having first removed therefrom a huge, orange-colored cat and a newspaper.

"Get down, Matey. The sofa is your place. I must put this paper away safe till I can find time to finish the story in it. It's called A Mad Love. 'Tisn't my favorite brand of fiction, but I'm reading it jest to see how long she can spin it out. It's at the sixty-second chapter now, and the wedding ain't any nearer than when it begun, far's I can see. When little Joe comes I have to read him pirate yarns. Ain't it strange how innocent little creatures like children like the blood-thirstiest stories?"

"Like my lad Davy at home," said Anne. "He wants tales that reek with gore."

Captain Jim's tea proved to be nectar. He was pleased as a child with Anne's compliments, but he affected a fine indifference.

"The secret is I don't skimp the cream," he remarked airily. Captain Jim had never heard of Oliver Wendell Holmes, but he evidently agreed with that writer's dictum that "big heart never liked little cream pot."

"We met an odd-looking personage coming out of your lane," said Gilbert as they sipped. "Who was he?"

Captain Jim grinned.

"That's Marshall Elliott—a mighty fine man with jest one streak of foolishness in him. I s'pose you wondered what his object was in turning himself into a sort of dime museum freak."

"Is he a modern Nazarite or a Hebrew prophet left over from olden times?" asked Anne.

"Neither of them. It's politics that's at the bottom of his freak. All those Elliotts and Crawfords and MacAllisters are dyed-in-the-wool politicians. They're born Grit or Tory, as the case may be, and they live Grit or Tory, and they die Grit or Tory; and what they're going to do in heaven, where there's probably no politics,

is more than I can fathom. This Marshall Elliott was born a Grit.
I'm a Grit myself in moderation, but there's no moderation about
Marshall. Fifteen years ago there was a specially bitter general
election. Marshall fought for his party tooth and nail. He was
dead sure the Liberals would win—so sure that he got up at a
public meeting and vowed that he wouldn't shave his face or cut
his hair until the Grits were in power. Well, they didn't go in—
and they've never got in yet—and you saw the result tonight for
yourselves. Marshall stuck to his word."

"What does his wife think of it?" asked Anne.

"He's a bachelor. But if he had a wife I reckon she couldn't
make him break that vow. That family of Elliotts has always
been more stubborn than natteral. Marshall's brother Alexander
had a dog he set great store by, and when it died the man actilly
wanted to have it buried in the graveyard, 'along with the other
Christians,' he said. Course, he wasn't allowed to; so he buried it
just outside the graveyard fence, and never darkened the church
door again. But Sundays he'd drive his family to church and sit by
that dog's grave and read his Bible all the time service was going
on. They say when he was dying he asked his wife to bury him
beside that dog; she was a meek little soul but she fired up at *that*.
She said *she* wasn't going to be buried beside no dog, and if he'd
rather have his last resting place beside the dog than beside her,
jest to say so. Alexander Elliott was a stubborn mule, but he was
fond of his wife, so he give in and said, 'Well, durn it, bury me
where you please. But when Gabriel's trump blows I expect my
dog to rise with the rest of us, for he had as much soul as any
durned Elliott or Crawford or MacAllister that ever strutted.'
Them was *his* parting words. As for Marshall, we're all used to
him, but he must strike strangers as right down peculiar-looking.
I've known him ever since he was ten—he's about fifty now—and
I like him. Him and me was out cod-fishing today. That's about
all I'm good for now—catching trout and cod occasional. But
'tweren't always so—not by no manner of means. I used to do
other things, as you'd admit if you saw my life-book."

Anne was just going to ask what his life-book was when the First Mate created a diversion by springing upon Captain Jim's knee. He was a gorgeous beastie, with a face as round as a full moon, vivid green eyes, and immense, white, double paws. Captain Jim stroked his velvet back gently.

"I never fancied cats much till I found the First Mate," he remarked, to the accompaniment of the Mate's tremendous purrs. "I saved his life, and when you've saved a creature's life you're bound to love it. It's next thing to giving life. There's some turrible thoughtless people in the world, Mistress Blythe. Some of them city folks who have summer homes over the harbor are so thoughtless that they're cruel. It's the worst kind of cruelty—the thoughtless kind. You can't cope with it. They keep cats there in the summer, and feed and pet 'em, and doll 'em up with ribbons and collars. And then in the fall they go off and leave 'em to starve or freeze. It makes my blood boil, Mistress Blythe. One day last winter I found a poor old mother cat dead on the shore, lying against the skin-and-bone bodies of her three little kittens. She'd died trying to shelter 'em. She had her poor stiff paws around 'em. Master, I cried. Then I swore. Then I carried them poor little kittens home and fed 'em up and found good homes for 'em. I knew the woman who left the cat and when she come back this summer I jest went over the harbor and told her my opinion of her. It was rank meddling, but I do love meddling in a good cause."

"How did she take it?" asked Gilbert.

"Cried and said she 'didn't think.' I says to her, says I, 'Do you s'pose that'll be held for a good excuse in the day of Jedgment, when you'll have to account for that poor old mother's life? The Lord'll ask you what He give you your brains for if it wasn't to think, I reckon.' I don't fancy she'll leave cats to starve another time."

"Was the First Mate one of the forsaken?" asked Anne, making advances to him which were responded to graciously, if condescendingly.

"Yes. I found *him* one bitter cold day in winter, caught in the branches of a tree by his durn-fool ribbon collar. He was almost starving. If you could have seen his eyes, Mistress Blythe! He was nothing but a kitten, and he'd got his living somehow since he'd been left until he got hung up. When I loosed him he give my hand a pitiful swipe with his little red tongue. He wasn't the able seaman you see now. He was meek as Moses. That was nine years ago. His life has been long in the land for a cat. He's a good old pal, the First Mate is."

"I should have expected you to have a dog," said Gilbert.

Captain Jim shook his head.

"I had a dog once. I thought so much of him that when he died I couldn't bear the thought of getting another in his place. He was a *friend*—you understand, Mistress Blythe? Matey's only a pal. I'm fond of Matey—all the fonder on account of the spice of devilment that's in him—like there is in all cats. But I *loved* my dog. I always had a sneaking sympathy for Alexander Elliott about *his* dog. There isn't any devil in a good dog. That's why they're more lovable than cats, I reckon. But I'm darned if they're as interesting. Here I am, talking too much. Why don't you check me? When I do get a chance to talk to anyone I run on turrible. If you've done your tea I've a few little things you might like to look at—picked 'em up in the queer corners I used to be poking my nose into."

Captain Jim's "few little things" turned out to be a most interesting collection of curios, hideous, quaint and beautiful. And almost every one had some striking story attached to it.

Anne never forgot the delight with which she listened to those old tales that moonlit evening by that enchanted driftwood fire, while the silver sea called to them through the open window and sobbed against the rocks below them.

Captain Jim never said a boastful word, but it was impossible to help seeing what a hero the man had been—brave, true, resourceful, unselfish. He sat there in his little room and made those things live again for his hearers. By a lift of the eyebrow, a twist of the lip, a gesture, a word, he painted a whole scene or character so that they saw it as it was.

Some of Captain Jim's adventures had such a marvellous edge that Anne and Gilbert secretly wondered if he were not drawing a rather long bow at their credulous expense. But in this, as they found later, they did him injustice. His tales were all literally true. Captain Jim had the gift of the born story-teller, whereby "unhappy, far-off things" can be brought vividly before the hearer in all their pristine poignancy.

Anne and Gilbert laughed and shivered over his tales, and once Anne found herself crying. Captain Jim surveyed her tears with pleasure shining from his face.

"I like to see folks cry that way," he remarked. "It's a compliment. But I can't do justice to the things I've seen or helped to do. I've 'em all jotted down in my life-book, but I haven't got the knack of writing them out properly. If I could hit on jest the right words and string 'em together proper on paper I could make a great book. It would beat *A Mad Love* holler, and I believe Joe'd like it as well as the pirate yarns. Yes, I've had some adventures in my time; and, do you know, Mistress Blythe, I still lust after 'em. Yes, old and useless as I be, there's an awful longing sweeps over me at times to sail out—out—out there—forever and ever."

"Like Ulysses, you would

'Sail beyond the sunset and the paths
Of all the western stars until you die,'"

said Anne dreamily.

"Ulysses? I've read of him. Yes, that's jest how I feel—jest how all us old sailors feel, I reckon. I'll die on land after all, I s'pose. Well, what is to be will be. There was old William Ford at the Glen who never went on the water in his life, 'cause he was afraid of being drowned. A fortune-teller had predicted he would be. And one day he fainted and fell with his face in the barn trough and was drowned. Must you go? Well, come soon and come often. The doctor is to do the talking next time. He knows a heap of things I want to find out. I'm sorter lonesome here by times. It's been worse since Elizabeth Russell died. Her and me was such cronies."

Captain Jim spoke with the pathos of the aged, who see their old friends slipping from them one by one—friends whose place can never be quite filled by those of a younger generation, even of the race that knows Joseph. Anne and Gilbert promised to come soon and often.

"He's a rare old fellow, isn't he?" said Gilbert, as they walked home.

"Somehow, I can't reconcile his simple, kindly personality with the wild, adventurous life he has lived," mused Anne.

"You wouldn't find it so hard if you had seen him the other day down at the fishing village. One of the men of Peter Gautier's boat made a nasty remark about some girl along the shore. Captain Jim fairly scorched the wretched fellow with the lightning of his eyes. He seemed a man transformed. He didn't say much— but the way he said it! You'd have thought it would strip the flesh from the fellow's bones. I understand that Captain Jim will never allow a word against any woman to be said in his presence."

"I wonder why he never married," said Anne. "He should have sons with their ships at sea now, and grandchildren climbing over him to hear his stories—he's that kind of a man. Instead, he has nothing but a magnificent cat."

But Anne was mistaken. Captain Jim had more than that. He had a memory.

10
LESLIE MOORE

"I'm going for a walk to the outside shore tonight," Anne told Gog and Magog one October evening. There was no one else to tell, for Gilbert had gone over the harbor. Anne had her little domain in the speckless order one would expect of anyone brought up by Marilla Cuthbert, and felt that she could gad shoreward with a clear conscience. Many and delightful had been her shore rambles, sometimes with Gilbert, sometimes with Captain Jim, sometimes alone with her own thoughts and new, poignantly-sweet dreams that were beginning to span life with their rainbows. She loved the gentle, misty harbor shore and the silvery, wind-haunted sand shore, but best of all she loved the rock shore, with its cliffs and caves and piles of surf-worn boulders, and its coves where the pebbles glittered under the pools; and it was to this shore she hied herself tonight.

There had been an autumn storm of wind and rain, lasting for three days. Thunderous had been the crash of billows on the rocks, wild the white spray and spume that blew over the bar, troubled and misty and tempest-torn the erstwhile blue peace of Four Winds Harbor. Now it was over, and the shore lay cleanwashed after the storm; not a wind stirred, but there was still a fine surf on, dashing on sand and rock in a splendid white turmoil—the only restless thing in the great, pervading stillness and peace.

"Oh, this is a moment worth living through weeks of storm and stress for," Anne exclaimed, delightedly sending her far gaze across the tossing waters from the top of the cliff where she stood. Presently she scrambled down the steep path to the little cove below, where she seemed shut in with rocks and sea and sky.

"I'm going to dance and sing," she said. "There's no one here to see me—the sea-gulls won't carry tales of the matter. I may be as crazy as I like."

She caught up her skirt and pirouetted along the hard strip of sand just out of reach of the waves that almost lapped her feet with their spent foam. Whirling round and round, laughing like a child, she reached the little headland that ran out to the east of the cove; then she stopped suddenly, blushing crimson; she was not alone; there had been a witness to her dance and laughter.

The girl of the golden hair and sea-blue eyes was sitting on a boulder of the headland, half-hidden by a jutting rock. She was looking straight at Anne with a strange expression—part wonder, part sympathy, part—could it be?—envy. She was bareheaded, and her splendid hair, more than ever like Browning's "gorgeous snake," was bound about her head with a crimson ribbon. She wore a dress of some dark material, very plainly made; but swathed about her waist, outlining its fine curves, was a vivid girdle of red silk. Her hands, clasped over her knee, were brown and somewhat work-hardened; but the skin of her throat and cheeks was as white as cream. A flying gleam of sunset broke through a low-lying western cloud and fell across her hair. For a moment she seemed the spirit of the sea personified—all its mystery, all its passion, all its elusive charm.

"You—you must think me crazy," stammered Anne, trying to recover her self-possession. To be seen by this stately girl in such an abandon of childishness—she, Mrs. Dr. Blythe, with all the dignity of the matron to keep up—it was too bad!

"No," said the girl, "I don't."

She said nothing more; her voice was expressionless; her manner slightly repellent; but there was something in her eyes—eager yet shy, defiant yet pleading—which turned Anne from her purpose of walking away. Instead, she sat down on the boulder beside the girl.

"Let's introduce ourselves," she said, with the smile that had never yet failed to win confidence and friendliness. "I am Mrs. Blythe—and I live in that little white house up the harbor shore."

"Yes, I know," said the girl. "I am Leslie Moore—Mrs. Dick Moore," she added stiffly.

Anne was silent for a moment from sheer amazement. It had not occurred to her that this girl was married—there seemed nothing of the wife about her. And that she should be the neighbor whom Anne had pictured as a commonplace Four Winds housewife! Anne could not quickly adjust her mental focus to this astonishing change.

"Then—then you live in that gray house up the brook," she stammered.

"Yes. I should have gone over to call on you long ago," said the other. She did not offer any explanation or excuse for not having gone.

"I wish you *would* come," said Anne, recovering herself somewhat. "We're such near neighbors we ought to be friends. That is the sole fault of Four Winds—there aren't quite enough neighbors. Otherwise it is perfection."

"You like it?"

"*Like* it! I love it. It is the most beautiful place I ever saw."

"I've never seen many places," said Leslie Moore, slowly, "but I've always thought it was very lovely here. I—I love it, too."

She spoke, as she looked, shyly, yet eagerly. Anne had an odd impression that this strange girl—the word "girl" would persist—could say a good deal if she chose.

"I often come to the shore," she added.

"So do I," said Anne. "It's a wonder we haven't met here before."

"Probably you come earlier in the evening than I do. It is generally late—almost dark—when I come. And I love to come just after a storm—like this. I don't like the sea so well when it's calm and quiet. I like the struggle—and the crash—and the noise."

"I love it in all its moods," declared Anne. "The sea at Four Winds is to me what Lover's Lane was at home. Tonight it seemed so free—so untamed—something broke loose in me, too, out of sympathy. That was why I danced along the shore in that wild way. I didn't suppose anybody was looking, of course. If Miss Cornelia Bryant had seen me she would have foreboded a gloomy prospect for poor young Dr. Blythe."

"You know Miss Cornelia?" said Leslie, laughing. She had an exquisite laugh; it bubbled up suddenly and unexpectedly with something of the delicious quality of a baby's. Anne laughed, too.

"Oh, yes. She has been down to my house of dreams several times."

"Your house of dreams?"

"Oh, that's a dear, foolish little name Gilbert and I have for our home. We just call it that between ourselves. It slipped out before I thought."

"So Miss Russell's little white house is *your* house of dreams," said Leslie wonderingly. "*I* had a house of dreams once—but it was a palace," she added, with a laugh, the sweetness of which was marred by a little note of derision.

"Oh, I once dreamed of a palace, too," said Anne. "I suppose all girls do. And then we settle down contentedly in eight-room houses that seem to fulfil all the desires of our hearts—because our prince is there. *You* should have had your palace really, though—you are so beautiful. You *must* let me say it—it *has* to be said—I'm nearly bursting with admiration. You are the loveliest thing I ever saw, Mrs. Moore."

"If we are to be friends you must call me Leslie," said the other with an odd passion.

"Of course I will. And *my* friends call me Anne."

"I suppose I am beautiful," Leslie went on, looking stormily out to sea. "I hate my beauty. I wish I had always been as brown and plain as the brownest and plainest girl at the fishing village over there. Well, what do you think of Miss Cornelia?"

The abrupt change of subject shut the door on any further confidences.

"Miss Cornelia is a darling, isn't she?" said Anne. "Gilbert and I were invited to her house to a state tea last week. You've heard of groaning tables."

"I seem to recall seeing the expression in the newspaper reports of weddings," said Leslie, smiling.

"Well, Miss Cornelia's groaned—at least, it creaked—positively. You couldn't have believed she would have cooked so much for two ordinary people. She had every kind of pie you could name, I think,—except lemon pie. She said she had taken the prize for lemon pies at the Charlottetown Exhibition ten years ago and had never made any since for fear of losing her reputation for them."

"Were you able to eat enough pie to please her?"

"*I* wasn't. Gilbert won her heart by eating—I won't tell you how much. She said she never knew a man who didn't like pie better than his Bible. Do you know, I love Miss Cornelia."

"So do I," said Leslie. "She is the best friend I have in the world."

Anne wondered secretly why, if this were so, Miss Cornelia had never mentioned Mrs. Dick Moore to her. Miss Cornelia had certainly talked freely about every other individual in or near Four Winds.

"Isn't that beautiful?" said Leslie, after a brief silence, pointing to the exquisite effect of a shaft of light falling through a cleft in the rock behind them, across a dark green pool at its base. "If I had come here—and seen nothing but just that—I would go home satisfied."

"The effects of light and shadow all along these shores are wonderful," agreed Anne. "My little sewing room looks out on the harbor, and I sit at its window and feast my eyes. The colors and shadows are never the same two minutes together."

"And you are never lonely?" asked Leslie abruptly. "Never—when you are alone?"

"No. I don't think I've ever been really lonely in my life," answered Anne. "Even when I'm alone I have real good company—dreams and imaginations and pretendings. I *like* to be alone now and then, just to think over things and *taste* them. But I love friendship—and nice, jolly little times with people. Oh, *won't* you come to see me—often? Please do. I believe," Anne added, laughing, "that you'd like me if you knew me."

"I wonder if *you* would like *me*," said Leslie seriously. She was not fishing for a compliment. She looked out across the waves that were beginning to be garlanded with blossoms of moonlit foam, and her eyes filled with shadows.

"I'm sure I would," said Anne. "And please don't think I'm utterly irresponsible because you saw me dancing on the shore at sunset. No doubt I shall be dignified after a time. You see, I haven't been married very long. I feel like a girl, and sometimes like a child, yet."

"I have been married twelve years," said Leslie.

Here was another unbelievable thing.

"Why, you can't be as old as I am!" exclaimed Anne. "You must have been a child when you were married."

"I was sixteen," said Leslie, rising, and picking up the cap and jacket lying beside her. "I am twenty-eight now. Well, I must go back."

"So must I. Gilbert will probably be home. But I'm so glad we both came to the shore tonight and met each other."

Leslie said nothing, and Anne was a little chilled. She had offered friendship frankly but it had not been accepted very graciously, if it had not been absolutely repelled. In silence they climbed the cliffs and walked across a pasture-field of which the feathery, bleached, wild grasses were like a carpet of creamy velvet in the moonlight. When they reached the shore lane Leslie turned.

"I go this way, Mrs. Blythe. You will come over and see me some time, won't you?"

Anne felt as if the invitation had been thrown at her. She got the impression that Leslie Moore gave it reluctantly.

"I will come if you really want me to," she said a little coldly.

"Oh, I do—I do," exclaimed Leslie, with an eagerness which seemed to burst forth and beat down some restraint that had been imposed on it.

"Then I'll come. Good-night—Leslie."

"Good-night, Mrs. Blythe."

Anne walked home in a brown study and poured out her tale to Gilbert.

"So Mrs. Dick Moore isn't one of the race that knows Joseph?" said Gilbert teasingly.

"No—o—o, not exactly. And yet—I think she *was* one of them once, but has gone or got into exile," said Anne musingly. "She is certainly very different from the other women about here.

You can't talk about eggs and butter to *her*. To think I've been imagining her a second Mrs. Rachel Lynde! Have you ever seen Dick Moore, Gilbert?"

"No. I've seen several men working about the fields of the farm, but I don't know which was Moore."

"She never mentioned him. I *know* she isn't happy."

"From what you tell me I suppose she was married before she was old enough to know her own mind or heart, and found out too late that she had made a mistake. It's a common tragedy enough, Anne. A fine woman would have made the best of it. Mrs. Moore has evidently let it make her bitter and resentful."

"Don't let us judge her till we know," pleaded Anne. "I don't believe her case is so ordinary. You will understand her fascination when you meet her, Gilbert. It is a thing quite apart from her beauty. I feel that she possesses a rich nature, into which a friend might enter as into a kingdom; but for some reason she bars everyone out and shuts all her possibilities up in herself, so that they cannot develop and blossom. There, I've been struggling to define her to myself ever since I left her, and that is the nearest I can get to it. I'm going to ask Miss Cornelia about her."

11
THE STORY OF LESLIE MOORE

"Yes, the eighth baby arrived a fortnight ago," said Miss Cornelia, from a rocker before the fire of the little house one chilly October afternoon. "It's a girl. Fred was ranting mad—said he wanted a boy—when the truth is he didn't want it at all. If it had been a boy he'd have ranted because it wasn't a girl. They had four girls and three boys before, so I can't see that it made much difference what this one was, but of course he'd have to be cantankerous, just like a man. The baby is real pretty, dressed up in its nice little clothes. It has black eyes and the dearest, tiny hands."

"I must go and see it. I just love babies," said Anne, smiling to herself over a thought too dear and sacred to be put into words.

"I don't say but what they're nice," admitted Miss Cornelia. "But some folks seem to have more than they really need, believe *me*. My poor cousin Flora up at the Glen had eleven, and such a slave as she is! Her husband suicided three years ago. Just like a man!"

"What made him do that?" asked Anne, rather shocked.

"Couldn't get his way over something, so he jumped into the well. A good riddance! He was a born tyrant. But of course it spoiled the well. Flora could never abide the thought of using it again, poor thing! So she had another dug and a frightful expense it was, and the water as hard as nails. If he *had* to drown himself there was plenty of water in the harbor, wasn't there? I've no patience with a man like that. We've only had two suicides in Four Winds in my recollection. The other was Frank West— Leslie Moore's father. By the way, has Leslie ever been over to call on you yet?"

"No, but I met her on the shore a few nights ago and we scraped an acquaintance," said Anne, pricking up her ears.

Miss Cornelia nodded.

"I'm glad, dearie. I was hoping you'd foregather with her. What do you think of her?"

"I thought her very beautiful."

"Oh, of course. There was never anybody about Four Winds could touch her for looks. Did you ever see her hair? It reaches to her feet when she lets it down. But I meant how did you like her?"

"I think I could like her very much if she'd let me," said Anne slowly.

"But she wouldn't let you—she pushed you off and kept you at arm's length. Poor Leslie! You wouldn't be much surprised if you knew what her life has been. It's been a tragedy—a tragedy!" repeated Miss Cornelia emphatically.

"I wish you would tell me all about her—that is, if you can do so without betraying any confidence."

"Lord, dearie, everybody in Four Winds knows poor Leslie's story. It's no secret—the *outside* that is. Nobody knows the *inside* but Leslie herself, and she doesn't take folks into her confidence. I'm about the best friend she has on earth, I reckon, and she's never uttered a word of complaint to me. Have you ever seen Dick Moore?"

"No."

"Well, I may as well begin at the beginning and tell you everything straight through, so you'll understand it. As I said, Leslie's father was Frank West. He was clever and shiftless—just like a man. Oh, he had heaps of brains—and much good they did him! He started to go to college, and he went for two years, and then his health broke down. The Wests were all inclined to be consumptive. So Frank came home and started farming. He married Rose Elliott from over harbor. Rose was reckoned the beauty of Four Winds—Leslie takes her looks from her mother, but she has ten times the spirit and go that Rose had, and a far better figure. Now you know, Anne, I always take the ground that us women ought to stand by each other. We've got enough to endure at the hands of the men, the Lord knows, so I hold we hadn't ought to clapper-claw one another, and it isn't often you'll find me running down another woman. But I never had much use for Rose Elliott. She was spoiled to begin with, believe *me*, and she was nothing but a lazy, selfish, whining creature. Frank was no hand to work, so they were poor as Job's turkey. Poor! They lived on potatoes and point, believe *me*. They had two children—Leslie and Kenneth. Leslie had her mother's looks and her father's brains, and something she didn't get from either of them. She took after her Grandmother West—a splendid old lady. She was the brightest, friendliest, merriest thing when she was a child, Anne. Everybody liked her. She was her father's favorite and she was awful fond of him. They were 'chums,' as she used to say. She couldn't see any of his faults—and he *was* a taking sort of man in some ways.

"Well, when Leslie was twelve years old, the first dreadful

thing happened. She worshipped little Kenneth—he was four years younger than her, and he *was* a dear little chap. And he was killed one day—fell off a big load of hay just as it was going into the barn, and the wheel went right over his little body and crushed the life out of it. And mind you, Anne, Leslie saw it. She was looking down from the loft. She gave one screech—the hired man said he never heard such a sound in all his life—he said it would ring in his ears till Gabriel's trump drove it out. But she never screeched or cried again about it. She jumped from the loft onto the load and from the load to the floor, and caught up the little bleeding, warm, dead body, Anne—they had to tear it from her before she would let it go. They sent for me—I can't talk of it."

Miss Cornelia wiped the tears from her kindly brown eyes and sewed in bitter silence for a few minutes.

"Well," she resumed, "it was all over—they buried little Kenneth in that graveyard over the harbor, and after a while Leslie went back to her school and her studies. She never mentioned Kenneth's name—I've never heard it cross her lips from that day to this. I reckon that old hurt still aches and burns at times; but she was only a child and time is real kind to children, Anne, dearie. After a while she began to laugh again—she had the prettiest laugh. You don't often hear it now."

"I heard it once the other night," said Anne. "It *is* a beautiful laugh."

"Frank West began to go down after Kenneth's death. He wasn't strong and it was a shock to him, because he was real fond of the child, though, as I've said, Leslie was his favorite. He got mopy and melancholy, and couldn't or wouldn't work. And one day, when Leslie was fourteen years of age, he hanged himself—and in the parlor, too, mind you, Anne, right in the middle of the parlor from the lamp hook in the ceiling. Wasn't that like a man? It was the anniversary of his wedding day, too. Nice, tasty time to pick for it, wasn't it? And, of course, that poor Leslie had to be the one to find him. She went into the parlor that morning, singing, with some fresh flowers for the vases, and there she saw her father hanging from the ceiling, his face as black as a coal. It was something awful, believe *me*!"

"Oh, how horrible!" said Anne, shuddering. "The poor, poor child!"

"Leslie didn't cry at her father's funeral any more than she had cried at Kenneth's. Rose whooped and howled for two, however, and Leslie had all she could do trying to calm and comfort her mother. I was disgusted with Rose and so was everyone else, but Leslie never got out of patience. She loved her mother. Leslie is clannish—her own could never do wrong in her eyes. Well, they buried Frank West beside Kenneth, and Rose put up a great big monument to him. It was bigger than his character, believe *me*! Anyhow, it was bigger than Rose could afford, for the farm was mortgaged for more than its value. But not long after Leslie's old grandmother West died and she left Leslie a little money— enough to give her a year at Queen's Academy. Leslie had made up her mind to pass for a teacher if she could, and then earn enough to put herself through Redmond College. That had been her father's pet scheme—he wanted her to have what he had lost. Leslie was full of ambition and her head was chock full of brains. She went to Queen's, and she took two years' work in one year and got her First; and when she came home she got the Glen school. She was so happy and hopeful and full of life and eagerness. When I think of what she was then and what she is now, I say—drat the men!"

Miss Cornelia snipped her thread off as viciously as if, Nerolike, she was severing the neck of mankind by the stroke.

"Dick Moore came into her life that summer. His father, Abner Moore, kept store at the Glen, but Dick had a sea-going streak in him from his mother; he used to sail in summer and clerk in his father's store in winter. He was a big, handsome fellow, with a little ugly soul. He was always wanting something till he got it, and then he stopped wanting it—just like a man. Oh, he didn't growl at the weather when it was fine, and he was mostly real pleasant and agreeable when everything went right. But he drank a good deal, and there were some nasty stories told of him and a girl down at the fishing village. He wasn't fit for Leslie to wipe her feet on, that's the long and short of it. And he was a Methodist! But he was clean mad about her—because of her good looks in the first place, and because she wouldn't have anything to say to him in the second. He vowed he'd have her—and he got her!"

"How did he bring it about?"

"Oh, it was an iniquitous thing! I'll never forgive Rose West. You see, dearie, Abner Moore held the mortgage on the West farm, and the interest was overdue some years, and Dick just went and told Mrs. West that if Leslie wouldn't marry him he'd get his father to foreclose the mortgage. Rose carried on terrible—fainted and wept, and pleaded with Leslie not to let her be turned out of her home. She said it would break her heart to leave the home she'd come to as a bride. I wouldn't have blamed her for feeling dreadful bad over it—but you wouldn't have thought she'd be so selfish as to sacrifice her own flesh and blood because of it, would you? Well, she was. And Leslie gave in—she loved her mother so much she would have done anything to save her pain. She married Dick Moore. None of us knew why at the time. It wasn't till long afterward that I found out how her mother had worried her into it. I was sure there was something wrong, though, because I knew how she had snubbed him time and again, and it wasn't like Leslie to turn face-about like that. Besides, I knew that Dick Moore wasn't the kind of man Leslie could ever fancy, in spite of his good looks and dashing ways. Of course, there was no wedding, but Rose asked me to go and see them married. I went, but I was sorry I did. I'd seen Leslie's face at her brother's funeral and at her father's funeral—and now it seemed to me I was seeing it at her own funeral. But Rose was smiling as a basket of chips, believe *me*!

"Leslie and Dick settled down on the West place—Rose couldn't bear to part with her dear daughter!—and lived there for the winter. In the spring Rose took pneumonia and died—a year too late! Leslie was heart-broken enough over it. Isn't it terrible the way some unworthy folks are loved, while others that deserve it far more, you'd think, never get much affection? As for Dick, he'd had enough of quiet married life—just like a man. He was for up and off. He went over to Nova Scotia to visit his relations—his father had come from Nova Scotia—and he wrote back to Leslie that his cousin, George Moore, was going on a voyage to Havana and he was going too. The name of the vessel was the *Four Sisters* and they were to be gone about nine weeks.

"It must have been a relief to Leslie. But she never said anything. From the day of her marriage she was just what she is now—cold and proud, and keeping everyone but me at a distance. I won't *be* kept at a distance, believe *me*! I've just stuck to Leslie as close as I knew how in spite of everything."

"She told me you were the best friend she had," said Anne.

"Did she?" exclaimed Miss Cornelia delightedly. "Well, I'm real thankful to hear it. Sometimes I've wondered if she really did want me around at all—she never let me think so. You must have thawed her out more than you think, or she wouldn't have said that much itself to you. Oh, that poor, heart-broken girl! I never see Dick Moore but I want to run a knife clean through him."

Miss Cornelia wiped her eyes again and having relieved her feelings by her blood-thirsty wish, took up her tale.

"Well, Leslie was left over there alone. Dick had put in the crop before he went, and old Abner looked after it. The summer went by and the *Four Sisters* didn't come back. The Nova Scotia Moores investigated, and found she had got to Havana and discharged her cargo and took on another and left for home; and that was all they ever found out about her. By degrees people began to talk of Dick Moore as one that was dead. Almost everyone believed that he was, though no one felt certain, for men have turned up here at the harbor after they'd been gone for years. Leslie never thought he was dead—and she was right. A thousand pities too! The next summer Captain Jim was in Havana—that was before he gave up the sea, of course. He thought he'd poke round a bit—Captain Jim was always meddle-some, just like a man—and he went to inquiring round among the sailors' boarding houses and places like that, to see if he could find out anything about the crew of the *Four Sisters*. He'd better have let sleeping dogs lie, in my opinion! Well, he went to one out-of-the-way place, and there he found a man and he knew at first sight it was Dick Moore, though he had a big beard. Captain Jim got it shaved off and then there was no doubt—Dick Moore it was—his body at least. His mind wasn't there—as for his soul, in my opinion he never had one!"

"What had happened to him?"

"Nobody knows the rights of it. All the folks who kept the boarding house could tell was that about a year before they had found him lying on their doorstep one morning in an awful con-dition—his head battered to a jelly almost. They supposed he'd got hurt in some drunken row, and likely that's the truth of it. They took him in, never thinking he could live. But he did—and he was just like a child when he got well. He hadn't memory or intellect or reason. They tried to find out who he was but they never could. He couldn't even tell them his name—he could only say a few simple words. He had a letter on him beginning 'Dear Dick' and signed 'Leslie,' but there was no address on it and the envelope was gone. They let him stay on—he learned to do a few odd jobs about the place—and there Captain Jim found him. He brought him home—and I've always said it was a bad day's work, though I s'pose there was nothing else he could do. He thought maybe when Dick got home and saw his old surroundings and familiar faces his memory would wake up. But it hadn't any effect. There he's been at the house up the brook ever since. He's just like a child, no more nor less. Takes fractious spells occa-sionally, but mostly he's just vacant and good humored and harmless. He's apt to run away if he isn't watched. That's the bur-den Leslie has had to carry for eleven years—and all alone. Old Abner Moore died soon after Dick was brought home and it was found he was almost bankrupt. When things were settled up there was nothing for Leslie and Dick but the old West farm. Leslie rented it to John Ward, and the rent is all she has to live on. Sometimes in summer she takes a boarder to help out. But most visitors prefer the other side of the harbor where the hotels and summer cottages are. Leslie's house is too far from the bathing shore. She's taken care of Dick and she's never been away from him for eleven years—she's tied to that imbecile for life. And after all the dreams and hopes she once had! You can imagine what it has been like for her, Anne, dearie—with her beauty and spirit and pride and cleverness. It's just been a living death."

"Poor, poor girl!" said Anne again. Her own happiness seemed to reproach her. What right had she to be so happy when another human soul must be so miserable?

"Will you tell me just what Leslie said and how she acted the night you met her on the shore?" asked Miss Cornelia.

She listened intently and nodded her satisfaction.

"*You* thought she was stiff and cold, Anne, dearie, but I can tell you she thawed out wonderful for her. She must have taken to you real strong. I'm so glad. You may be able to help her a good deal. I was thankful when I heard that a young couple was coming to this house, for I hoped it would mean some friends for Leslie; especially if you belonged to the race that knows Joseph. You *will* be her friend, won't you, Anne, dearie?"

"Indeed I will, if she'll let me," said Anne, with all her own sweet, impulsive earnestness.

"No, you must be her friend, whether she'll let you or not," said Miss Cornelia resolutely. "Don't you mind if she's stiff by times—don't notice it. Remember what her life has been—and is—and must always be, I suppose, for creatures like Dick Moore live forever, I understand. You should see how fat he's got since he came home. He used to be lean enough. Just *make* her be friends—you can do it—you're one of those who have the knack. Only you mustn't be sensitive. And don't mind if she doesn't seem to want you to go over there much. She knows that some women don't like to be where Dick is—they complain he gives them the creeps. Just get her to come over here as often as she can. She can't get away so very much—she can't leave Dick long, for the Lord knows what he'd do—burn the house down most likely. At nights, after he's in bed and asleep, is about the only time she's free. He always goes to bed early and sleeps like the dead till next morning. That is how you came to meet her at the shore likely. She wanders there considerable."

"I will do everything I can for her," said Anne. Her interest in Leslie Moore, which had been vivid ever since she had seen her driving her geese down the hill, was intensified a thousand fold by Miss Cornelia's narration. The girl's beauty and sorrow and loneliness drew her with an irresistible fascination. She had never known anyone like her; her friends had hitherto been whole- some, normal, merry girls like herself, with only the average trials of human care and bereavement to shadow their girlish dreams. Leslie Moore stood apart, a tragic, appealing figure of thwarted womanhood. Anne resolved that she would win entrance into the kingdom of that lonely soul and find there the comradeship it could so richly give, were it not for the cruel fet- ters that held it in a prison not of its own making.

"And mind you this, Anne, dearie," said Miss Cornelia, who had not yet wholly relieved her mind. "You mustn't think Leslie is an infidel because she hardly ever goes to church—or even that she's a Methodist. She can't take Dick to church, of course— not that he ever troubled church much in his best days. But you just remember that she's a real strong Presbyterian at heart, Anne, dearie."

12
LESLIE COMES OVER

Leslie came over to the house of dreams one frosty October night, when moonlit mists were hanging over the harbor and curling like silver ribbons along the seaward glens. She looked as if she repented coming when Gilbert answered her knock; but Anne flew past him, pounced on her, and drew her in.

"I'm so glad you picked tonight for a call," she said gaily. "I made up a lot of extra good fudge this afternoon and we want someone to help us eat it—before the fire—while we tell stories. Perhaps Captain Jim will drop in, too. This is his night."

"No. Captain Jim is over home," said Leslie. "He—he made me come here," she added, half defiantly.

"I'll say a thank-you to him for that when I see him," said Anne, pulling easy chairs before the fire.

"Oh, I don't mean that I didn't want to come," protested Leslie, flushing a little. "I—I've been thinking of coming—but it isn't always easy for me to get away."

"Of course it must be hard for you to leave Mr. Moore," said Anne, in a matter-of-fact tone. She had decided that it would be best to mention Dick Moore occasionally as an accepted fact, and not give undue morbidness to the subject by avoiding it. She was right, for Leslie's air of constraint suddenly vanished. Evidently she had been wondering how much Anne knew of the conditions of her life and was relieved that no explanations were needed. She allowed her cap and jacket to be taken, and sat down with a girlish snuggle in the big armchair by Magog. She was dressed prettily and carefully, with the customary touch of color in the scarlet geranium at her white throat. Her beautiful hair gleamed like molten gold in the warm firelight. Her sea-blue eyes were full of soft laughter and allurement. For the moment, under the influence of the little house of dreams, she was a girl again—a girl forgetful of the past and its bitterness. The atmosphere of the many loves that had sanctified the little house was all about her; the companionship of two healthy, happy, young folks of her own generation encircled her; she felt and yielded to the magic of her surroundings—Miss Cornelia and Captain Jim would scarcely have recognized her; Anne found it hard to believe that this was the cold, unresponsive woman she had met on the shore—this animated girl who talked and listened with the eagerness of a starved soul. And how hungrily Leslie's eyes looked at the book-cases between the windows!

"Our library isn't very extensive," said Anne, "but every book in it is a *friend*. We've picked our books up through the years, here and there, never buying one until we had first read it and knew that it belonged to the race of Joseph."

Leslie laughed—beautiful laughter that seemed akin to all the mirth that had echoed through the little house in the vanished years.

"I have a few books of father's—not many," she said. "I've read them until I know them almost by heart. I don't get many books. There's a circulating library at the Glen store—but I don't think the committee who pick the books for Mr. Parker know what books are of Joseph's race—or perhaps they don't care. It was so seldom I got one I really liked that I gave up getting any."

"I hope you'll look on our bookshelves as your own," said Anne. "You are entirely and wholeheartedly welcome to the loan of any book on them."

"You are setting a feast of fat things before me," said Leslie, joyously. Then, as the clock struck ten, she rose, half unwillingly.

"I must go. I didn't realize it was so late. Captain Jim is always saying it doesn't take long to stay an hour. But I've stayed two—and oh, but I've enjoyed them," she added frankly.

"Come often," said Anne and Gilbert. They had risen and stood together in the firelight's glow. Leslie looked at them—youthful, hopeful, happy, typifying all she had missed and must forever miss. The light went out of her face and eyes; the girl vanished; it was the sorrowful, cheated woman who answered the invitation almost coldly and got herself away with a pitiful haste.

Anne watched her until she was lost in the shadows of the chill and misty night. Then she turned slowly back to the glow of her own radiant hearthstone.

"Isn't she lovely, Gilbert? Her hair fascinates me. Miss Cornelia says it reaches to her feet. Ruby Gillis had beautiful hair—but Leslie's is *alive*—every thread of it is living gold."

"She is very beautiful," agreed Gilbert, so heartily that Anne almost wished he were a *little* less enthusiastic.

"Gilbert, would you like my hair better if it were like Leslie's?" she asked wistfully.

"I wouldn't have your hair any color but just what it is for the world," said Gilbert, with one or two convincing accompaniments. "You wouldn't be *Anne* if you had golden hair—or hair of any color but"—

"Red," said Anne, with gloomy satisfaction.

"Yes, red—to give warmth to that milk-white skin and those shining gray-green eyes of yours. Golden hair wouldn't suit you at all, Queen Anne—*my* Queen Anne—queen of my heart and life and home."

"Then you may admire Leslie's all you like," said Anne magnanimously.

13
A GHOSTLY EVENING

One evening, a week later, Anne decided to run over the fields to the house up the brook for an informal call. It was an evening of gray fog that had crept in from the gulf, swathed the harbor, filled the glens and valleys, and clung heavily to the autumnal meadows. Through it the sea sobbed and shuddered. Anne saw Four Winds in a new aspect, and found it weird and mysterious and fascinating; but it also gave her a little feeling of loneliness. Gilbert was away and would be away until the morrow, attending a medical pow-wow in Charlottetown. Anne longed for an hour of fellowship with some girl friend. Captain Jim and Miss Cornelia were "good fellows" each, in their own way; but youth yearned to youth.

"If only Diana or Phil or Pris or Stella could drop in for a chat," she said to herself, "how delightful it would be! This is such a *ghostly* night. I'm sure all the ships that ever sailed out of

Four Winds to their doom could be seen tonight sailing up the harbor with their drowned crews on their decks, if that shrouding fog could suddenly be drawn aside. I feel as if it concealed innumerable mysteries—as if I were surrounded by the wraiths of old generations of Four Winds people peering at me through that gray veil. If ever the dear dead ladies of this little house came back to revisit it they would come on just such a night as this. If I sit here any longer I'll see one of them there opposite me in Gilbert's chair. This place isn't exactly canny tonight. Even Gog and Magog have an air of pricking up their ears to hear the footsteps of unseen guests. I'll run over to see Leslie before I frighten myself with my own fancies, as I did long ago in the matter of the Haunted Wood. I'll leave my house of dreams to welcome back its old inhabitants. My fire will give them my good-will and greeting—they will be gone before I come back, and my house will be mine once more. Tonight I am sure it is keeping a tryst with the past."

Laughing a little over her fancy, yet with something of a creepy sensation in the region of her spine, Anne kissed her hand to Gog and Magog and slipped out into the fog, with some of the new magazines under her arm for Leslie.

"Leslie's wild for books and magazines," Miss Cornelia had told her, "and she hardly ever sees one. She can't afford to buy them or subscribe for them. She's really pitifully poor, Anne. I don't see how she makes out to live at all on the little rent the farm brings in. She never even hints a complaint on the score of poverty, but I know what it must be. She's been handicapped by it all her life. She didn't mind it when she was free and ambitious, but it must gall now, believe *me*. I'm glad she seemed so bright and merry the evening she spent with you. Captain Jim told me he had fairly to put her cap and coat on and push her out of the door. Don't be too long going to see her either. If you are she'll think it's because you don't like the sight of Dick, and she'll crawl into her shell again. Dick's a great, big, harmless baby, but that silly grin and chuckle of his do get on some people's nerves. Thank goodness, I've no nerves myself. I like Dick Moore better

now than I ever did when he was in his right senses—though the
Lord knows that isn't saying much. I was down there one day in
housecleaning time helping Leslie a bit, and I was frying dough-
nuts. Dick was hanging round to get one, as usual, and all at once
he picked up a scalding hot one I'd just fished out and dropped it
on the back of my neck when I was bending over. Then he
laughed and laughed. Believe *me*, Anne, it took all the grace of
God in my heart to keep me from just whisking up that stew-pan
of boiling fat and pouring it over his head."

Anne laughed over Miss Cornelia's wrath as she sped through
the darkness. But laughter accorded ill with that night. She was
sober enough when she reached the house among the willows.
Everything was very silent. The front part of the house seemed
dark and deserted, so Anne slipped round to the side door, which
opened from the veranda into a little sitting room. There she halt-
ed noiselessly.

The door was open. Beyond, in the dimly lighted room, sat
Leslie Moore, with her arms flung out on the table and her head
bent upon them. She was weeping horribly—with low, fierce,
choking sobs, as if some agony in her soul were trying to tear
itself out. An old black dog was sitting by her, his nose resting on
her lap, his big doggish eyes full of mute, imploring sympathy
and devotion. Anne drew back in dismay. She felt that she could
not intermeddle with this bitterness. Her heart ached with a sympathy she might not utter. To go in now would be to shut the
door forever on any possible help or friendship. Some instinct
warned Anne that the proud, bitter girl would never forgive the
one who thus surprised her in her abandonment of despair.

Anne slipped noiselessly from the veranda and found her way
across the yard. Beyond, she heard voices in the gloom and saw
the dim glow of a light. At the gate she met two men—Captain
Jim with a lantern, and another who she knew must be Dick
Moore—a big man, badly gone to fat, with a broad, round, red
face, and vacant eyes. Even in the dull light Anne got the impression that there was something unusual about his eyes.

"Is this you, Mistress Blythe?" said Captain Jim. "Now, now, you hadn't oughter be roaming about alone on a night like this. You could get lost in this fog easier than not. Jest you wait till I see Dick safe inside the door and I'll come back and light you over the fields. I ain't going to have Dr. Blythe coming home and finding that you walked clean over Cape Leforce in the fog. A woman did that once, forty years ago.

"So you've been over to see Leslie," he said, when he rejoined her.

"I didn't go in," said Anne, and told what she had seen. Captain Jim sighed.

"Poor, poor, little girl! She don't cry often, Mistress Blythe—she's too brave for that. She must feel terrible when she does cry. A night like this is hard on poor women who have sorrows. There's something about it that kinder brings up all we've suffered—or feared."

"It's full of ghosts," said Anne, with a shiver. "That was why I came over—I wanted to clasp a human hand and hear a human voice. There seem to be so many *inhuman* presences about tonight. Even my own dear house was full of them. They fairly elbowed me out. So I fled over here for companionship of my kind."

"You were right not to go in, though, Mistress Blythe. Leslie wouldn't have liked it. She wouldn't have liked me going in with Dick, as I'd have done if I hadn't met you. I had Dick down with me all day. I keep him with me as much as I can to help Leslie a bit."

"Isn't there something odd about his eyes?" asked Anne.

"You noticed that? Yes, one is blue and t'other is hazel—his father had the same. It's a Moore peculiarity. That was what told me he was Dick Moore when I saw him first down in Cuby. If it hadn't a-bin for his eyes I mightn't a-known him, what with his beard and fat. You know, I reckon, that it was me found him and brought him home. Miss Cornelia always says I shouldn't have done it, but I can't agree with her. It was the *right* thing to do—and so 'twas the only thing. There ain't no question in my mind about *that*. But my old heart aches for Leslie. She's only twenty-eight and she's eaten more bread with sorrow than most women do in eighty years."

They walked on in silence for a little while. Presently Anne said, "Do you know, Captain Jim, I never like walking with a lantern. I have always the strangest feeling that just outside the circle of light, just over its edge in the darkness, I am surrounded by a ring of furtive, sinister things, watching me from the shadows with hostile eyes. I've had that feeling from childhood. What is the reason? I never feel like that when I'm really in the darkness—when it is close all around me—I'm not the least frightened."

"I've something of that feeling myself," admitted Captain Jim. "I reckon when the darkness is close to us it is a friend. But when we sorter push it away from us—divorce ourselves from it, so to speak, with lantern light—it becomes an enemy. But the fog is lifting. There's a smart west wind rising, if you notice. The stars will be out when you get home."

They were out; and when Anne re-entered her house of dreams the red embers were still glowing on the hearth, and all the haunting presences were gone.

14
NOVEMBER DAYS

The splendor of color which had glowed for weeks along the shores of Four Winds Harbor had faded out into the soft gray-blue of late autumnal hills. There came many days when fields and shores were dim with misty rain, or shivering before the breath of a melancholy sea-wind—nights, too, of storm and tempest, when Anne sometimes wakened to pray that no ship might be beating up the grim north shore, for if it were so not even the great, faithful light, whirling through the darkness unafraid, could avail to guide it into safe haven.

"In November I sometimes feel as if spring could never come again," she sighed, grieving over the hopeless unsightliness of her frosted and bedraggled flower-plots. The gay little garden of the schoolmaster's bride was rather a forlorn place now, and the Lombardies and birches were under bare poles, as Captain Jim said. But the fir-wood behind the little house was forever green and staunch; and even in November and December there came gracious days of sunshine and purple hazes, when the harbor danced and sparkled as blithely as in midsummer, and the gulf was so softly blue and tender that the storm and the wild wind seemed only things of a long-past dream.

Anne and Gilbert spent many an autumn evening at the lighthouse. It was always a cheery place. Even when the east wind sang in minor and the sea was dead and gray, hints of sunshine seemed to be lurking all about it. Perhaps this was because the First Mate always paraded it in panoply of gold. He was so large and effulgent that one hardly missed the sun, and his resounding purrs formed a pleasant accompaniment to the laughter and conversation which went on around Captain Jim's fireplace. Captain Jim and Gilbert had many long discussions and high converse on matters beyond the ken of cat or king.

"I like to ponder on all kinds of problems, though I can't solve 'em," said Captain Jim. "My father held that we should never talk of things we couldn't understand, but if we didn't, doctor, the subjects for conversation would be mighty few. I reckon the gods laugh many a time to hear us, but what matters so long as we remember that we're only men and don't take to fancying that we're gods ourselves, really, knowing good and evil. I reckon our pow-pows won't do us or anyone much harm, so let's have another whack at the whence, why and whither this evening, doctor."

While they "whacked," Anne listened or dreamed. Sometimes Leslie went to the lighthouse with them, and she and Anne wandered along the shore in the eerie twilight, or sat on the rocks below the lighthouse until the darkness drove them back to the cheer of the driftwood fire. Then Captain Jim would brew them tea and tell them

> "tales of land and sea
> And whatsoever might betide
> The great forgotten world outside."

Leslie seemed always to enjoy those lighthouse carousals very much, and bloomed out for the time being into ready wit and beautiful laughter, or glowing-eyed silence. There was a certain tang and savor in the conversation when Leslie was present which they missed when she was absent. Even when she did not talk she seemed to inspire others to brilliancy. Captain Jim told his stories better, Gilbert was quicker in argument and repartee, Anne felt little gushes and trickles of fancy and imagination bubbling to her lips under the influence of Leslie's personality.

"That girl was born to be a leader in social and intellectual circles, far away from Four Winds," she said to Gilbert as they walked home one night. "She's just wasted here—wasted."

"Weren't you listening to Captain Jim and yours truly the other night when we discussed that subject generally? We came to the comforting conclusion that the Creator probably knew how to run His universe quite as well as we do, and that, after all, there are no such things as 'wasted' lives, saving and except when an individual wilfully squanders and wastes his own life—which Leslie Moore certainly hasn't done. And some people might think that a Redmond B.A., whom editors were beginning to honor, was 'wasted' as the wife of a struggling country doctor in the rural community of Four Winds."

"Gilbert!"

"If you had married Roy Gardner, now," continued Gilbert mercilessly, "*you* could have been 'a leader in social and intellectual circles far away from Four Winds.'"

"Gilbert *Blythe*!"

"You *know* you were in love with him at one time, Anne."

"Gilbert, that's mean—'pisen mean, just like all the men,' as Miss Cornelia says. I *never* was in love with him. I only imagined I was. *You* know that. You *know* I'd rather be your wife in our house of dreams and fulfilment than a queen in a palace."

Gilbert's answer was not in words; but I am afraid that both of them forgot poor Leslie speeding her lonely way across the fields to a house that was neither a palace nor the fulfilment of a dream.

The moon was rising over the sad, dark sea behind them and transfiguring it. Her light had not yet reached the harbor, the further side of which was shadowy and suggestive, with dim coves and rich glooms and jewelling lights.

"How the home lights shine out tonight through the dark!" said Anne. "That string of them over the harbor looks like a necklace. And what a coruscation there is up at the Glen! Oh, look, Gilbert, there is ours. I'm so glad we left it burning. I hate to come home to a dark house. *Our* homelight, Gilbert! Isn't it lovely to see?"

"Just one of earth's many millions of homes, Anne-girl—but ours—*ours*—our beacon in 'a naughty world.' When a fellow has a home and a dear, little, red-haired wife in it what more need he ask of life?"

"Well, he might ask *one* thing more," whispered Anne happily. "Oh, Gilbert, it seems as if I just *couldn't* wait for the spring."

15
CHRISTMAS AT FOUR WINDS

At first Anne and Gilbert talked of going home to Avonlea for Christmas; but eventually they decided to stay in Four Winds. "I want to spend the first Christmas of our life together in our own home," decreed Anne.

So it fell out that Marilla and Mrs. Rachel Lynde and the twins came to Four Winds for Christmas. Marilla had the face of a woman who had circumnavigated the globe. She had never been sixty miles away from home before; and she had never eaten a Christmas dinner anywhere save at Green Gables.

Mrs. Rachel had made and brought with her an enormous plum pudding. Nothing could have convinced Mrs. Rachel that a college graduate of the younger generation could make a Christmas plum pudding properly; but she bestowed approval on Anne's house.

"Anne's a good housekeeper," she said to Marilla in the spare room the night of their arrival. "I've looked into her bread box and her scrap pail. I always judge a housekeeper by those, that's what. There's nothing in the pail that shouldn't have been thrown away, and no stale pieces in the bread box. Of course, she was trained up with you—but, then, she went to college afterwards. I notice she's got my tobacco stripe quilt on the bed here, and that big round braided mat of yours before her living-room fire. It makes me feel right at home."

Anne's first Christmas in her own house was as delightful as she could have wished. The day was fine and bright; the first skim of snow had fallen on Christmas Eve and made the world beautiful; the harbor was still open and glittering.

Captain Jim and Miss Cornelia came to dinner. Leslie and Dick had been invited, but Leslie made excuse; they always went to her Uncle Isaac West's for Christmas, she said.

"She'd rather have it so," Miss Cornelia told Anne. "She can't bear taking Dick where there are strangers. Christmas is always a hard time for Leslie. She and her father used to make a lot of it."

Miss Cornelia and Mrs. Rachel did not take a very violent fancy to each other. "Two suns hold not their courses in one sphere." But they did not clash at all, for Mrs. Rachel was in the kitchen helping Anne and Marilla with the dinner, and it fell to Gilbert to entertain Captain Jim and Miss Cornelia,—or rather to be entertained by them, for a dialogue between those two old friends and antagonists was assuredly never dull.

"It's many a year since there was a Christmas dinner here, Mistress Blythe," said Captain Jim. "Miss Russell always went to her friends in town for Christmas. But I was here to the first Christmas dinner that was ever eaten in this house—and the schoolmaster's bride cooked it. That was sixty years ago today, Mistress Blythe—and a day very like this—just enough snow to make the hills white, and the harbor as blue as June. I was only a lad, and I'd never been invited out to dinner before, and I was too shy to eat enough. I've got all over *that*."

"Most men do," said Miss Cornelia, sewing furiously. Miss Cornelia was not going to sit with idle hands, even on Christmas. Babies come without any consideration for holidays, and there was one expected in a poverty-stricken household at Glen St. Mary. Miss Cornelia had sent that household a substantial dinner for its little swarm, and so meant to eat her own with a comfortable conscience.

"Well, you know, the way to a man's heart is through his stomach, Cornelia," explained Captain Jim.

"I believe you—when he *has* a heart," retorted Miss Cornelia. "I suppose that's why so many women kill themselves cooking—just as poor Amelia Baxter did. She died last Christmas morning, and she said it was the first Christmas since she was married that she didn't have to cook a big, twenty-plate dinner. It must have been a real pleasant change for her. Well, she's been dead a year, so you'll soon hear of Horace Baxter taking notice."

"I heard he was taking notice already," said Captain Jim, winking at Gilbert. "Wasn't he up to your place one Sunday lately, with his funeral blacks on, and a boiled collar?"

"No, he wasn't. And he needn't come neither. I could have had him long ago when he was fresh. I don't want any second-hand goods, believe *me*. As for Horace Baxter, he was in financial difficulties a year ago last summer, and he prayed to the Lord for help; and when his wife died and he got her life insurance he said he believed it was the answer to his prayer. Wasn't that like a man?"

"Have you really proof that he said that, Cornelia?"

"I have the Methodist minister's word for it—if you call *that* proof. Robert Baxter told me the same thing too, but I admit *that* isn't evidence. Robert Baxter isn't often known to tell the truth."

"Come, come, Cornelia, I think he generally tells the truth, but he changes his opinion so often it sometimes sounds as if he didn't."

"It sounds like it mighty often, believe *me*. But trust one man to excuse another. I have no use for Robert Baxter. He turned Methodist just because the Presbyterian choir happened to be singing 'Behold the bridegroom cometh' for a collection piece when him and Margaret walked up the aisle the Sunday after they were married. Served him right for being late! He always insisted the choir did it on purpose to insult him, as if he was of that much importance. But that family always thought they were much bigger potatoes than they really were. His brother Eliphalet imagined the devil was always at his elbow—but *I* never believed the devil wasted that much time on him."

"I—don't—know," said Captain Jim thoughtfully. "Eliphalet Baxter lived too much alone—hadn't even a cat or dog to keep him human. When a man is alone he's mighty apt to be with the devil—if he ain't with God. He has to choose which company he'll keep, I reckon. If the devil always was at Life Baxter's elbow it must have been because Life liked to have him there."

"Man-like," said Miss Cornelia, and subsided into silence over a complicated arrangement of tucks until Captain Jim deliberately stirred her up again by remarking in a casual way:

"I was up to the Methodist church last Sunday morning."

"You'd better have been home reading your Bible," was Miss Cornelia's retort.

"Come, now, Cornelia, *I* can't see any harm in going to the Methodist church when there's no preaching in your own. I've been a Presbyterian for seventy-six years, and it isn't likely my theology will hoist anchor at this late day."

"It's setting a bad example," said Miss Cornelia grimly.

"Besides," continued wicked Captain Jim, "I wanted to hear some good singing. The Methodists have a good choir; and you can't deny, Cornelia, that the singing in our church is awful since the split in the choir."

"What if the singing isn't good? They're doing their best, and God sees no difference between the voice of a crow and the voice of a nightingale."

"Come, come, Cornelia," said Captain Jim mildly, "I've a better opinion of the Almighty's ear for music than *that*."

"What caused the trouble in our choir?" asked Gilbert, who was suffering from suppressed laughter.

"It dates back to the new church, three years ago," answered Captain Jim. "We had a fearful time over the building of that church—fell out over the question of a new site. The two sites wasn't more'n two hundred yards apart, but you'd have thought they was a thousand by the bitterness of that fight. We was split up into three factions—one wanted the east site and one the south, and one held to the old. It was fought out in bed and at board, and in church and at market. All the old scandals of three generations were dragged out of their graves and aired. Three matches was broken up by it. And the meetings we had to try to settle the question! Cornelia, will you ever forget the one when old Luther Burns got up and made a speech? *He* stated his opinions forcibly."

"Call a spade a spade, Captain. You mean he got red-mad and raked them all, fore and aft. They deserved it too—a pack of incapables. But what would you expect of a committee of men? That building committee held twenty-seven meetings, and at the end of the twenty-seventh weren't no nearer having a church than when they begun—not so near, for a fact, for in one fit of hurrying things along they'd gone to work and tore the old church down, so there we were, without a church, and no place but the hall to worship in."

"The Methodists offered us their church, Cornelia."

"The Glen St. Mary church wouldn't have been built to this day," went on Miss Cornelia, ignoring Captain Jim, "if we women hadn't just started in and took charge. We said *we* meant to have a church, if the men meant to quarrel till doomsday, and we were tired of being a laughing-stock for the Methodists. We held *one* meeting and elected a committee and canvassed for subscriptions. We got them, too. When any of the men tried to sass us we told them they'd tried for two years to build a church and it was our turn now. We shut them up close, believe *me*, and in six months we had our church. Of course, when the men saw we were determined they stopped fighting and went to work, man-like, as soon as they saw they had to, or quit bossing. Oh, women can't preach or be elders; but they can build churches and scare up the money for them."

"The Methodists allow women to preach," said Captain Jim.

Miss Cornelia glared at him.

"I never said the Methodists hadn't common sense, Captain. What I say is, I doubt if they have much religion."

"I suppose you are in favor of votes for women, Miss Cornelia," said Gilbert.

"I'm not hankering after the vote, believe *me*," said Miss Cornelia scornfully. "*I* know what it is to clean up after the men. But some of these days, when the men realize they've got the world into a mess they can't get it out of, they'll be glad to give us the vote, and shoulder their troubles over on us. That's *their* scheme. Oh, it's well that women are patient, believe *me*!"

"What about Job?" suggested Captain Jim.

"Job! It was such a rare thing to find a patient man that when one was really discovered they were determined he shouldn't be forgotten," retorted Miss Cornelia triumphantly. "Anyhow, the virtue doesn't go with the name. There never was such an impatient man born as old Job Taylor over harbor."

"Well, you know, he had a good deal to try him, Cornelia. Even you can't defend his wife. I always remember what old William MacAllister said of her at her funeral, 'There's nae doot she was a Chreestian wumman, but she had the de'il's own temper.'"

"I suppose she *was* trying," admitted Miss Cornelia reluctantly, "but that didn't justify what Job said when she died. He rode home from the graveyard the day of the funeral with my father. He never said a word till they got near home. Then he heaved a big sigh and said, 'You may not believe it, Stephen, but this is the happiest day of my life!' Wasn't that like a man?"

"I s'pose poor old Mrs. Job did make life kinder uneasy for him," reflected Captain Jim.

"Well, there's such a thing as decency, isn't there? Even if a man is rejoicing in his heart over his wife being dead, he needn't proclaim it to the four winds of heaven. And happy day or not, Job Taylor wasn't long in marrying again, you might notice. His second wife could manage him. She made him walk Spanish, believe me! The first thing she did was to make him hustle round and put up a tombstone to the first Mrs. Job—and she had a place left on it for her own name. She said there'd be nobody to make Job put up a monument to *her*."

"Speaking of Taylors, how is Mrs. Lewis Taylor up at the Glen, doctor?" asked Captain Jim.

"She's getting better slowly—but she has to work too hard," replied Gilbert.

"Her husband works hard too—raising prize pigs," said Miss Cornelia. "He's noted for his beautiful pigs. He's a heap prouder of his pigs than of his children. But then, to be sure, his pigs are the best pigs possible, while his children don't amount to much. He picked a poor mother for them, and starved her while she was bearing and rearing them. His pigs got the cream and his children got the skim milk."

"There are times, Cornelia, when I have to agree with you, though it hurts me," said Captain Jim. "That's just exactly the truth about Lewis Taylor. When I see those poor, miserable children of his, robbed of all children ought to have, it p'isens my own bite and sup for days afterwards."

Gilbert went out to the kitchen in response to Anne's beckoning. Anne shut the door and gave him a connubial lecture.

"Gilbert, you and Captain Jim must stop baiting Miss Cornelia. Oh, I've been listening to you—and I just won't allow it."

"Anne, Miss Cornelia is enjoying herself hugely. You know she is."

"Well, never mind. You two needn't egg her on like that. Dinner is ready now, and Gilbert, *don't* let Mrs. Rachel carve the geese. I know she means to offer to do it because she doesn't think you can do it properly. Show her you can."

"I ought to be able to. I've been studying A-B-C-D diagrams of carving for the past month," said Gilbert. "Only don't talk to me while I'm doing it, Anne, for if you drive the letters out of my head I'll be in a worse predicament than you were in old geometry days when the teacher changed them."

Gilbert carved the geese beautifully. Even Mrs. Rachel had to admit that. And everybody ate of them and enjoyed them. Anne's first Christmas dinner was a great success and she beamed with housewifely pride. Merry was the feast and long; and when it was over they gathered around the cheer of the red hearth flame and Captain Jim told them stories until the red sun swung low over Four Winds Harbor, and the long blue shadows of the Lombardies fell across the snow in the lane.

"I must be getting back to the light," he said finally. "I'll jest have time to walk home before sun-down. Thank you for a beautiful Christmas, Mistress Blythe. Bring Master Davy down to the light some night before he goes home."

"I want to see those stone gods," said Davy with a relish.

16

NEW YEAR'S EVE AT THE LIGHT

The Green Gables folk went home after Christmas, Marilla under solemn covenant to return for a month in the spring. More snow came before New Year's, and the harbor froze over, but the gulf still was free, beyond the white, imprisoned fields. The last day of the old year was one of those bright, cold, dazzling winter days, which bombard us with their brilliancy, and command our admiration but never our love. The sky was sharp and blue; the snow diamonds sparkled insistently; the stark trees were bare and shameless, with a kind of brazen beauty; the hills shot assaulting lances of crystal. Even the shadows were sharp and stiff and clear-cut, as no proper shadows should be. Everything that was handsome seemed ten times handsomer and less attractive in the glaring splendor; and everything that was ugly seemed ten times uglier, and everything was either handsome or ugly. There was no soft blending, or kind obscurity, or elusive mistiness in that searching glitter. The only things that held their own individuality were the firs—for the fir is the tree of mystery and shadow, and yields never to the encroachments of crude radiance.

But finally the day began to realise that she was growing old. Then a certain pensiveness fell over her beauty which dimmed yet intensified it; sharp angles, glittering points, melted away into curves and enticing gleams. The white harbor put on soft grays and pinks; the far-away hills turned amethyst.

"The old year is going away beautifully," said Anne.

She and Leslie and Gilbert were on their way to the Four Winds Point, having plotted with Captain Jim to watch the New Year in at the light. The sun had set and in the southwestern sky hung Venus, glorious and golden, having drawn as near to her earth-sister as is possible for her. For the first time Anne and Gilbert saw the shadow cast by that brilliant star of evening, that faint, mysterious shadow, never seen save when there is white snow to reveal it, and then only with averted vision, vanishing when you gaze at it directly.

"It's like the spirit of a shadow, isn't it?" whispered Anne. "You can see it so plainly haunting your side when you look ahead; but when you turn and look at it—it's gone."

"I have heard that you can see the shadow of Venus only once in a lifetime, and that within a year of seeing it your life's most wonderful gift will come to you," said Leslie. But she spoke rather hardly; perhaps she thought that even the shadow of Venus could bring her no gift of life. Anne smiled in the

soft twilight; she felt quite sure what the mystic shadow promised her.

They found Marshall Elliott at the lighthouse. At first Anne
felt inclined to resent the intrusion of this long-haired, long-
bearded eccentric into the familiar little circle. But Marshall Elliott
soon proved his legitimate claim to membership in the household
of Joseph. He was a witty, intelligent, well-read man, rivalling
Captain Jim himself in the knack of telling a good story. They
were all glad when he agreed to watch the old year out with them.

Captain Jim's small nephew Joe had come down to spend
New Year's with his great-uncle, and had fallen asleep on the sofa
with the First Mate curled up in a huge golden ball at his feet.

"Ain't he a dear little man?" said Captain Jim gloatingly. "I do
love to watch a little child asleep, Mistress Blythe. It's the most
beautiful sight in the world, I reckon. Joe does love to get down
here for a night, because I have him sleep with me. At home he
has to sleep with the other two boys, and he doesn't like it. 'Why
can't I sleep with father, Uncle Jim?' say he. 'Everybody in the Bible
slept with their fathers.' As for the questions he asks, the minister
himself couldn't answer them. They fair swamp me. 'Uncle Jim, if I
wasn't *me* who'd I be?' and, 'Uncle Jim, what would happen if God
died?' He fired them two off at me tonight, afore he went to sleep.
As for his imagination, it sails away from everything. He makes up
the most remarkable yarns—and then his mother shuts him up in
the closet for telling stories. And he sits down and makes up
another one, and has it ready to relate to her when she lets him
out. He had one for me when he come down tonight. 'Uncle Jim,'
says he, solemn as a tombstone, 'I had a 'venture in the Glen today.'
'Yes, what was it?' says I, expecting something quite startling, but
nowise prepared for what I really got. 'I met a wolf in the street,'
says he, 'a 'normous wolf with a big, red mouf and *awful* long
teeth, Uncle Jim.' 'I didn't know there was any wolves up at the
Glen,' says I. 'Oh, he comed there from far, far away,' says Joe, 'and
I fought he was going to eat me up, Uncle Jim.' 'Were you scared?'
says I. 'No, 'cause I had a big gun,' says Joe, 'and I shot the wolf

dead, Uncle Jim,—solid dead—and then he went up to heaven and bit God,' says he. Well, I was fair staggered, Mistress Blythe."

The hours bloomed into mirth around the driftwood fire. Captain Jim told tales, and Marshall Elliott sang old Scotch ballads in a fine tenor voice; finally Captain Jim took down his old brown fiddle from the wall and began to play. He had a tolerable knack of fiddling, which all appreciated save the First Mate, who sprang from the sofa as if he had been shot, emitted a shriek of protest, and fled wildly up the stairs.

"Can't cultivate an ear for music in that cat nohow," said Captain Jim. "He won't stay long enough to learn to like it. When we got the organ up at the Glen church old Elder Richards bounced up from his seat the minute the organist began to play and scuttled down the aisle and out of the church at the rate of no-man's-business. It reminded me so strong of the First Mate tearing loose as soon as I begin to fiddle that I come nearer to laughing out loud in church than I ever did before or since."

There was something so infectious in the rollicking tunes which Captain Jim played that very soon Marshall Elliott's feet began to twitch. He had been a noted dancer in his youth. Presently he started up and held out his hands to Leslie. Instantly she responded. Round and round the firelit room they circled with a rhythmic grace that was wonderful. Leslie danced like one inspired; the wild, sweet abandon of the music seemed to have entered into and possessed her. Anne watched her in fascinated admiration. She had never seen her like this. All the innate richness and color and charm of her nature seemed to have broken loose and overflowed in crimson cheek and glowing eye and grace of motion. Even the aspect of Marshall Elliott, with his long beard and hair, could not spoil the picture. On the contrary, it seemed to enhance it. Marshall Elliott looked like a Viking of elder days, dancing with one of the blue-eyed, golden-haired daughters of the Northland.

"The purtiest dancing I ever saw, and I've seen some in my

time," declared Captain Jim, when at last the bow fell from his tired hand. Leslie dropped into her chair, laughing, breathless.

"I love dancing," she said apart to Anne. "I haven't danced since I was sixteen—but I love it. The music seems to run through my veins like quicksilver and I forget everything—everything—except the delight of keeping time to it. There isn't any floor beneath me, or walls about me, or roof over me—I'm floating amid the stars."

Captain Jim hung his fiddle up in its place, beside a large frame enclosing several banknotes.

"Is there anybody else of your acquaintance who can afford to hang his walls with banknotes for pictures?" he asked. "There's twenty ten-dollar notes there, not worth the glass over them. They're old Bank of P. E. Island notes. Had them by me when the bank failed, and I had 'em framed and hung up, partly as a reminder not to put your trust in banks, and partly to give me a real luxurious, millionairy feeling. Hullo, Matey, don't be scared. You can come back now. The music and revelry is over for tonight. The old year has just another hour to stay with us. I've seen seventy-six New Years come in over that gulf yonder, Mistress Blythe."

"You'll see a hundred," said Marshall Elliott.

Captain Jim shook his head.

"No; and I don't want to—at least, I think I don't. Death grows friendlier as we grow older. Not that one of us really wants to die though, Marshall. Tennyson spoke truth when he said that. There's old Mrs. Wallace up at the Glen. She's had heaps of trouble all her life, poor soul, and she's lost almost everyone she cared about. She's always saying that she'll be glad when her time comes, and she doesn't want to sojourn any longer in this vale of tears. But when she takes a sick spell there's a fuss! Doctors from town, and a trained nurse, and enough medicine to kill a dog. Life may be a vale of tears, all right, but there are some folks who enjoy weeping, I reckon."

They spent the old year's last hour quietly around the fire. A few minutes before twelve Captain Jim rose and opened the door.

"We must let the New Year in," he said.

Outside was a fine blue night. A sparkling ribbon of moonlight garlanded the gulf. Inside the bar the harbor shone like a pavement of pearl. They stood before the door and waited—Captain Jim with his ripe, full experience, Marshall Elliott in his vigorous but empty middle life, Gilbert and Anne with their precious memories and exquisite hopes, Leslie with her record of starved years and her hopeless future. The clock on the little shelf above the fireplace struck twelve.

"Welcome, New Year," said Captain Jim, bowing low as the last stroke died away. "I wish you all the best year of your lives, mates. I reckon that whatever the New Year brings us will be the best the Great Captain has for us—and somehow or other we'll all make port in a good harbor."

17
A FOUR WINDS WINTER

Winter set in vigorously after New Year's. Big, white drifts heaped themselves about the little house, and palms of frost covered its windows. The harbor ice grew harder and thicker, until the Four Winds people began their usual winter travelling over it. The safe ways were "bushed" by a benevolent Government, and night and day the gay tinkle of the sleigh-bells sounded on it. On moonlit nights Anne heard them in her house of dreams like fairy chimes. The gulf froze over, and the Four Winds light flashed no more. During the months when navigation was closed Captain Jim's office was a sinecure.

"The First Mate and I will have nothing to do till spring except keep warm and amuse ourselves. The last lighthouse keeper used always to move up to the Glen in winter; but I'd rather stay at the Point. The First Mate might get poisoned or

chewed up by dogs at the Glen. It's a mite lonely, to be sure, with
neither the light nor the water for company, but if our friends
come to see us often we'll weather it through."

Captain Jim had an ice boat, and many a wild, glorious spin
Gilbert and Anne and Leslie had over the glib harbor ice with
him. Anne and Leslie took long snowshoe tramps together, too,
over the fields, or across the harbor after storms, or through the
woods beyond the Glen. They were very good comrades in their
rambles and their fireside communings. Each had something to
give the other—each felt life the richer for friendly exchange of
thought and friendly silence; each looked across the white fields
between their homes with a pleasant consciousness of a friend
beyond. But, in spite of all this, Anne felt that there was always a
barrier between Leslie and herself—a constraint that never wholly vanished.

"I don't know why I can't get closer to her," Anne said one
evening to Captain Jim. "I like her so much—I admire her so
much—I *want* to take her right into my heart and creep right into
hers. But I can never cross the barrier."

"You've been too happy all your life, Mistress Blythe," said
Captain Jim thoughtfully. "I reckon that's why you and Leslie
can't get real close together in your souls. The barrier between
you is her experience of sorrow and trouble. She ain't responsible
for it and you ain't; but it's there and neither of you can cross it."

"My childhood wasn't very happy before I came to Green
Gables," said Anne, gazing soberly out of the window at the still,
sad, dead beauty of the leafless tree-shadows on the moonlit snow.

"Mebbe not—but it was just the usual unhappiness of a child
who hasn't anyone to look after it properly. There hasn't been any
tragedy in your life, Mistress Blythe. And poor Leslie's has been
almost *all* tragedy. She feels, I reckon, though mebbe she hardly
knows she feels it, that there's a vast deal in her life you can't
enter nor understand—and so she has to keep you back from
it—hold you off, so to speak, from hurting her. You know if we've

got anything about us that hurts we shrink from anyone's touch
on or near it. It holds good with our souls as well as our bodies, I
reckon. Leslie's soul must be near raw—it's no wonder she hides
it away."

"If that were really all, I wouldn't mind, Captain Jim. I would
understand. But there are times—not always, but now and
again—when I almost have to believe that Leslie doesn't—doesn't
like me. Sometimes I surprise a look in her eyes that seems to
show resentment and dislike—it goes so quickly—but I've seen
it, I'm sure of that. And it hurts me, Captain Jim. I'm not used to
being disliked—and I've tried so hard to win Leslie's friendship."

"You have won it, Mistress Blythe. Don't you go cherishing
any foolish notion that Leslie don't like you. If she didn't she
wouldn't have anything to do with you, much less chumming
with you as she does. I know Leslie Moore too well not to be sure
of that."

"The first time I ever saw her, driving her geese down the hill
on the day I came to Four Winds, she looked at me with the
same expression," persisted Anne. "I felt it, even in the midst of
my admiration of her beauty. She looked at me resentfully—she
did, indeed, Captain Jim."

"The resentment must have been about something else, Mistress Blythe, and you jest come in for a share of it because you
happened past. Leslie *does* take sullen spells now and again, poor
girl. I can't blame her, when I know what she has to put up with.
I don't know why it's permitted. The doctor and I have talked a
lot about the origin of evil, but we haven't quite found out all
about it yet. There's a vast of onunderstandable things in life, ain't
there, Mistress Blythe? Sometimes things seem to work out real
proper-like, same as with you and the doctor. And then again
they all seem to go catawampus. There's Leslie, so clever and
beautiful you'd think she was meant for a queen, and instead
she's cooped up over there, robbed of almost everything a woman'd value, with no prospect except waiting on Dick Moore all
her life. Though, mind you, Mistress Blythe, I daresay she'd

choose her life now, such as it is, rather than the life she lived with Dick before he went away. *That's* something a clumsy old sailor's tongue mustn't meddle with. But you've helped Leslie a lot—she's a different creature since you come to Four Winds. Us old friends see the difference in her, as you can't. Miss Cornelia and me was talking it over the other day, and it's one of the mighty few p'ints that we see eye to eye on. So jest you throw overboard any idea of her not liking you."

Anne could hardly discard it completely, for there were undoubtedly times when she felt, with an instinct that was not to be combated by reason, that Leslie harbored a queer, indefinable resentment towards her. At times, this secret consciousness marred the delight of their comradeship; at others it was almost forgotten; but Anne always felt the hidden thorn was there, and might prick her at any moment. She felt a cruel sting from it on the day when she told Leslie of what she hoped the spring would bring to the little house of dreams. Leslie looked at her with hard, bitter, unfriendly eyes.

"So you are to have *that*, too," she said in a choked voice. And without another word she had turned and gone across the fields homeward. Anne was deeply hurt; for the moment she felt as if she could never like Leslie again. But when Leslie came over a few evenings later she was so pleasant, so friendly, so frank, and witty, and winsome, that Anne was charmed into forgiveness and forgetfulness. Only, she never mentioned her darling hope to Leslie again; nor did Leslie ever refer to it. But one evening, when late winter was listening for the word of spring, she came over to the little house for a twilight chat; and when she went away she left a small, white box on the table. Anne found it after she was gone and opened it wonderingly. In it was a tiny white dress of exquisite workmanship—delicate embroidery, wonderful tucking, sheer loveliness. Every stitch in it was handwork; and the little frills of lace at neck and sleeves were of real Valenciennes. Lying on it was a card—"with Leslie's love."

"What hours of work she must have put on it," said Anne.

"And the material must have cost more than she could really afford. It is very sweet of her."

But Leslie was brusque and curt when Anne thanked her, and again the latter felt thrown back upon herself.

Leslie's gift was not alone in the little house. Miss Cornelia had, for the time being, given up sewing for unwanted, unwelcome eighth babies, and fallen to sewing for a very much wanted first one, whose welcome would leave nothing to be desired. Philippa Blake and Diana Wright each sent a marvellous garment; and Mrs. Rachel Lynde sent several, in which good material and honest stitches took the place of embroidery and frills. Anne herself made many, desecrated by no touch of machinery, spending over them the happiest hours of that happy winter.

Captain Jim was the most frequent guest of the little house, and none was more welcome. Every day Anne loved the simple-souled, true-hearted old sailor more and more. He was as refreshing as a sea-breeze, as interesting as some ancient chronicle. She was never tired of listening to his stories, and his quaint remarks and comments were a continual delight to her. Captain Jim was one of those rare and interesting people who "never speak but they say something." The milk of human kindness and the wisdom of the serpent were mingled in his composition in delightful proportions.

Nothing ever seemed to put Captain Jim out or depress him in any way.

"I've kind of contracted a habit of enj'ying things," he remarked once, when Anne had commented on his invariable cheerfulness. "It's got so chronic that I believe I even enj'y the disagreeable things. It's great fun thinking they can't last. 'Old rheumatiz,' says I, when it grips me hard, 'you've *got* to stop aching sometime. The worse you are the sooner you'll stop, mebbe. I'm bound to get the better of you in the long run, whether in the body or out of the body.'"

One night, by the fireside at the light Anne saw Captain Jim's "life-book." He needed no coaxing to show it and proudly gave it to her to read.

"I writ it to leave to little Joe," he said. "I don't like the idea of everything I've done and seen being clean forgot after I've shipped for my last v'yage. Joe, he'll remember it, and tell the yarns to his children."

It was an old leather-bound book filled with the record of his voyages and adventures. Anne thought what a treasure trove it would be to a writer. Every sentence was a nugget. In itself the book had no literary merit; Captain Jim's charm of story-telling failed him when he came to pen and ink; he could only jot roughly down the outline of his famous tales, and both spelling and grammar were sadly askew. But Anne felt that if anyone possessed of the gift could take that simple record of a brave, adventurous life, reading between the bald lines the tales of dangers staunchly faced and duty manfully done, a wonderful story might be made from it. Rich comedy and thrilling tragedy were both lying hidden in Captain Jim's "life-book," waiting for the touch of the master hand to waken the laughter and grief and horror of thousands.

Anne said something of this to Gilbert as they walked home.

"Why don't you try your hand at it yourself, Anne?"

Anne shook her head.

"No. I only wish I could. But it's not in the power of my gift. You know what my forte is, Gilbert—the fanciful, the fairylike, the pretty. To write Captain Jim's life-book as it should be written one should be a master of vigorous yet subtle style, a keen psychologist, a born humorist and a born tragedian. A rare combination of gifts is needed. Paul might do it if he were older. Anyhow, I'm going to ask him to come down next summer and meet Captain Jim."

"Come to this shore," wrote Anne to Paul. "I am afraid you cannot find here Nora or the Golden Lady or the Twin Sailors; but you will find one old sailor who can tell you wonderful stories."

Paul, however, wrote back, saying regretfully that he could not come that year. He was going abroad for two years' study.

"When I return I'll come to Four Winds, dear Teacher," he wrote.

"But meanwhile, Captain Jim is growing old," said Anne, sorrowfully, "and there is nobody to write his life-book."

18
SPRING DAYS

The ice in the harbor grew black and rotten in the March suns; in April there were blue waters and a windy, white-capped gulf again; and again the Four Winds light begemmed the twilights.

"I'm so glad to see it once more," said Anne, on the first evening of its reappearance. "I've missed it so all winter. The north-western sky has seemed blank and lonely without it."

The land was tender with brand-new, golden-green, baby leaves. There was an emerald mist on the woods beyond the Glen. The seaward valleys were full of fairy mists at dawn.

Vibrant winds came and went with salt foam in their breath. The sea laughed and flashed and preened and allured, like a beautiful, coquettish woman. The herring schooled and the fishing village woke to life. The harbor was alive with white sails making for the channel. The ships began to sail outward and inward again.

"On a spring day like this," said Anne, "I know exactly what my soul will feel like on the resurrection morning."

"There are times in spring when I sorter feel that I might have been a poet if I'd been caught young," remarked Captain Jim. "I catch myself conning over old lines and verses I heard the schoolmaster reciting sixty years ago. They don't trouble me at other times. Now I feel as if I had to get out on the rocks or the fields or the water and spout them."

Captain Jim had come up that afternoon to bring Anne a load

of shells for her garden, and a little bunch of sweet-grass which he had found in a ramble over the sand-dunes.

"It's getting real scarce along this shore now," he said. "When I was a boy there was a-plenty of it. But now it's only once in a while you'll find a plot—and never when you're looking for it. You jest have to stumble on it—you're walking along on the sand-hills, never thinking of sweet-grass—and all at once the air is full of sweetness—and there's the grass under your feet. I favor the smell of sweet-grass. It always makes me think of my mother."

"She was fond of it?" asked Anne.

"Not that I knows on. Dunno's she ever saw any sweet-grass. No, it's because it has a kind of motherly perfume—not too young, you understand—something kind of seasoned and whole-some and dependable—jest like a mother. The schoolmaster's bride always kept it among her handkerchiefs. You might put that little bunch among yours, Mistress Blythe. I don't like these boughten scents—but a whiff of sweet-grass belongs anywhere a lady does."

Anne had not been especially enthusiastic over the idea of surrounding her flower beds with quahog shells; as a decoration they did not appeal to her on first thought. But she would not have hurt Captain Jim's feelings for anything; so she assumed a virtue she did not at first feel, and thanked him heartily. And when Captain Jim had proudly encircled every bed with a rim of the big, milk-white shells, Anne found to her surprise that she liked the effect. On a town lawn, or even up at the Glen, they would not have been in keeping, but here, in the old-fashioned, sea-bound garden of the little house of dreams, they *belonged*.

"They *do* look nice," she said sincerely.

"The schoolmaster's bride always had cow-hawks round her beds," said Captain Jim. "She was a master hand with flowers. She *looked* at 'em—and touched 'em—*so*—and they grew like mad. Some folks have that knack—I reckon you have it, too, Mistress Blythe."

"Oh, I don't know—but I love my garden, and I love working

in it. To potter with green, growing things, watching each day to see the dear, new sprouts come up, is like taking a hand in creation, I think. Just now my garden is like faith—the substance of things hoped for. But bide a wee."

"It always amazes me to look at the little, wrinkled brown seeds and think of the rainbows in 'em," said Captain Jim. "When I ponder on them seeds I don't find it nowise hard to believe that we've got souls that'll live in other worlds. You couldn't hardly believe there was life in them tiny things, some no bigger than grains of dust, let alone color and scent, if you hadn't seen the miracle, could you?"

Anne, who was counting her days like silver beads on a rosary, could not now take the long walk to the lighthouse or up the Glen road. But Miss Cornelia and Captain Jim came very often to the little house. Miss Cornelia was the joy of Anne's and Gilbert's existence. They laughed side-splittingly over her speeches after every visit. When Captain Jim and she happened to visit the little house at the same time there was much sport for the listening. They waged wordy warfare, she attacking, he defending. Anne once reproached the Captain for his baiting of Miss Cornelia.

"Oh, I do love to set her going, Mistress Blythe," chuckled the unrepentant sinner. "It's the greatest amusement I have in life. That tongue of hers would blister a stone. And you and that young dog of a doctor enj'y listening to her as much as I do."

Captain Jim came along another evening to bring Anne some mayflowers. The garden was full of the moist, scented air of a maritime spring evening. There was a milk-white mist on the edge of the sea, with a young moon kissing it, and a silver gladness of stars over the Glen. The bell of the church across the harbor was ringing dreamily sweet. The mellow chime drifted through the dusk to mingle with the soft spring-moan of the sea. Captain Jim's mayflowers added the last completing touch to the charm of the night.

"I haven't seen any this spring, and I've missed them," said Anne, burying her face in them.

"They ain't to be found around Four Winds, only in the barrens away behind the Glen up yander. I took a little trip today to the Land-of-nothing-to-do, and hunted these up for you. I reckon they're the last you'll see this spring, for they're nearly done."

"How kind and thoughtful you are, Captain Jim. Nobody else—not even Gilbert"—with a shake of her head at him—"remembered that I always long for mayflowers in spring."

"Well, I had another errand, too—I wanted to take Mr. Howard back yander a mess of trout. He likes one occasional, and it's all I can do for a kindness he did me once. I stayed all the afternoon and talked to him. He likes to talk to me, though he's a highly eddicated man and I'm only an ignorant old sailor, because he's one of the folks that's *got* to talk or they're miserable, and he finds listeners scarce around here. The Glen folks fight shy of him because they think he's an infidel. He ain't that far gone exactly—few men is, I reckon—but he's what you might call a heretic. Heretics are wicked, but they're mighty int'resting. It's jest that they've got sorter lost looking for God, being under the impression that He's hard to find—which He ain't never. Most of 'em blunder to Him after awhile, I guess. I don't think listening to Mr. Howard's arguments is likely to do *me* much harm. Mind you, I believe what I was brought up to believe. It saves a vast of bother—and back of it all, God is good. The trouble with Mr. Howard is that he's a leetle *too* clever. He thinks that he's bound to live up to his cleverness, and that it's smarter to thrash out some new way of getting to heaven than to go by the old track the common, ignorant folks is travelling. But he'll get there sometime all right, and then he'll laugh at himself."

"Mr. Howard was a Methodist to begin with," said Miss Cornelia, as if she thought he had not far to go from that to heresy.

"Do you know, Cornelia," said Captain Jim gravely, "I've often thought that if I wasn't a Presbyterian I'd be a Methodist."

"Oh, well," conceded Miss Cornelia, "if you weren't a Presbyterian it wouldn't matter much what you were. Speaking of heresy, reminds me, doctor—I've brought back that book you lent me—that *Natural Law in the Spiritual World*—I didn't read more'n a third of it. I can read sense, and I can read nonsense, but that book is neither the one nor the other."

"It *is* considered rather heretical in some quarters," admitted Gilbert, "but I told you that before you took it, Miss Cornelia."

"Oh, I wouldn't have minded its being heretical. I can stand wickedness, but I can't stand foolishness," said Miss Cornelia calmly, and with the air of having said the last thing there was to say about *Natural Law.*

"Speaking of books, *A Mad Love* come to an end at last two weeks ago," remarked Captain Jim musingly. "It run to one hundred and three chapters. When they got married the book stopped right off, so I reckon their troubles were all over. It's real nice that that's the way in books anyhow, isn't it, even if 'tisn't so anywhere else?"

"I never read novels," said Miss Cornelia. "Did you hear how Geordie Russell was today, Captain Jim?"

"Yes, I called in on my way home to see him. He's getting round all right—but stewing in a broth of trouble, as usual, poor man. 'Course he brews up most of it for himself, but I reckon that don't make it any easier to bear."

"He's an awful pessimist," said Miss Cornelia.

"Well, no, he ain't a pessimist exactly, Cornelia. He only jest never finds anything that suits him."

"And isn't that a pessimist?"

"No, no. A pessimist is one who never expects to find anything to suit him. Geordie hain't got *that* far yet."

"You'd find something good to say of the devil himself, Jim Boyd."

"Well, you've heard the story of the old lady who said he was persevering. But no, Cornelia, I've nothing good to say of the devil."

"Do you believe in him at all?" asked Miss Cornelia seriously.

"How can you ask that when you know what a good Presbyterian I am, Cornelia? How could a Presbyterian get along without a devil?"

"*Do* you?" persisted Miss Cornelia.

Captain Jim suddenly became grave.

"I believe in what I heard a minister once call 'a mighty and malignant and *intelligent* power of evil working in the universe,'" he said solemnly. "I do *that*, Cornelia. You can call it the devil, or the 'principle of evil,' or the Old Scratch, or any name you like. It's *there*, and all the infidels and heretics in the world can't argue it away, any more'n they can argue God away. It's there, and it's working. But, mind you, Cornelia, I believe it's going to get the worst of it in the long run."

"I am sure I hope so," said Miss Cornelia, none too hopefully. "But speaking of the devil, I am positive that Billy Booth is possessed by him now. Have you heard of Billy's latest performance?"

"No, what was that?"

"He's gone and burned up his wife's new, brown broadcloth suit, that she paid twenty-five dollars for in Charlottetown, because he declares the men looked too admiring at her when she wore it to church the first time. Wasn't that like a man?"

"Mistress Booth *is* mighty pretty, and brown's her color," said Captain Jim reflectively.

"Is that any good reason why he should poke her new suit into the kitchen stove? Billy Booth is a jealous fool, and he makes his wife's life miserable. She's cried all the week about her suit. Oh, Anne, I wish I could write like you, believe *me*. Wouldn't I score some of the men round here!"

"Those Booths are all a mite queer," said Captain Jim. "Billy seemed the sanest of the lot till he got married and then this queer jealous streak cropped out in him. His brother Daniel, now, was always odd."

"Took tantrums every few days or so and wouldn't get out of bed," said Miss Cornelia with a relish. "His wife would have to do all the barn work till he got over his spell. When he died people wrote her letters of condolence; if I'd written anything it would have been one of congratulation. Their father, old Abram Booth, was a disgusting old sot. He was drunk at his wife's funeral, and kept reeling round and hiccuping 'I didn't dri—i—i—nk much but I feel a—a—awfully que—e—e—r.' I gave him a good jab in the back with my umbrella when he came near me, and it sobered him up until they got the casket out of the house. Young Johnny Booth was to have been married yesterday, but he couldn't be because he's gone and got the mumps. Wasn't that like a man?"

"How could he help getting the mumps, poor fellow?"

"I'd poor fellow him, believe *me*, if I was Kate Sterns. I don't know how he could help getting the mumps, but I *do* know the wedding supper was all prepared and everything will be spoiled before he's well again. Such a waste! He should have had the mumps when he was a boy."

"Come, come, Cornelia, don't you think you're a mite unreasonable?"

Miss Cornelia disdained to reply and turned instead to Susan Baker, a grim-faced, kind-hearted elderly spinster of the Glen, who had been installed as maid-of-all-work at the little house for some weeks. Susan had been up to the Glen to make a sick call, and had just returned.

"How is poor old Aunt Mandy tonight?" asked Miss Cornelia. Susan sighed.

"Very poorly—very poorly, Cornelia. I am afraid she will soon be in heaven, poor thing!"

"Oh, surely, it's not so bad as that!" exclaimed Miss Cornelia, sympathetically.

Captain Jim and Gilbert looked at each other. Then they suddenly rose and went out.

"There are times," said Captain Jim, between spasms, "when it would be a sin *not* to laugh. Them two excellent women!"

19
DAWN AND DUSK

In early June, when the sand-hills were a great glory of pink wild roses, and the Glen was smothered in apple-blossoms, Marilla arrived at the little house, accompanied by a black horse-hair trunk, patterned with brass nails, which had reposed undisturbed in the Green Gables garret for half a century. Susan Baker, who, during her few weeks' sojourn in the little house, had come to worship "young Mrs. Doctor," as she called Anne, with blind fervor, looked rather jealously askance at Marilla at first. But as Marilla did not try to interfere in kitchen matters, and showed no desire to interrupt Susan's ministrations to young Mrs. Doctor, the good handmaiden became reconciled to her presence, and told her cronies at the Glen that Miss Cuthbert was a fine old lady and knew her place.

One evening, when the sky's limpid bowl was filled with a red glory, and the robins were thrilling the golden twilight with jubilant hymns to the stars of evening, there was a sudden commotion in the little house of dreams. Telephone messages were sent up to the Glen, Doctor Dave and a white-capped nurse came hastily down, Marilla paced the garden walks between the quahog shells, murmuring prayers between her set lips, and Susan sat in the kitchen with cotton wool in her ears and her apron over her head.

Leslie, looking out from the house up the brook, saw that every window of the little house was alight, and did not sleep that night.

The June night was short; but it seemed an eternity to those who waited and watched.

"Oh, will it *never* end?" said Marilla; then she saw how grave the nurse and Doctor Dave looked, and she dared ask no more questions. Suppose Anne—but Marilla could not suppose it.

"Do not tell me," said Susan fiercely, answering the anguish in Marilla's eyes, "that God could be so cruel as to take that darling lamb from us when we all love her so much."

"He has taken others as well beloved," said Marilla hoarsely.

But at dawn, when the rising sun rent apart the mists hanging over the sand-bar, and made rainbows of them, joy came to the little house. Anne was safe, and a wee, white lady, with her mother's big eyes, was lying beside her. Gilbert, his face gray and haggard from his night's agony, came down to tell Marilla and Susan.

"Thank God," shuddered Marilla.

Susan got up and took the cotton wool out of her ears.

"Now for breakfast," she said briskly. "I am of the opinion that we will all be glad of a bite and sup. You tell young Mrs. Doctor not to worry about a single thing—Susan is at the helm. You tell her just to think of her baby."

Gilbert smiled rather sadly as he went away. Anne, her pale face blanched with its baptism of pain, her eyes aglow with the holy passion of motherhood, did not need to be told to think of her baby. She thought of nothing else. For a few hours she tasted of happiness so rare and exquisite that she wondered if the angels in heaven did not envy her.

"Little Joyce," she murmured, when Marilla came in to see the baby. "We planned to call her that if she were a girlie. There were so many we would have liked to name her for; we couldn't choose between them, so we decided on Joyce—we can call her Joy for short—Joy—it suits so well. Oh, Marilla, I thought I was happy before. Now I know that I just dreamed a pleasant dream of happiness. *This* is the reality."

"You mustn't talk, Anne—wait till you're stronger," said Marilla warningly.

"You know how hard it is for me *not* to talk," smiled Anne.

At first she was too weak and too happy to notice that Gilbert and the nurse looked grave and Marilla sorrowful. Then, as subtly, and coldly, and remorselessly as a sea-fog stealing landward, fear crept into her heart. Why was not Gilbert gladder? Why would he not talk about the baby? Why would they not let her have it with her after that first heavenly-happy hour? Was—was there anything wrong?

"Gilbert," whispered Anne imploringly, "the baby—is all right —isn't she? Tell me—tell me."

Gilbert was a long while in turning round; then he bent over Anne and looked in her eyes. Marilla, listening fearfully outside the door, heard a pitiful, heart-broken moan, and fled to the kitchen where Susan was weeping.

"Oh, the poor lamb—the poor lamb! How can she bear it, Miss Cuthbert? I am afraid it will kill her. She has been that built up and happy, longing for that baby, and planning for it. Cannot anything be done nohow, Miss Cuthbert?"

"I'm afraid not, Susan. Gilbert says there is no hope. He knew from the first the little thing couldn't live."

"And it is such a sweet baby," sobbed Susan. "I never saw one so white—they are mostly red or yallow. And it opened its big eyes as if it was months old. The little, little thing! Oh, the poor, young Mrs. Doctor!"

At sunset the little soul that had come with the dawning went away, leaving heartbreak behind it. Miss Cornelia took the wee, white lady from the kindly but stranger hands of the nurse, and dressed the tiny waxen form in the beautiful dress Leslie had made for it. Leslie had asked her to do that. Then she took it back and laid it beside the poor, broken, tear-blinded little mother.

"The Lord has given and the Lord has taken away, dearie," she said through her own tears. "Blessed be the name of the Lord."

Then she went away, leaving Anne and Gilbert alone together with their dead.

The next day, the small white Joy was laid in a velvet casket which Leslie had lined with apple-blossoms, and taken to the graveyard of the church across the harbor. Miss Cornelia and Marilla put all the little love-made garments away, together with the ruffled basket which had been befrilled and belaced for dimpled limbs and downy head. Little Joy was never to sleep there; she had found a colder, narrower bed.

"This has been an awful disappointment to me," sighed Miss

Cornelia. "I've looked forward to this baby—and I did want it to be a girl, too."

"I can only be thankful that Anne's life was spared," said Marilla, with a shiver, recalling those hours of darkness when the girl she loved was passing through the valley of the shadow.

"Poor, poor lamb! Her heart is broken," said Susan.

"I *envy* Anne," said Leslie suddenly and fiercely, "and I'd envy her even if she had died! She was a mother for one beautiful day. I'd gladly give my life for *that*!"

"I wouldn't talk like that, Leslie, dearie," said Miss Cornelia deprecatingly. She was afraid that the dignified Miss Cuthbert would think Leslie quite terrible.

Anne's convalescence was long, and made bitter for her by many things. The bloom and sunshine of the Four Winds world grated harshly on her; and yet, when the rain fell heavily, she pictured it beating so mercilessly down on that little grave across the harbor; and when the wind blew around the eaves she heard sad voices in it she had never heard before.

Kindly callers hurt her, too, with the well-meant platitudes with which they strove to cover the nakedness of bereavement. A letter from Phil Blake was an added sting. Phil had heard of the baby's birth, but not of its death, and she wrote Anne a congratulatory letter of sweet mirth which hurt her horribly.

"I would have laughed over it so happily if I had my baby," she sobbed to Marilla. "But when I haven't it just seems like wanton cruelty—though I know Phil wouldn't hurt me for the world. Oh, Marilla, I don't see how I can *ever* be happy again—*everything* will hurt me all the rest of my life."

"Time will help you," said Marilla, who was racked with sympathy but could never learn to express it in other than age-worn formulas.

"It doesn't seem *fair*," said Anne rebelliously. "Babies are born and live where they are not wanted—where they will be neglected—where they will have no chance. I would have loved my baby so—and cared for it so tenderly—and tried to give her every chance for good. And yet I wasn't allowed to keep her."

"It was God's will, Anne," said Marilla, helpless before the riddle of the universe—the *why* of undeserved pain. "And little Joy is better off."

"I can't believe *that*," cried Anne bitterly. Then, seeing that Marilla looked shocked, she added passionately, "Why should she be born at all—why should any one be born at all—if she's better off dead? I *don't* believe it is better for a child to die at birth than to live its life out—and love and be loved—and enjoy and suffer—and do its work—and develop a character that would give it a personality in eternity. And how do you know it was God's will? Perhaps it was just a thwarting of His purpose by the Power of Evil. We can't be expected to be resigned to *that*."

"Oh, Anne, don't talk so," said Marilla, genuinely alarmed lest Anne were drifting into deep and dangerous waters. "We can't understand—but we must have faith—we *must* believe that all is for the best. I know you find it hard to think so, just now. But try to be brave—for Gilbert's sake. He's so worried about you. You aren't getting strong as fast as you should."

"Oh, I know I've been very selfish," sighed Anne. "I love Gilbert more than ever—and I want to live for his sake. But it seems as if part of me was buried over there in that little harbor graveyard—and it hurts so much that I'm afraid of life."

"It won't hurt so much always, Anne."

"The thought that it may stop hurting sometimes hurts me worse than all else, Marilla."

"Yes, I know, I've felt that too, about other things. But we all love you, Anne. Captain Jim has been up every day to ask for you—and Mrs. Moore haunts the place—and Miss Bryant spends most of her time, I think, cooking up nice things for you. Susan doesn't like it very well. She thinks she can cook as well as Miss Bryant."

"Dear Susan! Oh, everybody has been so dear and good and lovely to me, Marilla. I'm not ungrateful—and perhaps—when this horrible ache grows a little less—I'll find that I can go on living."

20
LOST MARGARET

Anne found that she could go on living; the day came when she even smiled again over one of Miss Cornelia's speeches. But there was something in the smile that had never been in Anne's smile before and would never be absent from it again.

On the first day she was able to go for a drive Gilbert took her down to Four Winds Point, and left her there while he rowed over the channel to see a patient at the fishing village. A rollicking wind was scudding across the harbor and the dunes, whipping the water into white-caps and washing the sandshore with long lines of silvery breakers.

"I'm real proud to see you again, Mistress Blythe," said Captain Jim. "Sit down—sit down. I'm afeared it's mighty dusty here today—but there's no need of looking at dust when you can look at such scenery, is there?"

"I don't mind the dust," said Anne, "but Gilbert says I must keep in the open air. I think I'll go and sit on the rock down there."

"Would you like company or would you rather be alone?"

"If by company you mean yours I'd much rather have it than be alone," said Anne, smiling. Then she sighed. She had never before minded being alone. Now she dreaded it. When she was alone now she felt so dreadfully alone.

"Here's a nice little spot where the wind can't get at you," said Captain Jim, when they reached the rocks. "I often sit here. It's a great place jest to sit and dream."

"Oh—dreams," sighed Anne. "I can't dream now, Captain Jim—I'm done with dreams."

"Oh, no, you're not, Mistress Blythe—oh, no, you're not," said Captain Jim meditatively. "I know how you feel jest now—but if you keep on living you'll get glad again, and the first thing you know you'll be dreaming again—thank the good Lord for it! If it wasn't for our dreams they might as well bury us. How'd we stand living if it wasn't for our dream of immortality? And that's a dream that's *bound* to come true, Mistress Blythe. You'll see your little Joyce again some day."

"But she won't be my baby," said Anne, with trembling lips. "Oh, she may be, as Longfellow says, 'a fair maiden clothed with celestial grace'—but she'll be a stranger to me."

"God will manage better'n *that*, I believe," said Captain Jim.

They were both silent for a little time. Then Captain Jim said very softly:

"Mistress Blythe, may I tell you about lost Margaret?"

"Of course," said Anne gently. She did not know who "lost Margaret" was, but she felt that she was going to hear the romance of Captain Jim's life.

"I've often wanted to tell you about her," Captain Jim went on. "Do you know why, Mistress Blythe? It's because I want somebody to remember and think of her sometime after I'm gone. I can't bear that her name should be forgotten by all living souls. And now nobody remembers lost Margaret but me."

Then Captain Jim told the story—an old, old forgotten story, for it was over fifty years since Margaret had fallen asleep one day in her father's dory and drifted—or so it was supposed, for nothing was ever certainly known as to her fate—out of the channel, beyond the bar, to perish in the black thunder-squall which had come up so suddenly that long-ago summer afternoon. But to Captain Jim those fifty years were but as yesterday when it is past.

"I walked the shore for months after that," he said sadly, "looking to find her dear, sweet little body; but the sea never give her back to me. But I'll find her sometime, Mistress Blythe—I'll find her sometime. She's waiting for me. I wish I could tell you jest how she looked, but I can't. I've seen a fine, silvery mist hanging over the bar at sunrise that seemed like her—and then again I've seen a white birch in the woods back yander that made me think of her. She had pale, brown hair and a little white, sweet face, and long slender fingers like yours, Mistress Blythe, only browner, for she was a shore girl. Sometimes I wake up in the night and hear the sea calling to me in the old way, and it seems as if lost Margaret called in it. And when there's a storm and the waves are sobbing and moaning I hear her lamenting among them. And when they laugh on a gay day it's *her* laugh—lost Margaret's sweet, roguish, little laugh. The sea took her from me, but some day I'll find her, Mistress Blythe. It can't keep us apart forever."

"I am glad you have told me about her," said Anne. "I have often wondered why you had lived all your life alone."

"I couldn't ever care for anyone else. Lost Margaret took my heart with her—out there," said the old lover, who had been faithful for fifty years to his drowned sweetheart. "You won't mind if I talk a good deal about her, will you, Mistress Blythe? It's a pleasure to me—for all the pain went out of her memory years ago and jest left its blessing. I know you'll never forget her, Mistress Blythe. And if the years, as I hope, bring other little folks to your home, I want you to promise me that you'll tell *them* the story of lost Margaret, so that her name won't be forgotten among humankind."

21
BARRIERS SWEPT AWAY

"Anne," said Leslie, breaking abruptly a short silence, "you don't know how *good* it is to be sitting here with you again— working—and talking—and being silent together."

They were sitting among the blue-eyed grasses on the bank of the brook in Anne's garden. The water sparkled and crooned past them; the birches threw dappled shadows over them; roses bloomed along the walks. The sun was beginning to be low, and the air was full of woven music. There was one music of the wind in the firs behind the house, and another of the waves on the bar, and still another from the distant bell of the church near which the wee, white lady slept. Anne loved that bell, though it brought sorrowful thoughts now.

She looked curiously at Leslie, who had thrown down her sewing and spoken with a lack of restraint that was very unusual with her.

"On that horrible night when you were so ill," Leslie went on, "I kept thinking that perhaps we'd have no more talks and walks and *works* together. And I realized just what your friendship had come to mean to me—just what *you* meant—and just what a hateful little beast I had been."

"Leslie! Leslie! I never allow anyone to call my friends names."

"It's true. That's exactly what I am—a hateful little beast. There's something I've *got* to tell you, Anne. I suppose it will make you despise me, but I *must* confess it. Anne, there have been times this past winter and spring when I have *hated* you."

"I knew it," said Anne calmly.

"You *knew* it?"

"Yes, I saw it in your eyes."

"And yet you went on liking me and being my friend."

"Well, it was only now and then you hated me, Leslie. Between times you loved me, I think."

"I certainly did. But that other horrid feeling was always there, spoiling it, back in my heart. I kept it down—sometimes I forgot it—but sometimes it would surge up and take possession of me. I hated you because I *envied* you—oh, I was sick with envy of you at times. You had a dear little home—and love—and happiness—and glad dreams—everything I wanted—and never had—and never could have. Oh, never could have! *That* was what stung. I wouldn't have envied you, if I had had any *hope* that life would ever be different for me. But I hadn't—I hadn't—and it didn't seem *fair*. It made me rebellious—and it hurt me—and so I hated you at times. Oh, I was so ashamed of it—I'm dying of shame now—but I couldn't conquer it. That night, when I was afraid you mightn't live—I thought I was going to be punished for my wickedness—and I loved you so then. Anne, Anne, I never had anything to love since my mother died, except Dick's old dog—and it's so dreadful to have nothing to love—life is so *empty*—and there's *nothing* worse than emptiness—and I might have loved you so much—and that horrible thing had spoiled it—"

Leslie was trembling and growing almost incoherent with the violence of her emotion.

"Don't, Leslie," implored Anne, "oh, don't. I understand—don't talk of it any more."

"I must—I must. When I knew you were going to live I vowed that I would tell you as soon as you were well—that I wouldn't go an accepting your friendship and companionship without telling you how unworthy I was of it. And I've been so afraid—it would turn you against me."

"You needn't fear that, Leslie."

"Oh, I'm so glad—so glad, Anne." Leslie clasped her brown, work-hardened hands tightly together to still their shaking. "But I want to tell you everything, now I've begun. You don't remember the first time I saw you, I suppose—it wasn't that night on the shore—"

"No, it was the night Gilbert and I came home. You were driving your geese down the hill. I should think I *do* remember it! I thought you were so beautiful—I longed for weeks after to find out who you were."

"I knew who *you* were, although I had never seen either of you before. I had heard of the new doctor and his bride who were coming to live in Miss Russell's little house. I—I hated you that very moment, Anne."

"I felt the resentment in your eyes—then I doubted—I thought I must be mistaken—because *why* should it be?"

"It was because you looked so happy. Oh, you'll agree with me now that I *am* a hateful beast—to hate another woman just because she was happy,—and when her happiness didn't take anything from me! That was why I never went to see you. I knew quite well I ought to go—even our simple Four Winds customs demanded that. But I couldn't. I used to watch you from my window—I could see you and your husband strolling about your garden in the evening—or you running down the poplar lane to meet him. And it hurt me. And yet in another way I wanted to go over. I felt that, if I were not so miserable, I could have liked you and found in you what I've never had in my life—an intimate, *real* friend of my own age. And then you remember that night at the shore? You were afraid I would think you crazy. You must have thought *I* was."

"No, but I couldn't understand you, Leslie. One moment you drew me to you—the next you pushed me back."

"I was very unhappy that evening. I had had a hard day. Dick had been very—very hard to manage that day. Generally he is quite good-natured and easily controlled, you know, Anne. But some days he is very different. I was so heartsick—I ran away to the shore as soon as he went to sleep. It was my only refuge. I sat there thinking of how my poor father had ended his life, and wondering if I wouldn't be driven to it some day. Oh, my heart was full of black thoughts! And then you came dancing along the cove like a glad, light-hearted child. I—I hated you more then than I've ever done since. And yet I craved your friendship. The one feeling swayed me one moment; the other feeling the next. When I got home that night I cried for shame of what you must think of me. But it's always been just the same when I came over here. Sometimes I'd be happy and enjoy my visit. And at other times that hideous feeling would mar it all. There were times when everything about you and your house hurt me. You had so many dear little things I couldn't have. Do you know—it's ridiculous—but I had an especial spite at those china dogs of yours. There were times when I wanted to catch up Gog and Magog and bang their pert black noses together! Oh, you smile, Anne—but it was never funny to me. I would come here and see you and Gilbert with your books and your flowers, and your household gods, and your little family jokes—and your love for each other showing in every look and word, even when you didn't know it—and I would go home to—you know what I went home to! Oh, Anne, I don't believe I'm jealous and envious by nature. When I was a girl I lacked many things my schoolmates had, but

I never cared—I never disliked them for it. But I seem to have grown so hateful—"

"Leslie, dearest, stop blaming yourself. You are *not* hateful or jealous or envious. The life you have to live has warped you a little, perhaps—but it would have ruined a nature less fine and noble than yours. I'm letting you tell me all this because I believe it's better for you to talk it out and rid your soul of it. But don't blame yourself any more."

"Well, I won't. I just wanted you to know me as I am. That time you told me of your darling hope for the spring was the worst of all, Anne. I shall never forgive myself for the way I behaved then. I repented it with tears. And I *did* put many a tender and loving thought of you into the little dress I made. But I might have known that anything I made could only be a shroud in the end."

"Now, Leslie, that *is* bitter and morbid—put such thoughts away. I was so glad when you brought the little dress; and since I had to lose little Joyce I like to think that the dress she wore was the one you made for her when you let yourself love me."

"Anne, do you know, I believe I shall always love you after this. I don't think I'll ever feel that dreadful way about you again. Talking it all out seems to have done away with it, somehow. It's very strange—and I thought it so real and bitter. It's like opening the door of a dark room to show some hideous creature you've believed to be there—and when the light streams in your monster turns out to have been just a shadow, vanishing when the light comes. It will never come between us again."

"No, we are real friends now, Leslie, and I am very glad."

"I hope you won't misunderstand me if I say something else. Anne, I was grieved to the core of my heart when you lost your baby; and if I could have saved her for you by cutting off one of my hands I would have done it. But your sorrow has brought us closer together. Your perfect happiness isn't a barrier any longer. Oh, don't misunderstand, dearest—I'm *not* glad that your happiness isn't perfect any longer—I can say that sincerely; but since it isn't, there isn't such a gulf between us."

"I *do* understand that, too, Leslie. Now, we'll just shut up the past and forget what was unpleasant in it. It's all going to be different. We're both of the race of Joseph now. I think you've been wonderful—wonderful. And, Leslie, I can't help believing that life has something good and beautiful for you yet."

Leslie shook her head.

"No," she said dully. "There isn't any hope. Dick will never be better—and even if his memory were to come back—oh, Anne, it would be worse, even worse, than it is now. *This* is something you can't understand, you happy bride. Anne, did Miss Cornelia ever tell you how I came to marry Dick?"

"Yes."

"I'm glad—I wanted you to know—but I couldn't bring myself to talk of it if you hadn't known. Anne, it seems to me that ever since I was twelve years old life has been bitter. Before that I had a happy childhood. We were very poor—but we didn't mind. Father was so splendid—so clever and loving and sympathetic. We were chums as far back as I can remember. And mother was so sweet. She was very, very beautiful. I look like her, but I am not so beautiful as she was."

"Miss Cornelia says your are far more beautiful."

"She is mistaken—or prejudiced. I think my figure *is* better—mother was slight and bent by hard work—but she had the face of an angel. I used just to look up at her in worship. We all worshipped her,—father and Kenneth and I."

Anne remembered that Miss Cornelia had given her a very different impression of Leslie's mother. But had not love the truer vision? Still, it *was* selfish of Rose West to make her daughter marry Dick Moore.

"Kenneth was my brother," went on Leslie. "Oh, I can't tell you how I loved him. And he was cruelly killed. Do you know how?"

"Yes."

"Anne, I saw his little face as the wheel went over him. He fell on his back. Anne—Anne—I can see it now. I shall always see it.

Anne, all I ask of heaven is that that recollection shall be blotted out of my memory. O my God!"

"Leslie, don't speak of it. I know the story—don't go into details that only harrow your soul up unavailingly. It *will* be blotted out."

After a moment's struggle, Leslie regained a measure of self-control.

"Then father's health got worse and he grew despondent—his mind became unbalanced—you've heard all that, too?"

"Yes."

"After that I had just mother to live for. But I was very ambitious. I meant to teach and earn my way through college. I meant to climb to the very top—oh, I won't talk of that either. It's no use. You know what happened. I couldn't see my dear little heart-broken mother, who had been such a slave all her life, turned out of her home. Of course, I could have earned enough for us to live on. But mother *couldn't* leave her home. She had come there as a bride—and she had loved father so—and all her memories were there. Even yet, Anne, when I think that I made her last year happy I'm not sorry for what I did. As for Dick—I didn't hate him when I married him—I just felt for him the indifferent, friendly feeling I had for most of my schoolmates. I knew he drank some—but I had never heard the story of the girl down at the fishing cove. If I had, I *couldn't* have married him, even for mother's sake. Afterwards—I *did* hate him—but mother never knew. She died—and then I was alone. I was only seventeen and I was alone. Dick had gone off in the *Four Sisters*. I hoped he wouldn't be home very much more. The sea had always been in his blood. I had no other hope. Well, Captain Jim brought him home, as you know—and that's all there is to say. You know me now, Anne—the worst of me—the barriers are all down. And you still want to be my friend?"

Anne looked up through the birches, at the white paper-lantern of a half moon drifting downwards to the gulf of sunset. Her face was very sweet.

"I am your friend and you are mine, for always," she said. "Such a friend as I never had before. I have had many dear and beloved friends—but there is a something in you, Leslie, that I never found in anyone else. You have more to offer me in that rich nature of yours, and I have more to give you than I had in my careless girlhood. We are both women—and friends forever."

They clasped hands and smiled at each other through the tears that filled the gray eyes and the blue.

22
MISS CORNELIA ARRANGES MATTERS

Gilbert insisted that Susan should be kept on at the little house for the summer. Anne protested at first.

"Life here with just the two of us is so sweet, Gilbert. It spoils it a little to have anyone else. Susan is a dear soul, but she is an outsider. It won't hurt me to do the work here."

"You must take your doctor's advice," said Gilbert. "There's an old proverb to the effect that shoemakers' wives go barefoot and doctors' wives die young. I don't mean that it shall be true in my household. You will keep Susan until the old spring comes back into your step, and those little hollows on your cheeks fill out."

"You just take it easy, Mrs. Doctor, dear," said Susan, coming abruptly in. "Have a good time and do not worry about the pantry. Susan is at the helm. There is no use in keeping a dog and doing your own barking. I am going to take your breakfast up to you every morning."

"Indeed you are not," laughed Anne. "I agree with Miss Cornelia that it's a scandal for a woman who isn't sick to eat her breakfast in bed, and almost justifies the men in any enormities."

"Oh, Cornelia!" said Susan, with ineffable contempt. "I think you have better sense, Mrs. Doctor, dear, than to heed what Cornelia Bryant says. I cannot see why she must be always running down the men, even if she is an old maid. *I* am an old maid, but you never hear *me* abusing the men. I like 'em. I would have married one if I could. Is it not funny nobody ever asked me to marry him, Mrs. Doctor, dear? I am no beauty, but I am as good-looking as most of the married women you see. But I never had a beau. What do you suppose is the reason?"

"It may be predestination," suggested Anne, with unearthly solemnity.

Susan nodded.

"That is what I have often thought, Mrs. Doctor, dear, and a great comfort it is. I do not mind nobody wanting me if the Almighty decreed it so for His own wise purposes. But sometimes doubt creeps in, Mrs. Doctor, dear, and I wonder if maybe the Old Scratch has not more to do with it than anyone else. I cannot feel resigned *then*. But maybe," added Susan, brightening up, "I will have a chance to get married yet. I often and often think of the old verse my aunt used to repeat:

'There never was a goose so gray
   but sometime soon or late
Some honest gander came her way
   and took her for his mate!'

A woman cannot ever be sure of not being married till she is buried, Mrs. Doctor, dear, and meanwhile I will make a batch of cherry pies. I notice the doctor favors 'em, and I *do* like cooking for a man who appreciates his victuals."

Miss Cornelia dropped in that afternoon, puffing a little.

"I don't mind the world or the devil much, but the flesh *does* rather bother me," she admitted. "You always look as cool as a cucumber, Anne, dearie. Do I smell cherry pie? If I do, ask me to stay to tea. Haven't tasted a cherry pie this summer. My cherries have all been stolen by those scamps of Gilman boys from the Glen."

"Now, now, Cornelia," remonstrated Captain Jim, who had been reading a sea novel in a corner of the living room, "you shouldn't say that about those two poor, motherless little Gilman boys, unless you've got certain proof. Jest because their father ain't none too honest isn't any reason for calling them thieves. It's more likely it's been the robins took your cherries. They're turrible thick this year."

"Robins!" said Miss Cornelia disdainfully. "Humph! Two-legged robins, believe *me!*"

"Well, most of the Four Winds robins *are* constructed on that principle," said Captain Jim gravely.

Miss Cornelia stared at him for a moment. Then she leaned back in her rocker and laughed long and ungrudgingly.

"Well, you *have* got one on me at last, Jim Boyd, I'll admit. Just look how pleased he is, Anne, dearie, grinning like a Chessy-cat. As for the robins' legs, if robins have great, big, bare, sunburned legs, with ragged trousers hanging on 'em, such as I saw up in my cherry tree one morning at sunrise last week, I'll beg the Gilman boys' pardon. By the time I got down they were gone. I couldn't understand how they had disappeared so quick, but Captain Jim has enlightened me. They flew away, of course."

Captain Jim laughed and went away, regretfully declining an invitation to stay to supper and partake of cherry pie.

"I'm on my way to see Leslie and ask her if she'll take a boarder," Miss Cornelia resumed. "I'd a letter yesterday from a Mrs. Daly in Toronto, who boarded a spell with me two years ago. She wanted me to take a friend of hers for the summer. His name is Owen Ford, and he's a newspaper man, and it seems he's a grandson of the schoolmaster who built this house. John Selwyn's oldest daughter married an Ontario man named Ford, and this is her son. He wants to see the old place his grandparents lived in. He had a bad spell of typhoid in the spring and hasn't got rightly over it, so his doctor has ordered him to the sea. He doesn't want to go to the hotel—he just wants a quiet home place. I can't take him, for I have to be away in August. I've been appointed a delegate to the W. F. M. S. convention in Kingsport and I'm going. I don't know whether Leslie'll want to be bothered with him, either, but there's no one else. If she can't take him he'll have to go over the harbor."

"When you've seen her come back and help us eat our cherry pies," said Anne. "Bring Leslie and Dick, too, if they can come. And so you're going to Kingsport? What a nice time you will have. I must give you a letter to a friend of mine there—Mrs. Jonas Blake."

"I've prevailed on Mrs. Thomas Holt to go with me," said Miss Cornelia complacently. "It's time she had a little holiday, believe *me*. She has just about worked herself to death. Tom Holt can crochet beautifully, but he can't make a living for his family. He never seems to be able to get up early enough to do any work, but I notice he can always get up early to go fishing. Isn't that like a man?"

Anne smiled. She had learned to discount largely Miss Cornelia's opinions of the Four Winds men. Otherwise she must have believed them the most hopeless assortment of reprobates and ne'er-do-weels in the world, with veritable slaves and martyrs for wives. This particular Tom Holt, for example, she knew to be a kind husband, a much loved father, and an excellent neighbor. If he were rather inclined to be lazy, liking better the fishing he had been born for than the farming he had not, and if he had a harmless eccentricity for doing fancy work, nobody save Miss Cornelia seemed to hold it against him. His wife was a "hustler," who gloried in hustling; his family got a comfortable living off the farm; and his strapping sons and daughters, inheriting their mother's energy, were all in a fair way to do well in the world. There was not a happier household in Glen St. Mary than the Holts'.

Mrs. Cornelia returned satisfied from the house up the brook.

"Leslie's going to take him," she announced. "She jumped at the chance. She wants to make a little money to shingle the roof of her house this fall, and she didn't know how she was going to manage it. I expect Captain Jim'll be more than interested when he hears that a grandson of the Selwyns' is coming here. Leslie said to tell you she hankered after cherry pie, but she couldn't come to tea because she has to go and hunt up her turkeys.

They've strayed away. But she said, if there was a piece left, for you to put it in the pantry and she'd run over in the cat's light, when prowling's in order, to get it. You don't know, Anne, dearie, what good it did my heart to hear Leslie send you a message like that, laughing like she used to long ago. There's a great change come over her lately. She laughs and jokes like a girl, and from her talk I gather she's here real often."

"Every day—or else I'm over there," said Anne. "I don't know what I'd do without Leslie, especially just now when Gilbert is so busy. He's hardly ever home except for a few hours in the wee sma's. He's really working himself to death. So many of the over-harbor people send for him now."

"They might better be content with their own doctor," said Miss Cornelia. "Though to be sure I can't blame them, for he's a Methodist. Ever since Dr. Blythe brought Mrs. Allonby round folks think he can raise the dead. I believe Dr. Dave is a mite jealous—just like a man. He thinks Dr. Blythe has too many new-fangled notions! 'Well,' I says to him, 'it was a new-fangled notion saved Rhoda Allonby. If you'd been attending her she'd have died, and had a tombstone saying it had pleased God to take her away.' Oh, I do like to speak my mind to Dr. Dave! He's bossed the Glen for years, and he thinks he's forgotten more than other people ever knew. Speaking of doctors, I wish Dr. Blythe'd run over and see to that boil on Dick Moore's neck. It's getting past Leslie's skill. I'm sure I don't know what Dick Moore wants to start in having boils for—as if he wasn't enough trouble without that!"

"Do you know, Dick has taken quite a fancy to me," said Anne. "He follows me round like a dog, and smiles like a pleased child when I notice him."

"Does it make you creepy?"

"Not at all. I rather like poor Dick Moore. He seems so pitiful and appealing, somehow."

"You wouldn't think him very appealing if you'd see him on his cantankerous days, believe me. But I'm glad you don't mind him—it's all the nicer for Leslie. She'll have more to do when her boarder comes. I hope he'll be a decent creature. You'll probably like him—he's a writer."

"I wonder why people so commonly suppose that if two individuals are both writers they must therefore be hugely congenial," said Anne, rather scornfully. "Nobody would expect two blacksmiths to be violently attracted toward each other merely because they were both blacksmiths."

Nevertheless, she looked forward to the advent of Owen Ford with a pleasant sense of expectation. If he were young and likeable he might prove a very pleasant addition to society in Four Winds. The latch-string of the little house was always out for the race of Joseph.

23
OWEN FORD COMES

One morning Miss Cornelia telephoned down to Anne.

"The writer man has just arrived here. I'm going to drive him down to your place, and you can show him the way over to Leslie's. It's shorter than driving round by the other road, and I'm in a mortal hurry. The Reese baby has gone and fallen into a pail of hot water at the Glen, and got nearly scalded to death and they want me right off—to put a new skin on the child, I presume. Mrs. Reese is always so careless, and then expects other people to mend her mistakes. You won't mind, will you, dearie? His trunk can go tomorrow."

"Very well," said Anne. "What is he like, Miss Cornelia?"

"You'll see what he's like outside when I take him down. As for what he's like inside only the Lord who made him knows *that*. I'm not going to say another word, for every receiver in the Glen is down."

"Miss Cornelia evidently can't find much fault with Mr. Ford's looks, or she would find it in spite of the receivers," said Anne.

"I conclude therefore, Susan, that Mr. Ford is rather handsome than otherwise."

"Well, Mrs. Doctor, dear, I *do* enjoy seeing a well-looking man," said Susan candidly. "Had I not better get up a snack for him? There is a strawberry pie that would melt in your mouth."

"No, Leslie is expecting him and has his supper ready. Besides, I want that strawberry pie for my own poor man. He won't be home till late, so leave the pie and a glass of milk out for him, Susan."

"That I will, Mrs. Doctor, dear. Susan is at the helm. After all, it is better to give pie to your own men than to strangers, who may be only seeking to devour, and the doctor himself is as well-looking a man as you often come across."

When Owen Ford came Anne secretly admitted, as Miss Cornelia towed him in, that he was very "well-looking" indeed. He was tall and broad-shouldered, with thick, brown hair, finely-cut nose and chin, large and brilliant dark-gray eyes.

"And did you notice his ears and his teeth, Mrs. Doctor, dear?" queried Susan later on. "He has got the nicest-shaped ears I ever saw on a man's head. I am choice about ears. When I was young I was scared that I might have to marry a man with ears like flaps. But I need not have worried, for never a chance did I have with any kind of ears."

Anne had not noticed Owen Ford's ears, but she did see his teeth, as his lips parted over them in a frank and friendly smile. Unsmiling, his face was rather sad and absent in expression, not unlike the melancholy, inscrutable hero of Anne's own early dreams; but mirth and humor and charm lighted it up when he smiled. Certainly, on the outside, as Miss Cornelia said, Owen Ford was a very presentable fellow.

"You cannot realize how delighted I am to be here, Mrs. Blythe," he said, looking around him with eager, interested eyes. "I have an odd feeling of coming home. My mother was born and spent her childhood here, you know. She used to talk a great deal to me of her old home. I know the geography of it as well as of the one I lived in, and, of course, she told me the story of the building of the house, and of my grandfather's agonized watch for the *Royal William*. I had thought that so old a house must have vanished years ago, or I should have come to see it before this."

"Old houses don't vanish easily on this enchanted coast," smiled Anne. "This is a 'land where all things always seem the same'—nearly always, at least. John Selwyn's house hasn't even been much changed, and outside the rose-bushes your grandfather planted for his bride are blooming this very minute."

"How the thought links me with them! With your leave I must explore the whole place soon."

"Our latch-string will always be out for you," promised Anne. "And do you know that the old sea captain who keeps the Four Winds light knew John Selwyn and his bride well in his boyhood? He told me their story the night I came here—the third bride of the old house."

"Can it be possible? This *is* a discovery. I must hunt him up."

"It won't be difficult; we are all cronies of Captain Jim. He will be as eager to see you as you could be to see him. Your grandmother shines like a star in his memory. But I think Mrs. Moore is expecting you. I'll show you our 'cross-lots' road."

Anne walked with him to the house up the brook, over a field that was as white as snow with daisies. A boat-load of people were singing far across the harbor. The sound drifted over the water like faint, unearthly music wind-blown across a starlit sea. The big light flashed and beaconed. Owen Ford looked around him with satisfaction.

"And so this is Four Winds," he said. "I wasn't prepared to find it quite so beautiful, in spite of all mother's praises. What colors—what scenery—what charm! I shall get as strong as a horse in no time. And if inspiration comes from beauty, I should certainly be able to begin my great Canadian novel here."

"You haven't begun it yet?" asked Anne.

"Alack-a-day, no. I've never been able to get the right central idea for it. It lurks beyond me—it allures—and beckons—and recedes—I almost grasp it and it is gone. Perhaps amid this peace and loveliness, I shall be able to capture it. Miss Bryant tells me that you write."

"Oh, I do little things for children. I haven't done much since I was married. And I have no designs on a great Canadian novel," laughed Anne. "That is quite beyond me."

Owen Ford laughed too.

"I dare say it is beyond me as well. All the same I mean to have a try at it some day, if I can ever get time. A newspaper man doesn't have much chance for that sort of thing. I've done a good deal of short story writing for the magazines, but I've never had the leisure that seems to be necessary for the writing of a book. With three months of liberty I ought to make a start, though—if I could only get the necessary *motif* for it—the *soul* of the book."

An idea whisked through Anne's brain with a suddenness that made her jump. But she did not utter it, for they had reached the Moore house. As they entered the yard Leslie came out on the veranda from the side door, peering through the gloom for some sign of her expected guest. She stood just where the warm yellow light flooded her from the open door. She wore a plain dress of cheap, cream-tinted cotton voile, with the usual girdle of crimson. Leslie was never without her touch of crimson. She had told Anne that she never felt satisfied without a gleam of red somewhere about her, if it were only a flower. To Anne, it always seemed to symbolize Leslie's glowing, pent-up personality, denied all expression save in that flaming glint. Leslie's dress was cut a little away at the neck and had short sleeves. Her arms gleamed like ivory-tinted marble. Every exquisite curve of her form was outlined in soft darkness against the light. Her hair shone in it like flame. Beyond her was a purple sky, flowering with stars over the harbor.

Anne heard her companion give a gasp. Even in the dusk she could see the amazement and admiration on his face.

"Who is that beautiful creature?" he asked.

"That is Mrs. Moore," said Anne. "She is very lovely, isn't she?"

"I—I never saw anything like her," he answered, rather dazedly. "I wasn't prepared—I didn't expect—good heavens, one *doesn't* expect a goddess for a landlady! Why, if she were clothed in a gown of sea-purple, with a rope of amethysts in her hair, she would be veritable sea-queen. And she takes in boarders!"

"Even goddesses must live," said Anne. "And Leslie isn't a goddess. She's just a very beautiful woman, as human as the rest of us. Did Miss Bryant tell you about Mr. Moore?"

"Yes,—he's mentally deficient, or something of the sort, isn't he? But she said nothing about Mrs. Moore, and I supposed she'd be the usual hustling country housewife who takes in boarders to earn an honest penny."

"Well, that's just what Leslie is doing," said Anne crisply. "And it isn't altogether pleasant for her, either. I hope you won't mind Dick. If you do, please don't let Leslie see it. It would hurt her horribly. He's just a big baby, and sometimes a rather annoying one."

"Oh, I won't mind him. I don't suppose I'll be much in the house anyhow, except for meals. But what a shame it all is! Her life must be a hard one."

"It is. But she doesn't like to be pitied."

Leslie had gone back into the house and now met them at the front door. She greeted Owen Ford with cold civility, and told him in a business-like tone that his room and his supper were ready for him. Dick, with a pleased grin, shambled upstairs with the valise, and Owen Ford was installed as an inmate of the old house among the willows.

24
THE LIFE-BOOK OF CAPTAIN JIM

"I have a little brown cocoon of an idea that may possibly expand into a magnificent moth of fulfilment," Anne told Gilbert when she reached home. He had returned earlier than she had expected, and was enjoying Susan's cherry pie. Susan herself hovered in the background, like a rather grim but beneficent guardian spirit, and found as much pleasure in watching Gilbert eat pie as he did in the eating it.

"What is your idea?" he asked.

"I sha'n't tell you just yet—not till I see if I can bring the thing about."

"What sort of a chap is Ford?"

"Oh, very nice, and quite good-looking."

"Such beautiful ears, doctor, dear," interjected Susan with a relish.

"He is about thirty or thirty-five, I think, and he meditates writing a novel. His voice is pleasant and his smile delightful, and he knows how to dress. He looks as if life hadn't been altogether easy for him, somehow."

Owen Ford came over the next evening with a note to Anne from Leslie; they spent the sunset-time in the garden and then went for a moonlit sail on the harbor, in the little boat Gilbert had set up for summer outings. They liked Owen immensely and had that feeling of having known him for many years which distinguishes the freemasonry of the house of Joseph. "He is as nice as his ears, Mrs. Doctor, dear," said Susan, when he had gone. He had told Susan that he had never tasted anything like her strawberry shortcake and Susan's susceptible heart was his forever.

"He has got a way with him," she reflected, as she cleared up the relics of the supper. "It is real queer he is not married, for a man like that could have anybody for the asking. Well, maybe he is like me, and has not met the right one yet."

Susan really grew quite romantic in her musings as she washed the supper dishes.

Two nights later Anne took Owen Ford down to Four Winds Point to introduce him to Captain Jim. The clover fields along the harbor shore were whitening in the western wind, and Captain Jim had one of his finest sunsets on exhibition. He himself had just returned from a trip over the harbor.

"I had to go over and tell Henry Pollock he was dying.

Everybody else was afraid to tell him. They expected he'd take on turrible, for he's been dreadful determined to live, and been making no end of plans for the fall. His wife thought he oughter be told and that I'd be the best one to break it to him that he couldn't get better. Henry and me are old cronies—we sailed in the *Gray Gull* for years together. Well, I went over and sat down by Henry's bed and I says to him, says I, jest right out plain and simple, for if a thing's got to be told it may as well be told first as last, says I, 'Mate, I reckon you've got your sailing orders this time.' I was sorter quaking inside, for it's an awful thing to have to tell a man who hain't any idea he's dying that he is. But lo and behold, Mistress Blythe, Henry looks up at me, with those bright old black eyes of his in his wizened face and says, says he, 'Tell me something I don't know, Jim Boyd, if you want to give me information. I've known *that* for a week.' I was too astonished to speak, and Henry, he chuckled. 'To see you coming in here,' says he, 'with your face as solemn as a tombstone and sitting down there with your hands clasped over your stomach, and passing me out a blue-mouldy old item of news like that! It'd make a cat laugh, Jim Boyd,' says he. 'Who told you?' says I, stupid like. 'Nobody,' says he. 'A week ago Tuesday night I was lying here awake—and I jest knew. I'd suspicioned it before, but then I *knew*. I've been keeping up for the wife's sake. And I'd *like* to have got that barn built, for Eben'll never get it right. But anyhow, now that you've eased your mind, Jim, put on a smile and tell me something interesting.' Well, there it was. They'd been so scared to tell him and he knew it all the time. Strange how nature looks out for us, ain't it, and lets us know what we should know when the time comes? Did I never tell you the yarn about Henry getting the fish hook in his nose, Mistress Blythe?"

"No."

"Well, him and me had a laugh over it today. It happened nigh unto thirty years ago. Him and me and several more was out mackerel fishing one day. It was a great day—never saw such a school of mackerel in the gulf—and in the general excitement

Henry got quite wild and contrived to stick a fish hook clean through one side of his nose. Well, there he was; there was barb on one end and a big piece of lead on the other, so it couldn't be pulled out. We wanted to take him ashore at once, but Henry was game; he said he'd be jiggered if he'd leave a school like that for anything short of lockjaw; then he kept fishing away, hauling in hand over fist and groaning between times. Fin'lly the school passed and we come in with a load; I got a file and begun to try to file through that hook. I tried to be as easy as I could, but you should have heard Henry—no, you shouldn't either. It was well no ladies were around. Henry wasn't a swearing man, but he'd heard some few matters of that sort along shore in his time, and he fished 'em all out of his recollection and hurled 'em at me. Fin'lly he declared he couldn't stand it and I had no bowels of compassion. So we hitched up and I drove him to a doctor in Charlottetown, thirty-five miles—there weren't none nearer in them days—with that blessed hook still hanging from his nose. When we got there old Dr. Crabb jest took a file and filed that hook jest the same as I'd tried to do, only he weren't a mite particular about doing it easy!"

Captain Jim's visit to his old friend had revived many recollections and he was now in the full tide of reminiscences.

"Henry was asking me today if I remembered the time old Father Chiniquy blessed Alexander MacAllister's boat. Another odd yarn—and true as gospel. I was in the boat myself. We went out, him and me, in Alexander MacAllister's boat one morning at sunrise. Besides, there was a French boy in the boat—Catholic of course. You know old Father Chiniquy had turned Protestant, so the Catholics hadn't much use for him. Well, we sat out in the gulf in the broiling sun till noon, and not a bite did we get. When we went ashore old Father Chiniquy had to go, so he said in that polite way of his, 'I'm very sorry I cannot go out with you dis afternoon, Mr. MacAllister, but I leave you my blessing. You will catch a t'ousand dis afternoon.' Well, we did not catch a thousand, but we caught exactly nine hundred and ninety-nine—the biggest catch for a small boat on the whole north shore that summer. Curious, wasn't it? Alexander MacAllister, he says to Andrew Peters, 'Well, and what do you think of Father Chiniquy now?' 'Vell,' growled Andrew, 'I t'ink de old devil has got a blessing left yet.' Laws, how Henry did laugh over that today!"

"Do you know who Mr. Ford is, Captain Jim?" asked Anne, seeing that Captain Jim's fountain of reminiscence had run out for the present. "I want you to guess."

Captain Jim shook his head.

"I never was any hand at guessing, Mistress Blythe, and yet somehow when I come in I thought, 'Where have I seen them eyes before?'—for I *have* seen 'em."

"Think of a September morning many years ago," said Anne, softly. "Think of a ship sailing up the harbor—a ship long waited for and despaired of. Think of the day the *Royal William* came in and the first look you had at the schoolmaster's bride."

Captain Jim sprang up.

"They're Persis Selwyn's eyes," he almost shouted. "You can't be her son—you must be her—"

"Grandson; yes, I am Alice Selwyn's son."

Captain Jim swooped down on Owen Ford and shook his hand over again.

"Alice Selwyn's son! Lord, but you're welcome! Many's the time I've wondered where the descendants of the schoolmaster were living. I knew there was none on the Island. Alice—Alice— the first baby ever born in that little house. No baby ever brought more joy! I've dandled her a hundred times. It was from my knee she took her first steps alone. Can't I see her mother's face watching her—and it was near sixty years ago. Is she living yet?"

"No, she died when I was only a boy."

"Oh, it doesn't seem right that I should be living to hear that," sighed Captain Jim. "But I'm heart-glad to see you. It's brought back my youth for a little while. You don't know yet what a boon *that* is. Mistress Blythe here has the trick—she does it quite often for me."

Captain Jim was still more excited when he discovered that Owen Ford was what he called a "real writing man." He gazed at him as at a superior being. Captain Jim knew that Anne wrote, but he had never taken that fact very seriously. Captain Jim thought women were delightful creatures, who ought to have the vote, and everything else they wanted, bless their hearts; but he did not believe they could write.

"Jest look at *A Mad Love*," he would protest. "A woman wrote that and jest look at it—one hundred and three chapters when it could all have been told in ten. A writing woman never knows when to stop; that's the trouble. The p'int of good writing is to know when to stop."

"Mr. Ford wants to hear some of your stories, Captain Jim," said Anne. "Tell him the one about the captain who went crazy and imagined he was the Flying Dutchman."

This was Captain Jim's best story. It was a compound of horror and humor, and though Anne had heard it several times she laughed as heartily and shivered as fearsomely over it as Mr. Ford did. Other tales followed, for Captain Jim had an audience after his own heart. He told how his vessel had been run down by a steamer; how he had been boarded by Malay pirates; how his ship had caught fire; how he helped a political prisoner escape from a South African republic; how he had been wrecked one fall on the Magdalens and stranded there for the winter; how a tiger had broken loose on board ship; how his crew had mutinied and marooned him on a barren island—these and many other tales, tragic or humorous or grotesque, did Captain Jim relate. The mystery of the sea, the fascination of far lands, the lure of adventure, the laughter of the world—his hearers felt and realized them all. Owen Ford listened, with his head on his hand, and the First Mate purring on his knee, his brilliant eyes fastened on Captain Jim's rugged, eloquent face.

"Won't you let Mr. Ford see your life-book, Captain Jim?" asked Anne, when Captain Jim finally declared that yarn spinning must end for the time.

"Oh, he don't want to be bothered with *that*," protested Captain Jim, who was secretly dying to show it.

"I should like nothing better than to see it, Captain Boyd," said Owen. "If it is half as wonderful as your tales it will be worth seeing."

With pretended reluctance Captain Jim dug his life-book out of his old chest and handed it to Owen.

"I reckon you won't care to wrastle long with my old hand o' write. I never had much schooling," he observed carelessly. "Just wrote that there to amuse my nephew Joe. He's always wanting stories. Comes here yesterday and says to me, reproachful-like, as I was lifting a twenty-pound codfish out of my boat, 'Uncle Jim, ain't a codfish a dumb animal?' I'd been a-telling him, you see, that he must be real kind to dumb animals, and never hurt 'em in any way. I got out of the scrape by saying a codfish was dumb enough but it wasn't an animal, but Joe didn't look satisfied, and I wasn't satisfied myself. You've got to be mighty careful what you tell them little critters. *They* can see through you."

While talking, Captain Jim watched Owen Ford from the corner of his eye as the latter examined the life-book; and presently observing that his guest was lost in its pages, he turned smilingly to his cupboard and proceeded to make a pot of tea. Owen Ford separated himself from the life-book, with as much reluctance as a miser wrenches himself from his gold, long enough to drink his tea, and then returned to it hungrily.

"Oh, you can take that thing home with you if you want to," said Captain Jim, as if the "thing" were not his most treasured possession. "I must go down and pull my boat up a bit on the skids. There's a wind coming. Did you notice the sky tonight?

> 'Mackerel skies and mares' tails
> Make tall ships carry short sails.'"

Owen Ford accepted the offer of the life-book gladly. On their way home Anne told him the story of lost Margaret.

"That old captain is a wonderful old fellow," he said. "What a life he has led! Why, the man had more adventures in one week of his life than most of us have in a lifetime. Do you really think his tales are all true?"

"I certainly do. I am sure Captain Jim could not tell a lie; and besides, all the people about here say that everything happened as he relates it. There used to be plenty of his old shipmates alive to corroborate him. He's one of the last of the old type of P. E. Island sea-captains. They are almost extinct now."

25
THE WRITING OF THE BOOK

Owen Ford came over to the little house the next morning in a state of great excitement.

"Mrs. Blythe, this is a wonderful book—absolutely wonderful. If I could take it and use the material for a book I feel certain I could make the novel of the year out of it. Do you suppose Captain Jim would let me do it?"

"Let you! I'm sure he would be delighted," cried Anne. "I admit that it was what was in my head when I took you down last night. Captain Jim has always been wishing he could get somebody to write his life-book properly for him."

"Will you go down to the Point with me this evening, Mrs. Blythe? I'll ask him about the life-book myself, but I want you to tell him that you told me the story of lost Margaret and ask him if he will let me use it as a thread of romance with which to weave the stories of the life-book into a harmonious whole."

Captain Jim was more excited than ever when Owen Ford told him of his plan. At last his cherished dream was to be realized and his "life-book" given to the world. He was also pleased that the story of lost Margaret should be woven into it.

"It will keep her name from being forgotten," he said wistfully. "That's why I want it put in."

"We'll collaborate," cried Owen delightedly. "You will give the soul and I the body. Oh, we'll write a famous book between us, Captain Jim. And we'll get right to work."

"And to think my book is to be writ by the schoolmaster's grandson!" exclaimed Captain Jim. "Lad, your grandfather was my dearest friend. I thought there was nobody like him. I see now why I had to wait so long. It couldn't be writ till the right man come. You *belong* here—you've got the soul of this old north shore in you—you're the only one who *could* write it."

It was arranged that the tiny room off the living room at the lighthouse should be given over to Owen for a workshop. It was necessary that Captain Jim should be near him as he wrote, for consultation upon many matters of sea-faring and gulf lore of which Owen was quite ignorant.

He began work on the book the very next morning, and flung himself into it heart and soul. As for Captain Jim, he was a happy man that summer. He looked upon the little room where Owen worked as a sacred shrine. Owen talked everything over with Captain Jim, but he would not let him see the manuscript.

"You must wait until it is published," he said. "Then you'll get it all at once in its best shape."

He delved into the treasures of the life-book and used them freely. He dreamed and brooded over lost Margaret until she became a vivid reality to him and lived in his pages. As the book progressed it took possession of him and he worked at it with feverish eagerness. He let Anne and Leslie read the manuscript and criticize it; and the concluding chapter of the book, which the critics, later on, were pleased to call idyllic, was modelled upon a suggestion of Leslie's.

Anne fairly hugged herself with delight over the success of her idea.

"I knew when I looked at Owen Ford that he was the very man for it," she told Gilbert. "Both humor and passion were in his face, and that, together with the art of expression, was just what was necessary for the writing of such a book. As Mrs. Rachel would say, he was predestined for the part."

Owen Ford wrote in the mornings. The afternoons were generally spent in some merry outing with the Blythes. Leslie often went, too, for Captain Jim took charge of Dick frequently, in order to set her free. They went boating on the harbor and up the three pretty rivers that flowed into it; they had clam-bakes on the bar and mussel-bakes on the rocks; they picked strawberries on the sand-dunes; they went out cod-fishing with Captain Jim; they shot plover in the shore fields and wild ducks in the cove—at least, the men did. In the evenings they rambled in the low-lying, daisied, shore fields under a golden moon, or they sat in the living-room at the little house where often the coolness of the sea breeze justified a driftwood fire, and talked of the thousand and one things which happy, eager, clever young people can find to talk about.

Ever since the day on which she had made her confession to Anne Leslie had been a changed creature. There was no trace of her old coldness and reserve, no shadow of her old bitterness. The girlhood of which she had been cheated seemed to come back to her with the ripeness of womanhood; she expanded like a flower of flame and perfume; no laugh was readier than hers, no wit quicker, in the twilight circles of that enchanted summer. When she could not be with them all felt that some exquisite savor was lacking in their intercourse. Her beauty was illumined by the awakened soul within, as some rosy lamp might shine through a flawless vase of alabaster. There were hours when Anne's eyes seemed to ache with the splendor of her. As for Owen Ford, the "Margaret" of his book, although she had the soft brown hair and elfin face of the real girl who had vanished so long ago, "pillowed where lost Atlantis sleeps," had the personality of Leslie Moore, as it was revealed to him in those halcyon days at Four Winds Harbor.

All in all, it was a never-to-be-forgotten summer—one of those summers which come seldom into any life, but leave a rich heritage of beautiful memories in their going—one of those summers which, in a fortunate combination of delightful weather, delightful friends and delightful doings, come as near to perfection as anything can come in this world.

"Too good to last," Anne told herself with a little sigh, on the September day when a certain nip in the wind and a certain shade of intense blue on the gulf water said that autumn was hard by.

That evening Owen Ford told them that he had finished his book and that his vacation must come to an end.

"I have a good deal to do to it yet—revising and pruning and so forth," he said, "but in the main it's done. I wrote the last sentence this morning. If I can find a publisher for it it will probably be out next summer or fall."

Owen had not much doubt that he would find a publisher. He knew that he had written a great book—a book that would score a wonderful success—a book that would *live*. He knew that it would bring him both fame and fortune; but when he had written the last line of it he had bowed his head on the manuscript and so sat for a long time. And his thoughts were not of the good work he had done.

26
OWEN FORD'S CONFESSION

"I'm so sorry Gilbert is away," said Anne. "He had to go— Allan Lyons at the Glen has met with a serious accident. He will not likely be home till very late. But he told me to tell you he'd be up and over early enough in the morning to see you before you left. It's too provoking. Susan and I had planned such a nice little jamboree for your last night here."

She was sitting beside the garden brook on the little rustic seat Gilbert had built. Owen Ford stood before her, leaning against the bronze column of a yellow birch. He was very pale and his face bore the marks of the preceding sleepless night. Anne, glancing up at him, wondered if, after all, his summer had brought him the strength it should. Had he worked too hard over his book? She remembered that for a week he had not been looking well.

"I'm rather glad the doctor is away," said Owen slowly. "I wanted to see you alone, Mrs. Blythe. There is something I must tell somebody, or I think it will drive me mad. I've been trying for a week to look it in the face—and I can't. I know I can trust you—and, besides, you will understand. A woman with eyes like yours always understands. You are one of the folks people instinctively tell things to. Mrs. Blythe, I love Leslie. *Love* her! That seems too weak a word!"

His voice suddenly broke with the suppressed passion of his utterance. He turned his head away and hid his face on his arm. His whole form shook. Anne sat looking at him, pale and aghast. She had never thought of this! And yet—how was it she had never thought of it? It now seemed a natural and inevitable thing. She wondered at her own blindness. But—but—things like this did not happen in Four Winds. Elsewhere in the world human passions might set at defiance human conventions and laws—but not *here*, surely. Leslie had kept summer boarders off and on for ten years, and nothing like this had happened. But perhaps they had not been like Owen Ford; and the vivid, *living* Leslie of this summer was not the cold, sullen girl of other years. Oh, *somebody* should have thought of this! Why hadn't Miss Cornelia thought of it? Miss Cornelia was always ready enough to sound the alarm where men were concerned. Anne felt an unreasonable resentment against Miss Cornelia. Then she gave a little inward groan. No matter who was to blame the mischief was done. And Leslie—what of Leslie? It was for Leslie Anne felt most concerned.

"Does Leslie know this, Mr. Ford?" she asked quietly.

"No—no,—unless she has guessed it. You surely don't think I'd be cad and scoundrel enough to tell her, Mrs. Blythe. I couldn't help loving her—that's all—and my misery is greater than I can bear."

"Does *she* care?" asked Anne. The moment the question crossed her lips she felt that she should not have asked it. Owen Ford answered it with over-eager protest.

"No—no, of course not. But I could make her care if she were free—I know I could."

"She does care—and he knows it," thought Anne. Aloud she said, sympathetically but decidedly:

"But she is not free, Mr. Ford. And the only thing you can do is to go away in silence and leave her to her own life."

"I know—I know," groaned Owen. He sat down on the grassy bank and stared moodily into the amber water beneath him. "I know there's nothing to do—nothing but to say conventionally, 'Good-bye, Mrs. Moore. Thank you for all your kindness to me this summer,' just as I would have said it to the sonsy, bustling, keen-eyed housewife I expected her to be when I came. Then I'll pay my board money like any honest boarder and go! Oh, it's very simple. No doubt—no perplexity—a straight road to the end of the world! And I'll walk it—you needn't fear that I won't, Mrs. Blythe. But it would be easier to walk over red-hot ploughshares."

Anne flinched with the pain of his voice. And there was so little she could say that would be adequate to the situation. Blame was out of the question—advice was not needed—sympathy was mocked by the man's stark agony. She could only feel with him in a maze of compassion and regret. Her heart ached for Leslie! Had not that poor girl suffered enough without this?

"It wouldn't be so hard to go and leave her if she were only happy," resumed Owen passionately. "But to think of her living death—to realize what it is to which I do leave her! *That* is the worst of all. I would give my life to make her happy—and I can do nothing even to help her—nothing. She is bound forever to that poor wretch—with nothing to look forward to but growing old in a succession of empty, meaningless, barren years. It drives me mad to think of it. But I must go through my life, never seeing her, but always knowing what she is enduring. It's hideous—hideous!"

"It is very hard," said Anne sorrowfully. "We—her friends here—all know how hard it is for her."

"And she is so richly fitted for life," said Owen rebelliously. "Her beauty is the least of her dower—and she is the most beautiful woman I've ever known. That laugh of hers! I've angled all summer to evoke that laugh, just for the delight of hearing it. And her eyes—they are as deep and blue as the gulf out there. I never saw such blueness—and gold! Did you ever see her hair down, Mrs. Blythe?"

"No."

"I did—once. I had gone down to the Point to go fishing with Captain Jim but it was too rough to go out, so I came back. She had taken the opportunity of what she expected to be an afternoon alone to wash her hair, and she was standing on the veranda in the sunshine to dry it. It fell all about her to her feet in a fountain of living gold. When she saw me she hurried in, and the wind caught her hair and swirled it all around her—Danae in her cloud. Somehow, just then the knowledge that I loved her came home to me—and realized that I had loved her from the moment I first saw her standing against the darkness in that glow of light. And she must live on here—petting and soothing Dick, pinching and saving for a mere existence, while I spend my life longing vainly for her, and debarred, by that very fact, from even giving her the little help a friend might. I walked the shore last night, almost till dawn, and thrashed it all out over and over again. And yet, in spite of everything, I can't find it in my heart to be sorry that I came to Four Winds. It seems to me that, bad as everything is, it would be still worse never to have known Leslie. It's burning, searing pain to love her and leave her—but not to have loved her is unthinkable. I suppose all this sounds very crazy—all these terrible emotions always do sound foolish when we put them into our inadequate words. They are not meant to be spoken—only felt and endured. I shouldn't have spoken—but it has helped—some. At least, it has given me strength to go away respectably tomorrow morning, without making a scene. You'll write me now and then, won't you, Mrs. Blythe, and give me what news there is to give of her?"

"Yes," said Anne. "Oh, I'm so sorry you are going—we'll miss you so—we've all been such friends! If it were not for this you could come back other summers. Perhaps, even yet—by-and-by—when you've forgotten, perhaps—"

"I shall never forget—and I shall never come back to Four Winds," said Owen briefly.

Silence and twilight fell over the garden. Far away the sea was lapping gently and monotonously on the bar. The wind of evening in the poplars sounded like some sad, weird, old rune—some broken dream of old memories. A slender shapely young aspen rose up before them against the fine maize and emerald and paling rose of the western sky, which brought out every leaf and twig in dark, tremulous, elfin loveliness.

"Isn't that beautiful?" said Owen, pointing to it with the air of a man who puts a certain conversation behind him.

"It's so beautiful that it hurts me," said Anne softly. "Perfect things like that always did hurt me—I remember I called it 'the queer ache' when I was a child. What is the reason that pain like this seems inseparable from perfection? Is it the pain of finality—when we realize that there can be nothing beyond but retrogression?"

"Perhaps," said Owen dreamily, "it is the prisoned infinite in us calling out to its kindred infinite as expressed in that visible perfection."

"You seem to have a cold in the head. Better rub some tallow on your nose when you go to bed," said Miss Cornelia, who had come in through the little gate between the firs in time to catch Owen's last remark. Miss Cornelia liked Owen; but it was a matter of principle with her to visit any "high falutin" language from a man with a snub.

Miss Cornelia personated the comedy that ever peeps around the corner at the tragedy of life. Anne, whose nerves had been rather strained, laughed hysterically, and even Owen smiled.

Certainly, sentiment and passion had a way of shrinking out of sight in Miss Cornelia's presence. And yet to Anne nothing seemed quite as hopeless and dark and painful as it had seemed a few moments before. But sleep was far from her eyes that night.

27

ON THE SAND-BAR

Owen Ford left Four Winds the next morning. In the evening Anne went over to see Leslie, but found nobody. The house was locked and there was no light in any window. It looked like a home left soulless. Leslie did not run over on the following day—which Anne thought a bad sign.

Gilbert having occasion to go in the evening to the fishing cove, Anne drove with him to the Point, intending to stay awhile with Captain Jim. But the great light, cutting its swathes through the fog of the autumn evening, was in care of Alec Boyd and Captain Jim was away.

"What will you do?" asked Gilbert. "Come with me?"

"I don't want to go to the cove—but I'll go over the channel with you, and roam about on the sand-shore till you come back. The rock shore is too slippery and grim tonight."

Alone on the sands of the bar Anne gave herself up to the eerie charm of the night. It was warm for September, and the late afternoon had been very foggy; but a full moon had in part lessened the fog and transformed the harbor and the gulf and the surrounding shores into a strange, fantastic, unreal world of pale silver mist, through which everything loomed phantom-like. Captain Josiah Crawford's black schooner sailing down the channel, laden with potatoes for Bluenose ports, was a spectral ship bound for a far uncharted land, ever receding, never to be reached. The calls of unseen gulls overhead were the cries of the souls of doomed seamen. The little curls of foam that blew across the sand were elfin things stealing up from the sea-caves. The big, round-shouldered sand-dunes were the sleeping giants of some old northern tale. The lights that glimmered palely across the harbor were the delusive beacons on some coast of fairyland. Anne pleased herself with a hundred fancies as she wandered through the mist. It was delightful—romantic—mysterious to be roaming here alone on this enchanted shore.

But was she alone? Something loomed in the mist before her—took shape and form—suddenly moved towards her across the wave-rippled sand.

"Leslie!" exclaimed Anne in amazement. "Whatever are you doing—*here*—tonight?"

"If it comes to that, whatever are *you* doing here?" said Leslie, trying to laugh. The effort was a failure. She looked very pale and tired; but the love locks under her scarlet cap were curling about her face and eyes like little sparkling rings of gold.

"I'm waiting for Gilbert—he's over at the Cove. I intended to stay at the light, but Captain Jim is away."

"Well, *I* came here because I wanted to walk—and walk—and *walk*," said Leslie restlessly. "I couldn't on the rock shore—the tide was too high and the rocks prisoned me. I had to come here—or I should have gone mad, I think. I rowed myself over the channel in Captain Jim's flat. I've been here for an hour. Come—come—let us walk. I can't stand still. Oh, Anne!"

"Leslie, dearest, what is the trouble?" asked Anne, though she knew too well already.

"I can't tell you—don't ask me. I wouldn't mind your knowing—I wish you did know—but I can't tell you—I can't tell anyone. I've been such a fool, Anne—and oh, it hurts so terribly to be a fool. There's nothing so painful in the world."

She laughed bitterly. Anne slipped her arm around her.

"Leslie, is it that you have learned to care for Mr. Ford?"

Leslie turned herself about passionately.

"How did you know?" she cried. "Anne, how did you know? Oh, is it written in my face for everyone to see? Is it as plain as that?"

"No, no. I—I can't tell you how I knew. It just came into my mind, somehow. Leslie, don't look at me like that!"

"Do you despise me?" demanded Leslie in a fierce, low tone. "Do you think I'm wicked—unwomanly? Or do you think I'm just plain fool?"

"I don't think you any of these things. Come, dear, let's just talk it over sensibly, as we might talk over any other of the great crises of life. You've been brooding over it and let yourself drift into a morbid view of it. You know you have a little tendency to do that about everything that goes wrong, and you promised me that you would fight against it."

"But—oh, it's so—so shameful," murmured Leslie. "To love him—unsought—and when I'm not free to love anybody."

"There's nothing shameful about it. But I'm very sorry that you have learned to care for Owen, because, as things are, it will only make you more unhappy."

"I didn't *learn* to care," said Leslie, walking on and speaking passionately. "If it had been like that I could have prevented it. I never dreamed of such a thing until that day, a week ago, when he told me he had finished his book and must soon go away. Then—then I knew. I felt as if someone had struck me a terrible blow. I didn't say anything—I couldn't speak—but I don't know what I looked like. I'm so afraid my face betrayed me. Oh, I would die of shame if I thought he knew—or suspected."

Anne was miserably silent, hampered by her deductions from her conversation with Owen. Leslie went on feverishly, as if she found relief in speech.

"I was so happy all this summer, Anne—happier than I ever was in my life. I thought it was because everything had been made clear between you and me, and that it was our friendship which made life seem so beautiful and full once more. And it *was*, in part—but not all—oh, not nearly all. I know now why everything was different. And now it's all over—and he has gone. How can I live, Anne? When I turned back into the house this morning after he had gone the solitude struck me like a blow in the face."

"It won't seem so hard by and by, dear," said Anne, who always felt the pain of her friends so keenly that she could not speak easy, fluent words of comforting. Besides, she remembered how well-meant speeches had hurt her in her own sorrow and was afraid.

"Oh, it seems to me it will grow harder all the time," said Leslie miserably. "I've nothing to look forward to. Morning will come after morning—and he will not come back—he will never come back. Oh, when I think that I will never see him again I feel as if a great brutal hand had twisted itself among my heartstrings, and was wrenching them. Once, long ago, I dreamed of love— and I thought it must be beautiful—and *now*—it's like *this*. When he went away yesterday morning he was so cold and indifferent. He said 'Good-bye, Mrs. Moore' in the coldest tone in the world—as if we had not even been friends—as if I meant absolutely nothing to him. I know I don't—I didn't want him to care—but he *might* have been a little kinder."

"Oh, I wish Gilbert would come," thought Anne. She was racked between her sympathy for Leslie and the necessity of avoiding anything that would betray Owen's confidence. She knew why his good-bye had been so cold—why it could not have the cordiality that their good-comradeship demanded—but she could not tell Leslie.

"I couldn't help it, Anne—I couldn't help it," said poor Leslie.

"I know that."

"Do you blame me so very much?"

"I don't blame you at all."

"And you won't—you won't tell Gilbert?"

"Leslie! Do you think I would do such a thing?"

"Oh, I don't know—you and Gilbert are such *chums*. I don't see how you could help telling him everything."

"Everything about my own concerns—yes. But not my friends' secrets."

"I couldn't have *him* know. But I'm glad *you* know. I would feel guilty if there were anything I was ashamed to tell you. I hope Miss Cornelia won't find out. Sometimes I feel as if those terrible, kind brown eyes of hers read my very soul. Oh, I wish this mist would never lift—I wish I could just stay in it forever, hidden away from every living being. I don't see how I can go on with life. This summer has been so full. I never was lonely for a moment. Before Owen came there used to be horrible moments—when I had been with you and Gilbert—and then had to leave you. You two would walk away together and I would walk away *alone*. After Owen came he was always there to walk home with me—we would laugh and talk as you and Gilbert were doing—there were no more lonely, envious moments for me. And *now*! Oh, yes, I've been a fool. Let's have done talking about my folly. I'll never bore you with it again."

"Here is Gilbert, and you are coming back with us," said Anne, who had no intention of leaving Leslie to wander alone on the sand-bar on such a night and in such a mood. "There's plenty of room in our boat for three, and we'll tie the flat on behind."

"Oh, I suppose I must reconcile myself to being the odd one again," said poor Leslie with another bitter laugh. "Forgive me, Anne—that was hateful. I ought to be thankful—and I *am*—that I have two good friends who are glad to count me in as a third. Don't mind my hateful speeches. I just seem to be one great pain all over and everything hurts me."

"Leslie seemed very quiet tonight, didn't she?" said Gilbert, when he and Anne reached home. "What in the world was she doing over there on the bar alone?"

"Oh, she was tired—and you know she likes to go to the shore after one of Dick's bad days."

"What a pity she hadn't met and married a fellow like Ford long ago," ruminated Gilbert. "They'd have made an ideal couple, wouldn't they?"

"For pity's sake, Gilbert, don't develop into a matchmaker. It's an abominable profession for a man," cried Anne rather sharply, afraid that Gilbert might blunder on the truth if he kept on in this strain.

"Bless us, Anne-girl, I'm not matchmaking," protested Gilbert, rather surprised at her tone. "I was only thinking of one of the might-have-beens."

"Well, don't. It's a waste of time," said Anne. Then she added suddenly:

"Oh, Gilbert, I wish everybody could be as happy as we are."

28
ODDS AND ENDS

"I've been reading obituary notices," said Miss Cornelia, laying down the *Daily Enterprise* and taking up her sewing.

The harbor was lying black and sullen under a dour November sky; the wet, dead leaves clung drenched and sodden to the window sills; but the little house was gay with firelight and spring-like with Anne's ferns and geraniums.

"It's always summer here, Anne," Leslie had said one day; and all who were the guests of that house of dreams felt the same.

"The *Enterprise* seems to run to obituaries these days," quoth Miss Cornelia. "It always has a couple of columns of them, and I read every line. It's one of my forms of recreation, especially when there's some original poetry attached to them. Here's a choice sample for you:

> 'She's gone to be with her Maker,
> Never more to roam.
> She used to play and sing with joy
> The song of Home, Sweet Home.'

Who says we haven't any poetical talent on the Island! Have you ever noticed what heaps of good people die, Anne, dearie? It's kind of pitiful. Here's ten obituaries, and every one of them saints and models, even the men. Here's old Peter Stimson, who has 'left a large circle of friends to mourn his untimely loss.' Lord, Anne, dearie, that man was eighty, and everybody who knew him had been wishing him dead these thirty years. Read obituaries when you're blue, Anne, dearie—especially the ones of folks you know. If you've any sense of humor at all they'll cheer you up, believe *me*. I just wish *I* had the writing of the obituaries of some people. Isn't 'obituary' an awful ugly word? This very Peter I've been speaking of had a face exactly like one. I never saw it but I thought the word *obituary* then and there. There's only one uglier word that I know of, and that's *relict*. Lord, Anne, dearie, I may be an old maid, but there's this comfort in it—I'll never be any man's 'relict.'"

"It *is* an ugly word," said Anne, laughing. "Avonlea graveyard was full of old tombstones 'sacred to the memory of So-and-So, *relict* of the late So-and-So.' It always made me think of something worn-out and moth-eaten. Why is it that so many of the words connected with death are so disagreeable? I do wish that the custom of calling a dead body 'the remains' could be abolished. I positively shiver when I hear the undertaker say at a funeral, 'All who wish to see the remains please step this way.' It always gives me the horrible impression that I am about to view the scene of a cannibal feast."

"Well, all I hope," said Miss Cornelia calmly, "is that when I'm dead nobody will call me 'our departed sister.' I took a scunner at this sistering-and-brothering business five years ago when there was a traveling evangelist holding meetings at the Glen. I hadn't any use for him from the start. I felt in my bones that there was something wrong with him. And there was. Mind you, he was pretending to be a Presbyterian—Presby*tarian*, *he* called it—and all the time he was a Methodist. He brothered and sistered everybody. He had a large circle of relations, that man had. He clutched my hand fervently one night, and said imploringly, 'My *dear* sister Bryant, are you a Christian?' I just looked him over a bit, and then I said calmly, 'The only brother I ever had, *Mr.* Fiske, was buried fifteen years ago, and I haven't adopted any since. As for being a Christian, I was that, I hope and believe, when you were crawling about the floor in petticoats.' *That* squelched him, believe *me*. Mind you, Anne dearie, I'm not down on all evangelists. We've had some real fine, earnest men, who did a lot of good and made the old sinners squirm. But this Fiske-man wasn't one of them. I had a good laugh all to myself one evening. Fiske had asked all who were Christians to stand up. *I* didn't, believe *me!* I never had any use for that sort of thing. But most of them did, and then he asked all who wanted to be Christians to stand up. Nobody stirred for a spell, so Fiske started up a hymn at the top of his voice. Just in front of me poor little Ikey Baker was sitting in the Millison pew. He was a home boy, ten years old, and Millison just about worked him to death. The poor little creature was always so tired he fell asleep right off whenever he went to church or anywhere he could sit still for a few minutes. He'd been sleeping all through the meeting, and I was thankful to see the poor child getting a rest, believe *me*. Well, when Fiske's voice went soaring skyward and the rest joined in, poor Ikey wakened with a start. He thought it was just an ordinary singing and that everybody ought to stand up, so he scrambled to his feet mighty quick, knowing he'd get a combing down from Maria Millison for sleeping in meeting. Fiske saw him, stopped and shouted, 'Another soul saved! Glory Hallelujah!' And there was poor, frightened Ikey, only half awake and yawning, never thinking about his soul at all. Poor child, he never had time to think of anything but his tired, overworked little body.

"Leslie went one night and the Fiske-man got right after her—oh, he was especially anxious about the souls of the nice-looking girls, believe me!—and he hurt her feelings so she never went again. And then he prayed every night after that, right in public, that the Lord would soften her hard heart. Finally I went to Mr. Leavitt, our minister then, and told him if he didn't make Fiske stop that I'd just rise up the next night and throw my hymn book at him when he mentioned that 'beautiful but unrepentant young woman.' I'd have done it too, believe *me*. Mr. Leavitt did put a stop to it, but Fiske kept on with his meetings until Charley Douglas put an end to his career in the Glen. Mrs. Charley had been out in California all winter. She'd been real melancholy in the fall—religious melancholy—it ran in her family. Her father worried so much over believing that he had committed the unpardonable sin that he died in the asylum. So when Rose Douglas got that way Charley packed her off to visit her sister in Los Angeles. She got perfectly well and came home just when the Fiske revival was in full swing. She stepped off the train at the Glen, real smiling and chipper, and the first thing she saw staring her in the face on the black, gable-end of the freight shed, was the question, in big white letters, two feet high, 'Whither goest thou—to heaven or hell?' That had been one of Fiske's ideas, and he had got Henry Hammond to paint it. Rose just gave a shriek and fainted; and when they got her home she was worse than ever. Charley Douglas went to Mr. Leavitt and told him that every Douglas would leave the church if Fiske was kept there any longer. Mr. Leavitt had to give in, for the Douglases paid half his salary, so Fiske departed, and we had to depend on our Bibles once more for instructions on how to get to heaven. After he was gone Mr. Leavitt found out he was just a masquerading Methodist, and he felt pretty sick, believe *me*. Mr. Leavitt fell short in some ways, but he was a good, sound Presbyterian."

"By the way, I had a letter from Mr. Ford yesterday," said Anne. "He asked me to remember him kindly to you."

"I don't want his remembrances," said Miss Cornelia, curtly.

"Why?" asked Anne, in astonishment. "I thought you liked him."

"Well, so I did, in a kind of way. But I'll never forgive him for what he done to Leslie. There's that poor child eating her heart out about him—as if she hadn't had trouble enough—and him ranting round Toronto, I've no doubt, enjoying himself same as ever. Just like a man."

"Oh, Miss Cornelia, how did you find out?"

"Lord, Anne, dearie, I've got eyes, haven't I? And I've known Leslie since she was a baby. There's been a new kind of heartbreak in her eyes all the fall, and I know that writer-man was behind it

somehow. I'll never forgive myself for being the means of bringing him here. But I never expected he'd be like he was. I thought
he'd just be like the other men Leslie had boarded—conceited
young asses, every one of them, that she never had any use for.
One of them did try to flirt with her once and she froze him
out—so bad, I feel sure he's never got himself thawed since. So I
never thought of any danger."

"Don't let Leslie suspect you know her secret," said Anne hurriedly. "I think it would hurt her."

"Trust me, Anne, dearie. *I* wasn't born yesterday. Oh, a plague
on all the men! One of them ruined Leslie's life to begin with,
and now another of the tribe comes and makes her still more
wretched. Anne, this world is an awful place, believe *me*."

> "'There's something in the world amiss
> Will be unriddled by and by,'"

quoted Anne dreamily.

"If it is, it'll be in a world where there aren't any men," said
Miss Cornelia gloomily.

"What have the men been doing now?" asked Gilbert, entering.

"Mischief—mischief! What else did they ever do?"

"It was Eve ate the apple, Miss Cornelia."

"'Twas a he-creature tempted her," retorted Miss Cornelia triumphantly.

Leslie, after her first anguish was over, found it possible to go
on with life after all, as most of us do, no matter what our particular form of torment has been. It is even possible that she
enjoyed moments of it, when she was one of the gay circle in the
little house of dreams. But if Anne ever hoped that she was forgetting Owen Ford she would have been undeceived by the
furtive hunger in Leslie's eyes whenever his name was mentioned. Pitiful to that hunger, Anne always contrived to tell
Captain Jim or Gilbert bits of news from Owen's letters when
Leslie was with them. The girl's flush and pallor at such moments
spoke all too eloquently of the emotion that filled her being.

But she never spoke of him to Anne, or mentioned that night on the sand-bar.

One day her old dog died and she grieved bitterly over him.

"He's been my friend so long," she said sorrowfully to Anne. "He was Dick's old dog, you know—Dick had him for a year or so before we were married. He left him with me when he sailed on the *Four Sisters*. Carlo got very fond of me—and his dog-love helped me through that first dreadful year after mother died, when I was all alone. When I heard that Dick was coming back I was afraid Carlo wouldn't be so much mine. But he never seemed to care for Dick, though he had been so fond of him once. He would snap and growl at him as if he were a stranger. I was glad. It was nice to have one thing whose love was all mine. That old dog has been such a comfort to me, Anne. He got so feeble in the fall that I was afraid he couldn't live long—but I hoped I could nurse him through the winter. He seemed pretty well this morning. He was lying on the rug before the fire; then, all at once, he got up and crept over to me; he put his head on my lap and gave me one loving look out of his big, soft, dog eyes—and then he just shivered and died. I shall miss him so."

"Let me give you another dog, Leslie," said Anne. "I'm getting a lovely Gordon setter for a Christmas present for Gilbert. Let me give you one too."

Leslie shook her head.

"Not just now, thank you, Anne. I don't feel like having another dog yet. I don't seem to have any affection left for another. Perhaps—in time—I'll let you give me one. I really need one as a kind of protection. But there was something almost human about Carlo—it wouldn't be *decent* to fill his place too hurriedly, dear old fellow."

Anne went to Avonlea a week before Christmas and stayed until after the holidays. Gilbert came up for her, and there was a glad New Year celebration at Green Gables, when Barrys and Blythes and Wrights assembled to devour a dinner which had cost Mrs. Rachel and Marilla much careful thought and preparation. When they went back to Four Winds the little house was almost drifted over, for the third storm of a winter that was to prove phenomenally stormy had whirled up the harbor and heaped huge snow mountains about everything it encountered. But Captain Jim had shovelled out doors and paths, and Miss Cornelia had come down and kindled the hearth-fire.

"It's good to see you back, Anne, dearie! But did you ever see such drifts? You can't see the Moore place at all unless you go upstairs. Leslie'll be so glad you're back. She's almost buried alive over there. Fortunately Dick can shovel snow, and thinks it's great fun. Susan sent me word to tell you she would be on hand tomorrow. Where are you off to now, Captain?"

"I reckon I'll plough up to the Glen and sit a bit with old Martin Strong. He's not far from his end and he's lonesome. He hasn't many friends—been too busy all his life to make any. He's made heaps of money, though."

"Well, he thought that since he couldn't serve God and Mammon he'd better stick to Mammon," said Miss Cornelia crisply. "So he shouldn't complain if he doesn't find Mammon very good company now."

Captain Jim went out, but remembered something in the yard and turned back for a moment.

"I'd a letter from Mr. Ford, Mistress Blythe, and he says the life-book is accepted and is going to be published next fall. I felt fair uplifted when I got the news. To think that I'm to see it in print at last."

"That man is clean crazy on the subject of his life-book," said Miss Cornelia compassionately. "For my part, I think there's far too many books in the world now."

29
GILBERT AND ANNE DISAGREE

Gilbert laid down the ponderous medical tome over which he had been poring until the increasing dusk of the March evening made him desist. He leaned back in his chair and gazed meditatively out of the window. It was early spring—probably the ugliest time of the year. Not even the sunset could redeem the dead, sodden landscape and rotten-black harbor ice upon which he looked. No sign of life was visible, save a big black crow winging his solitary way across a leaden field. Gilbert speculated idly concerning that crow. Was he a family crow, with a black but comely crow wife awaiting him in the woods beyond the Glen? Or was he a glossy young buck of a crow on courting thoughts intent? Or was he a cynical bachelor crow, believing that he travels the fastest who travels alone? Whatever he was, he soon disappeared in congenial gloom and Gilbert turned to the cheerier view indoors.

The firelight flickered from point to point, gleaming on the white and green coats of Gog and Magog, on the sleek, brown head of the beautiful setter basking on the rug, on the picture frames on the walls, on the vaseful of daffodils from the window garden, on Anne herself, sitting by her little table, with her sewing beside her and her hands clasped over her knee while she traced out pictures in the fire—Castles in Spain whose airy turrets pierced moonlit cloud and sunset bar—ships sailing from the Haven of Good Hopes straight to Four Winds Harbor with precious burthen. For Anne was again a dreamer of dreams, albeit a grim shape of fear went with her night and day to shadow and darken her visions.

Gilbert was accustomed to refer to himself as "on old married man." But he still looked upon Anne with the incredulous eyes of a lover. He couldn't wholly believe yet that she was really his. It *might* be only a dream after all, part and parcel of this magic house of dreams. His soul still went on tip-toe before her, lest the charm be shattered and the dream dispelled.

"Anne," he said slowly, "lend me your ears. I want to talk with you about something."

Anne looked across at him through the fire-lit gloom.

"What is it?" she asked, gaily. "You look fearfully solemn, Gilbert. I really haven't done anything naughty today. Ask Susan."

"It's not of you—or ourselves—I want to talk. It's about Dick Moore."

"Dick Moore?" echoed Anne, sitting up alertly. "Why, what in the world have you to say about Dick Moore?"

"I've been thinking a great deal about him lately. Do you remember that time last summer I treated him for those carbuncles on his neck?"

"Yes—yes."

"I took the opportunity to examine the scars on his head thoroughly. I've always thought Dick was a very interesting case from a medical point of view. Lately I've been studying the history of trephining and the cases where it has been employed. Anne, I have come to the conclusion that if Dick Moore were taken to a good hospital and the operation of trephining performed on several places in his skull, his memory and faculties might be restored."

"Gilbert!" Anne's voice was full of protest. "Surely you don't mean it!"

"I do, indeed. And I have decided that it is my duty to broach the subject to Leslie."

"Gilbert Blythe, you shall *not* do any such thing," cried Anne vehemently. "Oh, Gilbert, you won't—you won't. You couldn't be so cruel. Promise me you won't."

"Why, Anne-girl, I didn't suppose you would take it like this. Be reasonable—"

"I won't be reasonable—I can't be reasonable—I *am* reasonable. It is you who are unreasonable. Gilbert, have you ever once thought what it would mean for Leslie if Dick Moore were to be restored to his right senses? Just stop and think! She's unhappy enough now; but life as Dick's nurse and attendant is a thousand times easier for her than life as Dick's wife. I know—I *know!*

It's unthinkable. Don't you meddle with the matter. Leave well enough alone."

"I *have* thought over that aspect of the case thoroughly, Anne. But I believe that a doctor is bound to set the sanctity of a patient's mind and body above all other considerations, no matter what the consequences may be. I believe it his duty to endeavor to restore health and sanity, if there is any hope whatever of it."

"But Dick isn't your patient in that respect," cried Anne, taking another tack. "If Leslie had asked you if anything could be done for him, *then* it might be your duty to tell her what you really thought. But you've no right to meddle."

"I don't call it meddling. Uncle Dave told Leslie twelve years ago that nothing could be done for Dick. She believes that, of course."

"And why did Uncle Dave tell her that, if it wasn't true?" cried Anne, triumphantly. "Doesn't he know as much about it as you?"

"I think not—though it may sound conceited and presumptuous to say it. And you know as well as I that he is rather prejudiced against what he calls 'these new-fangled notions of cutting and carving.' He's even opposed to operating for appendicitis."

"He's right," exclaimed Anne, with a complete change of front. "I believe myself that you modern doctors are entirely too fond of making experiments with human flesh and blood."

"Rhoda Allonby would not be a living woman today if I had been afraid of making a certain experiment," argued Gilbert. "I took the risk—and saved her life."

"I'm sick and tired of hearing about Rhoda Allonby," cried Anne—most unjustly, for Gilbert had never mentioned Mrs. Allonby's name since the day he had told Anne of his success in regard to her. And he could not be blamed for other people's discussion of it.

Gilbert felt rather hurt.

"I had not expected you to look at the matter as you do, Anne," he said a little stiffly, getting up and moving towards the office door. It was their first approach to a quarrel.

But Anne flew after him and dragged him back.

"Now, Gilbert, you are not 'going off mad.' Sit down here and I'll apologize bee-*yew*-ti-fully. I shouldn't have said that. But—oh, if you knew—"

Anne checked herself just in time. She had been on the very verge of betraying Leslie's secret.

"Knew what a woman feels about it," she concluded lamely.

"I think I do know. I've looked at the matter from every point of view—and I've been driven to the conclusion that it is my duty to tell Leslie that I believe it is possible that Dick can be restored to himself; there my responsibility ends. It will be for her to decide what she will do."

"I don't think you've any right to put such a responsibility on her. She had enough to bear. She is poor—how could she afford such an operation?"

"That is for her to decide," persisted Gilbert stubbornly.

"You say you think that Dick can be cured. But are you *sure* of it?"

"Certainly not. Nobody could be sure of such a thing. There may have been lesions of the brain itself, the effect of which can never be removed. But if, as I believe, his loss of memory and other faculties is due merely to the pressure on the brain centres of certain depressed areas of bone, then he can be cured."

"But it's only a possibility!" insisted Anne. "Now, suppose you tell Leslie and she decides to have the operation. It will cost a great deal. She will have to borrow the money, or sell her little property. And suppose the operation is a failure and Dick remains the same. How will she be able to pay back the money she borrows, or make a living for herself and that big helpless creature if she sells the farm?"

"Oh, I know—I know. But it is my duty to tell her. I can't get away from that conviction."

"Oh, I know the Blythe stubbornness," groaned Anne. "But don't do this solely on your own responsibility. Consult Doctor Dave."

"I *have* done so," said Gilbert reluctantly.

"And what did he say?"

"In brief—as you say—leave well enough alone. Apart from his prejudice against new-fangled surgery, I'm afraid he looks at the case from your point of view—don't do it, for Leslie's sake."

"There now," cried Anne triumphantly. "I do think, Gilbert, that you ought to abide by the judgment of a man nearly eighty, who has seen a great deal and saved scores of lives himself—surely his opinion ought to weigh more than a mere boy's."

"Thank you."

"Don't laugh. It's too serious."

"That's just my point. It *is* serious. Here is a man who is a helpless burden. He may be restored to reason and usefulness—"

"He was so very useful before," interjected Anne witheringly.

"He may be given a chance to make good and redeem the past. His wife doesn't know this. I do. It is therefore my duty to tell her that there is such a possibility. That, boiled down, is my decision."

"Don't say 'decision' yet, Gilbert. Consult somebody else. Ask Captain Jim what he thinks about it."

"Very well. But I'll not promise to abide by his opinion, Anne. This is something a man must decide for himself. My conscience would never be easy if I kept silent on the subject."

"Oh, your conscience!" moaned Anne. "I suppose that Uncle Dave has a conscience too, hasn't he?"

"Yes. But I am not the keeper of his conscience. Come, Anne, if this affair did not concern Leslie—if it were a purely abstract case, you would agree with me,—you know you would."

"I wouldn't," vowed Anne, trying to believe it herself. "Oh, you can argue all night, Gilbert, but you won't convince me. Just you ask Miss Cornelia what she thinks of it."

"You're driven to the last ditch, Anne, when you bring up Miss Cornelia as a reinforcement. She will say, 'Just like a man,' and rage furiously. No matter. This is no affair for Miss Cornelia to settle. Leslie alone must decide it."

"You know very well how she will decide it," said Anne, almost in tears. "She has ideals of duty, too. I don't see how you can take such a responsibility on your shoulders. *I* couldn't."

> "'Because right is right to follow right
> Were wisdom in the scorn of consequence,'"

quoted Gilbert.

"Oh, you think a couplet of poetry a convincing argument!" scoffed Anne. "That is so like a man."

And then she laughed in spite of herself. It sounded so like an echo of Miss Cornelia.

"Well, if you won't accept Tennyson as an authority, perhaps you will believe the words of a Greater than he," said Gilbert seriously. "'Ye shall know the truth and the truth shall make you free.' I believe that, Anne, with all my heart. It's the greatest and grandest verse in the Bible—or in any literature—and the *truest*, if there are comparative degrees of trueness. And it's the first duty of a man to tell the truth, as he sees it and believes it."

"In this case the truth won't make poor Leslie free," sighed Anne. "It will probably end in still more bitter bondage for her. Oh, Gilbert, I *can't* think you are right."

30
LESLIE DECIDES

A sudden outbreak of a virulent type of influenza at the Glen and down at the fishing village kept Gilbert so busy for the next fortnight that he had no time to pay the promised visit to Captain Jim. Anne hoped against hope that he had abandoned the idea about Dick Moore, and, resolving to let sleeping dogs lie, she said no more about the subject. But she thought of it incessantly.

"I wonder if it would be right for me to tell him that Leslie cares for Owen," she thought. "He would never let her suspect that he knew, so her pride would not suffer, and it *might* convince him that he should let Dick Moore alone. Shall I—shall I? No, after all, I cannot. A promise is sacred, and I've no right to betray Leslie's secret. But oh, I never felt so worried over anything in my life as I do over this. It's spoiling the spring—it's spoiling everything."

One evening Gilbert abruptly proposed that they go down and see Captain Jim. With a sinking heart Anne agreed, and they set forth. Two weeks of kind sunshine had wrought a miracle in the bleak landscape over which Gilbert's crow had flown. The hills and fields were dry and brown and warm, ready to break into bud and blossom; the harbor was laughter-shaken again; the long harbor road was like a gleaming red ribbon; down on the dunes a crowd of boys, who were out smelt fishing, were burning the thick, dry sand-hill grass of the preceding summer. The flames swept over the dunes rosily, flinging their cardinal banners against the dark gulf beyond, and illuminating the channel and the fishing village. It was a picturesque scene which would at other times have delighted Anne's eyes; but she was not enjoying this walk. Neither was Gilbert. Their usual good-comradeship and Josephian community of taste and view-point were sadly lacking. Anne's disapproval of the whole project showed itself in the haughty uplift of her head and the studied politeness of her remarks. Gilbert's mouth was set in all the Blythe obstinacy, but his eyes were troubled. He meant to do what he believed to be his duty; but to be at outs with Anne was a high price to pay. Altogether, both were glad when they reached the light—and remorseful that they should be glad.

Captain Jim put away the fishing net upon which he was working, and welcomed them joyfully. In the searching light of the spring evening he looked older than Anne had ever seen him. His hair had grown much grayer, and the strong old hand shook a little. But his blue eyes were clear and steady, and the staunch soul looked out through them gallant and unafraid.

Captain Jim listened in amazed silence while Gilbert said what he had come to say. Anne, who knew how the old man worshipped Leslie, felt quite sure that he would side with her, although she had not much hope that this would influence Gilbert. She was therefore surprised beyond measure when Captain Jim, slowly and sorrowfully, but unhesitatingly, gave it as his opinion that Leslie should be told.

"Oh, Captain Jim, I didn't think you'd say that," she exclaimed reproachfully. "I thought you wouldn't want to make more trouble for her."

Captain Jim shook his head.

"I don't want to. I know how you feel about it, Mistress Blythe—just as I feel meself. But it ain't our feelings we have to steer by through life—no, no, we'd make shipwreck mighty often if we did that. There's only the one safe compass and we've got to set our course by that—what it's right to do. I agree with the doctor. If there's a chance for Dick, Leslie should be told of it. There's no two sides to that, in my opinion."

"Well," said Anne, giving up in despair, "wait until Miss Cornelia gets after you two men."

"Cornelia'll rake us fore and aft, no doubt," assented Captain Jim. "You women are lovely critters, Mistress Blythe, but you're just a mite illogical. You're a highly eddicated lady and Cornelia isn't, but you're like as two peas when it comes to that. I dunno's you're any the worse for it. Logic is a sort of hard, merciless thing, I reckon. Now, I'll brew a cup of tea and we'll drink it and talk of pleasant things, jest to calm our minds a bit."

At least, Captain Jim's tea and conversation calmed Anne's mind to such an extent that she did not make Gilbert suffer so acutely on the way home as she had deliberately intended to do. She did not refer to the burning question at all, but she chatted amiably of other matters, and Gilbert understood that he was forgiven under protest.

"Captain Jim seems very frail and bent this spring. The winter has aged him," said Anne sadly. "I am afraid that he will soon be going to seek lost Margaret. I can't bear to think of it."

"Four Winds won't be the same place when Captain Jim 'sets out to sea,'" agreed Gilbert.

The following evening he went to the house up the brook. Anne wandered dismally around until his return.

"Well, what did Leslie say?" she demanded when he came in.

"Very little. I think she felt rather dazed."

"And is she going to have the operation?"

"She is going to think it over and decide very soon."

Gilbert flung himself wearily into the easy chair before the fire. He looked tired. It had not been an easy thing for him to tell Leslie. And the terror that had sprung into her eyes when the meaning of what he told her came home to her was not a pleasant thing to remember. Now, when the die was cast, he was beset with doubts of his own wisdom.

Anne looked at him remorsefully; then she slipped down on the rug beside him and laid her glossy red head on his arm.

"Gilbert, I've been rather hateful over this. I won't be any more. Please just call me red-headed and forgive me."

By which Gilbert understood that, no matter what came of it, there would be no I-told-you-so's. But he was not wholly comforted. Duty in the abstract is one thing; duty in the concrete is quite another, especially when the doer is confronted by a woman's stricken eyes.

Some instinct made Anne keep away from Leslie for the next three days. On the third evening Leslie came down to the little house and told Gilbert that she had made up her mind; she would take Dick to Montreal and have the operation.

She was very pale and seemed to have wrapped herself in her old mantle of aloofness. But her eyes had lost the look which had haunted Gilbert; they were cold and bright; and she proceeded to discuss details with him in a crisp, business-like way. There were plans to be made and many things to be thought over. When Leslie had got the information she wanted she went home. Anne wanted to walk part of the way with her.

"Better not," said Leslie curtly. "Today's rain has made the ground damp. Good-night."

"Have I lost my friend?" said Anne with a sigh. "If the

operation is successful and Dick Moore finds himself again Leslie will retreat into some remote fastness of her soul where none of us can ever find her."

"Perhaps she will leave him," said Gilbert.

"Leslie would never do that, Gilbert. Her sense of duty is very strong. She told me once that her Grandmother West always impressed upon her the fact that when she assumed any responsibility she must never shirk it, no matter what the consequences might be. That is one of her cardinal rules. I suppose it's very old-fashioned."

"Don't be bitter, Anne-girl. You know you don't think it old-fashioned—you know you have the very same idea of the sacredness of assumed responsibilities yourself. And you are right. Shirking responsibilities is the curse of our modern life—the secret of all the unrest and discontent that is seething in the world."

"Thus saith the preacher," mocked Anne. But under the mockery she felt that he was right; and she was very sick at heart for Leslie.

A week later Miss Cornelia descended like an avalanche upon the little house. Gilbert was away and Anne was compelled to bear the shock of the impact alone.

Miss Cornelia hardly waited to get her hat off before she began.

"Anne, do you mean to tell me it's true what I've heard—that Dr. Blythe has told Leslie Dick can be cured, and that she is going to take him to Montreal to have him operated on?"

"Yes, it is quite true, Miss Cornelia," said Anne bravely.

"Well, it's inhuman cruelty, that's what it is," said Miss Cornelia, violently agitated. "I did think Dr. Blythe was a decent man. I didn't think he could have been guilty of this."

"Dr. Blythe thought it was his duty to tell Leslie that there was a chance for Dick," said Anne with spirit, "and," she added loyalty to Gilbert getting the better of her, "I agree with him."

"Oh, no, you don't, dearie," said Miss Cornelia. "No person with any bowels of compassion could."

"Captain Jim does."

"Don't quote that old ninny to me," cried Miss Cornelia. "And I don't care who agrees with him. Think—*think* what it means to that poor hunted, harried girl."

"We *do* think of it. But Gilbert believes that a doctor should put the welfare of a patient's mind and body before all other considerations."

"That's just like a man. But I expected better things of you, Anne," said Miss Cornelia, more in sorrow than in wrath; then she proceeded to bombard Anne with precisely the same arguments with which the latter had attacked Gilbert; and Anne valiantly defended her husband with the weapons he had used for his own protection. Long was the fray, but Miss Cornelia made an end at last.

"It's an iniquitous shame," she declared, almost in tears. "That's just what it is—an iniquitous shame. Poor, poor Leslie!"

"Don't you think Dick should be considered a little, too?" pleaded Anne.

"Dick! Dick Moore! He's happy enough. He's a better-behaved and more reputable member of society now than he ever was before. Why, he was a drunkard and perhaps worse. Are you going to set him loose again to roar and to devour?"

"He may reform," said poor Anne, beset by foe without and traitor within.

"Reform your grandmother!" retorted Miss Cornelia. "Dick Moore got the injuries that left him as he is in a drunken brawl. He *deserves* his fate. It was sent on him for a punishment. I don't believe the doctor has any business to tamper with the visitations of God."

"Nobody knows how Dick was hurt, Miss Cornelia. It may not have been in a drunken brawl at all. He may have been waylaid and robbed."

"Pigs *may* whistle, but they've poor mouths for it," said Miss Cornelia. "Well, the gist of what you tell me is that the thing is settled and there's no use in talking. If that's so I'll hold my tongue. I don't propose to wear *my* teeth out gnawing files. When a thing has to be I give in to it. But I like to make mighty sure first that it *has* to be. Now, I'll devote *my* energies to comforting and sustaining Leslie. And after all," added Miss Cornelia, brightening up hopefully, "perhaps nothing can be done for Dick."

31
THE TRUTH MAKES FREE

Leslie, having once made up her mind what to do, proceeded to do it with characteristic resolution and speed. House-cleaning must be finished with first, whatever issues of life and death might await beyond. The gray house up the brook was put into flawless order and cleanliness, with Miss Cornelia's ready assistance. Miss Cornelia, having said her say to Anne, and later on to Gilbert and Captain Jim—sparing neither of them, let it be assured—never spoke of the matter to Leslie. She accepted the fact of Dick's operation, referred to it when necessary in a business-like way, and ignored it when it was not. Leslie never attempted to discuss it. She was very cold and quiet during these beautiful spring days. She seldom visited Anne, and though she was invariably courteous and friendly, that very courtesy was as an icy barrier between her and the people of the little house. The old jokes and laughter and chumminess of common things could not reach her over it. Anne refused to feel hurt. She knew that Leslie was in the grip of a hideous dread—a dread that wrapped her away from all little glimpses of happiness and hours of pleasure. When one great passion seizes possession of the soul all other feelings are crowded aside. Never in all her life had Leslie Moore shuddered away from the future with more intolerable terror. But she went forward as unswervingly in the path she had elected as the martyrs of old walked their chosen way, knowing the end of it to be the fiery agony of the stake.

The financial question was settled with greater ease than Anne had feared. Leslie borrowed the necessary money from Captain Jim, and, at her insistence, he took a mortgage on the little farm.

"So that is one thing off the poor girl's mind," Miss Cornelia told Anne, "and off mine too. Now, if Dick gets well enough to work again he'll be able to earn enough to pay the interest on it; and if he doesn't I know Captain Jim'll manage someway that Leslie won't have to. He said as much to me. 'I'm getting old, Cornelia,' he said, 'and I've no chick or child of my own. Leslie won't take a gift from a living man, but mebbe she will from a dead one.' So it will be all right as far as *that* goes. I wish everything else might be settled as satisfactorily. As for that wretch of a Dick, he's been awful these last few days. The devil was in him, believe *me*! Leslie and I couldn't get on with our work for the tricks he'd play. He chased all her ducks one day around the yard till most of them died. And not one thing would he do for us. Sometimes, you know, he'll make himself quite handy, bringing in pails of water and wood. But this week if we sent him to the well he'd try to climb down into it. I thought once, 'If you'd only shoot down there head-first everything would be nicely settled.'"

"Oh, Miss Cornelia!"

"Now, you needn't Miss Cornelia me, Anne, dearie. *Anybody* would have thought the same. If the Montreal doctors can make a rational creature out of Dick Moore they're wonders."

Leslie took Dick to Montreal early in May. Gilbert went with her, to help her, and make the necessary arrangements for her. He came home with the report that the Montreal surgeon whom they had consulted agreed with him that there was a good chance of Dick's restoration.

"Very comforting," was Miss Cornelia's sarcastic comment.

Anne only sighed. Leslie had been very distant at their parting. But she had promised to write. Ten days after Gilbert's return the letter came. Leslie wrote that the operation had been successfully performed and that Dick was making a good recovery.

"What does she mean by 'successfully'?" asked Anne. "Does she mean that Dick's memory is really restored?"

"Not likely—since she says nothing of it," said Gilbert. "She uses the word 'successfully' from the surgeon's point of view. The operation has been performed and followed by normal results. But it is too soon to know whether Dick's faculties will be eventually restored, wholly or in part. His memory would not be likely to return to him all at once. The process will be gradual, if it occurs at all. Is that all she says?"

"Yes—there's her letter. It's very short. Poor girl, she must be under a terrible strain. Gilbert Blythe, there are heaps of things I long to say to you, only it would be mean."

"Miss Cornelia says them for you," said Gilbert with a rueful smile. "She combs me down every time I encounter her. She makes it plain to me that she regards me as little better than a murderer, and that she thinks it a great pity that Dr. Dave ever let me step into his shoes. She even told me that the Methodist doctor over the harbor was to be preferred before me. With Miss Cornelia the force of condemnation can no further go."

"If Cornelia Bryant was sick, it would not be Doctor Dave or the Methodist doctor she would send for," sniffed Susan. "She would have you out of your hard-earned bed in the middle of the night, doctor, dear, if she took a spell of misery, that she would. And then she would likely say your bill was past all reason. But do not you mind her, doctor, dear. It takes all kinds of people to make a world."

No further word came from Leslie for some time. The May days crept away in a sweet succession and the shores of Four Winds Harbor greened and bloomed and purpled. One day in late May Gilbert came home to be met by Susan in the stable yard.

"I am afraid something has upset Mrs. Doctor, doctor, dear," she said mysteriously. "She got a letter this afternoon and since then she has just been walking round the garden and talking to herself. You know it is not good for her to be on her feet so much, doctor, dear. She did not see fit to tell me what her news was, and I am no pry, doctor, dear, and never was, but it is plain something has upset her. And it is not good for her to be upset."

Gilbert hurried rather anxiously to the garden. Had anything happened at Green Gables? But Anne, sitting on the rustic seat by the brook, did not look troubled, though she was certainly much excited. Her eyes were their grayest, and scarlet spots burned on her cheeks.

"What has happened, Anne?"

Anne gave a queer little laugh.

"I think you'll hardly believe it when I tell you, Gilbert. *I* can't believe it yet. As Susan said the other day, 'I feel like a fly coming to life in the sun—dazed-like.' It's all so incredible. I've read the letter a score of times and every time it's just the same—I can't believe my own eyes. Oh, Gilbert, you were right—so right. I can see that clearly enough now—and I'm so ashamed of myself— and will you ever really forgive me?"

"Anne, I'll shake you if you don't grow coherent. Redmond would be ashamed of you. *What* has happened?"

"You won't believe it—you won't believe it—"

"I'm going in to 'phone for Uncle Dave," said Gilbert, pretending to start for the house.

"Sit down, Gilbert. I'll try to tell you. I've had a letter, and oh, Gilbert, it's all so amazing—so incredibly amazing—we never thought—not one of us ever dreamed—"

"I suppose," said Gilbert, sitting down with a resigned air, "the only thing to do in a case of this kind is to have patience and go at the matter categorically. Whom is your letter from?"

"Leslie—and, oh, Gilbert—"

"Leslie! Whew! What has she to say? What's the news about Dick?"

Anne lifted the letter and held it out, calmly dramatic in a moment.

"There is *no* Dick! The man we have thought Dick Moore— whom everybody in Four Winds has believed for twelve years to be Dick Moore—is his cousin, George Moore, of Nova Scotia, who, it seems, always resembled him very strikingly. Dick Moore died of yellow fever thirteen years ago in Cuba."

32
MISS CORNELIA DISCUSSES THE AFFAIR

"And do you mean to tell me, Anne, dearie, that Dick Moore has turned out not to be Dick Moore at all but somebody else? Is *that* what you 'phoned up to me today?"

"Yes, Miss Cornelia. It is very amazing, isn't it?"

"It's—it's—just like a man," said Miss Cornelia helplessly. She took off her hat with trembling fingers. For once in her life Miss Cornelia was undeniably staggered.

"I can't seem to sense it, Anne," she said. "I've heard you say it—and I believe you—but I can't take it in. Dick Moore is dead—has been dead all these years—and Leslie is free?"

"Yes. The truth has made her free. Gilbert was right when he said that verse was the grandest in the Bible."

"Tell me everything, Anne, dearie. Since I got your 'phone I've been in a regular muddle, believe *me*. Cornelia Bryant was never so kerflummuxed before."

"There isn't a very great deal to tell. Leslie's letter was short. She didn't go into particulars. This man—George Moore—has recovered his memory and knows who he is. He says Dick took yellow fever in Cuba, and the *Four Sisters* had to sail without him. George stayed behind to nurse him. But he died very shortly afterwards. George did not write Leslie because he intended to come right home and tell her himself."

"And why didn't he?"

"I suppose his accident must have intervened. Gilbert says it is quite likely that George Moore remembers nothing of his accident, or what led to it, and may never remember it. It probably happened very soon after Dick's death. We may find out more particulars when Leslie writes again."

"Does she say what she is going to do? When is she coming home?"

"She says she will stay with George Moore until he can leave the hospital. She has written to his people in Nova Scotia. It seems that George's only near relative is a married sister much older than himself. She was living when George sailed on the *Four Sisters,* but of course we do not know what may have happened since. Did you ever see George Moore, Miss Cornelia?"

"I did. It is all coming back to me. He was here visiting his Uncle Abner eighteen years ago, when he and Dick would be about seventeen. They were double cousins, you see. Their fathers were brothers and their mothers were twin sisters, and they did look a terrible lot alike. Of course," added Miss Cornelia scornfully, "it wasn't one of those freak resemblances you read of in novels where two people are so much alike that they can fill each other's places and their nearest and dearest can't tell between them. In those days you could tell easy enough which was George and which was Dick, if you saw them together and near at hand. Apart, or some distance away, it wasn't so easy. They played lots of tricks on people and thought it great fun, the two scamps. George Moore was a little taller and a good deal fatter than Dick—though neither of them was what you would call fat—they were both of the lean kind. Dick had higher color than George, and his hair was a shade lighter. But their features were just alike, and they both had that queer freak of eyes—one blue and one hazel. They weren't much alike in any other way, though. George was a real nice fellow, though he was a scalawag for mischief, and some said he had a liking for a glass even then. But everybody liked him better than Dick. He spent about a month here. Leslie never saw him; she was only about eight or nine then and I remember now that she spent that whole winter over harbor with her grandmother West. Captain Jim was away, too—that was the winter he was wrecked on the Magdalens. I don't suppose either he or Leslie had ever heard about the Nova Scotia cousin looking so much like Dick. Nobody ever thought of him when Captain Jim brought Dick—George, I should say—home. Of course, we all thought Dick had changed considerable—he'd got so lumpish and fat. But we put that down to what had happened to him, and no doubt that was the reason, for, as I've said, George wasn't fat to begin with either. And there was no other way we could have guessed, for the man's senses were clean gone. I can't see that it is any wonder we were all deceived. But it's a staggering thing. And Leslie has sacrificed the best years of her life to nursing a man who hadn't any claim on her! Oh, drat the men! No matter what they do, it's the wrong thing. And no matter who they are, it's somebody they shouldn't be. They do exasperate me."

"Gilbert and Captain Jim are men, and it is through them that the truth has been discovered at last," said Anne.

"Well, I admit that," conceded Miss Cornelia reluctantly. "I'm sorry I raked the doctor off so. It's the first time in my life I've ever felt ashamed of anything I said to a man. I don't know as I shall tell him, though. He'll just have to take it for granted. Well, Anne, dearie, it's a mercy the Lord doesn't answer all our prayers. I've been praying hard right along that the operation wouldn't cure Dick. Of course I didn't put it just quite so plain. But that was what was in the back of my mind, and I have no doubt the Lord knew it."

"Well, He has answered the spirit of your prayer. You really wished that things shouldn't be made any harder for Leslie. I'm afraid that in my secret heart I've been hoping the operation wouldn't succeed, and I am wholesomely ashamed of it."

"How does Leslie seem to take it?"

"She writes like one dazed. I think that, like ourselves, she hardly realizes it yet. She says, 'It all seems like a strange dream to me, Anne.' That is the only reference she makes to herself."

"Poor child! I suppose when the chains are struck off a prisoner he'd feel queer and lost without them for a while. Anne, dearie, there's a thought keeps coming into my mind. What about Owen Ford? We both know Leslie was fond of him. Did it ever occur to you that he was fond of her?"

"It—did—once," admitted Anne, feeling that she might say so much.

"Well, I hadn't any reason to think he was, but it just appeared to me he *must* be. Now, Anne, dearie, the Lord knows I'm not a match-maker, and I scorn all such doings. But if I were you and writing to that Ford man I'd just mention, casual-like, what has happened. That is what *I'd* do."

"Of course I will mention it when I write him," said Anne, a trifle distantly. Somehow, this was a thing she could not discuss with Miss Cornelia. And yet, she had to admit that the same thought had been lurking in her mind ever since she had heard of Leslie's freedom. But she would not desecrate it by free speech.

"Of course there is no great rush, dearie. But Dick Moore's been dead for thirteen years and Leslie has wasted enough of her life for him. We'll just see what comes of it. As for this George Moore, who's gone and come back to life when everyone thought he was dead and done for, just like a man, I'm real sorry for him. He won't seem to fit in anywhere."

"He is still a young man, and if he recovers completely, as seems likely, he will be able to make a place for himself again. It must be very strange for him, poor fellow. I suppose all these years since his accident will not exist for him."

33
LESLIE RETURNS

A fortnight later Leslie Moore came home alone to the old house where she had spent so many bitter years. In the June twilight she went over the fields to Anne's, and appeared with ghost-like suddenness in the scented garden.

"Leslie!" cried Anne in amazement. "Where have you sprung from? We never knew you were coming. Why didn't you write? We would have met you."

"I couldn't write somehow, Anne. It seemed so futile to try and say anything with pen and ink. And I wanted to get back quietly and unobserved."

Anne put her arms about Leslie and kissed her. Leslie

returned the kiss warmly. She looked pale and tired, and she gave a little sigh as she dropped down on the grasses beside a great bed of daffodils that were gleaming through the pale, silvery twilight like golden stars.

"And you have come home alone, Leslie?"

"Yes. George Moore's sister came to Montreal and took him home with her. Poor fellow, he was sorry to part with me—though I was a stranger to him when his memory first came back. He clung to me in those first hard days when he was trying to realize that Dick's death was not the thing of yesterday that it seemed to him. It was all very hard for him. I helped him all I could. When his sister came it was easier for him, because it seemed to him only the other day that he had seen her last. Fortunately she had not changed much, and that helped him, too."

"It is all so strange and wonderful, Leslie. I think we none of us realize it yet."

"I cannot. When I went into the house over there an hour ago, I felt that it *must* be a dream—that Dick must be there, with his childish smile, as he had been for so long. Anne, I seem stunned yet. I'm not glad or sorry—or *anything*. I feel as if something had been torn suddenly out of my life and left a terrible hole. I feel as if I couldn't be *I*—as if I must have changed into somebody else and couldn't get used to it. It gives me a horrible lonely, dazed, helpless feeling. It's good to see you again—it seems as if you were a sort of anchor for my drifting soul. Oh Anne, I dread it all—the gossip and wonderment and questioning. When I think of that, I wish that I need not have come home at all. Dr. Dave was at the station when I came off the train—he brought me home. Poor old man, he feels very badly because he told me years ago that nothing could be done for Dick. 'I honestly thought so, Leslie,' he said to me today. 'But I should have told you not to depend on my opinion—I should have told you to go to a specialist. If I had, you would have been saved many bitter years, and poor George Moore many wasted ones. I blame myself very much, Leslie.' I told him not to do that—he had done what he thought right. He has always been so kind to me—I couldn't bear to see him worrying over it."

"And Dick—George, I mean? Is his memory fully restored?"

"Practically. Of course, there are a great many details he can't recall yet—but he remembers more and more every day. He went out for a walk on the evening after Dick was buried. He had Dick's money and watch on him; he meant to bring them home to me, along with my letter. He admits he went to a place where the sailors resorted—and he remembers drinking—and nothing else. Anne, I shall never forget the moment he remembered his own name. I saw him looking at me with an intelligent but puzzled expression. I said, 'Do you know me, Dick?' He answered, 'I never saw you before. Who are you? And my name is not Dick. I am George Moore, and Dick died of yellow fever yesterday! Where am I? What has happened to me?' I—I—fainted, Anne. And ever since I have felt as if I were in a dream."

"You will soon adjust yourself to this new state of things, Leslie. And you are young—life is before you—you will have many beautiful years yet."

"Perhaps I shall be able to look at it in that way after awhile, Anne. Just now I feel too tired and indifferent to think about the future. I'm—I'm—Anne, I'm lonely. I miss Dick. Isn't it all very strange? Do you know, I was really fond of poor Dick—George, I suppose I should say—just as I would have been fond of a helpless child who depended on me for everything. I would never have admitted it—I was really ashamed of it—because, you see, I had hated and despised Dick so much before he went away. When I heard that Captain Jim was bringing him home I expected I would just feel the same to him. But I never did—although I continued to loathe him as I remembered him before. From the time he came home I felt only pity—a pity that hurt and wrung me. I supposed then that it was just because his accident had made him so helpless and changed. But now I believe it was because there was really a different personality there. Carlo knew it, Anne—I know now that Carlo knew it. I always thought it strange that Carlo shouldn't have known Dick. Dogs are usually so faithful. But *he* knew it was not his master who had come back, although none of the rest of us did. I had never seen George Moore, you know. I remember now that Dick once mentioned casually that he had a cousin in Nova Scotia who looked as much like him as a twin; but the thing had gone out of my memory, and in any case I would never have thought it of any importance. You see, it never occurred to me to question Dick's identity. Any change in him seemed to me just the result of the accident.

"Oh, Anne, that night in April when Gilbert told me he thought Dick might be cured! I can never forget it. It seemed to me that I had once been a prisoner in a hideous cage of torture, and then the door had been opened and I could get out. I was still chained to the cage but I was not in it. And that night I felt that a merciless hand was drawing me back into the cage—back to a torture even more terrible than it had once been. I didn't blame Gilbert. I felt he was right. And he had been very good—he said that if, in view of the expense and uncertainty of the operation, I should decide not to risk it, he would not blame me in the least. But I knew how I ought to decide—and I couldn't face it. All night I walked the floor like a mad woman, trying to compel myself to face it. I couldn't, Anne—I thought I couldn't—and when morning broke I set my teeth and resolved that I *wouldn't*. I would let things remain as they were. It was very wicked, I know. It would have been a just punishment for such wickedness if I had just been left to abide by that decision. I kept to it all day. That afternoon I had to go up to the Glen to do some shopping. It was one of Dick's quiet, drowsy days, so I left him alone. I was gone a little longer than I had expected, and he missed me. He felt lonely. And when I got home, he ran to meet me just like a child, with such a pleased smile on his face. Some-how, Anne, I just gave way then. That smile on his poor vacant face was more than I could endure. I felt as if I were denying a child the chance to grow and develop. I knew that I must give him his chance, no matter what the consequences might be. So I came over and told Gilbert. Oh, Anne, you must have thought me hateful in those weeks before I went away. I didn't mean to be—but I couldn't think of anything except what I had to do, and everything and everybody about me were like shadows."

"I know—I understood, Leslie. And now it is all over—your chain is broken—there is no cage."

"There is no cage," repeated Leslie absently, plucking at the fringing grasses with her slender, brown hands. "But—it doesn't seem as if there were anything else, Anne. You—you remember what I told you of my folly that night on the sand-bar? I find one doesn't get over being a fool very quickly. Sometimes I think there are people who are fools forever. And to be a fool—of that kind—is almost as bad as being a—a dog on a chain."

"You will feel very differently after you get over being tired and bewildered," said Anne, who, knowing a certain thing that Leslie did not know, did not feel herself called upon to waste overmuch sympathy.

Leslie laid her splendid golden head against Anne's knee.

"Anyhow, I have *you*," she said. "Life can't be altogether empty with such a friend. Anne, pat my head—just as if I were a little girl—*mother* me a bit—and let me tell you while my stubborn tongue is loosed a little just what you and your comradeship have meant to me since that night I met you on the rock shore."

34
THE SHIP O' DREAMS COMES TO HARBOR

One morning, when a windy golden sunrise was billowing over the gulf in waves of light, a certain weary stork flew over the bar of Four Winds Harbor on his way from the Land of Evening Stars. Under his wing was tucked a sleepy, starry-eyed, little creature. The stork was tired, and he looked wistfully about him. He knew he was somewhere near his destination, but he could not yet see it. The big, white lighthouse on the red sandstone cliff had its good points; but no stork possessed of any gumption would leave a new, velvet baby there. An old gray house, surrounded by willows, in a blossomy brook valley, looked more promising, but did not seem quite the thing either. The staring green abode further on was manifestly out of the question. Then the stork brightened up. He had caught sight of the very place—a little white house nestled against a big, whispering fir-wood, with a spiral of blue smoke winding up from its kitchen chimney—a house which just looked as if it were meant for babies. The stork gave a sigh of satisfaction, and softly alighted on the ridge-pole.

Half an hour later Gilbert ran down the hall and tapped on the spare-room door. A drowsy voice answered him and in a moment Marilla's pale, scared face peeped out from behind the door.

"Marilla, Anne has sent me to tell you that a certain young gentleman has arrived here. He hasn't brought much luggage with him, but he evidently means to stay."

"For pity's sake!" said Marilla blankly. "You don't mean to tell me, Gilbert, that it's all over. Why wasn't I called?"

"Anne wouldn't let us disturb you when there was no need. Nobody was called until about two hours ago. There was no 'passage perilous' this time."

"And—and—Gilbert—will this baby live?"

"He certainly will. He weighs ten pounds and—why, listen to him. Nothing wrong with his lungs, is there? The nurse says his hair will be red. Anne is furious with her, and I'm tickled to death."

That was a wonderful day in the little house of dreams.

"The best dream of all has come true," said Anne, pale and rapturous. "Oh, Marilla, I hardly dare believe it, after that horrible day last summer. I have had a heartache ever since then—but it is gone now."

"This baby will take Joy's place," said Marilla.

"Oh, no, no, *no*, Marilla. He can't—nothing can ever do that. He has his own place, my dear, wee man-child. But little Joy has hers, and always will have it. If she had lived she would have been over a year old. She would have been toddling around on her tiny feet and lisping a few words. I can see her so plainly, Marilla. Oh, I know now that Captain Jim was right when he said God would manage better than that my baby would seem a stranger to me when I found her Beyond. I've learned *that* this past year. I've followed her development day by day and week by week—I always shall. I shall know just how she grows from year to year—and when I meet her again I'll know her—she won't be a stranger. Oh, Marilla, *look* at his dear, darling toes! Isn't it strange they should be so perfect?"

"It would be stranger if they weren't," said Marilla crisply. Now that all was safely over, Marilla was herself again.

"Oh, I know—but it seems as if they couldn't be quite *finished,* you know —and they are, even to the tiny nails. And his hands— *just* look at his hands, Marilla."

"They appear to be a good deal like hands," Marilla conceded.

"See how he clings to my finger. I'm sure he knows me already. He cries when the nurse takes him away. Oh, Marilla, do you think —you don't think, do you—that his hair is going to be red?"

"I don't see much hair of any color," said Marilla. "I wouldn't worry about it, if I were you, until it becomes visible."

"Marilla, he *has* hair—look at that fine little down all over his head. Anyway, nurse says his eyes will be hazel and his forehead is exactly like Gilbert's."

"And he has the nicest little ears, Mrs. Doctor, dear," said Susan. "The first thing I did was to look at his ears. Hair is deceitful and noses and eyes change, and you cannot tell what is going to come of them, but ears is ears from start to finish, and you always know where you are with them. Just look at their shape— and they are set right back against his precious head. You will never need to be ashamed of his ears, Mrs. Doctor, dear."

Anne's convalescence was rapid and happy. Folks came and worshipped the baby, as people have bowed before the kingship of the new-born since long before the Wise Men of the East knelt in homage to the Royal Babe of the Bethlehem manger. Leslie, slowly finding herself amid the new conditions of her life, hovered over it, like a beautiful, golden-crowned Madonna. Miss Cornelia nursed it as knackily as could any mother in Israel. Captain Jim held the small creature in his big brown hands and gazed tenderly at it, with eyes that saw the children who had never been born to him.

"What are you going to call him?" asked Miss Cornelia.

"Anne has settled his name," answered Gilbert.

"James Matthew—after the two finest gentlemen I've ever known—not even saving your presence," said Anne with a saucy glance at Gilbert.

Gilbert smiled.

"I never knew Matthew very well; he was so shy we boys couldn't get acquainted with him—but I quite agree with you that Captain Jim is one of the rarest and finest souls God ever clothed in clay. He is so delighted over the fact that we have given his name to our small lad. It seems he has no other namesake."

"Well, James Matthew is a name that will wear well and not fade in the washing," said Miss Cornelia. "I'm glad you didn't load him down with some high-falutin, romantic name that he'd be ashamed of when he gets to be a grandfather. Mrs. William Drew at the Glen has called her baby Bertie Shakespeare. Quite a combination, isn't it? And I'm glad you haven't had much trouble picking on a name. Some folks have an awful time. When the Stanley Flaggs' first boy was born there was so much rivalry as to who the child should be named for that the poor little soul had to go for two years without a name. Then a brother came along and there it was—'Big Baby' and 'Little Baby.' Finally they called Big Baby Peter and Little Baby Isaac, after the two grandfathers, and had them both christened together. And each tried to see if it couldn't howl the other down. You know that Highland Scotch family of MacNabs back of the Glen? They've got twelve boys and the oldest and the youngest are both called Neil—Big Neil and Little Neil in the same family. Well, I s'pose they ran out of names."

"I have read somewhere," laughed Anne, "that the first child is a poem but the tenth is very prosy prose. Perhaps Mrs. Mac-Nab thought that the twelfth was merely an old tale re-told."

"Well, there's something to be said for large families," said Miss Cornelia, with a sigh. "I was an only child for eight years and I did long for a brother and sister. Mother told me to pray for one—and pray I did, believe *me*. Well, one day Aunt Nellie came to me and said, 'Cornelia, there is a little brother for you upstairs in your ma's room. You can go up and see him.' I was so excited and delighted I just flew upstairs. And old Mrs. Flagg lifted up the baby for me to see. Lord, Anne, dearie, I never was so disappointed in my life. You see, I'd been praying for *a brother two years older than myself.*"

"How long did it take you to get over your disappointment?" asked Anne, amid her laughter.

"Well, I had a spite at Providence for a good spell, and for weeks I wouldn't even look at the baby. Nobody knew why, for I never told. Then he began to get real cute, and held out his wee hands to me and I began to get fond of him. But I didn't get really reconciled to him until one day a school chum came to see him and said she thought he was awful small for his age. I just got boiling mad, and I sailed right into her, and told her she didn't know a nice baby when she saw one, and ours was the nicest baby in the world. And after that I just worshipped him. Mother died before he was three years old and I was sister and mother to him both. Poor little lad, he was never strong, and he died when he wasn't much over twenty. Seems to me I'd have given anything on earth, Anne, dearie, if he'd only lived."

Miss Cornelia sighed. Gilbert had gone down and Leslie, who had been crooning over the small James Matthew in the dormer window, laid him asleep in his basket and went her way. As soon as she was safely out of earshot, Miss Cornelia bent forward and said in a conspirator's whisper:

"Anne, dearie, I'd a letter from Owen Ford yesterday. He's in Vancouver just now, but he wants to know if I can board him for

a month later on. *You* know what that means. Well, I hope we're
doing right."

"We've nothing to do with it—we couldn't prevent him from
coming to Four Winds if he wanted to," said Anne quickly. She
did not like the feeling of match-making Miss Cornelia's whispers
gave her; and then she weakly succumbed herself.

"Don't let Leslie know he is coming until he is here," she said.
"If she found out I feel sure she would go away at once. She
intends to go in the fall anyhow—she told me so the other day.
She is going to Montreal to take up nursing and make what she
can of her life."

"Oh, well, Anne, dearie," said Miss Cornelia, nodding sagely,
"that is all as it may be. You and I have done our part and we
must leave the rest to Higher Hands."

35
POLITICS AT FOUR WINDS

When Anne came downstairs again, the Island, as well as all
Canada, was in the throes of a campaign preceding a general election. Gilbert, who was an ardent Conservative, found himself
caught in the vortex, being much in demand for speech-making
at the various county rallies. Miss Cornelia did not approve of his
mixing up in politics and told Anne so.

"Dr. Dave never did it. Dr. Blythe will find he is making a mistake, believe *me*. Politics is something no decent man should
meddle with."

"Is the government of the country to be left solely to the
rogues then?" asked Anne.

"Yes—so long as it's Conservative rogues," said Miss Cornelia,
marching off with the honors of war. "Men and politicians are all
tarred with the same brush. The Grits have it laid on thicker than
the Conservatives, that's all—*considerably* thicker. But Grit or
Tory, my advice to Dr. Blythe is to steer clear of politics. First

thing you know, he'll be running an election himself, and going off to Ottawa for half the year and leaving his practice to go to the dogs."

"Ah, well, let's not borrow trouble," said Anne. "The rate of interest is too high. Instead, let's look at Little Jem. It should be spelled with a G. Isn't he perfectly beautiful? Just see the dimples in his elbows. We'll bring him up to be a good Conservative, you and I, Miss Cornelia."

"Bring him up to be a good man," said Miss Cornelia. "They're scarce and valuable; though, mind you, I wouldn't like to see him a Grit. As for the election, you and I may be thankful we don't live over harbor. The air there is blue these days. Every Elliott and Crawford and MacAllister is on the warpath, loaded for bear. This side is peaceful and calm, seeing there's so few men. Captain Jim's a Grit, but it's my opinion he's ashamed of it, for he never talks politics. There isn't any earthly doubt that the Conservatives will be returned with a big majority again."

Miss Cornelia was mistaken. On the morning after the election Captain Jim dropped in at the little house to tell the news. So virulent is the microbe of party politics, even in a peaceable old man, that Captain Jim's cheeks were flushed and his eyes were flashing with all his old-time fire.

"Mistress Blythe, the Liberals are in with a sweeping majority. After eighteen years of Tory mismanagement this down-trodden country is going to have a chance at last."

"I never heard you make such a bitter partisan speech before, Captain Jim. I didn't think you had so much political venom in you," laughed Anne, who was not much excited over the tidings. Little Jem had said "Wow-ga" that morning. What were principalities and powers, the rise and fall of dynasties, the overthrow of Grit or Tory, compared with that miraculous occurrence?

"It's been accumulating for a long while," said Captain Jim, with a deprecating smile. "I thought I was only a moderate Grit, but when the news came that we were in I found out how Gritty I really was."

"You know the doctor and I are Conservatives."

"Ah, well, it's the only bad thing I know of either of you, Mistress Blythe. Cornelia is a Tory, too. I called in on my way from the Glen to tell her the news."

"Didn't you know you took your life in your hands?"

"Yes, but I couldn't resist the temptation."

"How did she take it?"

"Comparatively calm, Mistress Blythe, comparatively calm. She says, says she, 'Well, Providence sends seasons of humiliation to a country, same as to individuals. You Grits have been cold and hungry for many a year. Make haste to get warmed and fed, for you won't be in long.' 'Well, now, Cornelia,' I says, 'mebbe Providence thinks Canada needs a real long spell of humiliation.' Ah, Susan, have *you* heard the news? The Liberals are in."

Susan had just come in from the kitchen, attended by the odor of delectable dishes which always seemed to hover around her.

"Now, are they?" she said, with beautiful unconcern. "Well, I never could see but that my bread rose just as light when Grits were in as when they were not. And if any party, Mrs. Doctor, dear, will make it rain before the week is out, and save our kitchen garden from entire ruination, that is the party Susan will vote for. In the meantime, will you just step out and give me your opinion on the meat for dinner? I am fearing that it is very tough, and I think that we had better change our butcher as well as our government."

One evening, a week later, Anne walked down to the Point, to see if she could get some fresh fish from Captain Jim, leaving Little Jem for the first time. It was quite a tragedy. Suppose he cried? Suppose Susan did not know just exactly what to do for him? Susan was calm and serene.

"I have had as much experience with him as you, Mrs. Doctor, dear, have I not?"

"Yes, with him—but not with other babies. Why, I looked after three pairs of twins, when I was a child, Susan. When they cried, I gave them peppermint or castor oil quite coolly. It's quite curious now to recall how lightly I took all those babies and their woes."

"Oh, well, if Little Jem cries, I will just clamp a hot water bag on his little stomach," said Susan.

"Not too hot, you know," said Anne anxiously. Oh, was it really wise to go?

"Do not you fret, Mrs. Doctor, dear. Susan is not the woman to burn a wee man. Bless him, he has no notion of crying."

Anne tore herself away finally and enjoyed her walk to the Point after all, through the long shadows of the sun-setting. Captain Jim was not in the living room of the lighthouse, but another man was—a handsome, middle-aged man, with a strong, clean-shaven chin, who was unknown to Anne. Nevertheless, when she sat down, he began to talk to her with all the assurance of an old acquaintance. There was nothing amiss in what he said or the way he said it, but Anne rather resented such a cool taking-for-granted in a complete stranger. Her replies were frosty, and as few as decency required. Nothing daunted, her companion talked on for several minutes, then excused himself and went away. Anne could have sworn there was a twinkle in his eye and it annoyed her. Who was the creature? There was something vaguely familiar about him but she was certain she had never seen him before.

"Captain Jim, who was that who just went out?" she asked, as Captain Jim came in.

"Marshall Elliott," answered the captain.

"Marshall Elliott!" cried Anne. "Oh, Captain Jim—it wasn't— yes, it *was* his voice—oh, Captain Jim, I didn't know him—and I was quite insulting to him! *Why* didn't he tell me? He must have seen I didn't know him."

"He wouldn't say a word about it—he'd just enjoy the joke. Don't worry over snubbing him—he'll think it fun. Yes, Marshall's shaved off his beard at last and cut his hair. His party is in, you know. I didn't know him myself first time I saw him. He was up in Carter Flagg's store at the Glen the night after election day, along with a crowd of others, waiting for the news. About twelve the 'phone came through—the Liberals were in. Marshall just got up and walked out—he didn't cheer or shout—he left the others do that, and they nearly lifted the roof off Carter's store, I reckon. Of course, all the Tories were over in Raymond Russell's store. Not much cheering *there*. Marshall went straight down the street to the side door of Augustus Palmer's barber shop. Augustus was in bed asleep, but Marshall hammered on the door until he got up and come down, wanting to know what all the racket was about.

"'Come into your shop and do the best job you ever did in your life, Gus,' said Marshall. 'The Liberals are in and you're going to barber a good Grit before the sun rises.'

"Gus was mad as hops—partly because he'd been dragged out of bed, but more because he's a Tory. He vowed he wouldn't shave any man after twelve at night.

"'You'll do what I want you to do, sonny,' said Marshall, 'or I'll jest turn you over my knee and give you one of those spankings your mother forgot.'

"He'd have done it, too, and Gus knew it, for Marshall is as strong as an ox and Gus is only a midget of a man. So he gave in and towed Marshall in to the shop and went to work. 'Now,' says he, 'I'll barber you up, but if you say one word to me about the Grits getting in while I'm doing it I'll cut your throat with this razor,' says he. You wouldn't have thought mild little Gus could be so bloodthirsty, would you? Shows what party politics will do for a man. Marshall kept quiet and got his hair and beard disposed of and went home. When his old housekeeper heard him come upstairs she peeked out of her bedroom door to see whether 'twas him or the hired boy. And when she saw a strange man striding down the hall with a candle in his hand she screamed blue murder and fainted dead away. They had to send for the doctor before they could bring her to, and it was several days before she could look at Marshall without shaking all over."

Captain Jim had no fish. He seldom went out in his boat that summer, and his long tramping expeditions were over. He spent a great deal of his time sitting by his seaward window, looking out over the gulf, with his swiftly-whitening head leaning on his hand. He sat there tonight for many silent minutes, keeping some tryst with the past which Anne would not disturb. Presently he pointed to the iris of the West:

"That's beautiful, isn't it, Mistress Blythe? But I wish you could have seen the sunrise this morning. It was a wonderful thing—wonderful. I've seen all kinds of sunrises come over that gulf. I've been all over the world, Mistress Blythe, and take it all in all, I've never seen a finer sight than a summer sunrise over the gulf. A man can't pick his time for dying, Mistress Blythe—jest got to go when the Great Captain gives His sailing orders. But if I could I'd go out when the morning comes across that water. I've watched it many a time and thought what a thing it would be to pass out through that great white glory to whatever was waiting beyant, on a sea that ain't mapped out on any airthly chart. I think, Mistress Blythe, that I'd find lost Margaret there."

Captain Jim had often talked to Anne of lost Margaret since he had told her the old story. His love for her trembled in every tone—that love that had never grown faint or forgetful.

"Anyway, I hope when my time comes I'll go quick and easy. I don't think I'm a coward, Mistress Blythe—I've looked an ugly death in the face more than once without blenching. But the thought of a lingering death does give me a queer, sick feeling of horror."

"Don't talk about leaving us, dear, *dear* Captain Jim," pleaded Anne, in a choked voice, patting the old brown hand, once so strong, but now grown very feeble. "What would we do without you?"

Captain Jim smiled beautifully.

"Oh, you'd get along nicely—nicely—but you wouldn't forget the old man altogether, Mistress Blythe—no, I don't think you'll ever quite forget him. The race of Joseph always remembers one another. But it'll be a memory that won't hurt—I like to think that my memory won't hurt my friends—it'll always be kind of pleasant to them, I hope and believe. It won't be very long now before lost Margaret calls me, for the last time. I'll be all ready to answer. I jest spoke of this because there's a little favor I want to ask you. Here's this poor old Matey of mine?"—Captain Jim reached out a hand and poked the big, warm, velvety, golden ball on the sofa. The First Mate uncoiled himself like a spring with a nice, throaty, comfortable sound, half purr, half meow, stretched his paws in air, turned over and coiled himself up again. "*He'll* miss me when I start on the Long V'yage. I can't bear to think of leaving the poor critter to starve, like he was left before. If anything happens to me will you give Matey a bite and a corner, Mistress Blythe?"

"Indeed I will."

"Then that is all I had on my mind. Your Little Jem is to have the few curious things I picked up—I've seen to that. And now I don't like to see tears in those pretty eyes, Mistress Blythe. I'll mebbe hang on for quite a spell yet. I heard you reading a piece of poetry one day last winter—one of Tennyson's pieces. I'd sorter like to hear it again, if you could recite it for me."

Softly and clearly, while the seawind blew in on them, Anne repeated the beautiful lines of Tennyson's wonder swan song—"Crossing the Bar." The old captain kept time gently with his sinewy hand.

"Yes, yes, Mistress Blythe," he said, when she had finished, "that's it, that's it. He wasn't a sailor, you tell me—I dunno how he could have put an old sailor's feelings into words like that, if he wasn't one. He didn't want any 'sadness o' farewells' and neither do I, Mistress Blythe—for all will be well with me and mine beyant the bar."

36
BEAUTY FOR ASHES

"Any news from Green Gables, Anne?"

"Nothing very especial," replied Anne, folding up Marilla's letter. "Jake Donnell has been there shingling the roof. He is a full-fledged carpenter now, so it seems he has had his own way in regard to the choice of a life-work. You remember his mother wanted him to be a college professor. I shall never forget the day she came to the school and rated me for failing to call him St. Claire."

"Does anyone ever call him that now?"

"Evidently not. It seems that he has completely lived it down. Even his mother has succumbed. I always thought that a boy with Jake's chin and mouth would get his own way in the end. Diana writes me that Dora has a beau. Just think of it—that child!"

"Dora is seventeen," said Gilbert. "Charlie Sloane and I were both mad about you when you were seventeen, Anne."

"Really, Gilbert, we must be getting on in years," said Anne, with a half-rueful smile, "when children who were six when we thought ourselves grown up are old enough now to have beaux. Dora's is Ralph Andrews—Jane's brother. I remember him as a little, round, fat, white-headed fellow who was always at the foot of his class. But I understand he is quite a fine-looking young man now."

"Dora will probably marry young. She's of the same type as Charlotta the Fourth—she'll never miss her first chance for fear she might not get another."

"Well, if she marries Ralph I hope he will be a little more up-and-coming than his brother Billy," mused Anne.

"For instance," said Gilbert, laughing, "let us hope he will be able to propose on his own account. Anne, would you have married Billy if he had asked you himself, instead of getting Jane to do it for him?"

"I might have." Anne went off into a shriek of laughter over the recollection of her first proposal. "The shock of the whole thing might have hypnotized me into some such rash and foolish act. Let us be thankful he did it by proxy."

"I had a letter from George Moore yesterday," said Leslie, from the corner where she was reading.

"Oh, how is he?" asked Anne interestedly, yet with an unreal feeling that she was inquiring about some one whom she did not know.

"He is well, but he finds it very hard to adapt himself to all the changes in his old home and friends. He is going to sea again in the spring. It's in his blood, he says, and he longs for it. But he told me something that made me glad for him, poor fellow. Before he sailed on the *Four Sisters* he was engaged to a girl at home. He did not tell me anything about her in Montreal, because he said he supposed she would have forgotten him and married someone else long ago, and with him, you see, his engagement and love was still a thing of the present. It was pretty hard on him, but when he got home he found she had never married and still cared for him. They are to be married this fall. I'm going to ask him to bring her over here for a little trip; he says he wants to come and see the place where he lived so many years without knowing it."

"What a nice little romance," said Anne, whose love for the romantic was immortal. "And to think," she added with a sigh of self-reproach, "that if I had had my way George Moore would never have come up from the grave in which his identity was buried. How I did fight against Gilbert's suggestion! Well, I am punished: I shall never be able to have a different opinion from Gilbert's again! If I try to have, he will squelch me by casting George Moore's case up to me!"

"As if even that would squelch a woman!" mocked Gilbert. "At least do not become my echo, Anne. A little opposition gives spice to life. I do not want a wife like John MacAllister's over the harbor. No matter what he says, she at once remarks in that drab, lifeless little voice of hers, 'That is very true, John, dear me!'"

Anne and Leslie laughed. Anne's laughter was silver and Leslie's golden, and the combination of the two was as satisfactory as a perfect chord in music.

Susan, coming in on the heels of the laughter, echoed it with a resounding sigh.

"Why, Susan, what is the matter?" asked Gilbert.

"There's nothing wrong with Little Jem, is there, Susan?" cried Anne, starting up in alarm.

"No, no, calm yourself, Mrs. Doctor, dear. Something has happened, though. Dear me, everything has gone catawampus with me this week. I spoiled the bread, as you know too well—and I scorched the doctor's best shirt bosom—and I broke your big platter. And now, on the top of all this, comes word that my sister Matilda has broken her leg and wants me to go and stay with her for a spell."

"Oh, I'm very sorry—sorry that your sister has met with such an accident, I mean," exclaimed Anne.

"Ah, well, man was made to mourn, Mrs. Doctor, dear. That sounds as if it ought to be in the Bible, but they tell me a person named Burns wrote it. And there is no doubt that we are born to trouble as the sparks fly upward. As for Matilda, I do not know what to think of her. None of our family ever broke their legs before. But whatever she has done she is still my sister, and I feel that it is my duty to go and wait on her, if you can spare me for a few weeks, Mrs. Doctor, dear."

"Of course, Susan, of course. I can get someone to help me while you are gone."

"If you cannot I will not go, Mrs. Doctor, dear, Matilda's leg to the contrary notwithstanding. I will not have you worried, and that blessed child upset in consequence, for any number of legs."

"Oh, you must go to your sister at once, Susan. I can get a girl from the cove, who will do for a time."

"Anne, will you let me come and stay with you while Susan is away?" exclaimed Leslie. "Do! I'd love to—and it would be an act of charity on your part. I'm so horribly lonely over there in that big barn of a house. There's so little to do—and at night I'm worse than lonely—I'm frightened and nervous in spite of locked doors. There was a tramp around two days ago."

Anne joyfully agreed, and next day Leslie was installed as an inmate of the little house of dreams. Miss Cornelia warmly approved of the arrangement.

"It seems Providential," she told Anne in confidence. "I'm sorry for Matilda Clow, but since she had to break her leg it couldn't have happened at a better time. Leslie will be here while Owen Ford is in Four Winds, and those old cats up at the Glen won't get the chance to meow, as they would if she was living over there alone and Owen going to see her. They are doing enough of it as it is, because she doesn't put on mourning. I said to one of them, 'If you mean she should put on mourning for George Moore, it seems to me more like his resurrection than his funeral; and if it's Dick you mean, I confess I can't see the propriety of going into weeds for a man who died thirteen years ago and good riddance then!' And when old Louisa Baldwin remarked to me that she thought it very strange that Leslie should never have suspected it wasn't her own husband I said, 'You never suspected it wasn't Dick Moore, and you were next-door neighbor to him all his life, and by nature you're ten times as suspicious as Leslie.' But you can't stop some people's tongues, Anne, dearie, and I'm real thankful Leslie will be under your roof while Owen is courting her."

Owen Ford came to the little house one August evening when Leslie and Anne were absorbed in worshipping the baby. He paused at the open door of the living room, unseen by the two within, gazing with greedy eyes at the beautiful picture. Leslie sat on the floor with the baby in her lap, making ecstatic dabs at his fat little hands as he fluttered them in the air.

"Oh, you dear, beautiful, beloved baby," she mumbled, catching one wee hand and covering it with kisses.

"Isn't him ze darlingest itty sing," crooned Anne, hanging over the arm of her chair adoringly. "Dem itty wee pads are ze very tweetest handies in ze whole big world, isn't dey, you darling itty man."

Anne, in the months before Little Jem's coming, had pored diligently over several wise volumes, and pinned her faith to one in especial, "Sir Oracle on the Care and Training of Children." Sir Oracle implored parents by all they held sacred never to talk "baby talk" to their children. Infants should invariably be addressed in classical language from the moment of their birth. So should they learn to speak English undefiled from their earliest utterance. "How," demanded Sir Oracle, "can a mother reasonably expect her child to learn correct speech, when she continually accustoms its impressionable gray matter to such absurd expressions and distortions of our noble tongue as thoughtless mothers inflict every day on the helpless creatures committed to their care? Can a child who is constantly called 'tweet itty wee singie' ever attain to any proper conception of his own being and possibilities and destiny?"

Anne was vastly impressed with this, and informed Gilbert that she meant to make it an inflexible rule never, under any circumstances, to talk "baby talk" to their children. Gilbert agreed with her, and they made a solemn compact on the subject—a compact which Anne shamelessly violated the very first moment Little Jem was laid in her arms. "Oh, the darling itty wee sing!" she had exclaimed. And she had continued to violate it ever since. When Gilbert teased her she laughed Sir Oracle to scorn.

"He never had any children of his own, Gilbert—I am positive he hadn't or he would never have written such rubbish. You just can't help talking baby talk to a baby. It comes natural—and it's *right*. It would be inhuman to talk to those tiny, soft, velvety little creatures as we do to great big boys and girls. Babies want love and cuddling and all the sweet baby talk they can get, and Little Jem is going to have it, bess his dear itty heartums."

"But you're the worst I ever heard, Anne," protested Gilbert, who, not being a mother but only a father, was not wholly convinced yet that Sir Oracle was wrong. "I never heard anything like the way you talk to that child."

"Very likely you never did. Go away—go away. Didn't I bring up three pairs of Hammond twins before I was eleven? You and Sir Oracle are nothing but cold-blooded theorists. Gilbert, *just* look at him! He's smiling at me—he knows what we're talking about. And oo dest agwees wif evy word muzzer says, don't oo, angel-lover?"

Gilbert put his arm about them. "Oh you mothers!" he said. "You mothers! God knew what He was about when He made you."

So Little Jem was talked to and loved and cuddled: and he throve as became a child of the house of dreams. Leslie was quite as foolish over him as Anne was. When their work was done and Gilbert was out of the way, they gave themselves over to shameless orgies of love-making and ecstasies of adoration, such as that in which Owen Ford had surprised them.

Leslie was the first to become aware of him. Even in the twilight Anne could see the sudden whiteness that swept over her beautiful face, blotting out the crimson of lip and cheeks.

Owen came forward, eagerly, blind for a moment to Anne.

"Leslie!" he said, holding out his hand. It was the first time he had ever called her by her name; but the hand Leslie gave him was cold; and she was very quiet all the evening, while Anne and Gilbert and Owen laughed and talked together. Before his call ended she excused herself and went upstairs. Owen's gay spirits flagged and he went away soon after with a downcast air.

Gilbert looked at Anne.

"Anne, what are you up to? There's something going on that I don't understand. The whole air here tonight has been charged with electricity. Leslie sits like the muse of tragedy; Owen Ford jokes and laughs on the surface, and watches Leslie with the eyes of his soul. You seem all the time to be bursting with some suppressed excitement. Own up. What secret have you been keeping from your deceived husband?"

"Don't be a goose, Gilbert," was Anne's conjugal reply. "As for Leslie, she is absurd and I'm going up to tell her so."

Anne found Leslie at the dormer window of her room. The little place was filled with the rhythmic thunder of the sea. Leslie sat with locked hands in the misty moonshine—a beautiful, accusing presence.

"Anne," she said in a low, reproachful voice, "did you know Owen Ford was coming to Four Winds?"

"I did," said Anne brazenly.

"Oh, you should have told me, Anne," Leslie cried passionately. "If I had known I would have gone away—I wouldn't have stayed here to meet him. You should have told me. It wasn't fair of you, Anne—oh, it wasn't fair!"

Leslie's lips were trembling and her whole form was tense with emotion. But Anne laughed heartlessly. She bent over and kissed Leslie's upturned, reproachful face.

"Leslie, you are an adorable goose. Owen Ford didn't rush from the Pacific to the Atlantic from a burning desire to see *me*. Neither do I believe that he was inspired by any wild and frenzied passion for Miss Cornelia. Take off your tragic airs, my dear friend, and fold them up and put them away in lavender. You'll never need them again. There are some people who can see through a grindstone when there is a hole in it, even if you cannot. I am not a prophetess, but I shall venture on a prediction. The bitterness of life is over for you. After this you are going to have the joys and hopes—and I daresay the sorrows, too—of a happy woman. The omen of the shadow of Venus did come true for you, Leslie. The year in which you saw it brought your life's best gift for you—your love for Owen Ford. Now, go right to bed and have a good sleep."

Leslie obeyed orders in so far that she went to bed: but it may be questioned if she slept much. I do not think she dared to dream wakingly; life had been so hard for this poor Leslie, the path on which she had had to walk had been so strait, that she could not whisper to her own heart the hopes that might wait on the future. But she watched the great revolving light bestarring the short hours of the summer night, and her eyes grew soft and bright and young once more. Nor, when Owen Ford came next day, to ask her to go with him to the shore, did she say him nay.

37
MISS CORNELIA MAKES A STARTLING ANNOUNCEMENT

Miss Cornelia sailed down to the little house one drowsy afternoon, when the gulf was the faint, bleached blue of hot August seas, and the orange lilies at the gate of Anne's garden held up their imperial cups to be filled with the molten gold of August sunshine. Not that Miss Cornelia concerned herself with painted oceans or sun-thirsty lilies. She sat in her favorite rocker in unusual idleness. She sewed not, neither did she spin. Nor did she say a single derogatory word concerning any portion of mankind. In short, Miss Cornelia's conversation was singularly devoid of spice that day, and Gilbert, who had stayed home to listen to her, instead of going a-fishing, as he had intended, felt himself aggrieved. What had come over Miss Cornelia? She did not look cast down or worried. On the contrary, there was a certain air of nervous exultation about her.

"Where is Leslie?" she asked—not as if it mattered much either.

"Owen and she went raspberrying in the woods back of her farm," answered Anne. "They won't be back before supper time—if even then."

"They don't seem to have any idea that there is such a thing as a clock," said Gilbert. "I can't get to the bottom of that affair. I'm certain you women pulled strings. But Anne, undutiful wife, won't tell me. Will you, Miss Cornelia?"

"No, I shall not. But," said Miss Cornelia, with the air of one determined to take the plunge and have it over, "I will tell you something else. I came today on purpose to tell it. I am going to be married."

Anne and Gilbert were silent. If Miss Cornelia had announced her intention of going out to the channel and drowning herself the thing might have been believable. This was not. So they waited. Of course Miss Cornelia had made a mistake.

"Well, you both look sort of kerflummexed," said Miss Cornelia, with a twinkle in her eyes. Now that the awkward moment of revelation was over, Miss Cornelia was her own woman again. "Do you think I'm too young and inexperienced for matrimony?"

"You know—it *is* rather staggering," said Gilbert, trying to gather his wits together. "I've heard you say a score of times that you wouldn't marry the best man in the world."

"I'm not going to marry the best man in the world," retorted Miss Cornelia. "Marshall Elliott is a long way from being the best."

"Are you going to marry Marshall Elliott?" exclaimed Anne, recovering her power of speech under this second shock.

"Yes. I could have had him any time these twenty years if I'd lifted my finger. But do you suppose I was going to walk into church beside a perambulating haystack like that?"

"I am sure we are very glad—and we wish you all possible happiness," said Anne, very flatly and inadequately, as she felt. She was not prepared for such an occasion. She had never imagined herself offering betrothal felicitations to Miss Cornelia.

"Thanks, I knew you would," said Miss Cornelia. "You are the first of my friends to know it."

"We shall be so sorry to lose you, though, dear Miss Cornelia," said Anne, beginning to be a little sad and sentimental.

"Oh, you won't lose me," said Miss Cornelia unsentimentally. "You don't suppose I would live over harbor with all those MacAllisters and Elliotts and Crawfords, do you? 'From the conceit of the Elliotts, the pride of the MacAllisters and the vain-glory of the Crawfords, good Lord deliver us.' Marshall is coming to live at my place. I'm sick and tired of hired men. That Jim Hastings I've got this summer is positively the worst of the species. He would drive anyone to getting married. What do you think? He upset the churn yesterday and spilled a big churning of cream over the yard. And not one whit concerned about it was he! Just gave a foolish laugh and said cream was good for the land. Wasn't that like a man? I told him I wasn't in the habit of fertilizing my back yard with cream."

"Well, I wish you all manner of happiness too, Miss Cornelia," said Gilbert, solemnly; "but," he added unable to resist the temptation to tease Miss Cornelia, despite Anne's imploring eyes, "I fear your day of independence is done. As you know, Marshall Elliott is a very determined man."

"I like a man who can stick to a thing," retorted Miss Cornelia. "Amos Grant, who used to be after me long ago, couldn't. You never saw such a weather-vane. He jumped into the pond to drown himself once and then changed his mind and swum out again. Wasn't that like a man? Marshall would have stuck to it and drowned."

"And he has a bit of a temper, they tell me," persisted Gilbert.

"He wouldn't be an Elliott if he hadn't. I'm thankful he has. It will be real fun to make him mad. And you can generally do something with a tempery man when it comes to repenting time. But you can't do anything with a man who just keeps placid and aggravating."

"You know he's a Grit, Miss Cornelia."

"Yes, he *is*," admitted Miss Cornelia rather sadly. "And of course there is no hope of making a Conservative of him. But at least he is a Presbyterian. So I suppose I shall have to be satisfied with that."

"Would you marry him if he were a Methodist, Miss Cornelia?"

"No, I would not. Politics is for this world, but religion is for both."

"And you may be a 'relict' after all, Miss Cornelia."

"Not I. Marshall will live me out. The Elliotts are long-lived, and the Bryants are not."

"When are you to be married?" asked Anne.

"In about a month's time. My wedding dress is to be navy blue silk. And I want to ask you, Anne, dearie, if you think it would be all right to wear a veil with a navy blue dress. I've always thought I'd like to wear a veil if I ever got married. Marshall says to have it if I want to. Isn't that like a man?"

"Why shouldn't you wear it if you want to?" asked Anne.

"Well, one doesn't want to be different from other people," said Miss Cornelia, who was not noticeably like anyone else on the face of the earth. "As I say, I do fancy a veil. But maybe it shouldn't be worn with any dress but a white one. Please tell me, Anne, dearie, what you really think. I'll go by your advice."

"I don't think veils are usually worn with any but white dresses," admitted Anne, "but that is merely a convention; and I am like Mr. Elliott, Miss Cornelia. I don't see any good reason why you shouldn't have a veil if you want one."

But Miss Cornelia, who made her calls in calico wrappers, shook her head.

"If it isn't the proper thing I won't wear it," she said, with a sigh of regret for a lost dream.

"Since you are determined to be married, Miss Cornelia," said Gilbert solemnly, "I shall give you the excellent rules for the management of a husband which my grandmother gave my mother when she married my father."

"Well, I reckon I can manage Marshall Elliott," said Miss Cornelia placidly. "But let us hear your rules."

"The first one is, catch him."

"He's caught. Go on."

"The second one is, feed him well."

"With enough pie. What next?"

"The third and fourth are—keep your eye on him."

"I believe you," said Miss Cornelia emphatically.

38
RED ROSES

The garden of the little house was a haunt beloved of bees and reddened by late roses that August. The little house folk lived much in it, and were given to taking picnic suppers in the grassy corner beyond the brook and sitting about in it through the twilights when great night moths sailed athwart the velvet gloom. One evening Owen Ford found Leslie alone in it. Anne and Gilbert were away, and Susan, who was expected back that night, had not yet returned.

The northern sky was amber and pale green over the fir tops. The air was cool, for August was nearing September, and Leslie wore a crimson scarf over her white dress. Together they wandered through the little, friendly, flower-crowded paths in silence. Owen must go soon. His holiday was nearly over. Leslie found her heart beating wildly. She knew that this beloved garden was to be the scene of the binding words that must seal their as yet unworded understanding.

"Some evenings a strange odor blows down the air of this garden, like a phantom perfume," said Owen. "I have never been able to discover from just what flower it comes. It is elusive and haunting and wonderfully sweet. I like to fancy it is the soul of Grandmother Selwyn passing on a little visit to the old spot she loved so well. There should be a lot of friendly ghosts about this little old house."

"I have lived under its roof only a month," said Leslie, "but I love it as I never loved the house over there where I have lived all my life."

"This house was builded and consecrated by love," said Owen. "Such houses *must* exert an influence over those who live in them. And this garden—it is over sixty years old and the history of a thousand hopes and joys is written in its blossoms. Some of those flowers were actually set out by the schoolmaster's bride, and she has been dead for thirty years. Yet they bloom on every summer. Look at those red roses, Leslie—how they queen it over everything else!"

"I love the red roses," said Leslie. "Anne likes the pink ones best, and Gilbert likes the white. But I want the crimson ones. They satisfy some craving in me as no other flower does."

"Those roses are very late—they bloom after all the others have gone—and they hold all the warmth and soul of the summer come to fruition," said Owen, plucking some of the glowing, half-opened buds. "The rose is the flower of love—the world has acclaimed it so for centuries. The pink roses are love hopeful and expectant—the white roses are love dead or forsaken—but the red roses—ah, Leslie, what are the red roses?"

"Love triumphant," said Leslie in a low voice.

"Yes—love triumphant and perfect. Leslie, you know—you understand. I have loved you from the first. And I *know* you love me—I don't need to ask you. But I want to hear you say it—my darling—my darling!"

Leslie said something in a very low and tremulous voice. Their hands and lips met; it was life's supreme moment for them and as they stood there in the old garden, with its many years of love and delight and sorrow and glory, he crowned her shining hair with the red, red rose of a love triumphant.

Anne and Gilbert returned presently, accompanied by Captain Jim. Anne lighted a few sticks of driftwood in the fireplace, for love of the pixy flames, and they sat around it for an hour of good fellowship.

"When I sit looking at a driftwood fire it's easy to believe I'm young again," said Captain Jim.

"Can you read futures in the fire, Captain Jim?" asked Owen.

Captain Jim looked at them all affectionately, and then back again at Leslie's vivid face and glowing eyes.

"I don't need the fire to read your futures," he said. "I see happiness for all of you—all of you—for Leslie and Mr. Ford—and the Doctor here and Mistress Blythe—and Little Jem—and children that ain't born yet but will be. Happiness for you all—though, mind you, I reckon you'll have your troubles and worries and sorrows, too. They're bound to come—and no house, whether it's a palace or a little house of dreams, can bar 'em out. But they won't get the better of you if you face 'em *together* with love and trust. You can weather any storm with them two for compass and pilot."

The old man rose suddenly and placed one hand on Leslie's head and one on Anne's.

"Two good, sweet women," he said. "True and faithful and to be depended on. Your husbands will have honor in the gates because of you—your children will rise up and call you blessed in the years to come."

There was a strange solemnity about the little scene. Anne and Leslie bowed as those receiving a benediction. Gilbert suddenly brushed his hand over his eyes; Owen Ford was rapt as one who can see visions. All were silent for a space. The little house of dreams added another poignant and unforgettable moment to its store of memories.

"I must be going now," said Captain Jim slowly at last. He took up his hat and looked lingeringly about the room.

"Good-night, all of you," he said, as he went out.

Anne, pierced by the unusual wistfulness of his farewell, ran to the door after him.

"Come back soon, Captain Jim," she called, as he passed through the little gate hung between the firs.

"Ay, ay," he called cheerily back to her. But Captain Jim had sat by the old fireside of the house of dreams for the last time.

Anne went slowly back to the others.

"It's so—so pitiful to think of him going all alone down to that lonely Point," she said. "And there is no one to welcome him there."

"Captain Jim is such good company for others that one can't imagine him being anything but good company for himself," said Owen. "But he must often be lonely. There was a touch of the seer about him tonight—he spoke as one to whom it had been given to speak. Well, I must be going, too."

Anne and Gilbert discreetly melted away; but when Owen had gone Anne returned, to find Leslie standing by the hearth.

"Oh, Leslie—I know—and I'm so glad, dear," she said, putting her arms about her.

"Anne, my happiness frightens me," whispered Leslie. "It seems too great to be real—I'm afraid to speak of it—to think of it. It seems to me that it must just be another dream of this house of dreams and it will vanish when I leave here."

"Well, you are not going to leave here—until Owen takes you. You are going to stay with me until that time comes. Do you think I'd let you go over to that lonely, sad place again?"

"Thank you, dear. I meant to ask you if I might stay with you. I didn't want to go back there—it would seem like going back into the chill and dreariness of the old life again. Anne, Anne, what a friend you've been to me—'a good, sweet woman—true and faithful to be adopted on'—Captain Jim summed you up."

"He said 'women,' not 'woman,'" smiled Anne. "Perhaps Captain Jim sees us both through the rose-colored spectacles of his love for us. But we can try to live up to his belief in us, at least."

"Do you remember, Anne," said Leslie slowly, "that I once said—that night we met on the shore—that I hated my good looks? I did—then. It always seemed to me that if I had been homely Dick would never have thought of me. I hated my beauty because it had attracted him, but now—oh, I'm glad that I have it. It's all I have to offer Owen,—his artist soul delights in it. I feel as if I do not come to him quite empty-handed."

"Owen loves your beauty, Leslie. Who would not? But it's foolish of you to say or think that that is all you bring him. He will tell you that—I needn't. And now I must lock up. I expected Susan back tonight, but she has not come."

"Oh, yes, here I am, Mrs. Doctor, dear," said Susan, entering unexpectedly from the kitchen, "and puffing like a hen drawing rails at that! It's quite a walk from the Glen down here."

"I'm glad to see you back, Susan. How is your sister?"

"She is able to sit up, but of course she cannot walk yet.

However, she is very well able to get on without me now, for her daughter has come home for her vacation. And I am thankful to be back, Mrs. Doctor, dear. Matilda's leg was broken and no mistake, but her tongue was not. She would talk the legs off an iron pot, that she would, Mrs. Doctor, dear, though I grieve to say it of my own sister. She was always a great talker and yet she was the first of our family to get married. She really did not care much about marrying James Clow, but she could not bear to disoblige him. Not but what James is a good man—the only fault I have to find with him is that he always starts in to say grace with such an unearthly groan, Mrs. Doctor, dear. It always frightens my appetite clear away. And speaking of getting married, Mrs. Doctor, dear, is it true that Cornelia Bryant is going to be married to Marshall Elliott?"

"Yes, quite true, Susan."

"Well, Mrs. Doctor, dear, it does *not* seem to me fair. Here is me, who never said a word against the men, and I cannot get married nohow. And there is Cornelia Bryant, who is never done abusing them, and all she has to do is to reach out her hand and pick one up, as it were. It is a very strange world, Mrs. Doctor, dear."

"There's another world, you know, Susan."

"Yes," said Susan with a heavy sigh, "but, Mrs. Doctor, dear, there is neither marrying nor giving in marriage there."

39
CAPTAIN JIM CROSSES THE BAR

One day in late September Owen Ford's book came at last. Captain Jim had gone faithfully to the Glen post-office every day for a month, expecting it. This day he had not gone, and Leslie brought his copy home with hers and Anne's.

"We'll take it down to him this evening," said Anne, excited as a schoolgirl.

The walk to the Point on that clear, beguiling evening along the red harbor road was very pleasant. Then the sun dropped down behind the western hills into some valley that must have been full of lost sunsets, and at the same instant the big light flashed on the white tower of the point.

"Captain Jim is never late by the fraction of a second," said Leslie.

Neither Anne nor Leslie ever forgot Captain Jim's face when they gave him the book—*his* book, transfigured and glorified. The cheeks that had been blanched of late suddenly flamed with the color of boyhood; his eyes glowed with all the fire of youth;' but his hands trembled as he opened it.

It was called simply *The Life-Book of Captain Jim*, and on the title page the names of Owen Ford and James Boyd were printed as collaborators. The frontispiece was a photograph of Captain Jim himself, standing at the door of the lighthouse, looking across the gulf. Owen Ford had "snapped" him one day while the book was being written. Captain Jim had known this, but he had not known that the picture was to be in the book.

"Just think of it," he said, "the old sailor right there in a real printed book. This is the proudest day of my life. I'm like to bust, girls. There'll be no sleep for me tonight. I'll read my book clean through before sun-up."

"We'll go right away and leave you free to begin it," said Anne.

Captain Jim had been handling the book in a kind of reverent rapture. Now he decidedly closed it and laid it aside.

"No, no, you're not going away before you take a cup of tea with the old man," he protested. "I couldn't bear to that—could you, Matey? The life-book will keep, I reckon. I've waited for it this many a year. I can wait a little longer while I'm enjoying my friends."

Captain Jim moved about getting his kettle on to boil, and setting out his bread and butter. Despite his excitement he did not move with his old briskness. His movements were slow and halting. But the girls did not offer to help him. They knew it would hurt his feelings.

"You just picked the right evening to visit me," he said, producing a cake from his cupboard. "Leetle Joe's mother sent me down a big basket full of cakes and pies today. A blessing on all good cooks, says I. Look at this purty cake, all frosting and nuts. 'Tain't often I can entertain in such style. Set in, girls, set in! We'll 'tak a cup o' kindness yet for auld lang syne.'"

The girls "set in" right merrily. The tea was up to Captain Jim's best brewing. Little Joe's mother's cake was the last word in cakes; Captain Jim was the prince of gracious hosts, never even permitting his eyes to wander to the corner where the life-book lay, in all its bravery of green and gold. But when his door finally closed behind Anne and Leslie they knew that he went straight to it, and as they walked home they pictured the delight of the old man poring over the printed pages wherein his own life was portrayed with all the charm and color of reality itself.

"I wonder how he will like the ending—the ending I suggested," said Leslie.

She was never to know. Early the next morning Anne awakened to find Gilbert bending over her, fully dressed, with an expression of anxiety on his face.

"Are you called out?" she asked drowsily.

"No. Anne, I'm afraid there's something wrong at the Point. It's an hour after sunrise now, and the light is still burning. You know it has always been a matter of pride with Captain Jim to start the light the moment the sun sets, and put it out the moment it rises."

Anne sat up in dismay. Through her window she saw the light blinking palely against the blue skies of dawn.

"Perhaps he has fallen asleep over his life-book," she said anxiously, "or become so absorbed in it that he has forgotten the light."

Gilbert shook his head.

"That wouldn't be like Captain Jim. Anyway, I'm going down to see."

"Wait a minute and I'll go with you," exclaimed Anne. "Oh,

yes, I must—Little Jem will sleep for an hour yet, and I'll call Susan. You may need a woman's help if Captain Jim is ill."

It was an exquisite morning, full of tints and sounds at once ripe and delicate. The harbor was sparkling and dimpling like a girl; white gulls were soaring over the dunes; beyond the bar was a shining, wonderful sea. The long fields by the shore were dewy and fresh in that first fine, purely-tinted light. The wind came dancing and whistling up the channel to replace the beautiful silence with a music more beautiful still. Had it not been for the baleful star on the white tower that early walk would have been a delight to Anne and Gilbert. But they went softly with fear.

Their knock was not responded to. Gilbert opened the door and they went in.

The old room was very quiet. On the table were the remnants of the little evening feast. The lamp still burned on the corner stand. The First Mate was asleep in a square of sunshine by the sofa.

Captain Jim lay on the sofa, with his hands clasped over the life-book, open at the last page, lying on his breast. His eyes were closed and on his face was a look of the most perfect peace and happiness—the look of one who has long sought and found at last.

"He is asleep?" whispered Anne tremulously.

Gilbert went to the sofa and bent over him for a few moments. Then he straightened up.

"Yes, he sleeps—well," he said quietly. "Anne, Captain Jim has crossed the bar."

They could not know precisely at what hour he had died, but Anne always believed that he had had his wish, and went out when the morning came across the gulf. Out on that shining tide his spirit drifted, over the sunrise sea of pearl and silver, to the haven where lost Margaret waited, beyond the storms and calms.

40
FAREWELL TO THE HOUSE OF DREAMS

Captain Jim was buried in the little over-harbor graveyard, very near to the spot where the wee white lady slept. His relatives put up a very expensive, very ugly "monument"—a monument at which he would have poked sly fun had he seen it in life. But his real monument was in the hearts of those who knew him, and in the book that was to live for generations.

Leslie mourned that Captain Jim had not lived to see the amazing success of it.

"How he would have delighted in the reviews—they are almost all so kindly. And to have seen his life-book heading the lists of the best sellers—oh, if he could just have lived to see it, Anne!"

But Anne, despite her grief, was wiser.

"It was the book itself he cared for, Leslie—not what might be said of it—and he had it. He had read it all through. That last night must have been one of the greatest happiness for him— with the quick, painless ending he had hoped for in the morning. I am glad for Owen's sake and yours that the book is such a success—but Captain Jim was satisfied—I *know*."

The lighthouse star still kept its nightly vigil; a substitute keeper had been sent to the Point, until such time as an all-wise government could decide which of many applicants was best fitted for the place—or had the strongest pull. The First Mate was at home in the little house, beloved by Anne and Gilbert and Leslie, and tolerated by a Susan who had small liking for cats.

"I can put up with him for the sake of Captain Jim, Mrs. Doctor, dear, for I liked the old man. And I will see that he gets bite and sup, and every mouse the traps account for. But do not ask me to do more than that, Mrs. Doctor, dear. Cats is cats, and take my word for it, they will never be anything else. And at least, Mrs. Doctor, dear, do keep him away from the blessed wee man. Picture to yourself how awful it would be if he was to suck the darling's breath."

"That might be fitly called a *cat*-astrophe," said Gilbert.

"Oh, you may laugh, doctor, dear, but it would be no laughing matter."

"Cats never suck babies' breaths," said Gilbert. "That is only an old superstition, Susan."

"Oh, well, it may be a superstition or it may not, doctor, dear. All that I know is, it has happened. My sister's husband's nephew's wife's cat sucked their baby's breath, and the poor innocent was all but gone when they found it. And superstition or not, if I find that yellow beast lurking near our baby I will whack him with the poker, Mrs. Doctor, dear."

Mr. and Mrs. Marshall Elliott were living comfortably and harmoniously in the green house. Leslie was busy with sewing, for she and Owen were to be married at Christmas. Anne wondered what she would do when Leslie was gone.

"Changes come all the time. Just as soon as things get really nice they change," she said with a sigh.

"The old Morgan place up at the Glen is for sale," said Gilbert, apropos of nothing in especial.

"Is it?" asked Anne indifferently.

"Yes. Now that Mr. Morgan has gone, Mrs. Morgan wants to go to live with her children in Vancouver. She will sell cheaply, for a big place like that in a small village like the Glen will not be very easy to dispose of."

"Well, it's certainly a beautiful place, so it is likely she will find a purchaser," said Anne, absently, wondering whether she should hemstitch or feather-stitch little Jem's "short" dresses. He was to be shortened the next week, and Anne felt ready to cry at the thought of it.

"Suppose we buy it, Anne?" remarked Gilbert quietly.

Anne dropped her sewing and stared at him.

"You're not in earnest, Gilbert?"

"Indeed I am, dear."

"And leave this darling spot—our house of dreams?" said Anne incredulously. "Oh, Gilbert, it's—it's unthinkable!"

"Listen patiently to me, dear. I know just how you feel about it. I feel the same. But we've always known we would have to move some day."

"Oh, but not so soon, Gilbert—not just yet."

"We may never get such a chance again. If we don't buy the Morgan place someone else will—and there is no other house in the Glen we would care to have, and no other really good site on which to build. This little house is—well, it is and has been what no other house can ever be to us, I admit, but you know it is out-of-the-way down here for a doctor. We have felt the inconvenience, though we've made the best of it. And it's a tight fit for us now. Perhaps, in a few years, when Jem wants a room of his own, it will be entirely too small."

"Oh, I know—I know," said Anne, tears filling her eyes. "I know all that can be said against it, but I love it so—and it's so beautiful here."

"You would find it very lonely here after Leslie goes—and Captain Jim has gone too. The Morgan place is beautiful, and in time we would love it. You know you have always admired it, Anne."

"Oh, yes, but—but—this has all seemed to come up so suddenly, Gilbert. I'm dizzy. Ten minutes ago I had no thought of leaving this dear spot. I was planning what I meant to do for it in the spring—what I meant to do in the garden. And if we leave this place who will get it? It *is* out-of-the-way, so it's likely some poor, shiftless, wandering family will rent it—and over-run it— and oh, that would be desecration. It would hurt me horribly."

"I know. But we cannot sacrifice our own interests to such considerations, Anne-girl. The Morgan place will suit us in every essential particular—we really can't afford to miss such a chance. Think of that splendid big lawn with those magnificent old trees; and of that splendid hardwood grove behind it—twelve acres of it. What a play place for our children! There's a fine orchard, too, and you've always admired that high brick wall around the garden with the door in it—you've thought it was so like a story-book garden. And there is almost as fine a view of the harbor and the dunes from the Morgan place as from here."

"You can't see the lighthouse star from it."

"Yes. You can see it from the attic window. *There's* another advantage, Anne-girl—you love big garrets."

"There's no brook in the garden."

"Well, no, but there is one running through the maple grove into the Glen pond. And the pond itself isn't far away. You'll be able to fancy you have your own Lake of Shining Waters again."

"Well, don't say anything more about it just now, Gilbert. Give me time to think—to get used to the idea."

"All right. There is no great hurry, of course. Only—if we decide to buy, it would be well to be moved in and settled before winter."

Gilbert went out, and Anne put away Little Jem's short dresses with trembling hands. She could not sew any more that day. With tear-wet eyes she wandered over the little domain where she had reigned so happy a queen. The Morgan place was all that Gilbert claimed. The grounds were beautiful, the house old enough to have dignity and repose and traditions, and new enough to be comfortable and up-to-date. Anne had always admired it; but admiring is not loving; and she loved this little house of dreams so much. She loved *everything* about it—the garden she had tended, and which so many women had tended before her—the gleam and sparkle of the little brook that crept so roguishly across the corner—the gate between the creaking fir trees—the old sandstone step—the stately Lombardies—the two tiny quaint glass cupboards over the chimney-piece in the living-room—the crooked pantry door in the kitchem—the two funny dormer windows upstairs—the little jog in the staircase—why, these things were a part of her! How could she leave them?

And how this little house, consecrated aforetime by love and joy, had been re-consecrated for her by her happiness and sorrow! Here she had spent her bridal moon; here wee Joyce had lived her one brief day; here the sweetness of motherhood had come again with Little Jem; here she had heard the exquisite music of her baby's cooing laughter; here beloved friends had sat by her fireside. Joy and grief, birth and death, had made sacred forever this little house of dreams.

And now she must leave it. She knew that, even while she had contended against the idea to Gilbert. The little house was outgrown. Gilbert's interests made the change necessary; his work, successful though it had been, was hampered by his location. Anne realized that the end of their life in this dear place drew nigh, and that she must face the fact bravely. But how her heart ached!

"It will just be like tearing something out of my life," she sobbed. "And oh, if I could hope that some nice folk would come here in our place—or even that it would be left vacant. That itself would be better than having it overrun with some horde who know nothing of the geography of dreamland, and nothing of the history that has given this house its soul and its identity. And if such a tribe come here the place will go to rack and ruin in no time—an old place goes down so quickly if it is not carefully attended to. They'll tear up my garden—and let the Lombardies get ragged—and the paling will come to look like a mouth with half the teeth missing—and the roof will leak—and the plaster fall—and they'll stuff pillows and rags in broken window panes—and everything will be out-at-elbows."

Anne's imagination pictured forth so vividly the coming degeneration of her dear little house that it hurt her as severely as if it had already been an accomplished fact. She sat down on the stairs and had a long, bitter cry. Susan found her there and enquired with much concern what the trouble was.

"You have not quarreled with the doctor, have you now, Mrs. Doctor, dear? But if you have, do not worry. It is a thing quite likely to happen with married couples, I am told, although I have had no experience that way myself. He will be sorry, and you can soon make it up."

"No, no, Susan, we haven't quarrelled. It's only—Gilbert is

going to buy the Morgan place, and we'll have to go and live at the Glen. And it will break my heart."

Susan did not enter into Anne's feelings at all. She was, indeed, quite rejoiced over the prospect of living at the Glen. Her one grievance against her place in the little house was its lonesome location.

"Why, Mrs. Doctor, dear, it will be splendid. The Morgan house is such a fine, big one."

"I hate big houses," sobbed Anne.

"Oh, well, you will not hate them by the time you have half a dozen children," remarked Susan calmly. "And this house is too small already for us. We have no spare room, since Mrs. Moore is here, and that pantry is the most aggravating place I ever tried to work in. There is a corner every way you turn. Besides, it is out-of-the-world down here. There is really nothing at all but scenery."

"Out of your world perhaps, Susan—but not out of mine," said Anne with a faint smile.

"I do not quite understand you, Mrs. Doctor, dear, but of course I am not well educated. But if Dr. Blythe buys the Morgan place he will make no mistake, and that you may tie to. They have water in it, and the pantries and closets are beautiful, and there is not another such cellar in P. E. Island, so I have been told. Why, the cellar here, Mrs. Doctor, dear, has been a heart-break to me, as well you know."

"Oh, go away, Susan, go away," said Anne forlornly. "Cellars and pantries and closets don't make a *home*. Why don't you weep with those who weep?"

"Well, I never was much hand for weeping, Mrs. Doctor, dear. I would rather fall to and cheer people up than weep with them. Now, do not you cry and spoil your pretty eyes. This house is very well and has served your turn, but it is high time you had a better."

Susan's point of view seemed to be that of most people. Leslie was the only one who sympathized understandingly with Anne. She had a good cry, too, when she heard the news. Then they both dried their tears and went to work at the preparations for moving.

"Since we must go let us go as soon as we can and have it over," said poor Anne with bitter resignation.

"You know you will like that lovely old place at the Glen after you have lived in it long enough to have dear memories woven about it," said Leslie. "Friends will come there, as they have come here—happiness will glorify it for you. Now, it's just a house to you—but the years will make it a home."

Anne and Leslie had another cry the next week when they shortened Little Jem. Anne felt the tragedy of it until evening when in his long nightie she found her own dear baby again.

"But it will be rompers next—and then trousers—and in no time he will be grown-up," she sighed.

"Well, you would not want him to stay a baby always, Mrs. Doctor, dear, would you?" said Susan. "Bless his innocent heart, he looks too sweet for anything in his little short dresses, with his dear feet sticking out. And think of the save in the ironing, Mrs. Doctor, dear."

"Anne, I have just had a letter from Owen," said Leslie, entering with a bright face. "And, oh! I have such good news. He writes me that he is going to buy this place from the church trustees and keep it to spend our summer vacations in. Anne, are you not glad?"

"Oh, Leslie, 'glad' isn't the word for it! It seems almost too good to be true. I sha'n't feel half so badly now that I know this dear spot will never be desecrated by a vandal tribe, or left to tumble down in decay. Why, it's lovely! It's lovely!"

One October morning Anne wakened to the realization that she had slept for the last time under the roof of her little house. The day was too busy to indulge regret and when evening came the house was stripped and bare. Anne and Gilbert were alone in it to say farewell. Leslie and Susan and Little Jem had gone to the Glen with the last load of furniture. The sunset light streamed in through the curtainless windows.

"It has all such a heart-broken, reproachful look, hasn't it?" said Anne. "Oh, I shall be so homesick at the Glen tonight!"

"We have been very happy here, haven't we, Anne-girl?" said Gilbert, his voice full of feeling.

Anne choked, unable to answer. Gilbert waited for her at the fir-tree gate, while she went over the house and said farewell to every room. She was going away; but the old house would still be there, looking seaward through its quaint windows. The autumn winds would blow around it mournfully, and the gray rain would beat upon it and the white mists would come in from the sea to enfold it; and the moonlight would fall over it and light up the old paths where the schoolmaster and his bride had walked. There on that old harbor shore the charm of story would linger; the wind would still whistle alluringly over the silver sand-dunes; the waves would still call from the red rock-coves.

"But we will be gone," said Anne through her tears.

She went out, closing and locking the door behind her. Gilbert was waiting for her with a smile. The lighthouse star was gleaming northward. The little garden, where only marigolds still bloomed, was already hooding itself in shadows.

Anne knelt down and kissed the worn old step which she had crossed as a bride.

"Good-bye, dear little house of dreams," she said.

. . .

ESSAY

from "Kindred Spirits" All: Green Gables Revisited

BY

CAROL GAY

. . . Few writers can characterize so adeptly, so quickly, and frequently, so poignantly, as Montgomery. She does it as well as Jewett and better than Harriet Beecher Stowe. And she has a sense of humor. There are always the shifting groups of girls, and, later, women, which Anne draws around her wherever she settles. And there are the memorable individuals that stand out so clearly. There is Rachel Lynde, who appears on the first page of *Anne of Green Gables*, "notable housewife," "one of those capable creatures who can manage their own concerns and those of other folks into the bargain." There are also . . . Miss Lavendar, whose pride let her lover leave her over a petty quarrel and who then retires to a life of solitude; Leslie Moore of *House of Dreams*, the gorgeous beauty married to a husband with the mind of a five-year-old; Mrs. Allan, of *Green Gables*, the minister's young wife, whose joy of following her husband to his next parish is marred by the grief of abandoning the grave of her first-born. Or Miss Patty, age seventy, and Miss Maria, age fifty, in *Anne of the Island*, who live together contentedly and quietly in a house called "Patty's Place" until one day they up and go to Europe. As Miss Patty declares, "I daresay I'd have gone to Europe before if the idea had occurred to me." When they hear of Anne's approaching marriage they write in *House of Dreams*: "We send you our best wishes. Maria and I have never married, but we have no objection to other people doing so." And there is Miss Cornelia Bryant who knows everyone around Four Winds Harbor in *House of Dreams* and who hates all men.

The life stories of these women, joyful and tragic, do not disturb the plot line of the novels. They are, indeed, the fabric of Montgomery's work, for the novels depend not on plot, but on the even flow of life, women's life. They revolve around a steady pattern of breakfast, dinner, and supper, and the intricate relationships between neighbors, mothers and sons, mothers and daughters, and the problems of growing up and raising children.

We need to look more closely at the lives of Marilla and Matthew Cuthbert as they are lived out within the narrow boundaries of Green Gables farm, for they reveal much. Through them, we catch glimpses of a harsh and rigid upbringing that stressed endurance, duty, and righteousness. We catch glimpses of marriage or a life beyond the farm passed by because of duty and obedience to family. Marilla and Matthew have survived the rigor of their upbringing and their harsh farm life and cling to the values that give it substance, just enough unsure of the methods that had produced them to bend a bit in the raising of Anne. Their lives have been lived mostly in silence. They are unused to expressing their feelings; the deeper emotions—love, sorrow, a sense of loss—remain deeply buried in their hearts, and the softer emotions—exuberance, mirth, joy—have disappeared. Matthew had looked as grim at twenty as he does at sixty. The silent strength, the repressed emotions, the deep goodness, and the lack of an imagination are common characteristics that Marilla and Matthew share with the older inhabitants of Avonlea. Marilla is the strongest of the two, and although Matthew does the outside work at the farm, it is Marilla who manages and runs the farm and takes care of him. The deep love that they share for each other is unexpressed; in fact, what they are most appalled by and yet most fascinated by are Anne's exuberant, imaginative outpourings and her direct and unconventional way of seeing and saying things.

Matthew does not represent an intrusion of the values of a patriarchal culture. If anything, he and the other members of the older generation in Avonlea are victims of that which Donovan (and of course others) define as "the masculine tyranny" of Calvinism. His humanity has survived because of the "feminine values" that predominate in his makeup. He is gentle, forgiving, soft. Indeed it is he who first recognizes (intuitively, for Matthew is not logical) the saving grace that Anne offers. At key points in Anne's upbringing, he insists on the softer act. At one point, when Anne has shone forth at a concert, Marilla concedes, "Anyhow, I was proud of Anne tonight, although I'm not going to tell her so," fearful of encouraging the sin of pride. "Well now," says Matthew, "I was proud of her and I did tell her so 'fore she went upstairs." His simple statement represents an enormous concession on the part of Matthew, who has not in sixty years made himself so vulnerable.

While the dimmed patriarchal shadows cast by Calvinism are an element in Avonlea's culture, they operate as something that the women have overcome. They seem to have seized the strength that the harshness and rigidity can instill; those softer ones who didn't survive or who became totally twisted never surface, for Montgomery peoples her landscape with the survivors. And their lives are based on what society defines as traditionally women's values. Their strength is fostered by a strong sense of sisterhood, and the "networking" that is everywhere expressed either implicitly or explicitly; and a large part of this "networking" is based on an intuitive recognition of imaginative insight. Perhaps the strongest example of it is expressed in a scene between Anne and her best friend Diana, in *Anne of Avonlea*:

> "Do you remember that evening when we first met, Diana, and 'swore' eternal friendship in your garden? We've kept that 'oath,' I think . . . we've never had a quarrel nor even a coolness. I shall never forget the thrill that went over me the day you told me you loved me. I had had such a lonely starved heart all through my childhood. I'm just beginning to realize how starved and lonely it really was . . . I should have been miserable if it hadn't been for that strange little dream-life of mine, wherein I imagined all the friends and love I craved. . . . And then I met you. You don't know what your friendship meant to me. I want to thank you

here and now, dear, for the warm and true affection you've always given me."

"And always, always will," sobbed Diana. "I shall *never* love anybody . . . any *girl* . . . half as well as I love you."

The close bond evidenced here is given expression in the catch-phrase of the series—"kindred spirit"—by which Anne identifies those who have the power of the imagination and whose values, like hers, are predominantly feminine. It serves as a common motif that appears throughout the series.

Although Maud Montgomery created in her fiction a landscape dominated by "woman's culture," she herself lived in a man's world. It was a world that brought her pain, confusion, and ultimately, like many other women writers, tragedy. In order to accommodate it, she lived an almost schizophrenic life as a minister's dutiful full-time wife, while maintaining at the same time an active, full-time career as a professional writer in which she consciously and unconsciously gave free rein to the intellectual and imaginative world she was afraid to reveal as a wife and mother. Montgomery reveals her "strange little dream-life" through her writings; Anne is one of the characters who expresses it. Anne, with her talkative ways, makes Marilla and Matthew and all her friends see things from a new perspective: the road leading to Green Gables becomes "The White Way of Delight," the small pond near the farm becomes "The Lake of Shining Waters." Marilla never manages to train her out of having too much to say; in fact it is her ability to communicate her feminine "romantic" way of looking at things, her "ladylikeness" and her strong "womanliness" that helps to illuminate the Avonlea landscape and every life she touches. Anne offers to her children and those around her, as well as to her readers, a romanticized and passionate way of viewing life and nature that will wrest happiness from it in spite of everything.

This romanticized, often sentimentalized, viewpoint is the major flaw of the Avonlea books just as it is one of their major strengths. Romance and sentiment are not strong enough weapons to win with. They merely offer escape. However Montgomery may not have realized, or wanted to accept, that you cannot substitute imagination for reality, her books show that a life lived without imagination is not worth living. She created through her Avonlea series a world where the traditional women's values of love, warmth, sensitivity, imagination, and quiet endurance survive and overcome, a world where kindred spirits are intuitively identified and cherished. It is a world that has enough reality for women and girls of the past seventy-five years to respond to with deep recognition, and thus, it serves as an important document in "the development of feminist consciousness." This helps explain Montgomery's lasting appeal, perhaps even more than her sense of humor, her descriptive skill, and her talent for creating lively, authentic characters.

Works Cited

Donovan, Josephine. *New England Local Color Literature: A Women's Tradition*. New York: Ungar, 1983.

Lerner, Gerda. *The Female Experience: An American Documentary*. Indianapolis, IN: Bobbs-Merrill, 1977.

————. *The Majority Finds Its Past: Placing Women in History*. New York: Oxford UP, 1979.

Carol Gay (1933–1985) was professor of English and Director of Graduate Studies at Youngstown State University in Ohio. She published widely on colonial American literature, the Transcendentalists, women's studies, and children's literature, and was a charter member and the first archivist of the Children's Literature Association.